DAWN OF WAR II

APOTHECARY GORDIAN DIDN'T pause an instant to consider, but fired off a stream of hellfire rounds. The ceramic hellfire shells smashed into the monster's carapace, allowing the payload of mutagenic acid to pour into the genestealer's torso, eating it away from within. With a hideous squeal – whether of rage, or pain, or frustration, or all three, Gordian couldn't say – the genestealer fell sprawling to the dust at the Apothecary's feet.

A WARHAMMER 40,000 NOVEL

DAWN OF
WAR II

Chris Roberson

A BLACK LIBRARY PUBLICATION

First published in Great Britain in 2009 by
BL Publishing,
Games Workshop Ltd.,
Willow Road, Nottingham,
NG7 2WS, UK.

10 9 8 7 6 5 4 3 2 1

Cover illustration by Cheol Joo Lee and Origin.

A CIP record for this book is available from the British Library.

ISBN13: 978 1 84416 686 2
ISBN10: 1 84416 686 4

Distributed in the US by Simon & Schuster
1230 Avenue of the Americas, New York, NY 10020, US.

See the Black Library on the Internet at
www.blacklibrary.com

Find out more about Games Workshop
and the world of Warhammer 40,000 at
www.games-workshop.com

Printed and bound in the US.

IT IS THE 41st millennium. For more than a hundred centuries the Emperor has sat immobile on the Golden Throne of Earth. He is the master of mankind by the will of the gods, and master of a million worlds by the might of his inexhaustible armies. He is a rotting carcass writhing invisibly with power from the Dark Age of Technology. He is the Carrion Lord of the Imperium for whom a thousand souls are sacrificed every day, so that he may never truly die.

YET EVEN IN his deathless state, the Emperor continues his eternal vigilance. Mighty battlefleets cross the daemon-infested miasma of the warp, the only route between distant stars, their way lit by the Astronomican, the psychic manifestation of the Emperor's will. Vast armies give battle in His name on uncounted worlds. Greatest amongst his soldiers are the Adeptus Astartes, the Space Marines, bio-engineered super-warriors. Their comrades in arms are legion: the Imperial Guard and countless planetary defence forces, the ever-vigilant Inquisition and the tech-priests of the Adeptus Mechanicus to name only a few. But for all their multitudes, they are barely enough to hold off the ever-present threat from aliens, heretics, mutants – and worse.

TO BE A man in such times is to be one amongst untold billions. It is to live in the cruellest and most bloody regime imaginable. These are the tales of those times. Forget the power of technology and science, for so much has been forgotten, never to be re-learned. Forget the promise of progress and understanding, for in the grim dark future there is only war. There is no peace amongst the stars, only an eternity of carnage and slaughter, and the laughter of thirsting gods.

PROLOGUE

PROSPERON WAS A dead world.

It had been that way since long before the moment Battle-Brother Aramus first set foot upon it. That much was clear now. But like the rest of the Space Marines of the Blood Ravens Fifth Company who had been sent to the planet, Aramus had been given his orders, and would carry them out, whatever the risks, whatever the costs.

The Blood Ravens had been tasked with recovering Imperial relics in advance of the encroaching tyranid horde which already held the planet's eastern hemisphere in its grip. There were several squads involved in the mission, each given a different objective. The squad of which Aramus was a part – ten Space Marines accompanied by the company Apothecary – had been dropped in the forests of Prosperon's western hemisphere, with orders to recover a relic held in the Templum Incarnatum, a shrine at the forest's heart.

When the Fifth Company had set out for the Prosperon system, weeks before, there was still some hope that the tyranid infestation could be expunged from the planet; one glimpse of the eastern horizon, though, hazed with an endless cloud of mycetic spores, was evidence enough that the infestation had progressed too far to be halted. Vox communication planet-side was all but impossible, impeded by the shadow in the warp cast by the tyranid fleet in high orbit. And when the air blew from the east, it carried with it the scent of fungus and rot, of mildew and stagnation – the smell of tyranoforming, the stench of a dying world.

It was a tragedy for the human inhabitants of Prosperon, to be sure, to see their home of millennia consumed by the Great Devourer. Those that had the means to do so had already fled, and those that didn't could only huddle together, pray to the Emperor to protect their souls, and await the inevitable. But for the Space Marines of the Fifth Company, there was still work to be done.

Sergeant Forrin had been the first to fall, brought down by a swarm of hormagaunts who overwhelmed the veteran campaigner with their vast numbers, their vicious scythes hacking again and again at the blood-red ceramite of Forrin's power armour, until finally the sergeant's bolter and chainsword could not hold the tyranid swarm at bay any longer. The rest of the squad had been deployed in a wide-spread tactical formation as they swept through the forest, and so were too far away to reach

Forrin in time to offer any assistance before it was too late. From a distance, and using the hellfire shells with which those with heavy bolters had been equipped given the extreme circumstances, the squad had dispatched the hormagaunt swarm, reducing them to a litter of blasted body parts and ichor carpeting the forest floor.

With the sergeant dead, the squad had been left momentarily leaderless, but the loss would not deter the Blood Ravens from their mission. Each Space Marine knew his duty and his role, and without Forrin to guide them, command fell to Battle-Brother Vela.

The squad continued through the forests of Prosperon, weapons ready, leaving the body of the sergeant to the attentions of Apothecary Gordian, who lingered behind to do the needful.

APOTHECARY GORDIAN READIED his reductor, crouching low over the mangled body of Sergeant Forrin. The hormagaunts had cracked open the ceramite of the sergeant's power armour like a nut's shell, and had torn the flesh beneath to ribbons, but it appeared to Gordian that the progenoid glands had not suffered damage. As he set to work, he repeated to himself the words of the Apothecary's Creed, which he carried in his heart. In his long years of service as Apothecary to the Fifth Company, Gordian had come to use the Creed as a kind of litany, a focussing agent to direct his mind to his task.

'He that may fight, heal him.'

With a steady hand, and the aid of the reductor, Gordian eased the progenoid gland from Forrin's abdomen. Had the sergeant yet lived, he would have been too far gone to be saved, the medical equipment in the narthecium that Gordian carried across his back ineffective against the extent of the sergeant's injuries. Had the sergeant yet lived, Gordian would have been left with no choice but to confer the Emperor's Mercy before extracting the gland.

'He that may fight no more, give him peace.'

Gordian had performed this manoeuvre countless times, more often than he cared to remember, but the repetition of the Creed helped him hold distractions at bay. This was no rote operation, to be carried out mindlessly, but was a solemn and holy responsibility. Reverentially, he eased the gland into a chrome bowl, and after cleaning it with a spray, slid it carefully into a self-locking tubular canister, one of ten he carried in his narthecium's rack.

'He that is dead, take from him the Chapter's due.'

That was the way he looked upon the gland, as the Chapter's due, a holy charge entrusted to a Space Marine in his initiation, that he surrendered back to the Chapter at the end of his life. Without the gene-seed carried within the progenoid gland of a fallen Space Marine, it would be impossible to create the zygote with which another Space Marine could be created. Were enough gene-seed to be lost, in time the Chapter itself would die, and the forces of the Imperium would be the poorer for it.

As Gordian was carefully reaffixing the protective canister in his narthecium, he heard a sound from behind him, and dropping his reductor to the ground spun with his bolter in his fist. It was a genestealer, scuttling towards the Apothecary with blinding speed, claws out and grasping, with flesh hooks stabbing out from its distended maw.

Apothecary Gordian didn't pause an instant to consider, but fired off a stream of hellfire rounds. The ceramic hellfire shells smashed into the monster's carapace, allowing the payload of mutagenic acid to pour into the genestealer's torso, eating it away from within. With a hideous squeal – whether of rage, or pain, or frustration, or all three, Gordian couldn't say – the genestealer fell sprawling to the dust at his feet.

As the monster twitched and writhed on the forest floor, Gordian fired another hellfire round into the base of its skull. After retrieving his reductor and checking to make sure the gene-seed canister was safely secured on his back, the Apothecary set out after the rest of the squad.

As he moved through the forest as quickly as possible, Gordian considered the empty canisters he carried. With one already used with Forrin's remains, he had nine left. And nine Space Marines remained.

Emperor protect and guide us, Gordian thought, if I should have to use all nine…

BATTLE-BROTHER VELA WAS the next to fall. He was taking point as the squad's vanguard formation moved through the dense undergrowth, the shrine still hours distant, when a lictor burst out of the jungle before them and was upon Vela in an eye-blink. Vela managed to hit one of the lictor's ventral limbs with his melta gun, searing it off at the joint, but the tyranid surged onwards with its remaining limbs, and Vela fell beneath it before he'd had a chance to take another shot.

Aramus rushed to assist, but before he'd reached Vela's side the lictor had driven a scything talon, as long as a man was tall, right through Vela's abdomen, shattering the ceramite on front and back and lancing through the body within.

The lictor reared back, hoisting Vela's body in the air, the Space Marine dangling like a puppet with cut strings. Then, a horrible screech sounding from the monster, it began shaking Vela's body loose from the talon, readying to attack one of the others.

Aramus raised his bolter, readying to fire. At this close range, he doubted even hellfire rounds would be enough to put the lictor down before it took another victim, but the Blood Ravens were not about to retreat, and could not outrun the lictor if they tried. As he prepared to fire, though, a voice buzzing in Aramus's ear-bead stopped him. It was Battle-Brother Vela, crackling over the comms, barely audible through the interference of the shadow in the warp.

'Kill… it…'

Aramus didn't waste the opportunity that Vela's fatal injury had granted them. He knew that the battle-brother was telling the rest of the squad he was already dead, and that there remained no reason not to unleash the harshest sanction available to them. If they hesitated, the odds were that another of their number would fall before the lictor's talons.

With a nod to the rest of the squad to withdraw to a safe distance, Aramus unclipped a frag grenade from his waist and, in a single motion, armed and threw it directly at the lictor, then dived for cover.

As the lictor turned its attention to Aramus, the frag grenade completed its tight arc through the air, striking the tyranid's carapace between the first and second upper limbs on the dorsal side. The grenade, set to detonate on impact, activated instantly. Aramus, still in midair in his dive for cover, could feel the concussive force of the blast rippling past him.

When he and the rest of the squad moved forward, all that remained of the lictor was a carpet of pulped remains, a few metres away from the place where Battle-Brother Vela lay.

Vela had shut down, rendered unconscious as his body struggled to combat his injuries, both those from the talon's puncture and the secondary effects of his proximity to the frag grenade's effects. It would fall to the Apothecary to determine whether Vela had a chance of recovering from his injuries, but in Aramus's experience Space Marines seldom recovered from injuries that looked as dire as Vela's did now.

They had hours to go until they reached their destination, and hours beyond that to reach the extraction point. Vela had fallen, whether he would rise again or not, and so command of the squad was now in the hands of Battle-Brother Durio.

Durio wasted no time, but ordered the remaining squad members to continue towards their target.

Aramus spared a glance at the broken and unconscious body of Vela, then racked his bolter and moved out.

* * *

APOTHECARY GORDIAN HAD known with a single look that Battle-Brother Vela was past the point of saving. Vela's body was doing its best to overcome the injuries – Larraman cells, borne by leucocytes to the site of the wound, formed instant scar tissue on contact with the air, as the sus-an membrane regulated his unconscious body in a state of suspension – but the damage was too severe, and the body was engaged in a losing battle. Even a Space Marine like Vela, a superhuman warrior in the service of the God-Emperor, was not immune to the effects of a giant hole punched through his body. It was only a matter of time before the rapid deterioration caused by the injuries overtook the body's attempts to heal itself, and Battle-Brother Vela would be no more.

'Rest easy, brother,' Gordian said, solemnly. 'Your name will be entered in the Book of Honour, and you shall be remembered whenever the Bell of Souls is rung.'

The unconscious Vela could not hear him, Gordian knew. But such words of comfort to the dying were an ineluctable part of the Apothecary's art, and Gordian would not omit them even if he could.

'I shall take the Chapter's due, Brother Vela.'

The steel tongs of the reductor flashing in the sun, Gordian set to work. A fallen battle-brother was a tremendous loss to the Chapter, but at least with the gene-seed retrieved another generation might rise one day to take his place.

'And then I will give you the Emperor's Peace.'

There would be only eight canisters left in the narthecium, now.

But for how long?

BATTLE-BROTHER MILIUS WAS the next to fall, though he took nearly a dozen tyranid warriors with him when he went. And Battle-Brother Qao managed to dispatch a broodlord and its retinue of genestealers before the damage done by the broodlord's acid maw finally claimed him. Battle-Brother Kraal was caught by a fragmentation spore mine, and while the mine managed only minor damage to his armour, a splinter of the spore shell was driven through into Kraal's flesh, flooding his system with toxins that his oolitic kidney was unable to overcome. Battle-Brother Javier, bolter flashing and chainsword whirring, took down four raveners single-handedly, but fell beneath the scything talons of the fifth, never to stand again.

Of the eleven Space Marines that had set out from the drop-pod that morning, only five reached their destination deep in the woods, the ancient Imperial shrine Templum Incarnatum, left untended and unguarded after the local population fled the encroaching tyranids. Unfortunately, the five Blood Ravens quickly discovered that they were not the first to arrive.

'Form up, squad,' Battle-Brother Durio called out in a harsh whisper, taking up a position at the edge of the clearing. The shrine was not large, perhaps no more than two or three times the height of one of the Space Marines, and half again as wide. A roughly pyramidal shape, it squatted at the centre of a circular clearing, surmounted by an Imperial aquila in bas-relief. There was a single entrance on the base of the structure, to the left of where Durio had gathered the squad, just a few dozen metres away. Their objective lay within, only a short walk from where they stood.

But it was not to be quite so easy.

In between the Space Marines and the shrine squatted something else, a monstrous creature that towered over the shrine. It was a carnifex, a screamer-killer, and it perched on the dead grasses of the clearing on its two massive hind-limbs, the scythes of its upper limbs rising from its back, and affixed to its middle-limbs the bio-plasma weapon-symbiote whose firing gave the monster its name.

The carnifex was motionless, facing the shrine. Was it sleeping, resting, or merely waiting? The Space Marines could not know. Who could guess the actions or intent of a creature of mindless appetite and destruction?

All that the Blood Ravens knew was that the carnifex was a living engine of destruction, and that it was all that stood between them and their objective. A rampaging screamer-killer would be all but unstoppable. If they could manage to disable or destroy it somehow before it shifted into motion, then they stood a good chance of–

A high-pitched screaming pierced the air as the carnifex surged into motion, spinning around to bring its weapon-symbiote to bear on the Space Marines.

'Apothecary, fall back and lay down covering fire! Siano, Quinzi, break right!' Durio shouted, diving to the left and firing his bolter at the carnifex as he went. 'Aramus, with me!'

Battle-Brother Quinzi dived clear to the right as the ball of blinding green fire spurted from the screamer-killer's weapon-symbiote, but Battle-Brother Siano was a fraction of an instant too slow, caught by the burst of bio-plasma as it shot past them. Knocked crashing back into the trees, which were immediately set ablaze, Siano was cooked alive in his power armour, his shouts of pain and outrage squawking over the static-laced comms.

Aramus hit the ground running, only metres behind Battle-Brother Durio, who was racing to the left around the carnifex's flank.

'Quinzi, krak grenades on my mark,' Durio shouted, firing hellfire rounds at the carnifex one-handed.

Intended for use against armoured vehicles and bunkers, the krak grenade in the early days of the Tyrannic War had been found to be just as effective against even the largest tyranids in close combat. The only problem was that you had to be extremely close to the target to get the krak grenade into position, which left you extremely close to the resultant blast. Even though krak charges imploded, instead of exploding, the blowback could be disastrous to anyone standing too close.

'Aramus, head for the shrine and acquire the objective!' Durio added, unclipping a krak grenade from his waist.

Without wasting an instant to confirm, Aramus powered on, shifting his trajectory as he ran and angling directly for the entrance to the shrine. The long, wickedly barbed tail of the screamer-killer lashed out, narrowly missing Aramus, but he paid it no mind, his every attention focussed only on speed.

Aramus was bare metres from the shrine's entrance as he heard the deafening scream of the carnifex's bio-plasma weapon building to another burst, and then the voice of Durio shouted out, 'Mark!'

The *thwump* of the krak grenades' implosion coincided with the final crescendo of the bio-plasma burst, just as Aramus dived through the open entrance into the Imperial shrine.

APOTHECARY GORDIAN EMERGED from behind the smouldering remains of the treeline, there no longer being any need for suppressing fire. The brief and horrible battle was over. The carnifex lay on its side, struggling to regain its footing, despite the fact that one of its lower limbs had been blown away at the second joint. One of its upper scything talons had been pulped to chitin and ichor by a krak grenade, but its weapon-symbiote appeared unharmed, and once it was upright and ambulatory – in a matter of moments, at most – it would be in a position to open fire once more.

But felling the carnifex had not come without a price. Battle-Brothers Siano and Quinzi both lay on the ground, motionless. There was no sign of Durio, living or dead, but Gordian had to assume the worst.

Gordian ran to nearest of the fallen Space Marines, reductor in hand. Siano had been burned alive by one of the bio-plasma bursts, but there was still a chance that his gene-seed had survived the conflagration that had claimed his life. Without sparing a glance at the carnifex, Gordian set to work.

When he finished with Siano's gene-seed, he would move onto the shattered remains of Battle-Brother Quinzi, laying only a few metres away. As he worked, Gordian didn't bother looking in the carnifex's direction. He was out of reach of the supine monster's remaining talons, for now, and knew that the high-pitched squeal of the weapon-symbiote would give some small warning of another ranged attack. He only hoped that a slight warning would be sufficient.

THEIR OBJECTIVE, AFTER the high cost of coming this far, seemed an insignificant thing. For an item that had already cost the lives of seven Space Marines, and had likely claimed two more, it was an anticlimax. It was a cylinder, about the thickness and length of a normal man's forearm, constructed of a substance that had the appearance of black glass; completely opaque, capped on either end with golden plugs covered in intricate scrollwork, and topped off with purity seals from which dangled ancient strips of curling brown paper.

Aramus didn't know what the relic contained. It appeared to be some sort of suspension unit, a miniature version of the sarcophagi into which badly injured – but not yet terminal – Space Marines were sometimes sealed, so that they could later be recovered and encased in Dreadnought assemblies. If it was a suspension unit, what was stored within? The finger bone of some forgotten saint, perhaps? Dust upon which the Emperor himself once trod when he still walked in mortal form? A scroll containing some hermetic and holy wisdom?

Aramus did not know, and didn't care to conjecture. It was enough for him that it was a relic, and that his squad of Blood Ravens had been dispatched to retrieve it, to prevent it being lost when the tyranids overran Prosperon.

Securing the cylinder in an impact-resistant case he carried at his hip for just that purpose, Aramus checked the action on his bolter and edged back towards the entrance to survey the surroundings from behind cover.

GORDIAN WAS PULLING the gland from the chest of Battle-Brother Quinzi with the now-incarnadine tongs of his reductor when he heard the sounds of the carnifex thrashing upright behind him, followed by the rising whine of the bio-plasma weapon charging. With Quinzi's gene-seed already exposed to the open air, he daren't risk fleeing, not until the gland was safely ensconced within the protective canister; not without risking the gene-seed's safety. Head down, Gordian worked as fast as he was able, while the scream behind him climbed ever higher.

ARAMUS SAW THE screamer-killer tottering on its hind-limbs, bringing its weapon-symbiote to bear on the Apothecary, who remained steadfastly at the side of the fallen Space Marine, reductor in hand. Aramus knew that the gene-seed the Apothecary carried was worth more than Aramus's own life.

Raising his bolter and firing hellfire round after hellfire round, Aramus raced out into the clearing, shouting and trying to attract the carnifex's attentions. If he could only distract the tyranid from Gordian, give the Apothecary a moment to complete his work and get clear, then the gene-seed that Gordian carried might be saved.

The tactic appeared to be working. As the hellfire rounds he fired slammed into the chitinous armour of the tyranid, the carnifex swung round to face Aramus, the scream of the bio-plasma weapon growing higher and louder by the instant.

'Apothecary, get clear,' Aramus shouted, weaving back and forth in serpentine fashion, trying to narrow his profile before the carnifex's weapon. 'I'll hold it here until you're gone.'

Aramus knew that the mission would fail, were he to die without delivering the relic to the extraction point. But better that the mission fail than the Chapter lose the future warriors which the Apothecary's gene-seed would help birth. Perhaps one of those future Space Marines might perform some great deed in the Emperor's service, and help expunge the stain of this mission's failure that Aramus's death would mean.

'Aramus!' Like a voice from beyond the grave, the sound of Battle-Brother Durio shouting from somewhere beyond the trees took Aramus momentarily aback. 'Do you have the objective?'

Aramus, still jinking back and forth across the clearing as the carnifex completed the charging of its bio-plasma weapon, glanced behind him, and saw the battered and broken form of Durio limping out of the forest. When the bio-plasma blast had taken out Quinzi, it appeared, Durio had been knocked deep into the trees and out of sight, though whether by a blow from the carnifex's scything talons or as a consequence of a misfiring krak grenade, Aramus couldn't say.

'Acknowledged,' Aramus answered simply, resisting the urge to tap the case strapped to his thigh, his hands occupied with firing bolter rounds at the carnifex.

'Then get the Apothecary clear,' Durio answered, 'and get him and the relic to the extraction point.' Durio held aloft another krak grenade, the last he carried. 'I'll see to our oversized friend here.'

The scream of the carnifex's weapon-symbiote had reached a fever pitch now, a deafening, screeching howl that cut through the air like a chainsword through soft flesh. The bio-plasma would fire at any moment.

Aramus didn't spare an instant to respond, but jinked back to the right, racing to the Apothecary's side. Durio limped forward into the clearing, heading directly for the carnifex, refusing to let the monster's attentions be diverted elsewhere.

'Apothecary!' Aramus shouted, skidding to a halt by Gordian's side. 'Are your ministrations complete?'

Gordian sealed the top of the eighth canister, and returned it to his narthecium. 'They are now, brother,' Gordian said, standing and raising his bolter.

'Then let's go!' Aramus surged into motion, rushing back into the surrounding forests, with the Apothecary following close behind.

'IGNORE THEM, MONSTER...'

As Aramus and Gordian tore through the forests, they could hear the voice of Durio crackling through the static on the comms.

'Your fight is with me…'

Even as they increased the distance between them and the clearing, the retreating Space Marines could hear the weapon-symbiote's scream climbing to its terminal crescendo.

'Let us finish this…'

The *thwump* of the krak grenade reached their ears a split second after the scream of the weapon-symbiote broke off, and the forest behind them erupted in green flame.

BATTLE-BROTHER ARAMUS AND Apothecary Gordian met relatively little resistance in their trek towards the extraction point. They encountered a gargoyle brood midway through their journey, but there were no more than a half-dozen of the bat-winged creatures in all, and firing together the bolters of the two Space Marines dealt with the gargoyles in short order. Further on they encountered a pair of warriors, but again Aramus and Gordian were able to make short work of them, sending streams of hellfire rounds into their carapaces, letting the acid do its work from within while the ceramic shells did their damage externally.

It was almost as if the price for their mission had already been paid with the lives of their fallen brothers, and that it was the Emperor's will that the pair of them should survive, the one carrying the mission's spoils – the relic – and the other carrying the Chapter's due – the gene-seed.

Finally, they reached the extraction point, at which the various squads deployed across this section of Prosperon were to rendezvous. To all indications,

Aramus and Gordian were the last to arrive, with the few surviving members of the other squads already taking up a defensive posture around the Thunderhawk, awaiting orders to board and strap in for lift-off. It was clear that Sergeant Forrin's was not the only squad to take casualties in the Prosperon undertaking, though none of the other squads had lost quite so many.

Brother-Captain Davian Thule, commander of the mission, was receiving mission reports from the other squad leaders when the newcomers arrived.

'Brother Aramus,' Captain Thule said, turning to face their approach. The captain's head was bare, his helmet under his arm, and Aramus could see the track of years in the lines etched across Thule's battle-hardened face. 'Report.'

Aramus unsealed the impact-resistant case from his hip, and proffered it to the captain. 'The relic has been recovered, brother-captain, as ordered.'

The captain accepted the case, and handed it on to a subordinate. 'And the rest of your squad? What of Sergeant Forrin? Or Brother Vela?'

Aramus opened his mouth to reply, but paused, glancing over at Apothecary Gordian.

The Apothecary had removed the straps that held the narthecium fast, and now held it protectively against his chest. 'To my shame, I was unable to recover the gene-seed of Battle-Brother Durio. The other eight' – he patted the casing of the narthecium – 'are sealed and ready for transport.'

Captain Thule nodded, seemingly satisfied, and returned his attention to Aramus.

'These last undertakings have taken their toll on the Chapter, and this day is no exception. The names of our honoured dead shall never be forgotten, and they rest now in the Emperor's glory. But their loss means that the Fifth Company finds itself in need of squad leaders.' He paused, regarding Aramus closely. 'Brother Aramus, I shall have my eye on you.'

Aramus drew himself up straight. 'Should that duty fall to me, sir, I hope only to be worthy of the honour, brother-captain.'

Thule mused for a moment, a grim smile quirking the corners of his thin-lipped mouth. He reached out and tapped the badges of penitence that Aramus, like all the battle-brothers of the Fifth Company, wore upon his armour at all times. 'You already carry a heavy burden as a member of "The Fated," Brother Aramus. Command is simply more weight to bear. Honour doesn't enter into it. Have faith in your Chapter, in your Emperor, and in your own strength, and your life – and death – will have purpose.'

Aramus nodded, and the captain turned to the others, still in defensive positions around the Thunderhawk, watchful of any incursions from the surrounding woods.

'Blood Ravens! Load up. I've no desire to linger on this Emperor-forsaken world an instant longer than is necessary.'

ARAMUS AND GORDIAN took up their positions within the troop transport compartment of the Thunderhawk, and as the engines revved to life they strapped themselves in, preparing for the pressures of lift-off and breaking orbit.

'Apothecary?' Aramus said, in a quiet voice. His eyes strayed to the narthecium held in Gordian's arms.

'Yes, Brother Aramus?' Gordian answered, glancing up and meeting his gaze.

'Our fallen brothers…' Aramus began, then broke off, struggling to form his thoughts into words. 'Do the heavy costs of our actions ever… That is, do you find yourself…'

'Am I burdened by the fact that when our brothers reach the ends of their lives and service, it falls to me to remove what is, in essence, the spark of life from their chests?'

Aramus nodded, in silence.

'It is a burden, perhaps,' Gordian said, after a moment's thought, 'but one I am honoured to carry. After all, as the Apothecary's Creed tells us, "While his gene-seed returns to the Chapter, a Space Marine cannot die." In that sense, at least, it is my function to ensure that each of our fallen brothers *never* dies, in essence.'

Aramus's lips drew into a tight line. 'But in the case of Brother Durio…'

A shadow passed over Gordian's face, and he nodded. 'In the case of Brother Durio,' Gordian said, his expression grave, 'I can only join you and the others in mourning his loss, and remember him when next the Bell of Souls rings.' He paused, and then said, 'That is why our charge is to recover the progenoid gland, whenever possible, to ensure that just such a loss can be avoided.'

Aramus considered the Apothecary's response for a moment, and managed a rueful chuckle. 'Even so,

Apothecary Gordian, you'll forgive me if I say that I hope not to find myself beneath your reductor for some long time to come.'

Aramus's chuckle failed to elicit even the slightest hint of a grin from Gordian, who instead regarded Aramus with an expression resembling pity.

'I join you in that hope, brother,' Gordian said, as the engines roared and the Thunderhawk lifted from the dead world of Prosperon. 'For all of the good such hopes will do either of us.'

CHAPTER ONE

THE SUN ROSE above the towering mountains to the east, sending shadows stretching out a hundred kilometres across the wind-sculpted desert sands. The relative cool of night clung to the shadows, like pools left behind by a retreating tide, but wherever the sunlight touched was already heating up, and quickly. By midday, the sun would beat down on the deserts like a hammer, hot enough to suck all the life and moisture from a man in a matter of hours.

Captain Davian Thule had little reason to concern himself over the heat of the midday sun, any more than he had reason to worry over the chill of the moonless desert night. Even without his blood-red power armour, his superhuman body was more than capable of handling even greater extremes of temperature and environment, but wearing his armour, as he'd done since first setting foot on Calderis a month before, he could survive everything from the cold of space to the heat of a close approach on a star's photosphere.

Thule regarded the mountains to the east, which marked the outer boundaries of human settlement on the desert world of Calderis, and the limits of his current search. Somewhere far beyond those towering peaks, past the globe's curve, lay the western hemisphere of the world, where dwelt tribes of feral orks. On this side stretched the eastern deserts, home to dozens of nomadic tribes of humans, descendants of Imperial colonists who claimed these lands in the name of the Imperium and the God-Emperor millennia before.

Few ever ventured to the Aurelia sub-sector, and fewer still came as far as Calderis, but the world had been for generations a recruiting world for the Blood Ravens, and the time had come once again for the Blood Trials.

'Any sign of it, sergeant?'

Thule turned to the Space Marine at his side. Though he wore only the gear of a Scout, not the full battle armour of an Astartes, Sergeant Cyrus was a full battle-brother of the Blood Ravens. For more than a century, Cyrus had trained the neophytes of the Chapter, doing his best to burn from them any hunger for glory, and instead to impart to them the skills and training necessary to survive life as a Space Marine in a hostile galaxy.

'No, sir,' Cyrus answered, looking up from the auspex in his hands. 'But I'm picking up movement to the north. It's inconclusive, but if I had to guess, I'd say it might be the souq we're after.'

On other worlds from which the Blood Ravens recruited, there were outpost-monasteries, and the populace was well familiar with the recruiting traditions of the Chapter. When it came time to perform the Blood Trials on such worlds, during which aspirants would compete for the honour of entering the Chapter as neophytes, a recruitment delegation would be sent from the *Omnis Arcanum*, the battle-barge that served as Chapter Fortress of the Blood Ravens, to conduct the trials. In many cases, it required nothing more than a Librarian to scan for any taint and a Chaplain to oversee the rites.

On a world like Calderis, that lacked an outpost-monastery, the Trials could be a more time-consuming prospect. But taking into consideration the fact that the majority of the population of Calderis was nomadic, never staying in the same place for more than a few months at a stretch, the time involved could often seem interminable. There were a few permanent settlements on the planet, like Argus Township at the desert's centre, but aside from those few spots on the map, the rest of the population could be found in small travelling groups of families spread out across the entire eastern hemisphere of the planet.

The recruiting mission to Calderis had been scheduled for this time of year because it was in this season that the nomadic tribes traditionally gathered in souqs, temporary settlements where anywhere from a handful of tribes to dozens of groups would gather together to barter and trade for goods, arrange marriages between families, and gather in worship of the God-Emperor on distant Holy Terra.

Nearly a week after setting out from Argus Township, though, the recruiting party had failed to find this region's souq, and aside from a few errant tribes they had encountered, had yet to screen for likely aspirants. They had intended to conduct the Blood Trials in another month in Argus Township, bringing with them all of the candidates culled from the desert tribes, but at the rate things were going, they'd hardly have enough aspirants for a decent-sized melee, much less enough to guarantee at least a few initiates to help bolster the depleted numbers of the Blood Ravens.

'Gather your scouts, sergeant,' Thule told Cyrus, turning to head back to the pair of Rhino transports that had brought the recruiting party into the desert. 'We shall track north, and hope that your guess is correct.'

As Thule crossed the rapidly heating sands to the Rhinos, he mused over the path that had brought him to this dry, desolate place. There had been a time when such a low priority undertaking would have been beneath his notice. For long years Thule had lead the Fifth Company – 'The Fated,' as they were called – with distinction and honour, claiming victory after victory, with never anything more than acceptable losses. Just under a year ago, though, Thule had found himself embroiled in the purge of Kronus, forced by circumstance to stand against fellow humans, servants of the Imperium who were not heretical, merely misguided. Though the Kronus undertaking had ended in victory for the Blood Ravens, it had left a stain on the Chapter, and on Captain Thule in particular. That stain, and other aspects of the undertaking which even at this late date remained obscured and hidden from many, Thule included, had lead to Thule's fall from grace. Once a favourite of the Secret Masters of the Blood Ravens, in the year since the Kronus undertaking he had fallen from favour. Though never censured or openly criticized for his handling of the purge, still Thule had found himself and his company assigned increasingly minor, less vital missions. This recruiting foray to the Aurelia sub-sector, surely, was his nadir.

From the glories of planet-wide combat and wars against a half-dozen armies' worth of enemies at once, to picking across a dried husk of a world for weeks and months at a time in search of a bare handful of aspirants – how much farther could Thule fall?

There would come a time, in the not too distant future, when Thule would curse himself for even thinking such a question – but only after realizing that it is *always* possible to fall farther.

As Sergeant Cyrus gathered his squad of Scouts, who he had deployed in a wide net around the area to search for any signs of recent human passage, Thule rejoined the rest of the party at the pair of Rhinos. A team of servitors was busy performing routine maintenance on the transports, overseen by a Chapter-serf, and standing between the two vehicles facing the rising sun was Chaplain Palmarius.

The sunlight glinted off the silver death's-head mask which obscured the face of the Fifth Company's spiritual leader, and glinted from the swept wings of the Imperial eagle that surmounted his crozius arcanum, the staff of office upon which the Chaplain leaned. Ribbons and scrolls fluttered in the dry wind from the purity seals which dotted his coal-black armour, and around his neck hung a pendant depicting a midnight-black raven with a teardrop of blood at its heart – the symbol of the Blood Ravens worked into a rosarius, the Chaplain's 'soul armour,' a symbol of the Ecclesiarchy and emblem of the bond between the Chapter and the Ministorum.

'The Emperor's blessings on you, captain,' the Chaplain intoned as Thule approached. Palmarius tilted his crozius arcanum in the captain's direction, dipping the staff's head only fractionally in a cursory benediction.

'Chaplain,' Captain Thule answered simply with a curt nod of his head. 'I trust the day finds you well?'

Palmarius merely turned one hand palm upwards, a gesture of indifference. 'Well enough, though I am eager to proceed with the Blood Trials. Our Chapter has suffered heavy losses, these last years, and none more so than the Fifth Company.'

Thule acknowledged the Chaplain's impatience with a knowing nod, then gestured to the collection of boys huddled in the shade of the nearest Rhino, being watched over by one of the Chapter serfs. 'Having only netted a bare handful of aspirants thus far, Chaplain, I'm sure you'll agree that we must continue our search for potential candidates, or risk returning to the Chapter with nothing but the desert sand which grits our teeth.'

'And the shame of failure,' put in a third voice from behind the captain.

Thule turned to see Librarian Niven approaching, his lean features shaded by the curve of the psychic hood upon his head, his force staff in hand. 'Just so, Librarian.'

'As you say,' the Chaplain allowed. 'But pray excuse me, as there are liturgies which must be attended to before we depart.'

As the Chaplain moved off to oversee the spiritual wellbeing of the party, and of Cyrus's neophyte Scouts in particular, Thule turned his attention to the Librarian.

'Librarian Niven.' Thule inclined his head, a brief but sincere token of respect. The captain had never been entirely comfortable around servants of the Librarium, and now was no exception.

'Captain, I wished to report…' Niven began, then paused, as though searching for the words.

'Yes, Librarian?' Thule leaned forward with interest. The ability of Librarians to peer through the veil of time was well-known, and well-trusted, in the Blood Ravens, for all that those in the Fifth Company had less experience with it than others. 'Something over tomorrow's horizon?'

Niven shook his head. 'I have no foreknowledge of future events, captain, not in this instance. Still I can't help feeling a sense of… foreboding.'

Thule narrowed his eyes, regarding the Librarian closely. The captain and the Librarian were never openly adversarial, both faithful to the Emperor and to the Chapter, but their very different personalities often seemed to put them at odds. But perhaps it was more than just their conflicting personalities that set Thule's nerves on edge. Since the days of Lucius in M.38, when the loss of the entire Fifth Company had led to their successors forever after being named 'The Fated,' the Secret Masters of the Chapter had seen to it that the Fifth had fewer Librarians than other Companies. So while the other Blood Ravens Companies had a far greater percentage of Librarians than any other Chapter – in the First Company, in fact, there were two entire combat squads of Librarians, which would have been unthinkable in any other Codex Chapter – in The Fated there were a bare handful, Niven among them.

'Foreboding, Librarian?' Thule asked, raising an eyebrow, causing the pair of golden studs affixed above the brow to dance and glitter in the bright sun.

The Librarian took a breath, appearing to centre himself, before answering. 'As you know, captain, I have only lately recovered from the injuries I sustained on Kronus, and while my body has mended, I sometimes feel that my spirit has yet to recover.'

Thule's lips tightened to a line. 'Are you suggesting, Niven,' he asked, his tone perched between outrage and disbelief, 'that I should be concerned about your soundness of mind?' The captain could not help recalling the names of other Librarians of the Blood Ravens, sorely tested in the battlefield, who went on to infamy – Phraius, Akios, Nox...

The Librarian drew himself up, anger fleeting briefly across his features, as though the mere suggestion was an offensive outrage. He regained his composure in the next instant, though, and shook his head, answering in measured tones.

'No, captain. There is no cause for concern on my account. It has been only weeks since I was last examined by the Chief Librarian himself, and deemed free from taint and perfectly able to serve.' Like all Librarians in the Blood Ravens, Thule knew, Niven was extensively monitored by the Chapter's Librarium for signs of corruption, to ensure that he had not fallen to the insidious lure of the Ruinous Powers or else succumbed to any of the other strains to which psykers were prone. 'Still, I cannot escape the sense that there is something… lurking at the edge of my awareness, some malevolent presence I can't yet identify. It brushes my thoughts but lightly, and yet it is there, nonetheless.'

Thule was thoughtful for a moment, considering Niven's words. There were four golden studs affixed to the captain's forehead, a pair over each brow, each of them reflecting a century of faithful service to the Blood Ravens. Thule might not have been comfortable around servants of the Librarium, principally because there were so few of them in the Fifth Company and his experience with them perforce was comparatively limited, but he had not survived long enough to earn four service-studs by ignoring the advice of Librarians. If he was to survive long enough to wear a fifth, it would be by making use of all information at his disposal. Thule knew too well that, just as the Blood Ravens' battle-cry held, 'Knowledge is power.'

'I will take your words under advisement, Brother-Librarian,' Captain Thule said at length. 'And if the nature of your lurking presence should make itself known to you, I trust you will not remain silent.'

Niven straightened, his expression hardening. If the admission of the Librarian's uncertainty about his premonition had served to hint, in part, of any weakness of character on his part, Niven was clearly not in any mood to allow any lingering questions about his fitness to serve. 'I shall, of course, do my duty, captain, as a Blood Raven.'

Thule nodded. 'I would expect nothing else, Librarian.'

A DAY AND a night passed before the party finally located the souq, a collection of a few dozen tents around a desert oasis. Transports like the Rhinos were rare on a world where most travelled by foot or by horseback, and so as the party approached, the locals gathered at the souq's southern edge, waiting with a mixture of fear and wonder. The anxiety and awe of the inhabitants only increased when Thule climbed down onto the desert sands, towering over even the tallest of the locals.

'The Blood Ravens come seeking aspirants for the Blood Trials,' Thule announced, without preamble.

It had been more than a generation since last the Blood Ravens came recruiting to Calderis, but the oldest among the souq's inhabitants still remembered the Blood Trials, and the youngest of them had been raised on stories of the God-Emperor upon his Golden Throne on distant Terra, and of the fabled Space Marines, giants among men, who protected the Imperium of Man from its innumerable foes out in the vast blackness of space.

The elders of the *ad hoc* community greeted Thule and the others in heavily-accented Low Gothic,

singing songs of praise, and invited the Blood
Ravens to join in a ceremonial sharing of water. In a
land in which the desert might swallow any unwary
traveller whole, never to be seen again, customs of
hospitality had been codified millennia before, and
no Calderian would ever dream of withholding
water from a visitor to their camp.

Thule accepted the water with the Chapter's
thanks, and in the name of the Emperor. Like the
other Space Marines, the captain had no need to
take in liquid sustenance, but drank in recognition
of the rituals importance to the Calderians. It was
just as well that he had no need to quench his thirst.
Pulled from the wells around which the souq had
been clustered, the water was brackish and saline;
potable, but only just. Thule's oolitic kidney, one of
the implants which had transformed him into an
Astartes, was of course capable of filtering any toxins
that entered his system, rendering them harmless,
but still did nothing to affect the foul taste of the
stuff on the tongue.

'Now,' Thule said, handing back the empty vessel
to the elders, 'gather all of the young men and boys
together for evaluation.'

Behind the elders, the parents of the souq
exchanged guarded glances, but seeing the looks of
stern warning on the Space Marines' faces, none
raised a voice in question or objection.

IT WAS AN incomparable honour to be selected as an
initiate into an Astartes Chapter, to be given the
chance to be transformed into a superhuman
machine of war, to serve the Imperium as no

mundane man ever could. But while Thule knew the honour that the merest chance of surviving the initiation would proffer upon the shoulders of the young aspirants, it was clear that many of the boys themselves were less clear on the matter.

'No,' the Librarian said, shaking his head and waving a hand in a dismissive gesture at the boy who stood snuffling on the dry ground before him. 'This one has a weak mind. He will not serve.'

'Agreed,' Chaplain Palmarius said, features hidden behind his silver death's-head. He had only recently finished judging the boy's intelligence with questions regarding his childish understanding of the Emperor, the Imperium, and Man's place in the universe. 'Unsuitable.'

The boy, eyes wide and nose running, looked from one to the other for a moment, uncomprehending, and then when he finally realized he had been dismissed scurried away back to his parents' side, sobbing with gratitude and relief. The pathetic boy acted as if he were a mouse allowed to climb back out of the snake's mouth after being swallowed.

Sergeant Cyrus, at a glance from Thule, motioned to one of his Scouts, who went and selected the next boy from the shuffling ranks at the souq's centre. There'd been more than a dozen in all when they'd started the examinations, and now only a handful remained, but so far none had passed muster and been chosen to join the recruiting party on their return to Argus Township for the Blood Trials.

As the resisting boy was dragged to stand before the Chaplain and Librarian, the winds shifted, carrying with them the stench of the livestock pens at the

western edge of the souq. It was the smell of
unwashed animals, of offal and sweat; the aroma of
beasts of burden who would work until they
dropped from the desert heat, and of others who
lived near lives of luxury, for the moment at least,
fattened and pampered but destined for the dinner
table.

Thule considered putting on the helmet that he
carried under his arm, if only to breathe for a
moment the familiar recycled air of his own power
armour, rather than the heat and stench of the pens.
But as the wind shifted again, coming now from the
north, it carried with it another unpleasant odour, if
perhaps a tantalizingly familiar one.

'Sergeant Cyrus,' Thule said in a low voice, calling
the Scout sergeant to his side as the Chaplain and
Librarian began their examination of the new candidate.

'Yes, captain?' Unlike most Blood Ravens, who
wore their hair close-cropped, Cyrus let his grow
long and unkempt, so that it now whipped around
his face like an errant halo in the hot desert winds.

'Have you yet found a source for those movement
traces you picked up en route?'

Cyrus narrowed his eyes, lips pursed, and shook
his head. It was clear that the sergeant felt it a personal failing that his auspex had registered
movement past the horizon that he'd subsequently
been unable to locate. 'No, sir.' He paused, considering. 'It could have been a sensor shadow, signals
bouncing off a sandstorm, maybe even mirroring
our own movements back at us.' He left off, gauging
the captain's response.

'But you don't believe that's the case?'

'No, sir,' Cyrus answered after a moment's pause. 'I think there's something out there – whether another caravan, or a string of horses that's run off from their masters, or something – but I don't know yet what it is.'

Thule considered, sniffing the air. 'I'm inclined to agree.' Thule glanced over at the examinations, which by the looks of displeasure on the Librarian's face were going no better than the previous had done. 'Sergeant, I want you to establish a picket, and send some of your Scouts out on a–'

Before Thule could complete his instructions, cries of alarm sounded from the far side of the souq. One of the elders rushed into the space set aside for the examinations, mouth open in a wide 'O' of terror, the whites showing all around the edges of his obsidian-dark eyes.

'*Ifriti!*' the old man yelped, rushing towards Thule and waving his arms as though he were attempting to take flight. '*Ifriti!*'

Cryus, who had already unslung the sniper rifle he always carried over his shoulder, shot Thule a questioning glance. 'Sir? What's he saying?'

The captain was already fitting his helmet into place and taking long strides in the direction from which the locals were fleeing.

'It's a word in the native dialect,' Thule said, referring to the language into which the old man had lapsed. He drew and racked his bolter. He finally knew what the familiar stench on the wind had been, and the movements in the desert distances that Cyrus had been unable to identify. 'It means "monster".'

Thule reached the far side of the cluster of tents. The skies to the north were blackened by a massive cloud of dust and sand, as though a storm were rushing down upon them. And across the deserts rang out a booming noise almost like thunder. But it was not thunder, and this was no storm. Or rather it was, but not one of wind, rain, or sand. The keen eyes of the Space Marines showed them what the Calderians could not yet see, but what the desert traditions had taught them that such a sandstorm meant. The dust-cloud was being kicked up in the wake of hundreds upon hundreds of tramping feet. And the thunderous booms were in fact shouts of animal rage, war cries issuing from the advancing horde.

'Blood Ravens!' Thule voxed over the comms, raising his bolter and taking aim. 'Defensive posture, severe threat.'

The examinations would have to wait. And in fact it remained to be seen whether the Blood Trials would be held or not. As it stood, Captain Thule and his party had more pressing concerns.

The feral orks thundered towards them, a ragtag motley of savage giants, primitive and barbaric, the weapons they wielded crudely made but no less deadly.

Thule fired his bolter into the advancing ranks, with his third shot managing to bring down one of the feral orks in the lead. He didn't allow himself to feel any sense of accomplishment. With one of the green-skinned monsters down, there were still hundreds upon hundreds more in the stampeding horde.

'Knowledge is power!' Thule called out the Blood Ravens' battle cry, drawing his power sword and hacking into the closest ork at hand. 'Guard it well!'

The greenskin tide closed around them, and the storm of sand engulfed the souq.

CHAPTER TWO

THE SPARRING HALL was draped in silence, punctuated only occasionally by the sound of fist striking flesh, or by the more muted thump of a diverted kick or parried blow. The two Space Marines, equally matched in strength and skill, made scarcely any utterance, their complete attention on the intricate dance of attack, counter-attack, and attack.

Had the strike cruiser *Armageddon* been manned at full capacity, the cavernous sparring hall would have been crowded with Blood Ravens, both full battle-brothers and initiate Scouts, testing their mettle, honing their combat skills, keeping their edge during the long trek through the immaterium from undertaking to undertaking. This was one of the Space Marines' favoured places onboard the strike cruiser, and seldom untenanted under normal circumstances. But the *Armageddon* was scarcely a fraction occupied, and aside from the hundred-odd Chapter serfs and innumerable servitors who serviced her, there were only four squads of Space Marines onboard, and none of them operating at full strength. Their recent undertaking on the planet Zalamis had been a victory for the Chapter, but had taken a heavy toll, and there wasn't one of the squads sent on the mission who hadn't lost at least one of their battle-brothers. And so it was that, as the *Armageddon* continued towards her new destination, the two Space Marines were the only occupants of the sparring hall.

Brother-Sergeant Thaddeus lifted his right leg high, as if to launch another kick, but instead stepped forward and delivered a roundhouse to Brother-Sergeant Aramus's midsection. Aramus managed to sidestep the kick, and riposted with a closed-fist punch aimed at Thaddeus's abdomen. The punch impacted, but the energy of the blow was absorbed as Thaddeus pulled away, sideswiping Aramus's arm away. Aramus was thrown slightly off-balance, and Thaddeus seized the advantage by whipping his right knee upwards in a front-knee kick, connecting with Aramus's groin.

A quick exhalation hissed through Aramus's teeth, but he recovered his stance immediately, and blocked Thaddeus's next blow with a sweep of his right arm, then followed with a left-handed punch thrown from the shoulder that caught Thaddeus in the solar plexus. Thaddeus grunted, all but inaudibly, and danced back out of the reach of Aramus's next blow.

Each of the two Space Marines was dressed in a blood-red chiton, their arms and legs bare. The same height, with similar builds and profiles, they could have easily been brothers, with Thaddeus's lighter complexion and Aramus's somewhat darker being the only significant difference between them. They were of an age, as well, each in the middle of his fourth decade of life, though with the life-extending benefits of the implants that had transformed them from mortals into superhuman Astartes, neither looked older than the middle of their third decade. And while they were not brothers by blood, merely battle-brothers of the Blood Ravens Chapter, in another sense they *were* the sons of the same mother – the same mother world at any rate, both native to the planet Meridian, capital of the Aurelia sub-sector.

'Hold,' Aramus said, his hands held up and palm-out towards Thaddeus, just as the latter was readying for another attack. Sweat ran in rivulets down both of their bodies, and even with the all-but-boundless stamina of an Astartes in his prime, both were growing increasingly winded after their long sparring match. 'A moment's rest.'

A sly grin tugged the corners of Thaddeus's mouth, as he considered Aramus's request. 'Do you concede the bout, then, brother?'

Aramus grinned in reply. 'Not hardly. If it comes to it, I can keep this up from here to Calderis.'

Thaddeus wiped the sweat from his brow with the back of a bare hand. 'If we should try that,' he said, chuckling, 'I think I'd succumb to boredom before I ever fell before your blows.'

'Perhaps we're too evenly matched, at that.' Aramus stuck out his hand. 'Then let's call it a draw, or a postponement if nothing else.'

'Agreed,' Thaddeus answered, grasping Aramus's wrist. His grin widened. 'But I'd have beaten you sooner or later, Aramus.'

Aramus tightened his grip around Thaddeus's wrist. 'A postponement, then.'

The two Space Marines moved to the side of the hall, where towels hung from a brass rail. They wiped the sweat and grime from their faces and arms in silence, their bodies gradually relaxing, heart-rates slowing and breathing returning to normal rhythms.

'That was a devious feint you made there at the beginning, Aramus,' Thaddeus said at length. He tapped his left temple, just above his ear. 'You almost had me then.'

Aramus's lips curled in a devious grin. 'If you weren't so damned hard-headed, I would have.' He stretched the fingers of his right hand, opening and closing his fist. 'Like hitting ceramite, that skull of yours.'

Thaddeus chuckled, and hung his towel around his thick neck. He paused for a moment, thoughtfully. 'Aramus, I meant to ask before. How is your squad faring?'

Aramus's lips tightened, the humour draining from his expression. It had been only a matter of months since he'd been promoted to the rank of brother-sergeant and given command of the Fifth Company's Third Squad, the third of six tactical squads in the company. Only a few months the commander of the Third Squad, and already Aramus had lost three battle-brothers in the undertaking on Zalamis. Counting himself, there were only seven Astartes in the squad at the moment, and barring reinforcements the Third Squad would be operating at partial strength for the time being. Aramus had hoped to redress the recent losses once they returned to the Fifth Company's battle-barge, *Scientia Est Potentia*, either by drawing Space Marines from other squads operating at or above full strength, or through the promotion of Blood Ravens Scouts to full battle-brother status. But en route to *Scientia Est Potentia* after the undertaking on Zalamis, the *Armageddon* had changed course, and was now bound for the Aurelia sub-sector.

'Well enough, Thaddeus,' Aramus replied in measured tones. 'We have been drilling, these last weeks, adapting battle plans and strategies to our reduced numbers.'

Thaddeus nodded, thoughtfully. His own command, the Seventh Squad, one of two assault squads in the Fifth Company, had suffered lighter losses on Zalamis and was currently at a strength of nine Space Marines in total, one of whom was still recovering from his injuries with the help of the company Apothecary.

'So,' Thaddeus said, finally. He brightened somewhat, and clapped his hands together, punctuating the end of the previous discussion. 'Aurelia, eh?'

'Aurelia,' Aramus replied, nodding. 'I'd not thought to come back this way, I'll admit.'

'Nor did I, brother.'

The two Blood Ravens had both been born and raised on Meridian, capital of the sub-sector, and both recruited into the Chapter during the same Blood Trials, more than two decades before. Unlike other Chapters of the Adeptus Astartes, though, many of whom had their own home worlds and who might well serve on the planets of their birth throughout the long years of service to their Chapter, the Blood Ravens were a Crusading Chapter, with no home but the massive fortress-monastery *Omnis Arcanum* and the ships of the fleet that followed in her wake. Once inducted into the Chapter, Blood Ravens seldom returned to their home worlds.

And while the desert world of Calderis was light years away from the world of their birth, it fell within the Aurelia sub-sector and so was governed by Meridian, which was much closer than either of them ever expected to come to their original home.

Not, that is, that the home recalled in the memories of the two Space Marines was the same. Aramus had been born into luxury, a member of the upper classes in their high-habs, while Thaddeus had grown up a ganger from the low-level habs. Born and raised only kilometres from one another, the two had effectively come from different worlds. But since passing the Blood Trials, and then their initiation into the ranks of the Astartes, they were battle-brothers, a bond more powerful and real than any ties of blood or kinship.

'Tell me, Thaddeus, do you suppose…' Aramus began, but left off as they felt the deck shifting beneath their feet.

Though the sparring hall looked the same as it had before, and the sound of their voices still echoed off the far walls in just the same way, still the two Blood Ravens could sense that the world had changed around them. It was as though there had been a man screaming in the next room all this while, and that the two had only noticed it now that the screaming had stopped and a palpable silence had taken its place.

The screaming they hadn't noticed had been the discharge of the strike cruiser's warp engines, the psychic trauma of it hidden from the passenger areas of the *Armageddon* by heavy shielding, that could not quite entirely block its effects from those within. Beyond the shielded hull had lain the incomprehensible dimensions of the immaterium, home of madness and monsters.

But the warp engines had gone silent, the discharge ended, and now there was nothing beyond the hull of the strike cruiser but the more familiar, saner dimensions of normal space. The *Armageddon* had made the transition from the immaterium back into real space.

Before either Space Marine could speak, an intercom chimed, hidden in the rafters high overhead, and a voice buzzed out.

'This is Sergeant Merrik. All squad leaders to the command deck for immediate briefing.'

Thaddeus and Aramus exchanged a glance, and then hurried towards the entrance to the sparring hall, all jests and jibes forgotten. They had learned as initiates that, when Merrik called, it didn't pay to keep him waiting.

SERGEANT MERRIK STOOD beside the captain's chair on the command dais, looking out over the railing at the command deck proper and the forward viewport beyond. Like the rest of the ships in the Blood Ravens fleet, the *Armageddon* was crewed almost entirely by servitors; half-human cyborgs wired directly into the ship's weapons, engines, and communications. At the control stations that ringed the command dais, dozens of servitors devoted their entire attentions to crystals and controls, monitoring the ship's myriad systems and processes. The only humans in evidence were Chapter serfs, some of the hundred or so onboard who served the ship and her crew, and none of these were responsible for anything other than routine maintenance and cleaning.

Merrik was dressed in full power armour, the ceramite enamelled blood-red; on his left shoulderguard the midnight-black raven with the teardrop of blood at its heart that was the symbol of the Blood Ravens, on his right shoulder-guard the upwardspointing arrow of a tactical squad with a number '1' emblazoned upon it. Each shoulder-guard, right and left, was the colour of ivory, and rimmed in midnight black. If his bearing and position on the dais were not evidence enough, to say nothing of the reputation of nearly two centuries of decorated service, these emblems and colours alone would mark him as the leader of Fifth Company's First Squad, first of six tactical squads. Onboard the strike cruiser *Armageddon*, however, Merrik was not merely squad leader, but acting Commander at Sail.

As was proper in a ship of the Adeptus Astartes, the only officers onboard the strike cruiser were Space Marines, Merrik chief among them. In the enginarium in the lower decks, where the massive warp engines were even now only beginning to spin down, Techmarine Martellus oversaw the ship's mechanical systems; that is, when his attention could be torn away from the empty Dreadnought assembly they were transporting back to the *Scientia Est Potentia*. The Dreadnought, lacking the biological component of an Astartes to guide it, had been only recently refitted and refurbished by the tech-priests of Mars, and was nearing the end of a years-long journey via one ship or another to its final home in the Fifth Company. Just who would be encased in the Dreadnought armour, just which Astartes would be granted the great honour of living beyond death within its shell, their remains suspended within and their minds animating the war-engine, none could say.

The ship's captain a Blood Raven, and a Techmarine of the Chapter at her engines – not only were the few officers onboard the *Armageddon* Space Marines, they were more importantly Blood Ravens. Even in the case of the ship's astropath, instead of a member of the Adeptus Astra Telepathica, the *Armageddon* instead employed Lexicanium Konan, a servant of the Blood Ravens Librarium. In fact, of all the ship's command functions, only that of Navigator was filled by any but Blood Ravens, the inscrutable Lord Principal in his dome an inhuman scion of the Navis Nobilite. But then, Sergeant Merrik found it difficult to imagine what kind of human could descend from the Navigator Houses, their third eye able to peer beyond the veil of space to guide a ship through the insane geometries of the empyrium, and yet still be found suitable for a place in the rolls of a Codex Chapter of the Adeptus Astartes.

Merrik's idle musings were interrupted by the sound of approaching feet. Not the heavy tread of a

Space Marine in power armour, but the lighter foot-falls of an unarmoured human. Merrik turned to face the Chapter serf who approached, his eyes lowered to the ground deferentially.

'Report,' Merrik said simply, without preamble.

Like all the Chapter serfs on board the *Armageddon*, and in fact on all the ships of the Blood Ravens fleet, this man was a fiercely loyal adherent of one of the lesser orders of the Blood Ravens' Cult. As the serf lifted his gaze momentarily to look upon the sergeant's face, Merrik recognized him as a one-time aspirant to the Blood Ravens Chapter, who had succeeded in the Blood Trials on his native world decades before, but who had been found unsuitable for initiation before the first of the implants had been administered. As often happened in the cases of such unfortunates, this man's life had been spared, and given new meaning, as a place was found for him in the service of the Chapter. Having served long years on board the *Armageddon*, he had risen to the rank of deck hand, and was one of a dozen such serfs who routinely relayed reports from the servitors to the officers – having learned enough of the binary-squeal language of the cyborgs to translate it into more easily comprehensible Low Gothic – or else relayed messages from one officer to another.

'Sir,' the Chapter serf answered with a deeper bow, 'passive sensors confirm that we have reached the outskirts of the Calderis system.'

'Time to planet-side?'

'Techmarine Martellus sends his compliments, sir,' the Chapter serf replied quickly, 'and says that with sublight engines at full burn we should make planetfall before the day is out.'

Sergeant Merrik dismissed the Chapter serf with a nod, and went back to regarding the forward viewport. At the centre of the heavily reinforced window he could see a star burning, baleful and red. Somewhere in the black void around that sun circled their destination, the desert world Calderis. And somewhere on that desert world, Merrik hoped, they would find Captain Thule and his recruiting party. Or, failing that, they would discover what had befallen Thule and his people, and then Merrik and the others would seek revenge.

'As you are all aware,' Sergeant Merrik said, once the squad leaders had gathered on the command deck, 'we are now inbound for Calderis, in the Aurelia sub-sector.'

There were four Space Marines gathered on the dais before him, all like Merrik encased in their full power armour. Together, they represented the leadership of the Blood Ravens onboard the *Armageddon*, with centuries of experience between them. The youngest, Sergeants Aramus and Thaddeus, had yet to earn a single service stud, while the oldest, Sergeant Tarkus, already had three service studs and was on his way to a fourth.

'Before leaving the Zalamis system some weeks back, our Lexicanium received an astropathic call from Librarian Niven, who accompanied Captain Thule on a recruiting mission to Calderis over two months ago. For reasons as yet unclear, Niven's telepathic message was fragmentary, garbled, but enough reached our Lexicanium to get the message across. Captain Thule and his party were under attack by a considerable number of feral orks, and Thule put out a call for reinforcements.'

Merrik paused, studying the faces before him, seeing the careful attention writ on each.

'The transport which carried the recruiting party to Calderis is not due to return for some time, and the *Armageddon* was the only Blood Ravens vessel in range to respond to the call. Now, I don't need to remind you that we are already operating on reduced strength after the recent action on Zalamis, but our orders in this instance are clear. We will go planet-side and offer whatever assistance the captain requires.'

'What is the latest from Librarian Niven?' Sergeant Tarkus asked.

Merrik regarded the veteran campaigner. It was the right question to ask at this moment, information whose omission in Merrik's summary was more than suspicious.

Only a few years Merrik's junior, Tarkus should have been given a command of his own by now. But he had served for so long beneath such an illustrious group of squad leaders – including Captain Davian Thule himself when he had still been merely Sergeant Thule – that Tarkus had not yet been given the chance. Recently, and despite Merrik's recommendations to the contrary, Thule had instead promoted the younger Battle-Brother Aramus to squad leadership and the rank of sergeant, and assigned Tarkus to act as Aramus's number two in the squad. Tarkus was a loyal Blood Raven and an exemplary Space Marine, so he would do as ordered, but Merrik could not help but wonder if his old friend resented once more being passed over for a younger, more visible Space Marine.

'There is no word, I'm afraid,' Merrik answered at last. 'After that first signal, our Lexicanium has had no further astropathic communication from Librarian Niven. Now that we have re-emerged in normal space, we are attempting to establish vox communication with Thule's party, but as yet have not made contact.'

The other Space Marines exchanged glances at that.

'The captain had only a handful of Blood Ravens with him, and most of those mere Scouts,' rumbled Sergeant Avitus, his voice tinged with a machine-like buzz, his eyes flashing darkly. The lower half of Avitus's jaw and most of his throat had been replaced by augmetic long years before, after a battle with a tyranid norn-queen left him with injuries that the Apothecaries and his own body could not repair, and which therefore the Techmarines were required to address. 'If there are as many greenskins down there as you suggest, is there any reason to suspect that Thule and his people are still alive?'

Merrik turned his gaze on Avitus. The leader of Ninth Squad, a Devastator squad, Avitus was a mountain of barely controlled rage. It was whispered in the halls of the *Scientia Est Potentia* that Avitus's soul had died months before, back on Kronus during the Battle of Victory Bay, leaving his body to go on and fight. It had been there that Avitus had watched as his battle-brothers had been gunned

down by misguided Imperial Guardsmen, killed by
the same Imperial citizens he'd sworn his life to protect. Avitus had survived the barrage, and repaid it
with a heavy flamer, scouring bunker after bunker of
Guardsmen before moving on to deal burning death
to the armed civilians who had thrown their lot in
with the renegade Governor-Militant. Avitus had
survived the undertaking on Kronus, but had carried
away with him nothing but disdain for the common
citizens of the Imperium, and precious little regard
for his battle-brothers in the Blood Ravens, as well.

'Until we have solid evidence to the contrary,' Merrik replied evenly, 'we will operate under the
assumption that Thule *is* still down there, and if he
is then he'll require reinforcing.'

'What of the native population?' Sergeant Aramus
put in. 'Calderis isn't heavily populated, as I understand it, but the numbers of inhabitants must still
number in the millions.'

'What of them?' Avitus snarled, a growling sound
buzzing from his throat. 'Pay them the slightest
mind, brother, and that's more consideration than
they'd ever give to you.'

'The planet below is Calderis, Brother-Sergeant
Avitus,' Tarkus said in a metered voice, 'not Kronus.
Perhaps you misheard the name?'

Avitus turned on Tarkus, eyes flashing. 'You'd protect disloyal, simpering *fools*, Tarkus?' The Devastator
took a step towards Tarkus, and given the fury evident on Avitus's face it looked as though they might
come to blows at any moment.

Tarkus just smiled, and held his hands out to
either side, palm upwards, as though he were giving

a benediction. 'The Emperor protects, Avitus. I merely carry out His will.'

Thaddeus chuckled, and Avitus turned his angry gaze on the younger sergeant, but the tension had broken. Avitus did not smile, but the rage in his face began to cool, and he took a step back, hands relaxing at his sides.

Merrik looked with admiration at Sergeant Tarkus. He knew that Tarkus was a man of faith, who unlike most other Blood Ravens regarded the Emperor as a god, and not merely as the mightiest of men. Was it Tarkus's faith that gave him such a dry wit, and the ability to dissolve tense situations with a few choice words? Or was it the other way around?

'The Emperor commands,' Merrik added, 'and we obey. And our orders now are to go down to Calderis and offer what assistance we can.' He paused, and looked from Avitus to the others, pointedly. 'And that is precisely what we will do.'

HOURS LATER, SERGEANT Aramus stood near the forward viewport, looking at the dun-coloured disc of the desert world Calderis as it hove into view. It would not be long now before they would be in range to descend to the planet in the trio of Thunderhawk gunships already prepared and ready in the launch bays of the *Armageddon*. Too impatient to wait below decks for the call to action, though, Aramus had returned to the command deck to watch their final approach with his own eyes, and not through images retransmitted to a data-slate.

'Greetings, brother-sergeant,' came a voice at his elbow.

Aramus turned to find Apothecary Gordian standing beside him, already dressed for the field in his white power armour with the Prime Helix emblazoned upon the right shoulder-guard and the blood raven upon the left, with his narthecium strapped across his back.

'Greetings, Apothecary,' Aramus answered, inclining his head minutely.

'What is the latest intelligence from the surface?' Gordian asked, coming to stand beside Aramus and peering out the viewport. 'Does our Lexicanium report any astropathic contact with Librarian Niven?'

'No,' Aramus said with a shake of his head. 'But en route from the system's edge, as I understand it, we were able to establish vox contact with Thule's party. The signal quality was weak and the message somewhat degraded, too much so for us to know much about the situation on the ground, but we have been given landing coordinates. Thule's forces are to meet us there.'

Gordian's eyes were fixed on the dun-coloured disc below them. 'I can't help but wonder what has become of Niven.' Gordian paused, and pointed a gauntleted hand at the viewport. 'Aramus, look at that.'

They had come close enough to Calderis now that the planet's small moon was visible, but more than that they could also now clearly distinguish what appeared to be vessels in orbit around the planet, now circling into view. And not just one or two, but some dozen or more.

'Sergeant Merrik?' Aramus said, turning to look towards the command dais where the Commander at Sail stood.

'We see them, brother-sergeant,' Merrik answered, stepping forward to lean on the brass rail that ran around the circumference of the command dais. He shot a glance to the servitors monitoring the ship's sensors. 'Report.'

The servitors sent back a cacophony of binary squeals in response.

'Thirteen ships in orbit, sir,' one of the Chapter serfs translated. 'No, fourteen. Most are civilian registry, but there are three Imperial Navy vessels, Dauntless-class light cruisers.'

Aramus could see the annoyance and curiosity playing across Merrik's face. There were typically few, if any ships in the vicinity of Calderis, or in fact anywhere in the Aurelia sub-sector, much less more than a dozen.

The servitor at the communications station squealed. 'Incoming hail from the lead Imperial Navy vessel, sir,' a Chapter serf relayed.

Merrik considered for a moment, then nodded. 'On speakers.'

An instant later, after another brief squeal, a voice buzzed from speakers mounted in the bulkheads around the command deck. It was a woman's voice, a velvet gauntlet over a fist of iron.

'Space Marines vessel, this is Fleet Admiral Laren Forbes of the Battlegroup Aurelia, onboard the *Sword of Hadrian*. Please identify.'

Merrik straightened, as though his posture would carry over the vox signal. 'You are addressing Brother-Sergeant Merrik of the Blood Ravens Fifth Company, Commander at Sail of the strike cruiser *Armageddon*.'

A smattering of static peppered the vox signal, and the admiral had to repeat her next question twice before it was successfully transmitted.

'*Armageddon*, have you come to offer assistance?'

'In what capacity might you expect us to assist?' Merrik replied, somewhat confused.

'Battlegroup Aurelia is responding to a distress call sent out by the Calderis civilian authority,' Admiral Forbes replied. 'On the authority of Governor Vandis of Meridian, we are in the process of evacuating key members of the planet's civilian population.'

Aramus knew what the admiral meant by 'key members' of the population, and by the expression on Merrik's face he could see the sergeant did, too. Even with a population as small as that of Calderis, there was simply no way an entire planet could be evacuated, whatever the threat. Instead, those who the admiral was taking off-world would be powerful politicians, noble families with ties to this Governor Vandis, and so on.

'And the civilian vessels?' Merrik asked, pointedly.

The admiral paused a moment before replying. 'We are not in a position to evacuate everyone, of course. Those with resources of their own have arranged for private transportation.'

Aramus could well imagine what that meant. Those lacking the prestige of the planet's political elite, but who had wealth enough of their own to call upon, had contracted civilian merchant trader vessels to whisk them out of harm's way.

As for those who lacked political prestige *and* wealth…?

Aramus could well imagine what remained for them.

'We have orders of our own to carry out, admiral,' Merrik replied, 'but we wish you good fortune in the successful completion of yours. *Armageddon* out.'

At a sign from Merrik the vox signal was cut, and the speakers overhead went silent.

'Come, Blood Ravens,' Merrik called to Aramus and Gordian, stepping down from the command dais and heading towards the corridor. 'We have responsibilities to attend.'

CHAPTER THREE

BROTHER-SERGEANT ARAMUS SETTLED into the acceleration chair in the troop transport compartment of the Thunderhawk, checking the safety on his bolter before stowing it at his side. The other members of Third Squad found their places around him, except for Brother Voire, who had taken the Thunderhawk's controls. Sergeant Tarkus had the seat across from Aramus, and was quietly muttering a prayer to the God-Emperor.

Aside from the Third Squad, a handful of Space Marines from Sergeant Merrik's First Squad had joined them, the rest riding in the second Thunderhawk with Sergeant Merrik and with Sergeant Avitus's Ninth Squad, while the third gunship carried Sergeant Thaddeus's Seventh Squad with their bulky jump packs.

'Thunderhawks,' came the voice of Techmarine Martellus over the gunship's vox-channel. 'You are cleared for departure.'

Techmarine Martellus had been left in command of the *Armageddon*, with every other able-bodied Blood Raven tapped for the planet-side mission. It had seemed to Aramus that Martellus had seemed merely annoyed by the additional responsibility, and that the Techmarine would much rather be below decks in the enginarium, ministering to his precious Dreadnought assembly.

Like most Astartes, Aramus was somewhat in awe of the hermetic knowledge that a Techmarine like Martellus possessed, but also like most Astartes he was likewise grateful that he himself had not been selected to journey to Mars to study alongside the devotees of the Machine God, the mysterious Adeptus Mechanicus. Techmarines, like their brother tech-priests, magi, and adepts in the Cult Mechanicus, revered the Omnissiah, and preached that biological life had no meaning unless married with the mechanical, and that only in the union between machine and man might perfection be approached. The Dreadnought, when bonded to the barely living form of a Blood Raven injured almost unto death, represented the ultimate exemplar of the Mechanicus beliefs.

As for Sergeant Aramus, he was a Blood Raven, and like most of his battle-brothers believed in no god. And unlike most Codex Chapters, the Blood Ravens did not even have a primarch in whose name they fought, and whose example they strove to follow. Since the Blood Ravens did not know from which primarch or Chapter they originally descended, they revered no one so much as the Immortal Emperor on Holy Terra, supreme master of all Space Marines and mightiest of men.

'All secure?' Voire called back from the flight deck.

The Space Marines in the troop transport compartment sounded off, one after another, confirming they were ready for launch.

'Go for launch,' Voire voxed to the servitors manning the launch bay controls.

A moment later, the launch bay doors opened. Guided by the machine spirit that governed the Thunderhawk's systems, Voire manoeuvred the gunship out into the vacuum using only the retro exhaust nozzles, and once the craft was clear of the doors he punched up a full burn. Propellant from the onboard fusion reactor pumped into the combustion chambers in each of the rocket boosters beneath the Thunderhawk's wings, which ignited to produce a high-pressure stream of gases, rapidly accelerating the craft forward.

'Insertion in three,' Voire intoned, 'two. One.'

With a sound like the screaming of the damned, the Thunderhawk hit the outer edges of the planet's atmosphere with a ballistic entry trajectory, coming in high and hot. The outer hull temperature soared as the atmospheric density grew higher and higher, but the ceramite layers and thermoplas fibre mesh employed in the Thunderhawk's construction were more than sufficient to keep the heat of atmospheric entry from bleeding into the interior of the craft.

'About to clear cloud cover,' Voire called back.

Hardly feeling the G-forces of acceleration within the confines of his power armour, Aramus swivelled a wall-mounted data-slate into position before him and called up a feed from the gunship's forward cameras. At first, all he could see was a swathe of dingy white, the heavy clouds that were at present smothering the eastern deserts. A moment later, the clouds parted like a curtain as the Thunderhawk shot downward like a bolter round, and the vistas below were revealed.

Directly below them, Aramus could make out the outlines of the township of Argus, their designated landing coordinates. A few kilometres on a side, Argus was laid out in a haphazard grid, roughly square in shape and aligned more-or-less north and south. It was an unremarkable sight, a small patch of urban development on the otherwise unbroken expanses of rock and sand that stretched out to the horizon in every direction. Or rather, it would have been an unremarkable sight, had the township itself and its inhabitants been the only elements visible on the data-slate.

However, Argus was not the only thing visible. Instead, it was all but surrounded by what appeared at first instance a motley-coloured ocean, a shifting tide of greens, blacks, browns, and reds, that verged on the boundaries of Argus township on three sides, north, east, and south. Smoke rose from that discoloured ocean, and periodically flashes of light flared up from within, signs of weapons-fire.

It was a horde of feral orks, threatening to engulf Argus completely. And it was into this maelstrom that the Blood Ravens were descending.

* * *

CAPTAIN DAVIAN THULE stood at the centre of a cavernous building, reviewing action reports by the dim light filtering in from the gaps in the roofing. It had been more than a week since he'd established a temporary headquarters in the shipping depot at the western edge of Argus, not far from the rudimentary space port that served the township.

Most of the crates and boxes that had filled the structure had been repurposed, in those early hours and days. Originally shipping containers from all over Calderis, from the other worlds of the Aurelia sub-sector and a few from even farther afield, had been stacked as makeshift furniture, arranged as tables and benches for the use of Thule and his people. Those who had owned the containers were in no position to contest their being commandeered – those who had survived the initial waves of the feral ork attacks were too busy trying to flee the planet to waste any time worrying about shipments that would never arrive.

Thule was alone in the depot at the moment, but for his ever-present, always silent companion of recent days. He glanced at the long, coffin-like crate upon which rested the insensate form of Librarian Niven, silent and unmoving.

'Niven,' Thule said in a quiet voice. 'I have found myself returning again and again to your talk of foreboding, the menace you felt brushing lightly at the edges of your awareness.' He paused, his thoughts interrupted by a faint boom, like the sound of thunder in the distance. 'I find it difficult to imagine the menace we now face 'lightly brushing' anything.'

The data-slate in Thule's hands told the story well enough. With only a handful of Astartes and Chapter serfs at his disposal, aided by the hardier natives who had been willing to stand and fight for their lives instead of merely lying down before the inevitable, Thule was barely managing to hold back the hordes of feral orks which broke like a surging tide against the walls of Argus Township. Thule's forces would not be able to hold out for much longer.

'We could use your agile mind and strong arm at our side, Librarian,' Thule went on.

But the Librarian would not be joining the fray. In the withdrawal from the desert, as Thule pulled his party back within the more easily defensible walls of Argus, Niven had been like the Emperor's own dark angel of vengeance. With his psychic hood serving to dampen any latent pyskers in the ork horde, the Librarian inspired the members of Thule's party from the vanguard, eldritch energies crackling from his gauntlets as his shouted battle cries rang out over the melee's din. Time and again the Librarian's psyker abilities allowed him to blunt the enemies' attacks, and he moved through the carnage with impossible speed, his blade snapping out lightning fast to slash against one greenskin enemy in one instant, then reappearing metres away to parry the blow of another ork in the next. Niven was a relentless combatant, seemingly tireless, lashing out time and again at the unwashed onslaught, striking fear into the enemies' soulless hearts.

But in the end, the overwhelming numbers of feral orks they faced had proved too much even for the

Librarian, and as he had been dealing the Emperor's vengeance upon a pair of massive orks, a cadre of others had fallen on him from behind, and the Librarian had gone down beneath their blows. Sergeant Cyrus and a group of his Scouts had come to the Librarian's aid, and picked the orks off him before they were able to inflict terminal damage, but even so the injuries sustained by Niven in the assault had been too grievous for his body to readily repair itself. He had lapsed into a state of suspended animation, his sus-an membrane helping to preserve his body and mind until his injuries could be repaired.

Now he lay in state like a fallen hero, unable to wake himself or to be woken by anyone else, except with the use of the appropriate chemical therapies and auto-suggestion that only a fully-trained Apothecary could deliver.

'Captain?' A voice from the far side of the depot disrupted Thule's reverie, and he turned to see one of Sergeant Cyrus's Scouts approaching, threading through the maze of discarded and destroyed crates at the depot's entrance.

Thule arched a brow in response.

'You asked to be informed when the contingent from the *Armageddon* arrived? They're touching down now.'

Thule nodded, and set the data-slate down atop a stack of crates. 'Very good.'

The newcomers, Thule knew, brought an Apothecary with them. Perhaps luck would be with them, and just as Sergeant Merrik and his squads served to reinforce Thule's position in the township until the recruitment party had done the needful, so too would the Apothecary help restore the Librarian to full health, strengthening their numbers that much more.

Thoughtfully, the captain crossed the floor in a few broad strides to the place where his bolter and power sword lay, ready for use. He holstered the bolter at his side, and then hefted the power sword. The blade had been presented to him in acknowledgement of valour in combat by the secret masters of the Blood Ravens when he'd still been a sergeant, and squad leader of the Fifth Company's Second Squad.

'Proceed to the landing site, Scout,' Thule ordered, his eyes on the blade. 'I will join you presently.'

The power sword was a relic of the Chapter, a weapon so ancient and honoured that it had been granted a name – Wisdom. It seemed a lifetime ago now that he had first borne Wisdom in battle – and, considering the extended lifespan of the Astartes, it *had* been a lifetime, or a normal human's lifetime at any rate. Into how many subsequent battles had he carried the power sword, and how often had it served those proud Blood Ravens who had carried the blade Wisdom before it had come to Thule's hand? The captain was hard-pressed to even estimate the answer to the former, and found the latter impossible to guess. Wisdom was an ancient weapon, dating back even to the earliest days of the Chapter's history, and might well have been forged in those dark days now lost forever in the records and remembrance of the Blood Ravens.

Thule buckled Wisdom at his side. With the Scout gone, he was alone again once more in the makeshift headquarters with the slumbering Librarian, locked in his dreamless sleep.

'You spoke of malevolence, Niven, of lurking, lightly-brushing evil.' Thule lifted his helmet from a nearby crate and fitted it over his head. 'I cannot help but wonder if you were sensing something other than this plague of orks which now besets us. And if so, what further horror might the future hold?'

Encased once more in his power armour, Thule was armed and ready for battle.

WITH THULE GONE, only Librarian Niven remained. But the sleeping psyker was not alone in the depot, whatever the captain had thought.

In the shadows that clung to the corners of the building, behind the haphazard pyramids of forgotten and neglected shipping crates, something was stirring. It was still small, but growing larger by the moment, watching from its place of hiding, waiting for the moment to strike.

And the moment to strike would come soon.

AS ORDERED, ARAMUS had mustered his squad on the cracked and pitted ferrocrete of the landing pad, at the southern end of the humble space port. Argus proper rose to their east, with the three Thunderhawk gunships that had ferried them to the surface parked to the west. Sergeants Thaddeus and Avitus had gathered their squads on either side of Aramus's, with Merrik and his First Squad in close formation only a short distance off. And all of them, squad leaders and battle-brothers alike, had their entire attention focused on the Space Marine who stood before them.

'Blood Ravens,' Captain Davian Thule said, his voice booming even over the plaintive howl of the winds from across the desert. 'It does my heart good to welcome you here. Calderis has long been a recruiting world of the Blood Ravens, and for generations we have come here to select only the best and most capable of Calderians to join the ranks of the Chapter.'

Beside the captain stood Chaplain Palmarius, his midnight-black power suit dusted with the dun-coloured sands that blew continually across the landing pad, and which were already gritting in the joints of Aramus's own armour. The Chaplain's face, as always, was completely hidden behind his silver skull mask, but through the eye slits Aramus could see Palmarius's eyes sliding back and forth, taking the measure of the reinforcements.

'If we fail in our duty here,' Thule went on, 'that proud tradition will be at an end, and never again will the sons of Calderis swell the ranks of the Blood Ravens.'

The captain pointed to a small knot of boys that huddled together against the scouring winds, flanked on either side by a Blood Ravens Scout. There were no more than a half-dozen of the boys, most of them bandaged or limping, and nearly all with a haunted look in their dark eyes, as though they had seen things that no mortal soul should be expected to survive.

'Two months ago we came to this world with the sacred charge of conducting the Blood Trials, of sifting through the populace of Calderis to find the most suitable candidates for our holy Chapter, and then to pit them one against another in combat to test their worthiness. More than a month since, the attack of the feral orks put paid to those plans. Many of the aspirants already gathered in our search fell before the greenskin tide, and these few you see before you are all that is left of the original number.'

Aramus regarded the boys. They looked numb, beyond pain and without fear. It was a look he had come to recognize during his own initiation into the ranks of the Space Marines, but he knew that if the boys were to survive whatever was to come and become initiates, they would face trials and pains far greater than any they had yet seen. Some of the injuries borne by the boys seemed severe, though, and might threaten to end their lives before their initiation ever began. Apothecary Gordian would have to examine them, once he finished seeing to the party's injured Librarian, whom Gordian had been ordered to attend as soon as they touched down.

'In the face of the encroaching orks, many of the civilians who dwelt in the deserts surrounding us have taken flight, seeking refuge behind the walls of Argus Township.' Thule waved a gauntleted fist towards the east and the walls of Argus proper. 'Once the principal urban centre on Calderis, Argus is now a place of final refuge, the last stand for humanity on the planet.'

Aramus glanced to the east, and saw the barricades being manned by more of the Blood Ravens Scouts.

With three gunships on the ferrocrete, panicked refugees had swarmed the barricades, desperate for any means of escape from Calderis and the orks threatening to overrun them. So far the Scouts had not been forced to open fire on the inhabitants to keep them from reaching the Thunderhawks – where their numbers and blind panic might drive them to do serious damage to the craft – but from Aramus's perspective it seemed as though it would only be a matter of time.

'If there are any potential Blood Ravens still among the surviving inhabitants of Calderis,' Thule continued, 'they are to be found in Argus, or else already en route through the deserts to the township. It falls to us to search the population for these potential recruits, to gather and protect any that we find, and to return to *Scientia Est Potentia* with them. If we must hold the Blood Trials onboard our own fortress-monastery, so be it, but at least then our sacred duty will have been discharged and we may return to the Fifth Company with honour.'

The captain paced for a moment, back and forth in front of the assembled squads, regarding each of them individually.

'The vessel which carried our recruiting party to Calderis is not due to return for another two months,' Thule went on, 'and I, for one, have no intention of remaining here for their return. With the *Armageddon* in orbit overhead, and her Thunderhawks here on the ground, there is no reason that we cannot complete the remainder of our mission in a matter of days, a week at the most, and then quit this world once and for all.'

Thule paused, the eyes behind his helmet gazing across the armoured forms before him.

'You have your orders. Search the population for potential aspirants, gather them together, and protect them. Is there a one of you who harbours any questions, or requires any clarification?'

A moment of silence passed, and then Aramus indicated with a raised gauntlet that he had a question.

'Captain?' Aramus began when Thule motioned him to speak. 'It is my understanding that the feral orks beyond the mountains have never before attacked the human settlements on this hemisphere. What drives them now to attack in such numbers?'

'We don't know,' Thule answered without hesitation. 'All that we *do* know is that they *have* attacked, and that it falls to us to respond. At this stage, nothing else matters.' He paused, his gaze sweeping the others. 'Are there any further questions or request for clarification?'

The assembled squads were silent, knowing that no reply was required if the answer was in the negative.

'In that case, there is nothing to be gained from further discussion. To your duty, Blood Ravens, and may the Emperor guide you!'

CHAPTER FOUR

THE DIN OF the feral ork horde hit Sergeant Thaddeus with the force of a tidal wave, followed quickly by the stench of the greenskins themselves. His assault squad, armed with bolters and chainswords, had been tasked with clearing a path through the ocean of orks to the south of Argus Township. Orbital surveillance transmitted by vox from the *Armageddon* had pinpointed a group of human refugees trapped beyond the besieging horde in that direction, and unless Thaddeus and the Blood Ravens of the Seventh Squad were able to escort them through to the relative safety of the walls of Argus, it would matter not at all whether there were among the refugees any potential candidates for initiation or not. And so, their jump packs granting them the ability to make prodigious leaps from the high city walls directly into the midst of the greenskin horde, Thaddeus ordered his men to engage.

'On your left,' Thaddeus voxed to his battle-brothers, as his own chainsword bit into the nearest of the green-skinned monsters, almost before the orks had realized the assault squad was among them.

The giant ork who had responded quickest to the sudden appearance of the Blood Ravens among them, and who had prompted Thaddeus's shout of warning, swung a massive, cruelly barbed and irregularly-shaped sword at the nearest of the Space Marines, who barely managed to dance back out of range of the sweeping blade. As the giant ork reversed his sword for another swing, a howl of incoherent rage reverberating through cracked teeth and rubbery lips, Thaddeus darted forward, chainsword whirring, and took a hunk from one of the ork's massive legs.

Bellowing in outraged pain, the ork backhanded Thaddeus with his free hand, the blow striking the Blood Raven with force almost sufficient to knock him off balance. As it was, Thaddeus managed to right himself in time to parry the ork's next thrust. Even with a large part of one of his legs sheared away, the ork continued to fight, merely shifting his weight onto his other leg and using the pain and rage to fuel his attacks.

It would take more than the loss of a bit of flesh and gristle for a full-grown ork to lie down. But then, brutal close combat was precisely the sort of fighting in which assault squads like the Seventh specialized.

'Thaddeus!' shouted Battle-Brother Loew. 'On your right.'

A stream of rounds from Loew's bolter streamed by Thaddeus's right shoulder before the sergeant could even respond, followed closely by an outraged roar from the direction in which the shots had been fired.

It was an impossibly loud roar, a sound of fury and of pain as inhuman as the bellowing calls of the greenskins but unlike any ork voice that Thaddeus had ever heard.

The ork with the barbed sword rushed forward for another lunge, and Thaddeus jinked to one side, at the same time sweeping his chainsword in and down, biting into the ork's as yet uninjured leg. This time Thaddeus's chainsword cut through the skin and meat of the greenskin's leg until it hit bone, and as the sergeant yanked his weapon free the whirling blade rasped against the sides of the wound, sending up a greenish-black mist of liquefied flesh, black ichor, and pulverized bone.

With one leg cut straight through to the bone and the other already missing a significant hunk of flesh, the ork was left unbalanced, and while the monster struggled to retain its footing, howling in pain, Thaddeus opened fire with his own bolter, sending a stream of rounds directly into the ork's wide chest, shattering the necklace of teeth that surrounded the tree-trunk neck. The force of the bolts' impact toppled the ork backwards, and without wasting an instant's advantage, Thaddeus leapt into the air a few metres and came crashing down on the supine monster's chest. Swinging his chainsword like a farmer cutting wheat with a scythe, Thaddeus cleaved the head of the ork from his massive shoulders, ending forever his bellowing rage.

Again Loew sent a stream of bolter fire across Thaddeus's back, and again the sergeant heard the inhuman roar of outrage and pain.

Raising his sword and swinging up the barrel of his bolter, Thaddeus spun around to view the source of the clamour, and found himself face to face with a monster from humanity's oldest nightmares. It was a giant boar, as large as a land speeder, each of its immense tusks as long as a man's leg, with viscous saliva glistening on its slavering jaws and falling like swollen raindrops onto the dry sands between its massive hooves. On the boar's back was an ork, dressed in barbaric finery with furs, necklaces of teeth, and a helmet made from another ork's bleached skull, in its hand a long lance with an explosive package strapped to its end, with a dozen more such lances in a quiver across the ork's back.

'That's more like it.' Thaddeus grinned and raised his whirring chainsword. 'I was beginning to worry that this would be too easy.'

'VOIRE, YOU'RE WITH ME.'

Sergeant Aramus walked up the middle of the narrow street, heading towards the northern extremity of Argus. In more peaceful times, this street would have been lined on either side with vendors selling their wares, calling out to passers-by from stalls cobbled together from discarded sheets of flak board or rockcrete slabs, accented with remnants of colourful cloth – the larger pieces used as awnings overhead to shade the bright desert sun, the smaller fragments used merely as garlands. Everything from produce to craftwork to antiquities recovered from the timeless desert sands, things built, borrowed, bought, or stolen offered at whatever price they could demand. Argus Township was seen by the Calderians as a permanently-stationed souq, the ancient structures first built by the early colonists in millennia past a static answer to the ever moving, always transient tent communities of the open desert, and like those migrating souqs Argus was perforce a place of trade, a temple to barter and a celebration of haggling. There was nothing that could be found on Calderis that could not be bought in the streets of Argus – or at least rented, for a time – and quite a few things on offer in the more discreet market stalls that could not be found anywhere else on the desert planet.

That was what Argus had been, before the coming of the feral orks. Now, it was a different matter entirely.

'The rest of you,' Aramus called to the five remaining members of Third Squad when Battle-Brother Voire had joined him. 'Two search parties, one under Sergeant Tarkus' – he nodded to his second – 'the other under Brother Cirrac.' He pointed to the intersection up ahead, where another street crossed the one he now walked upon. 'Tarkus, you take your team up the left branch, Cirrac, you take the right. We'll meet at the north wall, compare notes, and proceed from there.'

Argus was now a community under siege. The high city walls, designed to block out even the strongest of desert sandstorms, had been fortified by Thule's forces before the arrival of the *Armageddon*, and with the Scouts manning the barricades with the heaviest weaponry they had at their disposal, augmented by the braver Calderians who could be trained to operate a meltagun or fire a cannon, they had so far managed to keep incursions within the city by the orks beyond to a minimum. Already, though, there were breaks in the walls, here and there, which could fall before the orks should the greenskins organise their attacks in a concerted effort.

The streets of Argus, no longer a marketplace where anything and everything was on offer, were now filled with huddled masses of refugees, thousands upon thousands of desert-dwellers and town-denizens packed together in a space capable of supporting only a fraction of their number. The availability of foodstuffs had long been a problem, and now the supplies of fresh water were quickly being depleted. The presence of the Blood Ravens in the city was helping to calm the citizenry from outright panic, but it would be only a matter of time before they realized that even the Space Marines would be able only to delay the inevitable, and that the fall of Argus to the orks was an unavoidable inevitability.

'Aramus,' Voire said, pointing to a group cowering in the slim shade offered by a ramshackle stall in the lees of one of the ancient township buildings. There was an old woman, matriarch to an unmatched collection of men and women who were looking after an assortment of children of varying ages. Had they been an extended family, once upon a time, and the old woman the eldest surviving member? Or were they simply the straggling remains of one of the desert tribes, banded together out of familiarity when the rest of their families were lost in the flight across the burning sands?

Aramus saw the boy to which Voire was pointing. Perhaps ten years old, tall for his age and lean, the boy appeared bright and alert, and while he was no doubt as hungry as the rest of the refugees huddling in the shade of the stall around him, he was clean-limbed and healthy-seeming, the muscles of his calves and biceps not yet ravaged by starvation.

'Let's take a look,' Aramus answered, and diverted his course towards the stall.

Most of the men and women, like the children, averted their eyes at the approach of an Adeptus Astartes in full power armour with a bolter in hand, but the old woman kept her chin high and met Aramus's gaze, for all that she could not see his face behind his helmet.

'I am Sergeant Aramus of the Blood Ravens, seeking aspirants for our Chapter.'

The children at his feet began to whimper, and it seemed to Aramus as if they feared him perhaps as much as they feared the greenskins who had destroyed the only life they'd ever known.

Aramus didn't know that he could blame them. He tried to imagine what it must be like to look upon a Space Marine for the first time, barely able to remember what it was like to be human himself. But he could remember, and too well, the undertaking on Kronus, the Dark Crusade in which he, like the other Blood Ravens under Captain Thule's command, had been forced by circumstance to turn against the misguided citizens who had taken up arms against the Chapter. The injuries sustained by the Blood Ravens in that undertaking had healed, but there were some scars – those which could not be seen on the surface – which might never fade.

'Among the tribes of the desert,' the old woman began in heavily accented Low Gothic, her voice as dry as the deserts themselves, 'one who seeks favours with his face hidden is considered to be *cuffar*.' It was the Calderian term for a person who denied hospitality, or who was ungrateful. 'Am I to truck with *cuffar* for the lives of the last sons of my people?'

Aramus remained motionless, regarding the ancient woman. Like most Space Marines, he had little talent or patience for anything resembling diplomacy. He was built and trained as a warrior, and his few dealings with the common citizenry of the Imperium were typically restricted to barking orders at them in frenzied evacuations, or else rushing past them as they fled from the enemies that the Blood Ravens charged forward to meet. He had enough strength in one gauntleted hand to crush the old woman to a pulp...

And yet, what would it gain the Imperium if he were to do so? She was not his enemy. She was a scared old woman, defiant in the face of impossible odds, and insisting to the universe around her that it conform to her long-cherished traditions of propriety and hospitality in what little time remained to her in this life. So she failed to show the deference due to an Adeptus Astartes? What of it? In her eyes, Aramus had surely failed to show her the deference that was her due as elder of her now-lost desert tribe.

Before answering, Aramus reached up and removed his helmet. Holding it under his arm, with the dry wind buffeting against his bare neck and cheeks, he looked down again at the old woman, meeting her eyes with his own.

'I am Sergeant Aramus of the Blood Ravens,' he repeated in gentler tones, 'and I come seeking aspirants for our Chapter.'

The old woman nodded, and glanced around her at the children huddling terrified in the shade. 'And which of the sons of my tribe pleases your eye?'

Aramus pointed at the clean-limbed youngster whom Voire had indicated.

The ancient woman looked from Aramus to the boy and back again. 'And if he goes with you, he will become like you.' She pointed a bony finger at Aramus's armoured chest. '*Melik-a-sayf?*'

The old woman had no other word for what Aramus was, and so had used the Calderian term – 'Sword of the Emperor.'

'Perhaps,' Aramus answered. 'If he survives the Blood Trials, and the initiation that follows.'

The old woman narrowed her eyes. 'And if he does not become *melik-a-sayf*, he will die?'

'Perhaps,' Aramus said again. 'But there is the chance that he could fail the process and survive, to serve the Blood Ravens as a Chapter serf. It is not a common occurrence, but has been known to happen.'

The old woman nodded curtly, and waved a hand at the boy. 'Then take him. A slim chance at life is more than he will have if he remains here.'

* * *

'PICK YOUR TARGETS and fire at will!' Sergeant Avitus shouted, unleashing a stream of bolts from his heavy bolter at the heads and shoulders of the feral orks attempting to scale the city walls.

On either side of Avitus his battle-brothers in the Ninth Squad opened fire with heavy bolters, melta-guns and flamers, pouring death down upon the besieging greenskins. Captain Thule had tasked the Devastator squad with manning the eastern wall of Argus Township, where damage from earlier assaults had already weakened the integrity of the walls which the oncoming hordes of feral orks were now threatening to topple.

A firebomb lobbed by one of the lead orks smashed into Avitus's chest, wreathing him in sickly-green flames, but he paid it no mind, and returned the ork's fire with a few well-placed bolts of his own.

'Sergeant,' called Avitus's battle-brother Barabbas.

Avitus glanced over to see Barabbas indicating the ground beneath the wall to their right.

'They're resourceful,' Barabbas said, unclipping a frag grenade from his waist and tossing it out into the mass of orks below. The shrapnel tore into the greenskins, ruining flesh and smashing bone. 'You have to give them that.'

Avitus merely grunted in reply.

Like all the Blood Ravens, Avitus knew that these were feral orks, primitive tribes only a few stages removed from their earliest beginnings. In many ways orks were more fungal than animal, reproducing by the dispersal of spores, their green colouration from the algae that coursed through their crude blood and made up so much of their internal processes. A single world could be overrun, in time, if a single mature ork were to be killed on its surface. The dying ork would release spores, which would then develop into cocoons, which given time and suitable conditions would hatch into the more rudimentary of forms, that given the opportunity would eventually mature into fully-grown orks. Was that how the greenskin plague had come to Calderis? Ork Waaaghs had never touched the Aurelia system, or else the chances were that there would be no humans still living here. Perhaps nothing more than a single ork vessel, cast off from some mindlessly drifting space hulk, had crashed on the far side of the desert world, over across the mountains, at some point in the distant past, and the death of its passengers had over the course of centuries or even millennia eventually given rise to the untold thousands of greenskins who had covered the western hemisphere like a plague since time out of mind.

But these were not yet the most developed orks that waged their eternal Waaaghs across the stars. These were feral, primitive, little more than beasts. They lacked the technological sophistication to manufacture or repair engines of war – bikes, buggies, trucks, and so on – or even to devise firearms, and instead rode upon the backs of enormous beasts, and fought with little more than rocks and sticks, with primitive explosives being the pinnacle of their technological prowess.

Individually, any one of the feral orks presented hardly any threat, since a human with a ranged weapon could, with enough distance between him and his target, bring down any ork with a few well-placed rounds. And even though the lumbering creatures were all but immune to pain, and able to fight on even after receiving wounds that would fell even an Astartes, they were mindless fighting machines, bereft of any strategy or form, and a Space Marine with a sword in hand and his wits about him could best an ork in individual combat nine times out of ten.

The problem with feral orks, and with these feral orks in particular, came in their overwhelming numbers. Even with the addition of the forces from the *Armageddon* reinforcing them, Thule's defenders totalled little more than three dozen. Facing them were hundreds upon hundreds of greenskins, if not thousands, raging monsters with little thought for their own safety, and none at all for the safety of their fellow orks. This was perfectly exemplified in the strategy now being carried out beneath the walls of Argus, as Barabbas had pointed out.

'Burn them down!' Avitus shouted to the Blood Ravens fanned out to his right along the barricades. 'Concentrate fire!'

Lacking the technological sophistication to create siege engines, even something as rudimentary as a ladder, the feral orks had hit upon a novel approach to assaulting the high city walls. They simply piled the bodies of their fallen brethren one atop the other, creating an asymmetrical pyramid of ork bodies leaning against the walls of Argus. Some of the orks in the pile were dead, some were dying, and some had just had the misfortune of being knocked from their feet and had not stood up again before their brothers seized them and threw them upon the pile. Already the pyramid of greenskin bodies rose halfway to the top of the Argus walls, and was growing higher every passing moment.

Avitus had faced orks countless times in his century and a half of service to the Blood Ravens Chapter, but nearly all of those instances had been against the more developed orks who travelled between the stars in their salvaged space hulks. Like their feral cousins, the more developed orks had a similar lack of concern for their own longevity, and a disregard for the safety of their brother orks, and like the orks of Calderis they took to the field of battle in what were often incomprehensibly large numbers. But unlike the feral orks that Avitus and his squad now faced, the developed orks had mastered the machine, and brought to bear cannons, missiles, guns, munitions, and more.

The immense numbers of feral orks assaulting Argus made them an all but unbeatable foe, but their lack of technological sophistication meant, at least, that there was little chance that the Blood Ravens would not be able to carry out Captain Thule's orders and complete the recruitment search before withdrawing back to the *Armageddon*. If they had been developed orks which the Blood Ravens now faced, on the other hand, there would have been every chance that none of the Blood Ravens would have made it off Calderis alive.

A long wooden stick, sharpened to a point, bounced off the faceplate of Avitus's helmet, a spear thrown by one of the greenskins below.

'A spear?' Avitus said in disbelief.

Avitus, in a rare flash of humour, actually grinned, if only slightly, as he returned fire, ripping the green-skin's arm from its massive shoulder with a barrage of bolts.

Yes, the sergeant reflected as he continued to pour death down upon the attackers, at least these are merely feral orks that we face.

'SQUAD,' THADDEUS VOXED, pausing to reload his bolter before continuing, 'form up. We're approaching the edge.'

Thaddeus and his brothers in the Seventh Squad had pushed ever further south, each Space Marine an unstoppable juggernaut with bolter and chainsword in hand. For hours they had fought their way through the seemingly endless ocean of feral orks that stretched out beyond the walls of Argus, but Thaddeus's auspex indicated that they were now, finally and at long last, approaching the outer edge of the ork army, the far shore of the endless sea.

On the visor display within Thaddeus's helmet, runes representing each of the other eight members of the Seventh Squad were tinged green, indicating that each of them had survived the fight to this point. Though Thaddeus had issued orders that they were to maintain close formation as they pressed southwards, the hordes of orks had been so densely packed around them that at times they had lost sight of one another, each Space Marine left to fight his own way south against the overwhelming number of enemies until they regrouped again further along.

Now, as they neared the edge of the horde and the next phase of their mission, Thaddeus could only make visual contact with four of his battle-brothers, though most of the others were separated from him only by a matter of a few dozen metres at most. Only Battle-Brother Renzo trailed behind by a matter of several hundred metres.

'Renzo,' Thaddeus called over the vox-comm. 'Time to catch up. Hit your jump pack, and plot a trajectory to just south of our position.'

'Acknowledged,' Renzo voxed back. 'Apologies that I have lagged, sergeant.'

'Knowing you,' Thaddeus chuckled, 'it was all a ruse, so you could leapfrog the rest of us and get clear first.'

'As you say, sergeant.'

'Give me a full report on what you can see up there,' Thaddeus ordered, knowing that Renzo would be taking to the air any moment. It had been too long since they'd gotten any perspective.

Periodically through their trek south, Thaddeus and the others had employed their jump packs to take prodigious leaps, which allowed them not only to speed their journey south but also to survey the surrounding terrain, spot enemy dispersal patterns, and so on. It had been nearly an hour since their last jump, at which point they could still see nothing in all directions but the unbroken ocean of unwashed greenskins, but now that they neared the edge of the horde, Thaddeus needed to know what lay beyond.

Their orders had been to locate a group of human refugees fleeing north towards Argus, and then to escort them to the township safely or, failing that, at least select any potential aspirants from among the group to bring back with them. Thaddeus wasn't eager to leave the rest of the refugees behind, but knew that the Chapter's priorities were new recruits, and that if the other citizens had to be left behind to ensure the safety of an aspirant, so be it.

'Arcing up now,' Renzo voxed. 'Approaching apex. I can see the horde's edge and... Golden Throne!'

A feral ork made a charge at Thaddeus's position, and the sergeant swung his chainsword in a wide arc that took off the top of the greenskin's head before it even reached him. As he sidestepped the ork, who lurched by without even realizing yet that it was dead, Thaddeus glanced overhead to see Renzo beginning his descent a few hundred metres south of their position.

'What was that, Renzo?' Thaddeus voxed, charging towards the south through the gap left by the near-headless ork. 'Repeat!'

'Sergeant, it's not just ferals!' Renzo's voice sounded almost frenzied over the vox. 'There's...'

A deafening cracking sound split the air, and Renzo suddenly fell silent.

'That was heavy ordnance!' Thaddeus shouted, to no one in particular.

Renzo didn't answer.

Thaddeus couldn't risk taking a leap if it meant opening himself up to whatever had just taken out Renzo. So he redoubled his efforts to wade through the last of the greenskins before him, leaving the rest of the squad to contend with the hordes of feral orks pressing in on either side.

What had Renzo meant? That it wasn't 'just ferals'? What else was there...?

Thaddeus cleared the edge of the feral ork horde, and he had his answer.

Beyond the edge of the horde there was a wide stretch of open desert, a few hundred metres across. In the midst of this open stretch lay the broken and bloodied form of Battle-Brother Renzo, looking like a puppet whose strings had been cut. At the other side of the open ground, Thaddeus saw the source of the cracking sound, the thing that had brought the leaping Renzo back down to earth once and for all.

There were thousands of them. Orks with augmetic bionics, and others encased in piston-driven exoskeletons. Orks atop battlewagons and sitting astride combat bikes. Orks with flamethrowers, and rocket-launchers, and powerful energy cannons. There were war machines, mechanized walkers as tall as any Dreadnought. There were warbuggies, and trucks, and infantry beyond count.

These were no feral orks. That was what Renzo's dying words had meant. These were developed orks, spacefaring greenskins armed for war. But they were, as yet, not fighting. Instead, they were arranged in disciplined lines, facing the feral hordes that attacked Argus Township. And at the heart of the serried ranks of orks was a massive battlewagon, atop which stood an immense figure resplendent in spikes and skulls, a giant gun in one hand and a massive battleaxe in the other, his face painted blood-red. There could be little doubt that this was the warboss of this ork army.

The warboss appeared surprised to see Thaddeus standing at the edge of the feral horde, and many of the other developed orks were pointing towards the still form of Renzo on the desert sands, indicating the skies and jabbering in their inhuman tongue.

Thaddeus was no less surprised to see them. An ork army, highly armed and developed, led by what was to all appearances a powerful and bloodthirsty warboss. On a world where, as the Blood Ravens believed, only feral orks had been seen before.

The warboss seemed to come to some decision and, pointing his massive battleaxe in Thaddeus's direction, shouted a blood-curdling war cry at the top of his lungs. In response, the serried ranks of armoured and mechanised orks surged forward, answering their leader's war cry with shouts of their own, each of them rushing towards Thaddeus with weapons raised and ready.

'So much for this being too easy,' Thaddeus said as he raised his bolter and fired into the onrushing horde. The feral orks had already threatened to overrun Argus and kill every human on Calderis. Whatever the reason for the sudden appearance of the orks' more advanced cousins, their presence meant that now even the Blood Ravens had no guarantee of leaving the planet alive. 'Squad! Form on me. We have company.'

CHAPTER FIVE

IT HAD BEEN nearly two days since the Thunderhawks from the *Armageddon* had set down on the pitted ferrocrete landing pad of Argus Township's abused and neglected spaceport, nearly forty-eight hours since the four squads had mustered to receive the orders of Captain Davian Thule. Not yet two days, and already the battles with the orks had claimed their victims.

Apothecary Gordian laboured tirelessly over the still and all but lifeless form of Librarian Niven inside the makeshift headquarters of Captain Thule's forces. He knew that his brother Blood Ravens had already begun falling on the field of battle but, as yet, he had been unable to go to them and retrieve the vital gene-seed that each carried within their progenoid gland. The masses of orks on all sides, both feral and developed, meant that

Gordian had been unable to reach the fallen until it was too late, and the orks had already had their chance to despoil the bodies of the fallen Space Marines, cracking open the ceramite power armour they wore as though they were nothing more than rotten eggs, and then hacking and butchering the bodies within until nothing remained but pulp and gristle.

Battle-Brother Renzo of the Seventh Squad had been the first to fall, shattered into lifelessness by a barrage of heavy weapons fire thundering up from an ork battlewagon. When Thaddeus had voxed back to Thule's command centre with news of the appearance of the developed and organized orks, Thule had dispatched Sergeant Merrik's squad to assist, and had sent a pair of the better trained Scouts to pilot one of the Thunderhawks.

It was a risk, fielding in battle one of the gunships that the Blood Ravens were counting upon to carry them off the desert planet, but Thule considered the risk worth taking. As the gunship had swept in low, the lascannons beneath its attack wings had lanced out at the war-engines of the orks just as the four sets of heavy bolters mounted on the forward fuselage pumped round after round of bolter fire into the greenskin infantry. And as soon as the gunship had dipped low enough to the ground, Merrik and his First Squad had leapt out onto the desert sands, hitting the ground running with bolters firing, rushing to reinforce Thaddeus's Seventh Squad.

Of the nine Blood Ravens who had leapt from the Thunderhawk, only seven had survived long enough to offer assistance. A discharge from one of the orks' massive energy cannons pierced Battle-Brother Sten through the chest before he'd taken even a half-dozen steps, and Battle-Brother Xiao was crushed beneath one of the clanking feet of an ork mechanised walker only moments after entering the fray.

'Come on, Librarian,' Gordian said in a low voice laced with impatience, as the delicate instruments in his hand prodded the Larraman's organ implanted within Niven's chest cavity. 'I have other tasks to attend, once you are restored, so *heal*, Emperor damn you.'

One of the crucial implants that transformed a baseline human into a superhuman Astartes, the organ was liver-shaped, small enough to fit in the palm of a man's hand, but was one of the most vital of the nineteen implants that separated a Space Marine from common humanity. When an Astartes was wounded, the implant released Larraman cells into the bloodstream, which attached themselves to leucocytes in the blood and, once in contact with the air at the site of injury, immediately began forming an instant scar tissue, which staunched the flow of blood and served to protect the wounded area.

When Niven had been injured in the withdrawal to Argus, among other ills his Larraman's organ had been severely injured, preventing it from releasing the cells that would aid the body in healing itself. It was for this, and other reasons, that the Librarian had slipped into a state of suspended animation. Apothecary Gordian had already prepared the chemical therapies that, along with an appropriate auto-suggestion spoken aloud in the Librarian's hearing, would trigger the sus-an membrane to restore Niven to full consciousness. But until Gordian was able successfully to restore Niven's implants to full functioning, and his Larraman's organ in particular, if brought to full awareness his body would simply shut down again almost immediately.

Gordian yearned to be out in the field, reductor in hand, harvesting the precious gene-seed from the bodies of his fallen brothers – the risk to himself be damned! Or even fighting alongside the other battle-brothers, his bolter blazing in his hands. But Captain Thule's orders in this matter were clear. Their survival, Thule insisted, depended on the Librarian being restored to full health, and unless and until Niven had regained consciousness and the use of his facilities, and while the chance still remained that he *might* do so, Apothecary Gordian was to stay at his side.

Nearly two days into the undertaking on Calderis, and already three battle-brothers of the Blood Ravens had fallen, their gene-seed lost to the Chapter forever. How many more would fall, and how many more gene-seeds would be lost, before it was all said and done?

'Heal, damn you!' Gordian said, resisting the urge to strike a blow across the face of the unconscious Librarian. 'Heal, lest the rest of us perish in waiting for you to wake!'

CAPTAIN THULE TIGHTENED his grip on the hilt of Wisdom, as energy coruscated down the length of the power sword's blade. He stood with Sergeants Cyrus and Avitus atop the battlements at the south-eastern corner of the Argus city walls, looking out over the field of battle stretching before them.

'Here comes another,' Cyrus said, his hair whipping around his head in the hot desert winds.

Avitus hefted his heavy bolter. 'I've got this one…'

'No,' Thule said, shaking his head. He raised Wisdom once more, waiting for the moment to strike.

The captain had joined his sergeants on the battlements to survey the battle, but before he'd had time to as much as glance at the field, the feral orks had unveiled their newest innovation. The day before, they had taken to stacking the bodies of the living, dead and dying to act as makeshift siege engines. Only a prodigious amount of firepower and the careful attention of Cyrus's Scouts and Avitus's Devastator squad had kept the greenskins from successfully scaling the walls and taking the city.

Now, the orks had hit upon a new strategy. Using long planks of sturdy material, perhaps ripped from the remains of one of the smaller townships that dotted the far edge of the desert, and which the orks had doubtless already overrun, the greenskins had constructed a sort of seesaw, with a pile of dead bodies acting as the fulcrum, set far to one end of the plank.

One of their number – living, of course, and heavily armed – would stand on the end closest to the fulcrum, the other end of the plank rising in the air as his weight pressed his end down. Then, after a brief countdown, a dozen or more of his brethren would jump together onto the other end of the plank, and as their combined weight brought that end quickly down to earth, the end upon which the heavily armed ork stood was thrust suddenly upwards. More often than not, the ork thus catapulted skywards merely flailed back to earth atop his own brothers, precision and aim being beyond the orks' conception. But when the makeshift contraption functioned as intended – as it had just done once more – then the now skywards-streaking ork would arc up and over the city walls of Argus, a living missile.

Had any of the orks succeeded in landing within the walls of Argus, they could play havoc, killing the native refugees indiscriminately until the Blood Ravens were able to stop them. Even now, Sergeant Aramus and his squad were involved in a race against time to find any potential recruits among the refugees, but so far had only managed to find a bare handful. Fortunately, the orks had so far managed to catapult one of their number in the correct direction, and with the appropriate height and velocity, only a scant few times, and in each instance the Blood Ravens had ended the catapulted ork's life before he even touched down. The deadweight of the orks' bodies plummeting to earth had caused more than a few injuries to the refugees upon which the bodies landed, but these losses were inconsequential when compared to the damage a living ork could do if successfully catapulted in.

Under other circumstances, it might have been an enjoyable diversion, picking errant orks out of the sky with bolter and melta fire, almost a kind of sport. But Thule and his men had more serious matters on their mind than a tally of who had hit the most airborne orks, and the consequences of a miss were too grave to allow any levity.

Thule raised Wisdom, the blade coursing with energy.

'I tire of this,' Thule said, as the ork catapulted through the sky towards him, an axe in either hand and an inhuman war cry on its rubbery lips.

The ork's trajectory carried it down towards the city, its path passing less than a metre from where Thule and the others stood.

Thule scarcely grunted as he swept Wisdom up and out, the blade biting through the top of the ork's skull and continuing on through its massive body, splitting it in half lengthwise.

'Now, where were we?' Thule said, as the severed halves of the catapulted ork continued on their downward trajectory towards the streets below.

'Troop movements, captain,' Cyrus answered

From the streets below a wailing cry rose up, shouts of grief and dismay as yet another ork fell from the sky and crushed the life out of some hapless refugee.

'Precisely,' Thule answered, paying the cries of grief no mind. 'So, the First and Seventh are still in the field. Now, what have they learned about these new ork forces?'

THERE WAS, IN fact, very little that the many humans knew about orks – whether feral, developed, or otherwise. Over the millennia many a magos biologis of the Adeptus Mechanicus had devoted their lives to the study of the greenskins, motivated by a desire to understand and comprehend the enemy, and thus be better positioned to defeat him. With their reverence for wisdom and knowledge, this was of course a strategy that the Blood Ravens could well appreciate. After all, since the days of the Great Father himself, Azariah Vidya, the Blood Ravens Chapter had always believed that knowledge, alongside faith of course, was the greatest weapon available in the fight against the Emperor's enemies. To defeat an enemy, one had first to understand them.

But how could a human mind – whether a supremely trained tactician like Thule and his fellow Blood Ravens, or a psyker like Librarian Niven and the other servants of the Librarium, or even an augmented consciousness like a magos of the Adeptus Biologis – ever hope to comprehend the crude, base motivations that drove an inhuman monster like an ork? The human heretic could be understood at least in the light of his madness, and a xenos like an eldar or a tau could be comprehended if one took the trouble of studying his culture and history enough to grasp his psychology. But an ork was merely one step up from animal, driven by primitive appetites and raw desires, seeking only combat and conquest. Perhaps only the tyranids, unstoppable and innumerable offspring of the Great Devourer, were less comprehensible to humans than the mind of the ork.

It would not be until much later, long after the information would be of any use to Captain Thule and his party, that it would be discovered that the developed orks who had appeared on Calderis were under the command of Warlord Zagmor Gorgrim, whose name in Low Gothic would translate into something roughly equivalent to Wild-Lightning Bloodface.

Once a warboss in the Waaagh of the Arch-Arsonist of Charadon, Gorgrim had gained in power and prestige as he led his warband to victory after victory. In time, Gorgrim had splintered his warband off from the forces of the Arch-Arsonist, commandeering a massive space hulk of his own and leading his warband to new systems and unspoiled territories.

Gorgrim had hit upon an innovation in the waging of war, a rare thing in a species born with skills and knowledge already encoded into their genetic strand. Having perhaps a few hundred fully-grown orks in his warband at the point that he struck out on his own, when Gorgrim's space hulk chanced upon a world inhabited by feral orks, he saw the advantage in recruitment. Taking his warband to the surface, he bested the local warlord in single combat, and then declared that all of the planet's inhabitants were henceforth to consider themselves part of Gorgrim's horde. But that only a select few would be allowed to leave on board Gorgrim's space hulk, and the rest left behind to die as Gorgrim unleashed an orbital bombardment that would wipe clean the surface of the planet of any life.

Understandably motivated, the feral orks on the planet quickly turned against one another in mortal combat, lashing out with swords, clubs, fists, and teeth to claim their place among Gorgrim's horde.

In the end, some few thousand feral orks survived the ensuing melee, and accompanied Gorgrim and his warband back up to the space hulk that hung in orbit above the world. And then Gorgrim set off in search of other contests, other conquests.

And so Gorgrim's horde continued through the stars for years upon years. When it fell upon a world inhabited by any species other than orks, such as humans, they would wage Waaagh, wiping the world clean of the human stain in the name of their terrible gods, Gork and Mork. And if they came upon any world on which feral orks dwelt, then Gorgrim would best their strongest warrior in personal combat, claim the rest of the ork population as his own, and then issue the challenge – prove yourself worthy to join the horde, or stay behind and die. And if feral orks shared a world with another species, then Gorgrim would goad them to first eradicate all non-ork life from the world, and only then fight for the privilege of joining the horde.

Warlord Gorgrim and his horde had arrived on Calderis some months before the arrival of Captain Thule and his recruitment party, and Gorgrim had goaded the countless numbers of feral orks on the western hemisphere into savage combat, demanding that they prove their worth in order to join his horde. First the orks would eradicate the humans from the far side of the planet, and then they would turn against one another. When only a handful of feral orks remained, they would leave the planet with Gorgrim's horde, returning to the space hulk which even now drifted at anchor above Calderis's lone moon, before Gorgrim bombarded the planet from orbit, killing all who remained.

What Gorgrim had not taken into account, that about which he could not have known, was the presence of Captain Thule and his Blood Ravens on the desert world, on a recruitment mission of their own.

It was, perhaps, a dark irony that both Gorgrim's horde and Thule's Blood Ravens came to the desert world of Calderis seeking new recruits, and each might have successfully completed their recruitment search without incident had it not been for the other.

But when the orks of Gorgrim's horde finally came into contact with the Blood Ravens of Captain Thule, it was clear that matters had grown far, far more complicated than any simple search for recruits.

THE SQUAD HAD spread out so wide that Sergeant Merrik had lost sight of the nearest of the others, keeping track of them on his visor's display. He knew that the odds were against them, but he was a Blood Raven, and would not give up without a fight. He fired his bolter at the ork bike slewing his way, then leapt to one side just in time to avoid a blow from the massive battleaxe the biker wielded.

'Knowledge is power!' Merrik shouted, calling out the battle cry of the Blood Ravens Chapter. 'Guard it well!'

The ork biker was coming around for another run. A cloud of greasy smoke billowed from the exhausts of the warbike, and as the ork brought his forks back around to face Merrik once more, the warbiker opened fire with the twin-linked guns mounted beneath the handlebars. The guns were heavy calibre, but poorly balanced, so that when they were fired the bike bucked and spun wildly out of control. Even so, the sands at Merrik's feet kicked up in sprays wherever the shots hit home, and were even a scant handful of them to find their mark on Merrik's body, even his ceramite power armour may not be enough to protect him.

Merrik was a trained Adeptus Astartes with long years of experience, and he had an advantage that the orks did not – the ability to strategise beyond the immediate moment. Orks were vicious fighters, but largely creatures of instinct, and seldom thought beyond the next exchange in any confrontation.

As the warbike roared and rumbled its way towards him, Merrik caught sight of a warbuggy heading in the opposite direction only a few dozen metres away. On the rear of the warbuggy was a pintle-mounted flamethrower, fuelled by the same promethium tank that powered the vehicle's engine. The ork manning the flamethrower was sending gouts of flame indiscriminately into the melee around him, while the warbuggy's driver careened on in search of fresh targets.

Firing a few more rounds from his bolter towards the onrushing warbiker, Merrik feigned as if to flee, turning and running away at an angle from the warbike's trajectory. Merrik didn't have to glance back to imagine the grin of vicious triumph on the warbiker's face; the sprays of sand kicking up all around Merrik's pounding feet were enough evidence that the warbike was changing course to follow him.

Merrik continued on, looking for all the world like he had lost all courage and was fleeing the field of battle, but as he heard the rumbling sound of the warbike closing at his heels, he suddenly jinked to the left and then lunged back in the opposite direction.

Through the corner of his eye Merrik could see the warbiker looking at him with bewildered confusion, but the warbiker didn't have long to be confused. In the next instant, the flamethrowing warbuggy careened into the warbiker's path, both of them moving much too fast to turn away from the collision, much less stop. As the warbike and warbuggy collided at high speed, the promethium tanks fuelling the flamethrower were sparked into a conflagration, and bike, buggy, and the three orks who manned them were caught in a fiery holocaust that engulfed them entirely, hot enough to reduce metal to slag and flesh to dust and ash.

Merrik didn't have the luxury of basking in his victory, he knew. He spun around, raising his bolter, looking for the next target.

But it was too late. Before Merrik saw it coming, he could hear the thunderous sound of its approaching footfalls and the clanking of its joints. By the time he caught sight of the enormous monstrosity, the massive mechanized walker was already bearing down on him, opening fire with bunker-busting rounds that hammered into his power armour, knocking him to the ground.

Merrik moaned, struggling to regain his footing before the walker opened fire again. He only needed a moment's grace. But seeing the walker take another lumbering step forward, its massive guns trained on his supine form, Merrik knew that he didn't have a moment.

'Knowledge is…' Merrik began, and then the thunderous roar of the walker's guns sounded again.

IN THE MAKESHIFT headquarters of the shipping depot, Apothecary Gordian at last whispered the words of auto-suggestion into the ear of the sleeping Librarian, the final signal to his suspended mind.

In the next instant, Librarian Niven lurched up
into a sitting position, eyes wide and wild.

'It comes!' Niven shouted, disoriented and all but
incoherent.

Gordian put a hand on Niven's shoulders,
attempting to calm him. The transition from suspended animation to full wakefulness was often a
disorienting one, and Astartes who woke after long
periods of suspension often took time to come to
their complete senses.

'Rest easy, Librarian,' Gordian said in reassuring
tones. 'Your body is mended, and now there is work
for you to do.'

'No!' Niven wheeled around and grabbed hold of
Gordian's arm in a vice-like grip. 'You don't understand. It comes!'

Gordian pried Niven's hand from his arm, trying to
remain patient. 'What comes, Librarian?' The Apothecary paused, eyes narrowing. 'What is it you see?'

Niven struggled to climb to his feet, but failed.

'The Great Devourer!' the Librarian shouted, saliva
flecking the corners of his mouth. 'It comes!'

'Sergeant Aramus?' Brother Voire called from the
entrance to the warehouse. They'd nearly completed
their sweep of this part of Argus Township, and once
they searched the last few buildings in the area for
any huddled refugees, they would be finished with
their search.

'What is it, Voire?' Aramus called from the street
outside.

'There's something in here I think you'll want to
see,' Voire said, his tone dark and foreboding.

Aramus voxed to Sergeant Tarkus and Battle-Brother Cirrac to have their teams continue their searches of the surrounding buildings, and then went to join Voire in the warehouse.

From the rolling door at the entrance, the warehouse looked no different from any one of a dozen similar structures they'd searched in the previous day. Having begun their quest for potential aspirants at the north end of the township, they'd worked their way east, and then south, before finally returning to the west. So it was that they were now checking the buildings closest to the space port, and to the warehouse in which Thule had established his headquarters.

Brother Voire was standing near an overturned crate, with markings in Low Gothic stamped on the sides. Within the crate was something that, in the low light that filtered through the open door, seemed strangely pearlescent, its shape rounded and bulbous.

'What do you make of it?' Voire asked.

Aramus crouched down, and prodded at the contents of the crate with the point of his combat knife.

'It appears to be xenos.'

He straightened, lips drawn into a line.

'And it looks like something has hatched out of it.'

CHAPTER SIX

'THERE IS NO doubt about it,' Captain Thule said, standing over the crate and examining the remains of the object within. 'It is definitely xenos.'

Sergeant Aramus stood at the captain's side, his bolter in hand and ready to fire, eyes scanning the darkened warehouse around them. 'It has a tyranid look to it,' the sergeant offered.

Thule nodded. 'That it does.' He glanced in Aramus's direction. 'And your squad found this while searching for candidates?'

'Yes, captain,' Aramus answered. The rest of the squad was still engaged in the search, in fact. On finding the xenos object, only recently broken open, though, Aramus had made the decision that it should be brought to the captain's attention, and so gone to fetch Thule from the barricades.

Thule shook his head in disbelief. 'And yet, how did it come to be here? In a *shipping* container, no less?'

As soon as Sergeant Tarkus and the rest of Aramus's Third Squad completed their search of the remaining refugees for any potential aspirants, Thule's orders were for the surviving Blood Ravens to withdraw to the extraction point for immediate departure. Already the trio of Thunderhawks were prepared and ready for takeoff on the landing pad of the space port.

Beyond the walls of the warehouse could be heard the faint din of the battle being waged against the orks to the north, east, and south, a constant susurration of noise like the endless beating of waves against a rocky shores. From time to time the background noise was punctuated by the sound of powerful engines firing, as ships lifted off from the spaceport to the west, Navy and merchant ships alike carrying those with the influence and means away from the threat to the safety of the vessels waiting in orbit above.

Aramus indicated the Low Gothic writing stencilled on the side of the crate. 'It would appear that the container originated on another world in the Aurelia sub-sector. The jungle world of Typhon Primaris, whose system neighbours Calderis.'

'Brought *from* Typhon Primaris,' Thule repeated with incredulity. 'And brought *to* Calderis.' He looked from the egg within the crate to Aramus and back again. 'By what madness would someone bring a xenos organism *to* an inhabited world?'

Aramus could only shrug, the movement obscured by his heavy power armour such that his shoulder-guards only bobbed fractionally on either side. 'I don't know, sir.' He paused, and then added, 'When I saw that the thing had... well, had *hatched*, though, I thought you should be apprised immediately.'

Thule nodded. 'You thought correctly, sergeant.' The captain ran his gaze around the darkened warehouse, thoughtfully. 'We are only some hundred metres or so from the shipping depot in which I've made my headquarters. With all the effort we've put into strategising against the orks beyond the city walls, I'd never have dreamed that we'd have to consider such a threat from within the township itself.'

'Have there been any reports that might suggest a xenos sighting, sir?'

Before Thule could answer, there was a scraping sound from behind them, and the noise of crates being toppled.

The two Blood Ravens whirled around, impossibly fast, Aramus with his bolter raised and ready to fire, Thule with Wisdom coruscating in his gauntleted grip.

The pair of men who stood at the warehouse entrance saw the bolter trained on them and the power sword drawn against them, and likewise saw the aggressive poses of the Space Marines who held them. Stricken white as ghosts as all the blood fled their faces, the two men shot their hands up into the air in an attitude of surrender.

'Don't shoot!' shouted one of the men, who wore the finely-wrought robes of a member of the Argus Township gentry, a corded belt straining over his prodigious belly. Here was a Calderian who had not missed many meals when the foodstores of the general populace began to run empty.

'Noble Astartes, we present no threat,' the other said, as calmly as possible. He was dressed flamboyantly in a brocade jacket with epaulettes on each shoulder, knee-high boots, a duelling pistol in a lacquered holster at his hip, and an augmetic patch over one eye. No Calderian, whether gentry or otherwise, this was an off-worlder, a rogue trader by the look of him.

'Stand fast, sergeant,' Captain Thule ordered, pointedly not sheathing the power sword Wisdom. The captain turned his baleful gaze on the two men. 'What is your business here?'

The Calderian flustered, flapping his hands overhead like tethered birds attempting to take wing. 'Th-this… this *is* my business,' he managed, with some difficulty.

Captain Thule raised the point of Wisdom until the tip of the power sword was aimed directly at the Calderian's heart. 'You waste my already-too-precious time. I'll ask again, what is your business here?'

The Calderian, a guilty look on his face, glanced to the rogue trader beside him, seeking assistance.

'What my corpulent friend is attempting to explain, proud sons of the Emperor,' the rogue trader began, his tone oily and obsequious, 'is that he is the master of this warehouse. This place is, as he inelegantly attempted to phrase his response, *his* business.'

Captain Thule was quickly losing what little patience remained to him. Though it was something of a break in etiquette, Aramus stepped forward to address the pair, in large part out of a desire to spare them testing the captain's patience and thereby earning his ire. 'Have you a ship, man?'

The rogue trader inclined his head in an abbreviated bow. 'Humbly,' he said, without a trace of humility in his tone, 'that felicity is mine.'

'Then why are you here?' Aramus indicated the warehouse, and the township beyond, and the hordes of orks beyond the city walls. 'Why have you not fled?'

The rogue trader glanced in the warehouse-master's direction. 'My companion here has retained my services to escort him from this world to some safe harbour, but expressed a desire to salvage a few items of value – both commercial and sentimental – from the warehouse before quitting the planet.'

Captain Thule took a step forward, his gaze boring into the warehouse-master. 'As master of this place, you are responsible for what is stored within.'

It was not a question, only a bald statement of fact, but the warehouse-master still stammered a reply in the affirmative.

'What do you know about *that*?' Captain Thule said, swinging his power sword around and thrusting its point towards the container and the hatched xenos egg within.

The warehouse-master and rogue trade exchanged a glance, neither willing yet to speak.

'Answer!' Thule boomed, brandishing Wisdom.

'I-I-I…' the warehouse-master stammered.

'You,' Thule said, pointing to the rogue trader. 'What is your role in this?'

'Well, you see, Noble Astartes,' the rogue trader began, waving his hands as though conjuring his words from thin air, 'I am only lately arrived on Calderis, and so surely I can't be expected to…'

Before the rogue trader could finish his prevarication, there came a sound of screeching metal from the far side of the warehouse.

Annoyance boiling over, Thule turned to see who this new interloper might be. 'What is it *now*?'

It was at that moment that the tyranid warrior leapt from the shadows of the darkened warehouse, talons scything and toxins dripping from its gaping maw.

SERGEANT THADDEUS HAD seen Sergeant Merrik fall before the ork mechanised walker, but been too far away to do anything to help. It had been only a short while since Sergeant Avitus had relayed Captain Thule's orders to prepare for withdrawal, and with their extraction almost within sight, Thaddeus had made a private vow that no other Blood Raven would fall on Calderis if he could help it.

The spacefaring orks, led by the blood-faced Warlord, were proving a much deadlier enemy than their feral cousins had done. So long as he had kept his chainsword whirring and his feet moving, and so long as he was able to face off against the feral orks singly and not in large numbers, Thaddeus had been reasonably assured of escaping serious injury. Only the primitive explosives which the feral orks lobbed at him, whether lashed to the end of spears or configured as crude grenades, had given the enemy much in the way of ranged attacks, and so long as

Thaddeus was constantly aware of the greenskins in close quarters, ready to parry any of their attacks with his chainsword, he maintained the upper hand. And with his jump pack, he had been able to leap away, if the numbers of orks in close range ever proved too many for him to overcome.

Out on the open deserts, though, facing the more sophisticated orks of Gorgrim's horde, there were countless variables more to consider at each passing moment. No longer was he able to contend himself only with those orks close enough to make close combat attacks, only occasionally having to dodge or outrun the crude explosives lobbed his way; now, facing off against the artillery and energy cannons and heavy weapons of Gorgrim's horde, Thaddeus found himself facing possible danger from all sides, at all times. And if he found himself overwhelmed by numbers, he could not simply leap away, for fear that he would, like Brother Renzo, simply be shot out of the sky before ever touching down again.

All of which, of course, made the withdrawal to the extraction point that much more complicated a proposition. There were fourteen Space Marines of the Blood Ravens Chapter still standing and fighting against Gorgrim's horde by this point.

Thaddeus swore on the name of the Great Father, Azariah Vidya, that he would see all fourteen of them reach the extraction point. And even if he couldn't get them all out alive, it was worth his life to die in the attempt.

AVITUS AND HIS Devastator squad manned the walls. The sergeant itched to join the action against the spacefaring orks out in the desert, and had done since Sergeant Thaddeus had first voxed back word of their discovery, but Thule had ordered the Ninth Squad to safeguard the township until the last possible moment.

Though Avitus was a Blood Raven, and knew his duty, the assignment rankled. What did he care about the safety of the quavering inhabitants of Argus, much less of the snivelling desert-dwellers who had taken refuge there? He knew all too well that the Calderians would not hesitate to sacrifice the lives of Argus and the rest of the Space Marines, if it meant even a few moments more life for themselves. He had learned the real value that the common citizens of the Imperium placed on the Adeptus Astartes back on Kronus during the Dark Crusade, and never again would he be fool enough to place undue value on the lives of normal men and women.

Sergeant Cyrus and his Scouts had been dispatched to gather and protect the aspirants selected to accompany the Blood Ravens back to the *Armageddon*, and had now likely already reached the space port to the west of the city, preparing to depart in the Thunderhawks. When Thule had been called away by Aramus, who had discovered something of interest in his search through the city, Avitus was tempted to quit the barricades, and withdraw to the extraction point himself. But he was a Space Marine, and given his orders he would fulfil them to the best of his ability, however odious the task might be.

So now he waited for the word from Captain Thule, for leave either to proceed to the space port for extraction or else join Thaddeus and the others in the action against Gorgrim's horde, for the moment busying himself with picking off feral orks as they attempted to scramble up the township's walls.

But when the next vox came from Thule, it was not the word which Avitus had been expecting.

Captain Thule's next communication was a single word, one which brought a chill even to the spine of a hardened and world-weary veteran like Sergeant Avitus.

It was a word that could conjure nightmares, and brought back memories of the titanic struggle against the norn-queen that had cost Avitus his jaw and most of his throat.

'Tyranid!'

ARAMUS LOOKED ON as Captain Thule parried the tyranid's rending claw with the power sword Wisdom, the energy that crackled along the blade's length sending up sparks as it rebounded against the diamond-hard chitin of the monster's claw.

'Captain, to your left!' Aramus shouted, then fired a stream of bolter rounds at the tyranid's torso as Thule leaned out of the line of fire.

Against the chitinous armour of a tyranid, even a relative juvenile such as the warrior who faced them now, the bolts were all but ineffective. Aramus cursed himself for not bringing hellfire rounds to the planet's surface – with a mutagenic acid vial at the bolt's core, the rounds would at least have stood a chance of doing some significant damage – but no one had anticipated the presence of the Great Devourer's offspring lurking on Calderis.

'For the Emperor!' Thule shouted, charging the tyranid once more, power sword swinging through the air in a whirling blur. The tyranid warrior leapt aside with blinding speed, its movements impossibly fast thanks to the adrenal glands that pulsed on its back, launching a salvo of diamond-hard spines at Thule from its spinefist as it went.

The tyranid was barely mature, having only recently hatched, but was already a fearsome monster. Tyranids passed quickly through their juvenile stages, and in short order were already all but unstoppable killing machines. This one had evidently been skulking around the shadows of Argus for days, picking its prey carefully as it grew, perhaps dining upon a stray animal or two until it had grown large enough to begin to cull the weaker members of the unsuspecting refugees who crowded the streets of Argus Township.

And if one or two, or a handful, or even a dozen or more refugees went missing over the course of a few days, who would notice? There were so many crammed into the township, and confusion ran so high, that families and groups were continually being separated from one another. And even if they *had* noticed the loss of one of their number, to whom would they raise the alarm? Their leaders and politicians had already fled from the world, most of them now safely on board the ships of Admiral Forbes's Battlegroup Aurelia, and the Blood Ravens had concerns of their own to occupy their attentions.

'Aramus!' shouted Captain Thule, his power armour already dotted with toxic-laden spines that had buried themselves in the ceramite, but none of which had, as yet, pierced through into the flesh beneath. 'Flanking manoeuvre.'

Aramus didn't waste time or breath in acknowledgment, but sprang into motion. He had a frag grenade in one fist, his bolter in the other, and while he wished fervently that he had heavier weaponry, or perhaps even a krak grenade or two, he knew too well that wishing was not going to alter the odds one whit, nor magically change the contents of his personal armoury.

Of the warehouse-master and the rogue trader, there had been no sign since the moment after the tyranid warrior attacked. Aramus hoped that they had gotten clear, and had not been hit by an errant spine disgorged by the tyranid's spinefist – or, in fact, by any errant weapons fire from Aramus's own bolter – and that perhaps they had already reached the space port and the rogue trader's own vessel. The two men were hardly exemplars of the Imperial population, both seemingly of a low and somewhat devious nature, but any human lives lost unnecessarily to a xenos enemy stung Aramus's sense of responsibility, and if the two were to escape with their lives, the dangers which Thule and the sergeant now faced might not be in vain.

Aramus waited until Thule had pulled away, then lobbed a frag grenade at the warrior. The grenade hit the ground between the tyranid's rear limbs, and the resulting blast was directed upwards into the warrior's lower body. The shrapnel pitted and cracked the tyranid's chitin here and there, with an evil-smelling ichor oozing out from between the cracks, but aside from some minor surface damage the warrior seemed not to be significantly injured.

Still, they had succeeded in cracking the tyranid's armoured shell, and if they could do that, it meant that they might be able to do real harm to the body within, as well.

'Stand clear!' Captain Thule ordered, waving Aramus back. 'I shall take the battle to *it*.'

Wisdom was like a living thing in the fist of the Blood Ravens captain, the energy that coruscated along its blade leaving streaked traces in midair, so swiftly did Thule swing it through the air. Even in the face of daunting odds, Aramus could not help but admire the technique with which Thule bore the blade, or the strength that powered his swings and thrusts.

When the warrior had first attacked, Aramus had offered to call for additional Blood Ravens to assist them. But beyond making his initial, curt announcements to the others that a tyranid had been spotted in Argus, Thule had refused to call on the others again. They had already lost four of their brothers in the preceding days to the orks, feral and otherwise, and it was Thule's opinion that the rest of them would be needed to successfully complete their mission and escort the aspirants off of Calderis. If the price of that success was to be the lives of Aramus and Thule himself at the rending talons and tusks of this tyranid, then that was a cost that the sergeant and captain would have to pay.

CAPTAIN DAVIAN THULE closed with the monster, lunging forward, Wisdom whistling through the stale air of the warehouse. In close quarters as they were there was little opportunity for feints and evasion, and subtly was seldom of much use against a tyranid in any case. What mattered most in a contest against an offspring of the Great Devourer were speed and strength.

Had Thule and Aramus been properly armed, a contest against a single tyranid warrior would have been no contest at all. Enough well-placed hellfire rounds and a krak grenade would have been sufficient to fell the inhuman beast. But the Blood Ravens had come to Calderis armed for a conflict with orks, little expecting a need for the weaponry and tactics developed over the long years of the Tyrannic Wars.

With a wordless, keening cry, the tyranid met Thule's power sword with one of its forelimbs, and though Wisdom managed to sheer off the chitinous tip of the warrior's claw, the remaining portion of the limb was left no less able to strike.

Wisdom shifted in Thule's grip, and the captain swung the power sword backhanded at the tyranid's thorax, but before the blade impacted the warrior was able to fire the barbed strangler which was fused to one of its middle limbs, the seed-pod vomited from the muscled tube at speed. Just as Wisdom was rebounding off the tyranid's armoured skin, the seed-pod struck Thule's sword-arm at the shoulder, sticking in place as though held by the strongest of adhesives. Before Thule had realised the seed-pod had stuck, it had already begun to grow to maturity, impossibly fast, spreading out in all directions with blinding speed, shooting out hooked tendrils that wrapped themselves around his neck, shoulder, and sword-arm, binding as tightly as any forged manacles.

'Captain!' Thule heard Aramus shout.

Thule struggled to break free of the barbed strangler, or to shift his power sword to his free hand if he could not, but having gained a momentary advantage the killing instincts of the tyranid warrior would not relent. The spinefist bound to the warrior's other mid-limb fired another salvo of diamond-hard spines, which at this close range grouped together over an area no more than a few centimetres in diameter at the centre of Thule's abdomen, just below his sternum. The spines buried themselves in the ceramite, some of them a centimetre or more deep, and together sent cracks spidering through the outer skin of the captain's armour.

Thule heard Aramus's bolter firing, again and again, saw the muzzle-flashes from the corner of his eye, but already his vision was becoming obscured as the barbed strangler continued to grow and wrap itself around Thule's helmet.

The warrior swung down its massive rending claw, punching directly at the worst of the spidering cracks on Thule's abdomen, once, then again, and on the third impact the claw punched through the cracked ceramite and buried itself in the muscle and soft tissue within.

As the warrior drove its claw deeper and deeper into Thule body, captain and tyranid were pulled only centimetres apart. Through the sliver of vision afforded to Thule through his barb-obscured eye slits, Thule could see the pits and cracks on the tyranid's carapace where Aramus's bolts had struck true. It looked like the crater-pocked surface of a moon, oozing foul ichor.

The barbed strangler had all but immobilised Thule's sword arm, and the claw impaling him prevented him from moving to either side, but if he could only manage to shift Wisdom in his grasp a fraction, and then…

Captain Thule reached out with his free hand and grabbed hold of the tyranid's upper body.

'If I die, monster,' he seethed through clenched teeth, 'I won't die alone.'

Thule twisted his wrist as far as he was able, straining with pain, bringing Wisdom's blade around, its point aimed directly at the crater-pocked area of the tyranid's carapace. Then, ignoring the throbbing pain of the impaling claw, feeling his strength ebb from him as the toxins coursed through his system, Thule wrenched his sword-arm inwards, bracing himself with his other hand on the warrior's carapace, and buried Wisdom halfway to the hilt in the tyranid's body.

ARAMUS WATCHED THE tyranid warrior shove the tendril-wrapped body of Captain Thule off its claw. As the captain crumpled to the ground, the tyranid reached down with one of its forelimbs and yanked the power sword from its side with an inhuman screech, and then tossed Wisdom away to the farthest corner of the warehouse.

Aramus rushed forward, bolter firing, but then the tyranid let out a final ear-splitting cry and toppled forward onto the still body of Captain Thule, and it was all over.

CHAPTER SEVEN

His own enhanced strength augmented by the servos of his power armour, Sergeant Aramus strained as he lifted the massive bulk of the felled tyranid warrior from off Captain Thule, and with a grunt of effort shoved it aside. Having already confirmed to his satisfaction that the tyranid was no further threat, Aramus knelt by Thule's side as soon as the warrior flopped lifeless onto the cold rockcrete of the warehouse floor.

The captain's wounds were grave, perhaps even fatal, but it appeared that he was not dead yet. He lived, if only barely. Aramus lacked an Apothecary's expert knowledge of Astartes physiology, but it seemed to him that the rending claw of the tyranid warrior appeared to have done some serious damage to Thule's internal organs, and perhaps even to the implants that made him an Adeptus Astartes.

If Thule were to survive, he would need the attention of Apothecary Gordian. Assuming Gordian had followed Thule's orders, he would have already withdrawn to the extraction site, awaiting the rest of the team to arrive so the Blood Ravens could quit Calderis once and for all. There was little to gain from summoning Gordian here, though, Aramus knew; better that Thule should be brought to him, so that the captain could be returned to the *Armageddon* where he might receive better treatment than battlefield conditions would allow.

There was little time to waste. Aramus spent a precious few moments attempting to locate the captain's power sword, but after searching amongst the toppled crates and containers where the tyranid had thrown it with its dying movements, Aramus could not locate it.

Wisdom, it appeared, had been lost.

Holstering his bolter, Aramus bent and, straining with the effort, lifted Thule up and over his shoulder, and then hurried from the warehouse.

Sergeant Thaddeus and the remains of the First and Seventh Squads were fighting their way through the massed orks, both the ferals native to Calderis and the well-armed members of Gorgrim's horde who goaded them on. They were working their way west towards the extraction point, but it was beginning to look doubtful that they would reach the space port before the appointed time.

The fourteen survivors had cut, blasted, and punched their way through the main line of Gorgrim's horde, and now found themselves making only slow progress, with the barbaric feral orks before them and on their right flank, and the more sophisticated forces of Warlord Gorgrim at their rear and on their left flank. Had Thaddeus only had the members of his assault squad to consider, they could have made faster progress by employing their jump packs, leaping over the vast numbers of orks which they were now obliged to battle their way through. But the surviving members of the late Sergeant Merrik's First Squad were not equipped with jump packs, and since there was simply no way that eight Astartes with jump packs could carry with them six fully armed and armoured Space Marines, the brutal calculus of their situation dictated that a hastier withdrawal for the assault squad would mean that the tactical squad would need to be left behind to fend for themselves. And since Thaddeus had already vowed to leave no Blood Raven behind, that meant that they would all extract together – or not at all.

The sheer overwhelming numbers of the feral orks in their path were slowing them down, giving the elements of Gorgrim's horde behind the opportunity to catch up and attack from the rear. But even the enhanced senses and keen tactical mind of an Adeptus Astartes was hard pressed to constantly monitor threats from all directions, and it was only by acting together as a well-oiled machine that the Blood Ravens had even survived this long.

'Thaddeus!'

Sergeant Thaddeus heard the voice of Battle-Brother Loew calling over the vox. Loew had been tasked with covering their rear, while Thaddeus was among those concerning themselves with the enemy before them.

'To your rear!' Loew shouted again.

Thaddeus dealt a blow to the feral ork before him with his chainsword, lopping the ork's left arm off at the elbow. The ork scarcely seemed to notice, but swung with his right, and Thaddeus was forced to lunge to one side to avoid the ork's next strike. Then he unleashed a stream of bolt rounds from his bolt pistol at the ork's head, and danced back out of the way as the ork's body gradually came to realise it was no longer receiving signals from its brain.

Finally free to see what Loew had been warning him about, Thaddeus turned just in time to see a massive figure, more machine than flesh, thundering towards him. One of Gorgrim's shock troops, a large percentage of the ork's body had been replaced with crude cybernetics – the top half of the ork's head was hidden behind an inverted bowl of tarnished metal, with the red glow of augmetics where his eyes would have been, and his shoulders on either side ended in massive metallic joints from which swung a pair of bionic arms, both terminating in gargantuan power claws.

Thaddeus began to raise his chainsword, but the cyborg ork was already barrelling forward too quickly for him to take an appropriate defensive posture, and was already too close for Thaddeus to get clear of its charge. His only option was to face the cyborg's attack as best as he was able, and look for a shift in advantage in which to regain the upper hand – provided he survived the initial attack.

Then a Blood Raven rammed into the cyborg ork from the side, knocking him to one side and diverting him from the collision with Thaddeus.

'Thought you could use some help,' Brother Loew voxed, as he fired his bolter at short range into the cyborg ork's body. Thaddeus could almost hear Loew's taunting grin as he spoke.

Loew's bolter rounds ricocheted ineffectually off the grimy metal of the ork's bionics, as the cyborg ork regained his footing and turned to deal with the Space Marine who had diverted his path.

'Loew, look out!' Thaddeus shouted, but the cyborg ork moved impossibly fast, belying its ungainly appearance.

With a mechanical buzz of outrage, the cyborg ork swung its two massive power-clawed fists together, taking hold of Loew's arms at either elbow.

Loew shouted in defiance, but the cyborg ork held his arms pinned to his sides, the grip of the power-claws tightening all the while, threatening to crack the Blood Raven's ceramite armour like an egg's shell.

Thaddeus was already in motion, chainsword whirring as he rushed to Loew's aid, but before he reached the pair the damage had already been done.

'Knowledge is power!' Thaddeus cried as he drove his chainsword up to the hilt into the ork's back. The chainsword sent up curls of smoke as its teeth bit and chewed into the cyborg ork's body, ripping into metal and flesh alike, but it wasn't until Thaddeus had yanked the chainsword free and taken another swipe at the linkages between the cyborg ork's shoulders and bionic arms that the power-claws finally loosened their grip on Loew's arms.

Still howling in buzzing rage, the cyborg ork toppled over, sparking and bleeding green ichor, legs twitching and cybernetic eyes flashing. Thaddeus leapt over the bionic greenskin's flailing body and landed at Loew's side.

'It looks bad, I know,' Loew said, voice laced with pain as he raised his eyes from the mangled ruins of his arms on either side. The armour had broken, large chunks of it falling away, and the flesh and bone within had been pulped, so that the arms hung from Loew's shoulders uselessly. 'But you should see the other combatant.'

Thaddeus snarled, but didn't waste a moment either in unnecessary sympathy or pointless self-recrimination.

'Those arms of yours weren't good for much, anyway,' Thaddeus said, as he sheathed his chainsword temporarily, and hauled Loew's moaning form over his shoulder. 'And you never *could* manage to use your punches effectively when we sparred.'

'When my arms are back,' Loew said, his voice scarcely above a whisper, 'I'll make you eat those words.'

'Perhaps,' Thaddeus said, drawing his chainsword once more and turning back to the fray. 'But don't think this means that I'll go easy on you in the sparring hall until they do.'

Thaddeus motioned the other twelve Space Marines forward.

'Come on, Blood Ravens! I don't want to carry all of you, so let's keep this train moving!'

The First and Seventh Squads fought on. It looked doubtful that they would reach the extraction point in time, but they weren't about to stop trying.

'SERGEANT,' SCOUT XENAKIS said as he jogged to the edge of the landing pad. 'Scout Jutan reports that Thunderhawk Three will be ready for takeoff in another ten minutes.'

Sergeant Cyrus stood on the pitted ferrocrete, looking east at Argus Township. Pillars of black smoke curled up from several points in the city, where the firebombs lobbed by the feral orks had made it over the wall and found fuel down below. If left unchecked, the fires might consume the township whole before the orks were able to claim her.

'And the aspirants?' Cyrus asked, not taking his eyes off the Argus skyline.

'Scout Muren has all twelve of them belted-in on board Thunderhawk Two,' Xenakis answered in clipped tones.

Twelve aspirants. All of these weeks of fighting and bleeding – and dying, Cyrus reminded himself – and all they had to show for it were twelve aspirants. Would even a single one of them survive the Blood Trials that would follow, much less the examinations and initiations required to become a Blood Raven?

And at what cost? Cyrus had brought ten Blood Raven Scouts with him to act as Captain Thule's retinue. Now, only five were left. Five Scouts, neophytes that stood on the precipice of becoming full Adeptus Astartes themselves, their lives snuffed out on the unforgiving and uncaring sands of Calderis.

'And Watral has Thunderhawk One ready for lift-off?' Cyrus asked.

'Yes, sergeant.'

'Tell him there may be a change in plans, and to be prepared for lift-off at any moment.'

It came as small consolation to remember that the five Scouts who survived would be the better for their experiences here. Battle-hardened, tried and tested, when they joined the ranks of the Blood Ravens as full battle-brothers, they would carry with them the lessons they had learned on this Emperor-forsaken world, and would be the better warriors for it.

Cyrus hoped that they remembered the other lessons he had tried to teach them, as well. For the better part of two centuries Cyrus had served as sergeant to a squad of Blood Ravens Scouts, doing his best to burn out any hunger for glory they might still harbour, and to impart the martial skills and mental toughness which any warrior needed in order to survive in a hostile galaxy. It was not, after all, arms and armour that made an Astartes, but a tactical mind and a trained body. That was why Cyrus opted not to wear the power armour of an Adeptus Astartes, unlike some other Scout sergeants, but instead wore only the lighter gear of a Scout, as a symbol to the neophytes whom he led of what truly mattered in combat.

'Dismissed,' Cyrus said, glancing over in Xenakis's direction.

Scout Xenakis nodded, and rushed off to fulfil his orders.

Cyrus turned from Argus and surveyed the space port. Aside from the three Blood Ravens

Thunderhawks, there were scant few craft in evidence. The last of the Imperial Navy vessels had left some time before, ferrying away the last few Calderians with the political clout to demand safe passage off-world. Most of the civilian craft had departed, as well, with only a single ship left, which was parked, it seemed, as far from the Thunderhawks as practicable.

As Cyrus glanced in its direction, he saw a pair of figures hurrying from Argus towards the civilian ship. One was a rogue trader in a brocade coat with an augmetic eyepatch, the other a man in the robes of a Calderian merchant, and between them they struggled to carry a heavily-wrapped object about as long as a man was tall. They scurried aboard the ship, evidently eager to depart without any contact with Cyrus and his Scouts.

It hardly mattered to Cyrus whether the rogue trader and his passenger wanted to exchange pleasantries with him. He had already been forced to harden his heart to the countless thousands of Calderians they would be forced to leave to their fate. As he had always striven to impress upon the Scouts in his charge, there were grim realities of war that could not be altered, only accepted, and it was a wise Space Marine who concentrated on his duties and on those aspects of the war that *could* be altered.

At the moment, it was just such an alterable aspect of war that occupied Cyrus's thoughts. What he intended for Thunderhawk One was contrary to Captain Thule's orders – in the letter, if perhaps not the spirit – but nearly two centuries of experience in battle had given Cyrus a certain flexibility in regards to orders, in particular, and to the precepts of the

Codex Astartes in general. So long as he served Emperor and Chapter faithfully, Cyrus reasoned, the occasional lapses in strict adherence to commands could be overlooked.

He only hoped his superiors would agree, when all was said and done.

SERGEANT AVITUS FIRED one last burst from his heavy bolter down into the scrambling ranks of feral orks at the base of the city walls before giving the signal. The appointed hour had arrived, and it was time to pull back from the city walls.

'Barabbas, Philetus!' he voxed to the battle-brothers he'd set up as team leaders. 'Pull your teams back to the rendezvous point.'

With the whole of the city walls of Argus Township to man in these last hours, and only eight Blood Ravens of the Ninth Squad at his disposal, Avitus had opted for a divisional tactic, splitting the squad into two teams, one centred around the north-east corner of the Argus wall, the other around the south-east corner, each with operational autonomy. Avitus, heavy bolter firing so often the barrel scarcely had time to cool down between magazine reloads, had roamed between the two strongpoints, overseeing the operations.

'Acknowledged,' Barabbas voxed back.

'Do we have to leave so soon?' Philetus replied, chuckling ruefully.

'Silence, Blood Ravens,' Avitus barked back. 'Keep nonessential vox to a minimum.'

'Acknowledged,' a chastened Philetus responded.

Avitus would have to have a talk with Battle-Brother Philetus onboard the *Armageddon*, provided they both returned alive. He knew that other squad leaders allowed some degree of levity in their commands – others, like Sergeant Thaddeus, even seemed to encourage jocularity among their battle-brothers – but Avitus saw no place for such levity in combat. Battle was a deadly serious business, and a light heart and a laughing spirit were no asset in an environment in which death might come screaming towards you at any moment. If the Space Marines under his command deigned to waste their time in banter and jibes back in the barracks, that was their business – though there, too, it was a pastime which Avitus was always quick to discourage – but in combat he would allow no such nonsense.

The runes on Avitus's visor display showed green for each of the seven Space Marines in his Devastator squad, and his auspex showed that all seven had withdrawn from the wall and were moving towards the west, the two teams angling together, one north-west and the other south-west, so that their paths converged somewhere near the city's centre.

Avitus remained on the wall, covering their retreat, firing his heavy bolter first to the north along the Argus wall, then along to the south, and then north again. He succeeded in keeping some of the orks back, but the quicker-witted among the greenskins had already worked out that the fire from above had abated somewhat, and had redoubled their efforts to construct siege towers from the bodies of their fallen brothers. And the makeshift catapults further out continued to fling ork after ork into the air, and without the whole of the Ninth Squad on hand to shoot them down if they happened to overfly the wall, they began in small numbers to catapult successfully into the city behind Avitus, some even managing to survive the fall.

It was time for Avitus to follow his squad in withdrawal. Once he had left the wall, there would be nothing stopping the rest of the orks from climbing and catapulting over, and then Argus would be all but lost. But Avitus cared nothing about that. He had been given his orders, and he had carried them out. If the citizens below fell to claws and jaws of the ork horde once he'd quit his post, what did it matter to him?

Avitus fired another burst of bolter shells into the greenskins scaling the wall, then leapt down on the city side, hitting the ground running. He would catch up with his squad in a matter of moments, and then they would double-time to the extraction point and get off this world at last. And none too soon for Avitus's tastes.

'THE DEVOURER IS at hand,' Librarian Niven intoned for the hundredth time. 'We must make ready.'

Apothecary Gordian led the Librarian out onto the landing pad. It was not uncommon that Space Marines who had been in states of suspended animation for prolonged periods often had a period of disorientation upon revival. The mind of an Astartes was a highly trained tool, but one that had to be kept properly honed in order to maintain full functioning. The catalepsean node, one of the nineteen organs implanted in the Space Marine's body during the process of initiation, regulated the body's circadian rhythms and responses to sleep deprivation, and with it an Astartes was capable of remaining awake for long periods while at the same time getting the benefits of slumber by switching off different regions of the brain sequentially. It could not substitute for proper sleep entirely – even a Space Marine had to sleep eventually – but it meant that a Space Marine could survive long periods in the field while never losing awareness of their surroundings.

As a consequence, the minds of even the most highly trained Adeptus Astartes were not acquainted with long periods of inactivity, used instead to a near-constant influx of stimulation and information. When a Space Marine entered a state of suspended animation, however, their body regulated at the threshold between life and death by their sus-an membrane, the brain received virtually no stimulus, not even the low-level rapid eye movement activity experienced in dreams. Thus deprived of stimulus, the mind of a Space Marine in suspended animation would, when revived, temporarily find it difficult once more to process the cascade of new information flooding in. And in the case of a psyker like Librarian Niven, who experienced the world with a greater number of senses than the average Space Marine, the process of acclimatising once more to their world beyond their skulls could be an even more difficult one.

Still, Niven's repeated insistence that the Great Devourer was upon them was troubling. Gordian had heard Thule's all-points vox about the tyranid that had been discovered in the city, and a short while later had received a point-to-point vox from

Sergeant Aramus, who was bringing the injured Thule to the spaceport and calling ahead for Gordian's assistance. But from all accounts, there was only the single tyranid in Argus Township, perhaps only the one on all of Calderis, and if Aramus's estimation was correct it had been hatched from a seed brought to this world for unknown reasons. A single tyranid warrior was a threat, as evidenced by the injuries sustained by Captain Thule, but it was hardly a cause for general alarm, much less the repeated litany of the Librarian's warnings about the Great Devourer.

But were Niven's warnings more than just the distress of a recently revived mind, struggling to make sense of the incoming flood of sensory information? Was there more to the tyranid threat than was immediately obvious?

The two Thunderhawks on the landing pad were ready for lift-off, each with a Scout of the Blood Ravens Chapter at the helm. The aspirants gathered in the recent weeks had been loaded onto one of them, and the Blood Ravens of the Third Squad stood sentry around the other, waiting for the arrival of their squad leader and the captain. Chaplain Palmarius was on board the Thunderhawk with the aspirants, instructing them in any number of hymns and liturgies which Palmarius felt would be of use at the present moment, all the while taking the measure of each of the dozen aspirants, already beginning the lengthy examinations that would only end when they were installed as full battle-brothers – if they only lived that long.

As Apothecary Gordian escorted Librarian Niven across the landing pad, and entrusted him to the

care of the Third Squad who guarded the Thunderhawks, he received a vox message from Sergeant
Aramus.

'Aramus to squad. We're at the spaceport and in
need of assistance.'

Brother Voire of the Third Squad led Librarian
Niven to the Thunderhawk, while Brother Cirrac
and Gordian both turned to look for the source of
Aramus's transmission. A moment later they both
caught sight of Aramus hurrying towards the landing
pad, struggling under the unwieldy weight of the
motionless Captain Thule.

'Battle-brother, with me!' Apothecary Gordian said
to Cirrac, taking to his heels and rushing to intercept
Sergeant Aramus.

'Apothecary,' Aramus said as Gordian and Cirrac
helped ease Thule from the sergeant's shoulders.
'He's badly wounded, but still lives. He needs immediate assistance.'

Gordian didn't bother telling Aramus that he
could see that perfectly well for himself, but
motioned to Cirrac to help him carry the captain to
the Thunderhawk his battle-brothers guarded.

'We'll get him on board,' Gordian said, 'and then
I'll see what needs he has.'

Aramus followed, glancing first at the city behind
him, and then to the landing pad.

'Where is the other gunship?' Aramus said, looking from one Thunderhawk to the other.

Gordian glanced back over his shoulder at him
impatiently. 'Sergeant Cyrus countermanded the
captain's orders. He said he would let the results
judge his actions.'

Before Aramus could pose another question, Sergeant Avitus and his Devastator squad pounded onto the ferrocrete behind him.

'That's it, the township is empty,' Avitus said calmly, casually disregarding in his count the thousands upon thousands of refugees still within the city walls. With barely a glance at the others as they loaded the motionless body of Thule onboard, Avitus directed his squad to load up and prepare for lift-off.

THADDEUS AND THE other twelve survivors had fought as long and hard as they were able, and still had only covered a fraction of the distance to the space port. The designated time for lift-off had arrived, and there was no chance that they would reach the extraction point on time.

With the orks pressing in on all sides, Thaddeus had gathered all fourteen of the Blood Ravens under his command into a defensive ring, with the injured Space Marines like Brother Loew placed in the middle, and all those still able to fight standing shoulder to shoulder with their weapons trained outwards.

'Stand fast, men,' Thaddeus ordered. 'Whatever happens here today, your names shall be entered in the Book of Honour, and should we fall, all of us will be remembered in every ringing of the Bell of Souls.'

The orks pressed closer, the feral orks in their barbaric splendour side by side with their better armed and armoured cousins of Gorgrim's horde. Power-claws and explosive-tipped spears, crude swords and flamethrowers, all bore down on the fourteen Space Marines, all eyes filled with the lust for blood and murder in Warlord Gorgrim's name.

Just as the encircling greenskins closed the distance to the ring of defenders, a bolt of blinding blue las-fire lanced down out of the sky and drew a line of screaming death across a dozen or more orks. Before the orks could even look up to the heavens to see whence this burning agony came, a torrent of metal storm frag rounds ripped into the orks on the opposite side of the defenders' ring, the high-explosive charges detonating on impact and sending the deadly fragmentation casings flying out in all directions.

'What the Throne…?' Thaddeus said as he looked up from the carnage wreaked upon the ork attackers, just as a Thunderhawk gunship roared overhead at speed.

'Cyrus to Blood Ravens,' crackled the voice of the pilot over the vox-comms. 'Thought you could use a bit of assistance.'

With the ranks of the orks in disarray, the ring of defenders opened fire, thinning the numbers of enemies around them even further.

'You were not wrong, Sergeant Cyrus,' Thaddeus voxed back with a grin.

'When you failed to reach the space port,' Cyrus replied, 'I decided you might prefer an extraction point a little closer to home.'

'Acknowledged,' Thaddeus said, chuckling. Then, to the Blood Ravens under his command, he added, 'Let's help clear a landing strip, Space Marines, and then we can be up and out of here.'

The gunship roared back for another pass, and though the orks howled in outrage and frustration, they were not prepared for an aerial attack, and were soon set to scatter. It would be a minor victory, but a victory savoured by the Space Marines involved nonetheless.

BY THE TIME Thunderhawk One landed, loaded, and lifted off again, Thunderhawks Two and Three had already blasted up from the Argus space port, with all surviving members of the recruiting party and the *Armageddon* reinforcements present and accounted for. In all, four full battle-brothers and five neophyte Scouts had been lost in the undertaking, and another half-dozen had received wounds that would not soon heal, Captain Thule chief among them.

As the Thunderhawks rumbled up to escape velocity, towards the strike cruiser *Armageddon* waiting in orbit, Sergeant Aramus looked at an image of the planet below on a data-slate, taking a last look at the city they'd fought these last days to defend.

With the Blood Ravens gone, nothing remained to prevent the orks, Gorgrim's horde and their feral cousins, from overrunning Argus Township. There were still pockets of resistance and refuge out in the vastness of the deserts, and it would be long months before the orks managed to completely wipe humanity from the face of the planet, but for all intents and purposes Calderis was now lost to the orks.

'The Emperor protect them,' Aramus said of the humans who remained below, but he harboured little hope that any power, whether on Holy Terra or anywhere else in the universe, would turn an eye towards the last bloody days of Calderis.

Aramus tried to remember the lessons that Sergeant Cyrus had taught them, when he and Thaddeus had been mere neophytes themselves, about the ways a Space Marine must harden his heart against the grim realities of war, and focus only on his duty.

Looking down at Argus Township, unable to avoid picturing the horrors that would soon descend upon the innocents within its crumbling walls, Aramus found it harder and harder to think of anything *but* the grim realities of war.

CHAPTER EIGHT

DEEP WITHIN THE strike cruiser *Armageddon*, at its safest, most highly defensible and defended heart, lay the Apothecarion. Here in this vast dimly-lit chamber, in self-locking, sterile tubes, were housed the gene-seed of the Blood Ravens who had fallen during the undertaking on Zalamis. On the *Armageddon*'s return to the fortress-monastery *Omnis Arcanum* and the rest of the Blood Raven fleet, the tubes would be handed over to the servants of the Chief Apothecary, who would oversee the removal of the progenoid glands from within. These would then be used to create new zygotes, which would allow another generation of Blood Ravens to be initiated. Perhaps even some of the aspirants even now being received onboard by Chaplain Palmarius might survive to have the resultant organs implanted into their bodies, and the gene-seed extracted from the dying bodies of Blood Ravens on distant Zalamis would find new life in aspirants drawn from the desert world of Calderis. Just as the Apothecary's Creed held, 'While his gene-seed returns to the Chapter, a Space Marine cannot die.'

But it was not the broader scope of Space Marines surviving through the inheritance of their gene-seed that now occupied Gordian's attentions, but the more immediate survival of Captain Thule in the here and now. The captain lived, but only just, and unless Gordian wanted to surrender to the inevitable and ready his reductor to begin the extraction process, quick action was required.

With the flip of a switch, Gordian summoned a fleet of medical servitors from their resting places in niches around the circumference of the Apothecarion.

The lead servitor clanked to a stop at Gordian's side, as the Apothecary withdrew his probes from the body of Captain Thule.

'It is time,' Gordian said to the lead servitor. 'Prepare the sarcophagus.'

SERGEANT ARAMUS STOOD on the command deck of the *Armageddon*, near the captain's chair atop the dais, looking down at the bustle of activity that surrounded him. On all sides Chapter serfs hustled back and forth as servitors buzzed and clicked in their binary speak, preparing the strike cruiser to break orbit and depart the Calderis system. The question still remained as to where they were headed, of course...

'Sir,' one of the Chapter serfs said, approaching with eyes averted. 'The Lord Principal sends his compliments, and requests whether he may yet know our destination and heading.'

Aramus regarded the Chapter serf. He had scarcely noticed the presence of the deck hands in his previous visits to the command deck, and had certainly never been addressed by one. He found it impossible to guess the Chapter serf's age. Half a century? A century? Certainly older than Aramus himself, who hadn't set foot on a space-going vessel before his recruitment into the Blood Ravens, little more than two decades past. This Chapter serf had likely served on the *Armageddon* longer than Aramus had been alive. It was almost certain that he had served on the command deck as long as Aramus had been a Blood Raven. And yet here Aramus was, in a position to issue commands, which the Chapter serf would follow, or suffer the consequences.

Aramus tried to imagine what his life might have been like, had he failed the examinations or the initiation as a boy, and been taken on by the Blood Ravens as a Chapter serf. Would he be half so loyal, half so proud to serve, if he was denied the opportunity to be an Adeptus Astartes, and was instead relegated to the level of serf?

He didn't know, and likely couldn't know. He learned to love the Chapter and to honour the Emperor through the course of his indoctrination as an initiate and neophyte, and his every view of the universe and of life and duty was coloured by those early lessons. Had he not received that instruction, he would perforce be a different person, and might see the world from a different vantage point.

All of which, of course, was simply a distraction from the present moment. Musing on what might have been, ruminating fruitlessly on the difference between himself and a Chapter serf, imagining how life might have turned out had this event not happened or that event had – all of it was simply a means by which he was distracting himself from the matter at hand, and from the awesome responsibility he suddenly found himself shouldering.

'Inform the Navis dome that we have yet to determine our course,' Sergeant Aramus replied at length, 'and will notify him when the situation changes.'

'Sir,' the Chapter serf answered with a low bow, and then backed away.

With Sergeant Merrik dead on the planet below, and Captain Thule currently out of commission pending Apothecary Gordian's treatment of his injuries, command of the strike cruiser *Armageddon* fell, per Blood Ravens Chapter protocols, to the ranking tactical squad leader. There being only two tactical squads onboard, the First and the Third – and as the First was at present leaderless, with one of the battle-brothers, Brother Nord, acting as temporary leader only – that meant that the leader of Third Squad would be the new Commander at Sail.

At least until Captain Thule regains consciousness and returns to his post, Sergeant Aramus kept reminding himself.

It wasn't that he hadn't fancied that one day he might progress in the ranks so far as to command such a vessel. But it had been only a short while, in Aramus's estimation, since Captain Thule had first intimated to him on Prosperon that he was on track for a command of his own, and now he suddenly found himself in command of an entire strike cruiser? And, according to protocol, in ultimate command of all of the squads who sailed on board her? A Space Marine less than half his life, and already Aramus held in his hands the lives – and deaths, potentially – of more than three dozen Blood Ravens, including the Scouts in the count. And if one included the dozen aspirants culled from Calderis, or the hundred or so Chapter serfs, or the countless servitors who manned the ship…

Having barely grown accustomed to commanding ten Space Marines, Aramus now found himself with considerably more responsibility.

'Sergeant?'

Aramus turned at the sound of approaching footsteps, and found Apothecary Gordian climbing the command dais to join him. 'Yes, Apothecary?' He paused, and then added, unable to mask the tinge of optimism from his voice. 'Have you news of Captain Thule?'

Gordian nodded, slowly, his expression dour. 'There is news, sergeant, but none of it good.'

Aramus took a breath and let out a ragged sigh. 'Are his wounds fatal, then?'

'Yes,' Gordian answered, 'and no. There are any number of lacerations, breakages, and contusions, but most importantly there is a degree of systemic organ failure. In particular, the captain's oolitic kidney has been badly damaged, rendering it incapable of filtering out the tyranid toxins coursing through his body.'

'So the captain will die,' Aramus said, his tone flat and affectless.

'No,' Gordian replied, 'and yes. Were his oolitic kidney functioning, his body might in time recover from its other injuries, but if not, the toxins would kill him in short order. I have placed the captain in a sarcophagus, which will maintain his body in its present state, almost indefinitely.'

'To what end?' Aramus was perplexed. 'Surely his organs won't repair themselves while he is held in suspension?'

Gordian chuckled, the amusement of an expert hearing the uninformed speculation of the layman. 'No, sergeant, surely not. But if I were to be able to purge the toxins from the captain's body first, then it might be possible to repair the oolitic kidney. But in order to purge the toxins, I'd need to devise an effective antitoxin.'

'Then why don't you?' Aramus asked with mounting impatience.

'In order to craft such an antitoxin, I'd need access to a source of pure biotoxin from a tyranid of the same phylum as that which attacked Thule.'

Aramus glanced over at the forward viewports, where the dun-coloured disc of Calderis now turned. 'But there was only one tyranid on the planet, so far as we know. Where would we find another of the same phylum?'

Gordian affected a shrug. 'Perhaps discover whence the tyranid came, and then journey there to find another of the same strain?'

Aramus's eyes narrowed. He recalled what they had learned in the warehouse, and the madness it portended.

The question of their destination was, therefore, decided for him. As was the question of whether he'd be required to continue to act as Commander at Sail. It appeared, despite his hopes to the contrary, that the command was his, after all.

A SHORT WHILE later, Aramus stood on the command deck, awaiting the arrival of the other squad leaders. They were also to be joined by Admiral Forbes of the Imperial Navy's Battlegroup Aurelia, who was compiling an after-action report for her superiors about the events on the planet below, and out of deference to the Blood Ravens Chapter had requested permission to come aboard personally to seek their input rather than delegating the task to a subordinate.

'You wished to see me?' The voice sounded from just behind Aramus, and he turned to find Sergeant Tarkus already climbing the steps onto the command dais.

'Sergeant Tarkus.' Aramus acknowledged his arrival with a nod.

In the recent action on Calderis, Aramus had seen little of Third Squad's second in command, not once he'd divided their numbers to more effectively search Argus Township for recruits. Now, before meeting with the others, he'd summoned Tarkus to join him first, for they had something to discuss.

'It's about the disposition of the tactical squads,' Aramus said, as Tarkus came to stand beside him, looking out at the forward viewports.

Tarkus nodded, his expression all but unreadable.

Perhaps due to the fact that Third Squad saw little enemy action on Calderis, tasked with scouring

Argus Township for candidates, they had sustained virtually no injuries, and had not lost a single battle-brother. Their numbers already depleted by the undertaking on Zalamis, however, there were still only seven Space Marines in the squad. The other tactical squad, alternatively, First Squad, had suffered only light casualties on Zalamis, but had lost three of their number – including their squad leader Sergeant Merrik – in the undertaking on Calderis, and now were operating almost at half-strength, only six Blood Ravens in all.

'I'm transferring you to First Squad,' Aramus continued, 'effective immediately, and naming you squad leader.'

Tarkus blinked, his unflappable expression breaking for the briefest moment. 'Sir?'

'You're the most likely candidate, sergeant. And it's no secret that it's high time you had a command of your own.'

After a brief pause, Tarkus replied. 'Chapter protocols are quite explicit in this matter, Sergeant Aramus. In the event that a squad leader falls in combat, command of the squad should either devolve to the squad second in command, or else the next available junior squad leader should be promoted to take his place. By all rights *you* should take First Squad – assuming Brother Nord isn't capable of doing so – and I should take temporary command of Third.'

Aramus shook his head. 'With the loss not only of their leader, but also of his second, Brother Xiao, First Squad is in desperate need of restructuring. I'll have enough to occupy my attention ramping up to the responsibilities of Commander at Sail, and while Battle-Brother Nord did a commendable job as acting squad leader after Merrik's loss, I don't think he's yet ready for a command of his own.'

Tarkus narrowed his eyes. 'Very well,' he finally replied. 'Until we return to *Scientia Est Potentia* and a more permanent placement can be assigned, I will take command of First Squad. But I'd like it noted that I made reference to Chapter protocols, and advised against this move.'

'So noted,' Aramus answered with a smile. 'Now, Sergeant Tarkus, one squad leader to another, I would very much like your input on the plans for our coming actions.'

LIBRARIAN SEJS NIVEN sat in his darkened quarters, meditating.

Having finally convinced Apothecary Gordian that he was, despite all evidence to the contrary, fully restored from his period of prolonged suspended animation, on their return to the *Armageddon* Niven had sought solitude, and a quiet space in which to gather his thoughts. He had performed the cleansing rituals, strengthening himself against the warping influence of the Ruinous Powers, and now reflected on the events of the preceding months. In a short while, he would need to respond to the new Commander at Sail's summons to the command deck, but in the meantime, he worked to get his thoughts in order.

Since he had been an initiate of the Blood Ravens, more than a century before, and had been selected for induction into the Blood Ravens Librarium, Niven had worked tirelessly to develop the strength of will required by any psykers who sought to serve as Space Marine Librarians. Perhaps more than in any other Chapter, the Librarians of the Blood Ravens were ceaselessly called upon to combat the tainting effects of the warp, or the beguiling allure of the xenos. In his long lifetime of service, Niven had never shrunk from his duties, and never once failed to meet the challenge. And each time he had been examined by his superiors – whether by Codicers and Epistolaries as a junior servant of the Librarium, or by the Chief Librarian himself once he had ascended in the ranks – he had been found completely free from taint himself, and perfectly able to serve.

And yet, ever since sustaining critical injuries in the undertaking on Kronus, Niven had felt somewhat troubled, ill at ease. And from the moment he set foot upon the desert world of Calderis, in fact since the moment that he and Captain Thule's company first emerged from the empyrean into the normal space of the Aurelia sub-sector, Niven had felt his thoughts shadowed by some unknown malevolence that he could not identify. The unease, and the sense of some power lurking just beyond the edge of his psyker's perception, only redoubled once he was revived from his extended state of suspended animation.

Now, with the discovery that a tyranid warrior had been loose in Argus Township, Niven wondered whether that was all that he had been sensing, or whether there was more. Had a single offspring of the Great Devourer been enough to raise his mental alarms? Or had perhaps the fact that the warrior had been dispatched so quickly – though at the cost of the captain's severe injuries – only belied the fact that there was some other presence that yet stalked the corridors of Niven's mind?

The Librarian's meditations were interrupted by the arrival of Lexicanium Konan, the ship's astropath. The young servant of the Librarium was dressed in simple robes, hands tucked into the sleeves, his eyes downcast while approaching his superior.

'Master?' Konan said, inching his way into the Librarian's quarters. 'Have you a moment?'

It was a mark of the strength of the Blood Ravens Librarium, and of the prowess of the Librarians it produced, that a mere Lexicanium could serve on a Space Marine strike cruiser as her astropath. In other Chapters, Niven knew, only Librarians who had advanced to the rank of Epistolary were able to master the ability to project their minds across warp space itself, a feat that no normal psyker could endure without first undergoing the tortuous ritual of Soul Binding. Niven often wondered if the Blood Ravens had such powerful Librarians because they recruited such naturally gifted psykers, or if they recruited such gifted psykers because they had powerful Librarians. Or, in fact, if it even mattered at all.

'Yes, Konan,' Niven answered the Lexicanium. 'What troubles your thoughts?'

'I have been attempting to make contact with the astropaths of the Blood Ravens fleet, Master, both those onboard the *Scientia Est Potentia* and those on other ships, and so far have experienced difficulty. It is as if...'

Konan paused, searching for words.

'Yes, Lexicanium? It is as if…?'

'It is as if there is some interference, something that occludes my ability to peer across the vast distances of the empyrean.'

Niven narrowed his eyes, studying Konan's features. 'Tell me, Lexicanium. What do your senses tell you about this… interference? And please, spare no details…'

ARAMUS STOOD FACING the gathered squad leaders – Sergeants Tarkus, Thaddeus, Avitus, and Cyrus – Librarian Niven, and Chaplain Palmarius. And despite some grumbles and sidelong glances, Aramus had also invited Admiral Laren Forbes to join their debriefing. Standing ramrod straight in her navy uniform, the auburn hair falling carelessly to her collar the only exception to her otherwise flawless military precision, the admiral had arrived onboard from her flagship the *Sword of Hadrian* shortly before the appointed hour for the gathering, and Aramus had deemed it the most efficient use of time to include her in their discussions. Tarkus and Avitus raised the objection that any discussions of Blood Ravens leadership matters, and in particular the state of health of their company captain, were not fit for disclosure to outside parties; but Thaddeus appeared to agree with Aramus that time was of the essence, and that if Forbes could get the input that she needed for her after-action report right away, allowing the *Armageddon* to be more quickly on its way, so much the better. Cyrus, for his part, did not seem to have an opinion on the matter one way or the other. Not that it would have mattered, in the final analysis, if he did, no more than the objections of Tarkus and Avitus mattered in the long run. Sergeant Aramus was the Commander at Sail, and onboard the *Armageddon* his word was law.

'And so,' Aramus was concluding, 'taking into consideration Apothecary Gordian's need for a pure sample of tyranid biotoxin, I have requested that the Lord Principal prepare to depart for Typhon Primaris at the first available opportunity.'

Aramus had outlined to the others the state of Captain Thule's health, having already recounted the details of their encounter with the tyranid warrior in the Argus Township warehouse, and the evidence that suggested that the tyranid had been brought in larval form from the neighbouring system of Typhon Primaris.

'I have requested that Lexicanium Konan send word to the *Scientia Est Potentia* of our plans,' Aramus said, 'along with the details of our undertaking on Calderis and the disposition of Captain Thule's recruitment efforts.'

'However,' Librarian Niven said, raising a hand, 'the Lexicanium has reported to me' – he paused meaningfully, emphasizing the fact that while Lexicanium Konan acted as astropath for the *Armageddon*, and was therefore beneath the Commander at Sail's chain of command, as a servant of the Blood Ravens' Librarium he was subject to Librarian Niven's personal authority – 'that he has experienced some difficulty making astropathic contact out of the Aurelia sub-sector. It remains to be discovered whether the attempted communication will, or will not, reach the fortress-monastery as intended.'

'If I may,' Admiral Forbes put forward, 'I can task the astropaths onboard the *Sword of Hadrian* to relay your message through Imperial Navy astropathic channels, as well. Perhaps they'll have better luck.'

Librarian Niven regarded the admiral through narrowed eyes, as though turning his gaze upon a civilian was almost painful. 'I'm sure that won't be necessary.'

'The offer is appreciated, admiral,' Aramus replied. 'I'll have Lexicanium Konan put the message through to your astropaths before we depart.'

The Librarian turned his gaze upon Sergeant Aramus, his expression no less pained, but then inclined his head in an acknowledging nod. Like the others, he knew that no Blood Raven should ever question a command in front of someone from outside the Chapter.

'Techmarine Martellus reports that the ship is ready to depart,' Aramus went on, 'so as soon as we have word from the Navis dome that they have our course through the immaterium plotted, we will be on our way. Now, any questions?'

Thaddeus lifted a hand. 'We go to Typhon Primaris in search of tyranids. Are we expecting an isolated outbreak, as we found on Calderis, or a full-blown infestation?'

'Sergeant,' Admiral Forbes broke in, 'if I may?' She addressed her answer to Thaddeus, but clearly was speaking to them all. 'It is our understanding from intelligence received from the office of Governor

Vandis on Meridian that there have been uncon-firmed reports of xenos activity on Calderis, but to my knowledge they have yet to be substantiated or investigated.'

'So there's your answer, Thaddeus,' Aramus said. 'In short, we don't know.'

'If it *is* a full-blown infestation,' Tarkus put in, 'it may well prove more than a handful of Blood Ravens and a single strike cruiser can handle.'

'On that point,' Admiral Forbes piped up, her tone almost cheerful, 'might a Dauntless-class light cruiser might be of some assistance?'

Aramus raised a brow. 'Admiral?'

'The rest of Battlegroup Aurelia will transport the Calderis refugees to Meridian, as per the governor's orders, but I'm placing the *Sword of Hadrian* at your disposal as support for your operation.' She paused, and grinned ruefully, 'Gentlemen, I'm sure that noble Astartes have no need to concern themselves with such matters, but speaking as an officer in the Imperial Navy who has spent nearly two *years* sec-onded as adjutant to a sub-sector governor who has no more pressing business for three Dauntless-class light cruisers than to send us on trifling errands like ferrying his distant relatives and most generous donors out of harm's way, I am *bored*. And the thought of an action with the promise of actual *action* to it is an all but irresistible one.'

Aramus allowed himself a grin, a rare display of emotion before a non-Astartes. 'Then your offer is accepted, Admiral Forbes.' He turned to regard the others. 'And if there are no further questions or con-cerns, you can consider yourselves dismissed.'

CHAPTER NINE

AFTER LITTLE MORE than a day of travelling through the immaterium, the *Armageddon* shuddered through the transition from warp to normal space, and the verdant globe of Typhon Primaris hung before them like an emerald against the black velvet of night. Shortly after the strike cruiser emerged into real space, they received confirmation that Admiral Forbes's flagship the *Sword of Hadrian* had followed, and together the two craft crawled at sublight speeds towards their destination.

As the green globe grew steadily larger in the forward viewports, the Chapter serfs and servitors controlling all aspects of the strike cruiser's final approach, Sergeant Aramus conferred on the command dais with Sergeants Tarkus and Thaddeus.

'When last I was here,' Tarkus said, tapping one of the three half-century service studs affixed to his forehead, 'I had yet to earn this third stud.'

'A recruiting mission?' Aramus asked. 'Or some other undertaking?'

Tarkus quirked a fractional smile at the Commander at Sail. 'If an Astartes ever came to Typhon Primaris for any reason other than the search for aspirants, I'll eat my power armour.'

'I may have to contact the Librarium Sanatorium and see what secrets about this world their records hold,' Thaddeus grinned, referring to the unparalleled archives kept secure on board the First Company's battle-barge, the *Omnis Arcanum*. 'I should very much like to see you eat your way through your ceramite, Tarkus.'

Aramus ignored the jibe, and replied, 'I understand that once he had completed the Blood Trials on Calderis, his next port of call was to be Typhon Primaris, where he would search for still more recruits.'

It was true that Typhon Primaris was rarely visited. In fact, Aramus would not have been surprised to discover that the majority of ships that had appeared in the skies above the jungle world in past centuries had been those of the Blood Ravens, who visited it as a recruiting world, just as they did the other Aurelian worlds, Calderis and Meridian. But like Calderis, there was no outpost-monastery on Typhon Primaris; unlike Meridian's, where Aramus and Thaddeus had been brought after their Blood Trials two decades before. There wasn't a sufficiently large population on Typhon to justify a permanent presence for the Chapter, and so instead periodic visits, once a generation or so, were deemed more than sufficient for the Blood Ravens' purposes.

'What is the terrain?' Aramus asked Tarkus, turning his attentions to their impending planetfall. 'What conditions may we expect to find on the surface?'

'Jungles,' Tarkus replied simply. 'Lowland swamps, creeping vines, high humidity and soaring temperatures. All of the insects and animals are poisonous, to one degree or another, and even the plants bite.'

'Charming,' Thaddeus said, glancing ruefully at the forward viewport.

'And if there *are* tyranids abroad?' Aramus added.

Tarkus narrowed his gaze. 'Then I expect matters will become even more *charming*' – he glanced pointedly at Thaddeus – 'if by "charming" you mean dangerous, deadly, and dark.'

'THUNDERHAWKS,' CRACKLED THE voice of Techmarine Martellus over the gunship's vox-channel. 'You are cleared for departure.'

Once again, as in the skies above Calderis, Techmarine Martellus had been left in command of the *Armageddon*. And once again, Martellus had merely expressed annoyance at being pulled away from his consuming passion, the careful maintenance and constant cleaning of the Dreadnought assembly stored below decks. Until it was animated by the introduction of a Blood Raven trapped at the point between life and death, the assembly was merely a lifeless shell, but nevertheless it represented to a servant of the Adeptus Mechanicus like Martellus the apotheosis of the union between man and machine, a liturgy of praise to the Omnissiah in riveted adamantium.

Apothecary Gordian, too, had opted to remain on board, in order that he might better be able to monitor the condition of Captain Thule. Chaplain Palmarius had suggested that he stay on board to continue the examination of the aspirants from Calderis, but Sergeant Aramus had pointed out that the low numbers of candidates culled from the desert world might be offset if they were to return from Typhon Primaris with additional aspirants. So Palmarius joined Librarian Niven, and together they would examine and evaluate the young men of the jungles just as they previously had those of the deserts. The principal objective of the operation, as Sergeant Aramus had outlined the mission, was to locate a tyranid life form and retrieve a sample of pure biotoxin, but a secondary objective was the recruitment of as many potential candidates as could be found.

Chapter protocols called for Blood Trials, of course, but it was unlikely that time would permit a full search for candidates *and* a properly conducted series of Trials, and so it was decided that perhaps, in this rare instance, protocols might be temporarily set aside. Chaplain Palmarius had already begun drafting plans to hold *ad hoc* Blood Trials in the sparring hall of the *Armageddon*, pitting the aspirants against one another on the sparring floor, and then allowing only the winners to progress as initiates. There were those who questioned whether it was appropriate that aspirants should fight, bleed, and possibly even die in the same space in which the Blood Ravens honed their skills and strengthened their arms, but the Chaplain was the authority in these matters, and Sergeant Aramus was willing to defer to Palmarius's judgement.

'Ready for lift-off, sir,' called Scout Jutan from the pilot's controls. Sergeant Cyrus had trained all of his Scout squad in the operation of Thunderhawks, and in order to free as many of the full battle-brothers as possible for the impending search through the jungles, Sergeant Aramus had tapped the Scouts to act as the flight crews for the trio of Thunderhawks in this impromptu undertaking. Jutan and Muren acted as pilot and co-pilot for Thunderhawk One, Scouts Xenakis and Tubach were the flight crew for Thunderhawk Two, and Scout Watral was pilot for Thunderhawk Three, with Sergeant Cyrus himself acting as co-pilot.

Aramus realized that the Scout was waiting for some response.

'Acknowledged,' he said, with a wave of his hand. 'Launch away.'

Manoeuvring only using the retro exhaust nozzles, Jutan eased the gunship through the launch bay doors. Once they were in open vacuum he toggled the rocket boosters for full burn, angling for insertion.

With the keening sounds of atmospheric entry screaming through the hull, the Blood Ravens descended upon the jungle world.

TYPHON PRIMARIS WAS sparsely populated, no more than a few hundred thousand hardy souls who dwelt in the ruins of their former glory. The villages of the Typhonians were typically clustered around the bases of the massive stepped pyramids which dotted the landscape, their towering profiles softened by the millennia worth of creeping vines and lichens that covered them. The earliest origins of man on the jungle world had been lost, but were impossibly ancient, possibly dating back even to before the end of the Age of Strife, when man first ventured out into the void. Those first men on Typhon Primaris had built a grand civilization, far from the cradle of the human race, Holy Terra; a civilisation of monumental architecture, vast tracts of developed lands, populous cities, and a highly organised society. At least, such was the supposition based on what little evidence of them remained. For, as so often was the case in such ancient societies, the ancients of Typhon had been unable to keep their civilization from tumbling into decay, and in the end the jungles had reclaimed their cities, their farms, and their entire societies. Only the massive stepped pyramids remained, all but completely obliterated by century upon century of wild growth, as mute tombstones of the unknown ancients who had once lived and thrived there.

When the servants of the Emperor first arrived, on their crusade to unite the myriad worlds upon which the seed of mankind had taken root, they had found only primitive tribes of pale-skinned, green-eyed jungle-dwellers who – aside from a complex matrilocal kinship structure that completely baffled the missionaries of the Adeptus Ministorum who later came to instruct the natives in the proper belief in the Emperor's divinity – displayed none of the sophistication their ancestors must once have mastered and then, inevitably, lost.

Now, aside from irregular visits from agents of Governor Vandis, the nominal Imperial authority over the planet, and the once-a-generation recruiting expeditions of the Blood Ravens, Typhon Primaris was rarely visited at all and so remained much as those early crusaders and missionaries had found it, with the only marked change being that the Typhonians now revered the 'Sky-Father,' as they named the God-Emperor on distant Holy Terra, rather than the jungle spirits worshipped by their ancestors.

But it was a well-established fact, on many worlds reunited with the Imperium of Mankind during the Emperor's crusades, that folk beliefs were tenacious, and even after exposure to the light and truth of the God-Emperor, many such superstitions had a habit of persisting...

'You are welcome, Sons of the Sky-Father!'

The headman of the village held his arms wide in greeting as he called out to Sergeant Aramus and the others in heavily accented Low Gothic, standing in the deepening shadows at the edge of the village. He was ancient, his face lined with wrinkles, but his emerald-green eyes sparked with lively intelligence, and he was nimble on his feet for all that his legs were bowed and bent with age. His skin was as pale as that of his fellow villagers, but his was veined with age, rendered almost translucent. Was it his age, though, that gave a brittle tone to his words, and that slight twitch to the corner of his mouth?

'I am Sergeant Aramus of the Blood Ravens,' the sergeant answered, 'seeking aspirants for our Chapter.'

Aramus had decided it wisest not to announce outright that the Blood Ravens had come in search of tyranids, to forestall any panic that the news of a potential infestation might have on the Typhonian natives. Instead, they would operate under the pretext that they were merely searching for potential candidates for the Blood Trials, and carry out their search for tyranids through the surrounding jungles without alarming the villagers. Sergeant Avitus had initially objected, saying he cared little for the fears and concerns of ignorant villagers, until Aramus explained that he, too, cared little for their fears, at least held in the balance against Captain Thule's life, but that their search through the jungle would be easier to carry out if they didn't have to contend with hundreds of terrified Typhonians tramping through the jungles in flight from a xenos threat that might not even exist.

The headman peered up at Aramus's face in puzzlement for a moment. 'Aspirants, you say?'

Aramus nodded. 'We seek young men and boys, strong in body and mind, to join us in the Blood Ravens, and in the service of... the service of the Sky-Father.'

The headman blinked a few times, and then his puzzled look faded as a smile stretched across his face. He brought his hand together in a clap, and motioned for his people to come forward. 'Aspirants! Yes, of course! Come, libations and gifts for the mighty Sons of the Sky-Father!'

Aramus glanced over at Sergeants Thaddeus and Tarkus, each of them already studying his auspex, searching for any sign of xenos activity in the area, and of tyranids in particular.

The headman capered back and forth before them, singing greetings to each of the Blood Ravens in turn, as the villagers struggled to reach high enough to drape wreaths of jungle flowers around the Astartes' necks.

Watching the headman, and remembering the puzzled look he had worn, for just a moment, Aramus began to suspect that, in fact, the headman had been surprised to hear that the Blood Ravens had come seeking aspirants. But if the headman hadn't expected that they had come on a recruiting mission, what *had* he thought was the purpose of their visit?

On the command deck of the *Sword of Hadrian*, the air filled with the sound of her officers carrying out their duties and the high binary squeal of servitors at work. Fleet Admiral Laren Forbes studied a dataslate distractedly, sitting cross-legged in the captain's chair, while a steaming cup of caffeine at her elbow gradually cooled to room temperature, untouched.

'Admiral?' The light cruiser's first officer ascended the command dais, carrying a data-slate of his own.

'Yes, Commander Mitchels?' She looked up, taking him in at a glance.

The first officer was fair-haired, and fair-complexioned. Under normal circumstances, with his close-cropped hair neatly trimmed and his uniform jacket buttoned to the neck, he appeared some spectral vision crammed into the suit of a man, a ghost in the clothing of the living. But when worries or anxieties plagued him, a blush would rise in his cheek, growing redder as his anxieties mounted, until finally he was crimson, fringed by the halo of his white hair.

Mitchels was not quite the reddest he'd ever gotten, but he was definitely pinker than the norm, which suggested that there was something troubling him.

'What's bothering you, commander?' the admiral asked, musing that it paid to have a subordinate who carried around a barometer of their internal moods on their epidermis.

'I've received word from the ship's lead astropath, ma'am.'

He paused, glancing again at his data-slate as though to confirm what he'd already read there before ever approaching the dais, as though the information might have changed as he mounted the steps.

'Yes, Mitchels?'

'Well, ma'am, it appears that since we transitioned back to normal space, the astropaths are having difficulty making contact with the rest of the Aurelia Battlegroup. Or with Meridian, for that matter.'

'Mmmm,' Forbes hummed, thoughtfully. She picked up her cup of caffeine, and almost spat out the now lukewarm contents on the deck. Setting the cup back down on the arm of the captain's chair, she reached out to accept the data-slate the first officer proffered. She looked it over, seeing in detail the report that Mitchels had just relayed in brief. 'Very well.' She handed the data-slate back, and stood up. 'Keep me informed. This bears watching, Mitchels.'

'Yes, ma'am,' the commander responded with a quick salute, and then descended the dais back to the base of the command deck.

Forbes looked up at the wide forward viewports before her, at the emerald disc of the jungle world spinning beneath them. The only word from the *Armageddon* had been a curt transmission from a techmarine that the landing parties had reached the planet's surface successfully and had begun their search. No word yet about any xenos presence, tyranid or otherwise.

The admiral only hoped that the difficulty in astropathic communication was due merely to some sort of vagary in warp topography – perhaps the empyrean equivalent of a seasonal squall if such a thing existed – and might pass quickly.

Because if that was *not* the case, and the interference did *not* pass, then it was highly suggestive of only one other cause that Forbes knew, one other circumstance that affected all astropathic communications.

But Forbes did not dwell on *that* particular circumstance. She merely offered a prayer to the Emperor and the souls of all of the admirals and captains of the *Sword of Hadrian* who had preceded her that she was wrong. Because if it *was* what she feared, then matters were about to become far, far more complicated.

THE HEADMAN HAD hastily arranged a reception in the Blood Ravens' honour, and though it was not in the Space Marines' habit to socialize amiably with common citizens, the headman had insisted, saying that he would gather together all of the young men and boys of the village at the fete, that the 'Sons of the Sky-Father' might examine them each in turn. And though none of the Blood Ravens had any desire to spend any more time than was absolutely necessary being feted, and draped with garlands of jungle flowers, and hearing the endless choruses of praise and devotion sung by the villagers, the promise of a quick recruiting survey was too attractive to pass up and so Aramus had accepted the headman's invitation.

However, Aramus had stipulated that not all of their party would be joining the celebration. Aramus would be there, as would Sergeant Cyrus and his Scouts, and Librarian Niven and Chaplain Palmarius. But the rest of the Blood Ravens who had accompanied them to the surface would, he explained to the headman, be required to go out into the jungle on training exercises, and would not return until long after the celebration had finished.

The sun was already setting over the green-shrouded bulk of the stepped pyramid to the west of the village when Aramus and the others arrived at the village centre, where the headman had had his people construct a scaffold for them. Rising nearly half a metre from the jungle floor, the scaffold was little more than a wide wooden platform, on which were arranged woven blankets and cushions to make a place for each of the Blood Ravens in Aramus's party. But while Aramus had been willing to accept the headman's hospitality, however reluctantly, he was not prepared to clamber onto a rickety wooden platform and attempt to sit on a pile of pillows while wearing full power armour, and he was not about to order any of the others to do so, either. So the Blood Ravens instead simply arranged themselves in a single file before the platform, at parade rest, and waited for the headman to begin whatever ceremony he'd concocted.

'Praised be your name, Sky-Father!' the headman began in a loud, booming voice, turning in his hands a long wooden tube filled with rocks or seeds. As the tube reversed, the objects within tumbled from one to the other, sounding something like falling rain. 'Yours is the will!' A villager on the far side of the clearing beat a quick tattoo on a skin drum, sounding like distant thunder. 'Yours is the power!' Another villager struck a rudimentary gong fashioned from hull plating discarded by some earlier visiting vessel, sounding like lightning's thunderclap. 'Yours is the glory!'

Aramus exchanged a glance with the Blood Ravens standing nearest him. 'Don't worry,' he voxed privately to the others. 'This can't last long.'

'Now, Sky-Father,' the headman called out to the heavens, 'let us sing each of the Thousand Hymns of Praise, to thank you for the arrival of your mighty Sons!'

As the villagers began to intone the first of the thousand hymns, Aramus grimaced. He was wrong. This *could* last long.

OUT IN THE jungles of Typhon Primaris, the squads of Blood Ravens split up and fanned out, tracking the spoor of monsters, searching for any sign of tyranids.

And they were not alone…

CHAPTER TEN

Sergeant Thaddeus and his battle-brothers of the Seventh Squad ghosted through the darkened jungle. With the canopy of trees overhead so tightly woven, their jump packs would have been of little use on Typhon Primaris, and had been left behind at the Thunderhawk. Unencumbered by the weight, the Space Marines of the Seventh Squad moved with even more ease than normal, and considering that they were all masters of the arts of infiltration, able to move through virtually any environment without being seen – even with their jump packs on – without the bulk and weight of their packs they were even stealthier.

Still, as they moved all but silently through the trees, the darkness surrounding them taxing even their enhanced vision, Thaddeus found himself wishing that he still had his jump pack, with the ability to leap great distances should trouble rear up before him. Or failing that, an armoured vehicle in which to ride. Thaddeus was an Adeptus Astartes, with the courage and fortitude that implied, but after the undertaking on Prosperon, and the heavy losses suffered by the Blood Ravens at the talons of the Great Devourer, he had learned caution at the mention of the word 'tyranid.' And while Blood Ravens did not make use of the heaviest equipment often employed by other Chapters, still Thaddeus knew that he would not complain were a Predator Destructor or two to be offered him. Several centimetres of forged adamantium between him and an onslaught of tyranids would not be something he would readily refuse.

So far, though, there had been no sign of tyranids, neither any spoor on the jungle tracks nor any positive readings on Thaddeus's auspex. But with the life of Captain Thule in the balance, the Space Marines of the Seventh Squad would continue to search until all hope was lost, and perhaps even beyond that.

Still, a Predator Destructor might come in handy, were their search to prove successful.

ONCE THE SEEMINGLY interminable rounds of hymns had completed, and the headman had clapped for the next stage of the fete to begin, a few dozen boys and young men had been brought forward. Now, Chaplain Palmarius and Librarian Niven evaluated the potential aspirants by the flickering light of the torches set around the village centre, examining them one by one.

Sergeant Aramus kept watch from his station near the unused scaffolding and its unnecessary cushions, periodically required to refuse politely the offers of food, drink, and other comforts made by the villagers.

'Do our offerings offend, noble Son of the Sky-Father?' the headman asked, sidling near, after the most recent tray of food was being taken away.

'No.' Like all Space Marines, Aramus could subsist for long periods of time without sustenance, but more to the point, he simply wasn't in any mood to eat.

The headman smiled. 'Then perhaps you worry that our cuisine will not agree with your digestion?' He motioned to the retreating tray. 'I am informed that off-worlders often find the spices we employ... difficult to take on first eating.'

Aramus shook his head. 'Again, no.' As though a Space Marine had any need to fear such things. One of his implants, the preomnor, was a predigestive stomach capable of processing a wide variety of poisonous or otherwise indigestible material – if he so chose, Aramus could consume and digest the scaffolding and the cushions and all, without any concern but that he might receive a few splinters along the way. And if a Space Marine should happen to ingest something that the preomnor was incapable of processing, the neuroglottis implanted at the back of his mouth would allow him to detect the fact in time for him to spit it out before swallowing any of it. 'We don't wish to offer offence, headman. We merely eat in our own time.'

The headman raised his hands in a dismissive gesture. 'Then no offence is taken.' He came to stand at

Aramus's side, and together the two looked at the ongoing evaluation of the village youth.

'It is a great honour that you do us,' the headman said. 'Our boys are raised with the promise that, if they are devout and dutiful, they might one day be allowed the chance to serve the Sky-Father as you do now.'

Aramus nodded. 'As you say.' He paused, and then added, 'But it appeared to me that, though you did not seem surprised or alarmed in any way by our unannounced arrival, you *did* seem surprised to learn we were here for just such a recruiting mission.'

The headman's already pale face blanched somewhat, and his eyes found sudden interest in the hard-packed dirt at his feet.

'Tell me, headman,' Aramus continued, 'what was it that you supposed we were here to accomplish?'

The headman shuffled his feet for a moment before answering. 'Well, noble Son of the Sky-Father, we thought you had been sent by one of the vessels who have visited our jungle in these recent months.'

Aramus turned to regard the old man more closely, narrowing his gaze. 'Vessels? Imperial vessels?'

The headman shrugged. 'Perhaps. We did not know for certain.' He waved a hand towards the surrounding jungles. 'They landed out in the green, and did not venture into our villages. But when you descended from the sky, we assumed that the vessels *had* been from the Sky-Father, and that those on board might have seen…' He paused suddenly, glancing sidelong at Aramus before continuing. 'That they might have seen… *things*… which would lead to our being chastened.' He glanced around the village circle at the others gathered around, who even now that the hymns of praise had ceased were busying themselves in acts of contrition and worship. 'We had hoped that a renewed devotion on our part might spare us the Sky-Father's wrath, if the chastisement was still to follow your search for recruits.'

Aramus remained silent, studying the old man's face. What was it that the villagers had done that led them to expect chastisement?

'If you are not come to chastise us,' the old man went on, 'then perhaps the visitations of the jungle spirits themselves will serve as sufficient punishment in themselves.'

Aramus arched an eyebrow.

'Jungle spirits?'

SERGEANT AVITUS AND the rest of his Devastator squad smashed through the undergrowth, their heavy weapons loaded and ready for action. For hours they had made their way through the twilit jungle, and now that the sun had long since set, they continued on through the murky blackness of the jungle at night.

The eight members of the Ninth Squad were spread out in a wide formation, to cover as much ground as possible as they swept through the jungle. Creeping vines and hanging mosses draped from the branches overhead like ragged curtains, and gnarled roots snatched at the boots of their power armour as they trudged along. Out in the darkness, countless pairs of eyes reflected back what little light there was, like pairs of miniature stars in the blackness, but still they'd had no sign of xenos activity, tyranid or otherwise.

'Barabbas?' Avitus called over the vox. 'Anything?'

'Negative, sergeant,' the battle-brother voxed back. 'Just more muck and mire.'

Avitus was about to continue on through the rolls when a voice over the vox-comms interrupted him.

'Sergeant Avitus?'

The rune for Brother Philetus blinked on Avitus's visor display. 'Go ahead,' Avitus answered gruffly.

'I've found something you might want to take a look at.'

'Tyranid spoor?' Avitus hefted his heavy bolter, ready for action.

'No, sir. It's…' Philetus paused before finishing. 'I'm not sure *what* it is.'

Avitus voxed to the others. 'Converge on Philetus's position, squad.'

A few moments later Avitus and the rest of the squad joined Philetus, who stood before some sort of crudely constructed wooden structure in the midst of a jungle clearing a few metres across. Roughly pyramidal in shape, it recalled the outline of the stepped pyramids all but obscured by the millennia of greenery creeping over them, but this was skeletal, an outer frame supporting a platform within.

'Is it cultist?' Barabbas said, playing a light over the structure and the objects within.

On the platform within the frame were arranged vessels of wine, plates of food – much of it already despoiled – stacks of knives and axes, woven blankets and other craftworks.

'I don't believe so,' Philetus answered. He pointed to the markings carved in the wood of the frame. 'Those aren't Chaos symbols. I don't know *what* they are, but it doesn't hurt my eyes to look on them, like every other Chaos symbol I've ever seen.'

Avitus agreed. 'This isn't like the work of any heretic I've ever come across.'

'But it's clearly an offering of some kind,' Barabbas answered.

'Undoubtedly,' Philetus agreed. 'But to whom?'

'Or to what?' Barabbas said.

'It hardly matters,' Avitus said dismissively. 'We're here to find tyranids, not to waste time in speculating on local lapses in Imperial faith.'

The other members of the squad exchanged glances, but it hardly mattered if they agreed with the sergeant's assessment or not. The squad was his to command as he willed, and theirs was to follow orders.

'Move out,' Avitus said, shouldering past the frame and heading out of the clearing on the far side. 'Burn it down if you like, but don't waste any more time worrying about it.'

THE HEADMAN REGARDED Sergeant Aramus nervously, clearly only now realizing that he had said more than he should. Having assumed early on that the Blood Ravens had come to chastise the village for whatever lapse the unknown spacefarers had witnessed, he had been less than circumspect in referring to those same lapses even after discovering the true reason for the Blood Ravens' visit – or, at least, the purported reason for their visit.

'You see,' the headman finally responded, 'dozens of generations ago, when the missionaries came from the sky and brought with them the good news of the Sky-Father and his star-spanning empire, we were forbidden from holding the beliefs of our forefathers. We were told only to revere the Sky-Father, and to have no other gods before him. For generation upon generation, we did as we had been instructed, not wanting to bring the reprisals of the Sky-Father down on our heads. But even so, there were always those among us who insisted that the jungle spirits worshipped by our forefathers still dwelt in the green, and that one day they would return to wreak their vengeance on those of us who had abandoned the faith of our forefathers.'

The headman paused for a moment, his gaze fixed on the flickering light of a nearby torch, as though lost in memory.

'In recent months,' he continued at length, 'the promised vengeance was finally visited upon us.'

Aramus leaned forward. 'In what way?'

The headman took a deep breath, and let out a ragged sigh, his shoulders slumped. 'There are spirits that walk abroad in the dark jungles around us,' he said, 'that much is true. And while it had been many generations since they have been seen, they now return to us. No longer the helpmates of our forefathers' stories, though, they are now vicious, vengeful creatures. And any who are foolhardy enough to venture too far from the borders of our village are seized, never to be seen again.'

'Seized?' Aramus repeated. 'What becomes of them?'

The headman shrugged again. 'Who can say? All that is known is that they are never seen again.' He glanced around at the gathered villagers still caught up in their ecstatic worship of the distant God-Emperor. 'We tried to appease the jungle spirits by offering libations, victuals, and other such valuables, but it was no use. The anger of the spirits would not be abated by such trifles.'

SERGEANT TARKUS'S TEAM had found evidence of xenos activity – or at least of spacefaring activity – but so far none of it had been tyranid.

Tarkus and First Squad had been tasked with searching the swampy lowlands that stretched south of the headman's village, out where the trees became sparser and more widely spaced, and the ground underfoot squelched with every step. The lowlands were virtually bogs, the ground as much liquid as solid, and even in the dead of night swarms of stinging insects drifted like endless, buzzing clouds.

Where the ground was most level, and least wet, they had found evidence of landing sites. At least one of them, based on the burn patterns of the retro rockets that had eased the craft to ground and the main rockets that had thrown it back to the heavens, was of Imperial manufacture, but the footprint at another site was highly suggestive of eldar activity.

What the eldar would be doing on a backwater world like Typhon Primaris – of no interest or strategic importance even to the galactic power whose flag had been figuratively planted there – none could say, but there was no denying the clear suggestion that some xenos craft, at least, had visited the world.

Both landing sites, Imperial and xenos, suggested recent visits, no less than a few weeks and no more than a few months in the past. None of these visitors was in evidence now, however, so beyond making note of each site and the state in which it had been found, there was little else for Tarkus's team to do there.

They pressed on, into the darkness.

THE HEADMAN PAUSED, and glanced over at Sergeant Aramus.

'It was believed that the visitors to our world had seen the offering sites to the jungle spirits, and had returned to the Sky-Father with word that we had failed him, and lapsed back to the faith of our forefathers. It was for this heresy that we had assumed you came to chasten us.'

Aramus drew his lips into a tight line. It was true that there was a considerable degree of variation in religious practices from culture to culture, and from planet to planet, but it was also true that the agents of the Inquisition and the Ministorium were always on the watch for heresy, as any deviation from the prescribed practices of the Imperial faith might, if allowed to continue too far, be corrupted to the worship of the Ruinous Powers.

'But the offerings were of no use, anyway,' the headman continued. 'And now even the village offers little hope of sanctuary. Already there are several other settlements within a day's travel of here who have gone silent in recent weeks, seemingly swallowed by the jungle itself.'

The headman turned his eyes to the dark shadows beyond the little circle of firelight, the blackness of the jungle that stretched endlessly beyond the boundaries of the village.

'The jungle spirits have returned to seek vengeance, and I fear there is nothing else but vengeance that will satisfy them.'

SERGEANT THADDEUS WAS bored. Only by checking the chronometer runes in his visor display was he able to keep track of the time passing. One stretch of jungle appeared nearly the same as any other by daylight, but in the grey illumination of his enhanced vision by night, it was all virtually indistinguishable.

He was beginning to think they had come on a fool's errand. Perhaps Aramus and Thule had misread the shipping information on the crate that had held the hatched tyranid egg, or the shipping information had been a lie to begin with, and there had never been any tyranids on the jungle planet. There was certainly no sign of any here now. If so, there was nothing that could be done for Thule, nothing to stop the toxins from wrecking his body and destroying him entirely. It was regrettable, as the Fifth Company had rarely had a better captain than Thule.

Thaddeus had already begun to mourn Captain Thule, he realized. He had already begun thinking of him in the past tense.

All Space Marines died, Thaddeus knew. And almost all of them died in combat, or at least as the result of wounds received in combat. He had never heard of a Blood Raven who died of old age. But it seemed that Blood Ravens of the Fifth Company, and their captains in particular, were more prone to fatal injuries on the field of battle than most. It was not that the Fifth was any less covered in glory than the other companies of the Chapter, and the Fifth had just as many victories to its credit as any other. But it seemed that, more often than with the other companies, the victories of the Fifth often came at a heavy price.

Perhaps it was something to do with the name by which the Fifth was known – the Fated – and the circumstances surrounding how the company came to earn the name. Like all Blood Ravens of the Fifth Company, Thaddeus and the rest of his squad wore on their power armour badges of penitence and shame, symbolizing that they fought to redeem their company. With blood – that of their enemies, but even more so their own – the Fated would wash away the sins of the past. It was always hoped that at some point in the future the Fated would be completely redeemed, and that the events of M.38 that had so darkened the company's history might be forever forgotten, and only a bright and glorious future remain. But that day had not yet arrived, and Thaddeus often wondered whether he would ever live to see it.

Had the Blood Ravens Chapter itself begun in just such a way? Were the secret beginnings of the Chapter which were now lost to history something like the dark days that had befallen the Fated in M.38, and had the Chapter as a whole striven to redeem itself, until finally those blighted pages in the historical records were finally expunged and the shame forever forgotten?

It was a strangely comforting thought. And it suggested to Thaddeus that, if so, then the heavy costs paid by the Fifth for so many of its victories might well have been worth it. If the Fifth Company in some future age was no longer 'The Fated,' and no longer went to battle wearing signs of penitence and shame, then it would be a future well worth dying for.

Thaddeus mused as he and the rest of his squad moved through the darkened forest. Occupied with his thoughts as he was, though, there was still a portion of his awareness fully focused on his surroundings, on every sound, every smell, every glint or rustle in the shadows around him.

Even so, like the rest of his squad he was caught completely by surprise when the clutch of lictors leapt out from the concealing foliage around them, bearing down upon them with scything talons and rending claws.

The tyranids *were* here, and they were attacking!

CHAPTER ELEVEN

Sᴇʀɢᴇᴀɴᴛ Aʀᴀᴍᴜs ᴡᴀs about to question the village headman further when a vox-comm interrupted him.

'Enemy contact!' the voice buzzed in Aramus's ear.

Without sparing a moment in apologising to the headman, Aramus slammed his helmet down over his head, and saw the rune for Sergeant Thaddeus flaring brightly on his visor display.

'Thaddeus, report,' Aramus replied.

Over the vox, Aramus could hear the sound of bolters firing, and the whirr of chainswords.

'Lictors, Aramus,' Thaddeus replied, the strain of battle sounding in his voice. 'Five, six… No, a clutch of seven of the bastards. They just came out of nowhere.'

'Losses?'

'None yet,' Thaddeus answered. 'We're holding our own. But Aramus?'

'Yes?' Aramus drew his bolter, checking the action and chambering a round.

'This lictor strain appears to lack toxin symbiotes.'

So the search wasn't over yet.

'Acknowledged, Thaddeus.' He toggled his vox-comms for a general call. 'Blood Ravens, Seventh Squad has made enemy contact. Repeat, enemy contact made. Tyranids *are* on planet. But we still need to locate toxin-bearing specimens.'

Flashing runes on his visor signalled the squads' acknowledgement, none wasting time or effort in vocal response.

'Gather your people,' Aramus said aloud, turning to the headman. 'These are no jungle spirits that bedevil you, but something far, far worse.'

Battle-Brother Voire and the rest of the Third Squad received Sergeant Aramus's instructions. They were only a few kilometres from the village, and in hours of searching had found nothing of interest. Voire's auspex had mapped the terrain, and their current position was less than half an hour's travel from the point at which Thaddeus had encountered the tyranids.

'Lictors are outriders,' Voire said to Brother Cirrac, who had come to stand beside him as they considered their next action. 'They move ahead of tyranid ground swarms, searching out lifeforms to be absorbed.'

'And any enemies to attack,' Cirrac replied, darkly.

Voire indicated the map of the area displayed on his auspex. 'If Thaddeus and his squad

encountered lictors here' – he pointed at the spot
on the map – 'likely moving in this direction' – he
drew his gauntleted finger across the map from
southwest to north-east, opposite the trajectory
along which the Seventh Squad had been moving
– 'then it stands to reason that the main body of
any tyranid swarm in the region might be in this
direction.' He pointed to the lower left quadrant of
the map display, to the south-west of the village.

Cirrac nodded. 'Seems likely,' he allowed.

'In which case,' Voire said, glancing around at the
jungle surrounding them, apparently – or decep-
tively? – empty, 'we should proceed to the
south-west and see what we find.'

'Or what finds us,' Cirrac replied grimly.

'Either way,' Voire said, racking his bolter. 'It
beats an endless slog through this mess.'

Cirrac grinned. 'Then lead on, battle-brother,
lead on.'

THERE WERE EIGHT Space Marines in the Seventh
Squad, all armed with bolters and chainswords.
They had fought together through the masses of
Gorgrim's hordes and the feral orks on Calderis,
and through the bloody undertaking on Zalamis,
and in all that time had lost only two battle-
brothers, one on each world. It often seemed to
Thaddeus that, working together, there was no
threat they could not face and overcome. His faith
in the Seventh, and in their collective strength, was
all but boundless.

Now, faced with only a bare handful of tyranid
lictors, he was finding that faith sorely tested.

'Stand fast, squad!' Thaddeus shouted, meeting the scything talon of the lead lictor with his own chainsword. 'No quarter given or asked!'

When he had been faced with the overwhelming numbers of feral orks outside Argus Township, Thaddeus had gone to battle with a grin on his lips. Even when he had first seen the serried ranks of Gorgrim's horde, even after seeing Brother Renzo fall, he had fought with a lightness in his heart. Just as sparring was an enjoyable contest of skill and strength, so too did Thaddeus view combat. Though he was dutiful in his service to Emperor and Chapter, and ever mindful of the solemn responsibility he bore as a Space Marine and as a Blood Raven, still Thaddeus found something to enjoy in the clash of metal on metal, in pitting muscle against muscle, strength against strength.

But on Prosperon, when facing the inhuman, ravenous offspring of the Great Devourer, Thaddeus had for the first time caught a glimpse that combat might be anything but something to be enjoyed. On Prosperon, his squad sent on some minor mission and forced to run the gauntlet of tyranid forces on all sides, taking heavy casualties inbound and out, Thaddeus had felt the first inklings of what he thought might be *fear*.

Now, with a clutch of lictors crashing into them from all angles, leaping out of the darkness with their talons and claws hungry for human blood and carnage, Thaddeus felt that unfamiliar sensation return. There was no smile on his lips tonight.

Thaddeus fired another hellfire round from his bolter, and reversed the chainsword in his hands for another blow.

'SERGEANT CYRUS,' ARAMUS voxed, as he crossed the village centre to the place where Librarian Niven and Chaplain Palmarius were evaluating the village youths.

'Sir?' Sergeant Cyrus voxed back.

'What's your position?'

'Checking the pickets, sir,' Cyrus answered. As soon as the news of the Seventh Squad's encounter with enemy elements had come through, Blood Ravens protocols dictated that those Blood Ravens not in the battlefield should immediately go to a defensive posture, barring orders to the contrary. It had taken merely a quick glance exchanged between Sergeants Aramus and Cyrus across the village centre to set those plans in motion, and the Scout sergeant had moved off with his squad before Aramus had even taken a single step forward.

'Good,' Aramus voxed back. If it seemed somewhat strange for Aramus to be giving orders to one of the Space Marines who taught him how to be a Blood Raven in the first place, who was in large part responsible for making him the Space Marine he now was, Aramus didn't let it get in the way of his duty. 'I'm leaving you and your squad here in defence of the village. The headman will be pulling all of his people here to the centre of the village, which should be more easily defensible.'

'And you, sir?'

'I'll be joining my squad in the field,' Aramus answered.

'Acknowledged,' Cyrus replied. 'Good hunting, sir.'

'Obliged, Cyrus. Aramus out.'

He cut the vox-comms just as he reached the place where the Librarian and Chaplain were examining the most recent prospect, as though nothing whatsoever amiss was going on around them.

'Sergeant,' Chaplain Palmarius said by way of greeting, the firelight glinting off his silver death's-head mask.

'Any luck?' Aramus said, indicating the youths gathered a short distance off, who regarded the Blood Ravens with expressions comingling awe and terror.

'None,' Librarian Niven said, sounding annoyed.

'I find in each of them,' Chaplain Palmarius explained, 'certain impurities of belief incompatible with further instruction in the Imperial faith.'

'Impurities?' Aramus prompted for more. 'Are we dealing with cultists, then?' He glanced across the open space to the place where the headman was huddled with a group of his followers.

'I find no evidence of allegiance with the Ruinous Powers,' Palmarius said, 'but a full examination of the village entire by the Inquisition would be necessary to prove that there is none whatsoever. But still the responses of each of the candidates thus far suggests a lack of fidelity to the essential tenets upon which Imperial faith is built. Instruction can build a foundation of faith in the heart of an aspirant, but not if the soil upon which it would be based is treacherous and shifting.'

'Never mind their hearts,' Librarian Niven put in, 'it is their *minds* which concern me, and they are, each and every one of them, weak and easily led.'

Aramus glanced over at the boys and young men who remained to be examined. If the previous examinations had produced no suitable candidates, he harboured little hope that the remainder would, either. But even the hope of a bare few aspirants to the Chapter was enough to justify that the evaluations be completed. Though none of these boys looked capable of surviving the Blood Trials, much less the torment of initiation that would follow, they would not stop looking until they had exhausted all the possibilities close at hand.

'Continue your search,' Aramus finished, gesturing towards the remaining boys. 'I go to join the others in the field, and if fortune is with us we shall soon have the biotoxin sample we need and will be able to leave this world behind.'

'The sooner,' Chaplain Palmarius said, glancing around at the village surrounding them, distaste clearly readable even behind his inscrutable mask, 'the better.'

'On that,' Librarian Niven answered, turning back to the next boy, who stood quavering on the hard-packed earth, 'we are agreed.'

SERGEANT AVITUS AND his team had continued crashing through the jungle for several minutes after hearing Sergeant Thaddeus's report of tyranid contact, making even more of a clamour than before.

Avitus had hoped to lure the tyranids out by making as much noise with their passage as possible, presenting easy targets that might prove irresistible to the tyranid mind. But after a few minutes of tromping through the underbrush failed to draw any enemy elements out of the wood, Avitus had to admit that it was impossible truly to understand the mind of the tyranid, or to understand what motivated such a creature.

'Perhaps we should head to the west,' Brother Barabbas suggested, 'towards the position where the other tyranids were sighted.'

'Perhaps,' Avitus acknowledged.

'And leave all this excitement behind?' Philetus replied, his grin audible in his tone.

Again Philetus displayed such unwarranted and inappropriate levity on the battlefield, and even after being chastened after they'd returned from Calderis to the *Armageddon*.

'The Blood Raven does not seek excitement,' Avitus said, his voice even, 'but instead seeks after knowledge, and does the duty that is set before him.' Avitus paused, and then added, 'There are times when I wonder if there is anything of the Blood Raven in you at all, Brother Philetus.'

Philetus's eyes flashed behind his helmet, as he stiffened. Avitus knew that Philetus would view the sergeant's words as a grave insult, but didn't care. In Avitus's eyes, there *was* little of the Blood Ravens Chapter to be found in either Philetus's words or his actions, and it was his duty as a squad leader to voice his concerns.

'I....' Philetus began, his gauntleted hands tightening into fists at his sides. For the briefest moment, Avitus thought that his battle-brother might actually attempt to strike him, but the moment passed and the tension bled from Philetus's arms as his fists loosened at his sides. 'I am sorry, sergeant,' Philetus finally answered, chastened. 'I will endeavour in future to–'

Just what it was that Philetus would endeavour to do in future would remain a mystery, tragically, for it was at that moment that a hormagaunt brood erupted from the undergrowth around them, and immediately swarmed all over the nearest Blood Raven, flesh hooks snaring and talons scything.

Philetus went down under the swarm of hormagaunts, and he never got up again.

Avitus didn't bother issuing orders, trusting his squad to know their duty. He opened fire with his heavy bolter, hellfire shells ripping into the carapaces of the gaunts in the line of fire, bursting the toxin sacs which clung to their torsos like popped balloons.

SERGEANT TARKUS AND First Squad continued through the swampy lowlands. They had yet to make enemy contact, but had made another discovery, almost as unsettling.

'What do you make of it, sergeant?' Battle-Brother Nord asked, nudging with the tip of his boot the small form that twitched on the squelching ground before them.

It was a bird. Or rather, it *had* been a bird. With bright plumage and an oversized beak, it was typical of the tropical varieties that flourished everywhere on Typhon Primaris, cawing from the treetops and flashing like varicoloured dancers as they swooped through the open spaces.

But the bright, rainbow hues of this particular bird had become muted, sullied, and though its extended wings twitched spasmodically from moment to moment, there was no other sign of life to it. The beak was opened wide, black tongue lolling from within, and it seemed that the creature was gasping for air.

Tarkus prodded the wretched bird with the point of his combat knife, and then stood up, his expression thoughtful.

'Ever seen anything like that before, Nord?' Tarkus asked the battle-brother, seeing in this a teachable moment.

Nord was young for a Space Marine, barely at the beginning of his third decade of life. It had been only ten years or so since he'd been an aspirant like the trembling boys that they had lifted off Calderis, or whom the Librarian and Chaplain now examined in the village centre. He had the makings of a fine Blood Raven, but Tarkus had quickly surmised that Sergeant Aramus had been correct, and that Nord was not quite ready for a command of his own.

Nord wore a thoughtful expression for a moment before answering. 'On Prosperon,' he answered at last. 'The animals there were poisoned in just such a manner.'

Tarkus nodded, sheathing his combat knife. 'Mycetic poisoning,' he replied.

Mycetic spores, and their effects on living creatures, were perhaps one of the most insidious aspects of a tyranid invasion. Typically released into the atmosphere in the middle stages of the invasion, mycetic spores grew rapidly on contact with any organic material. Reproducing at an alarming rate, they would send rhizomes burrowing deep into the host's organic tissue, releasing enzymes that began to break down the organic matter itself, rendering it gradually into raw biomass. In essence, the affected plants and animals were digested alive within their own skins, long before their bodies were ever consumed. All that remained was for a tyranid ripper swarm to come along and consume the resultant biomass, which would be eventually converted into yet more tyranids.

'It's the lungs,' Tarkus went on, stepping past the doomed bird, his eyes scanning the lowlands before them. 'Aerobic creatures develop mycetic infestations in the lungs after exposure to high concentrations of airborne spores.'

Nord followed Tarkus, with the rest of the squad falling in behind him. 'But that only happens after exposure to high concentrations.'

Tarkus nodded. 'And death occurs within twenty-four hours. So the bird can't have travelled far.'

The sergeant raised his bolter, his enhanced senses straining to pierce the midnight gloom before them.

'One thing's for certain,' he said, darkly. 'We're not looking at the early stages of an invasion here.'

* * *

BATTLE-BROTHER VOIRE AND the rest of Third Squad were making their way steadily south-west, heading ever deeper into the shadow-laced forest, when they finally made enemy contact. They had reached a wide clearing, able for the first time in what seemed hours to see the sky unobstructed above them.

'I'm picking up movement,' Brother Cirrac voxed, studying his auspex.

'Which direction?' Voire replied, his bolter raised and ready.

Cirrac pointed into the shadows of a stand of trees ahead and to the left of their current path, the boundary of the clearing in which they stood.

'Human?' Voire asked.

Cirrac shook his head. 'Too small, too many of them.'

Voire was thoughtful. 'Could be native fauna.'

Cirrac nodded. 'Possibly. With the high amount of plant matter in between us and them it's hard to say.'

Voire motioned the rest of the squad forward. 'We need to check it out. Cirrac, I think the honour should be yours, as spotter.'

'Should I thank you?' Cirrac jibed, slipping away his auspex and drawing his bolter. 'Somehow it doesn't feel like I should.'

As Brother Cirrac ghosted forward towards the stand of trees, hardly making a sound, Voire instructed the rest of the squad to fan out in an arc facing the treeline. If Cirrac did manage to flush something out, they would need to be in a position to deal with whichever path it took.

The blood-red of Cirrac's power armour looked almost black in the low light, even with the Astartes' enhanced vision augmented by their helmets' visors, a shadow merging with shadows as he slipped through the trees and into the darkness beyond.

The Blood Ravens of Third Squad waited in silence for any response from him.

In the next moment, the thunderous sound of bolter fire cracked the silence, and Cirrac crashed backwards through the trees, firing into the darkness as he withdrew as quickly as possible.

'No,' Cirrac said through gritted teeth, 'definitely not native fauna.'

Even over the sound of Cirrac's bolter fire a chittering sound could now be heard, starting softly and growing ever louder, sounding like bone clicking against bone, like countless teeth gnashing again and again.

'Report!' Voire voxed, aiming his bolter at the trees. 'What did you find?'

'Trouble,' Cirrac answered cryptically.

Before Voire or the others could respond, the trees ahead of them shattered like kindling. Out of the ruined foliage burst a swarm of rippers, exploding into the clearing, hundreds upon hundreds of them, their razor-sharp jaws and claws clacking as they raced towards the Blood Ravens.

SERGEANT ARAMUS RAN through the darkness to join his squad, with little concern for stealth or secrecy. The Blood Ravens were engaging multiple targets already, in an ever-broadening range of positions, and there was considerable evidence now that they were not dealing with an initial tyranid outbreak or an isolated infestation, but that the tyranid invasion was much farther along than any of them had anticipated. Aramus's place was on the front line, engaging the enemy, not back in the village in relative safety, however temporary that safety might be.

The runes on his helmet's visors indicated that at least two of the Blood Ravens had fallen, Battle-Brother Philetus of the Ninth Squad, and Battle-Brother Loew of the Seventh. They had anticipated only a minor outbreak of tyranids on Typhon Primaris, at best, and Aramus had not expected that they might take any significant casualties. So confident had Aramus been that this would be little more than a search and retrieval mission that Apothecary Gordian had been allowed to remain on board the strike cruiser *Armageddon* tending to the injured Captain Thule.

Were the gene-seeds of Philetus and Loew already lost, or might it be possible that their bodies could be taken back to the *Armageddon* in time for Gordian's reductor to do its work, before the progenoid glands corrupted beyond use? And was it worth the risk to have Sergeants Avitus and Thaddeus task their squads with retrieving their fallen brothers from the battlefield, if doing so served to increase the risk that even more of them might fall to the enemy in the attempt?

As he tracked through the darkness, racing to the position where his own Third Squad was already engaged with a tyranid swarm, Aramus found himself wondering what Captain Thule would have done in this situation. Was the life of the captain worth the risk of so many others? Aramus believed that Thule was worth the risk, but at the same time he wasn't sure how much his estimation was motivated by a desire to surrender authority for the squads back to a revived and healed Captain Thule, freeing him to be responsible once more only for himself and the Space Marines of Third Squad.

Now was not the time for such self-examination, though. Blood Ravens prized knowledge and its pursuit, and considered self-knowledge as worthy of study as any other, but on the battlefield there were more pressing concerns, like the safety of the Space Marines under his command. He would have to save any questioning about his own motivations and assumptions until the battle was won or lost.

Up ahead he could already hear the sound of Third Squad's bolters firing continuously, and the counterpoint of the ripper swarm's maddening chittering. Pushing aside any lingering questions or doubts, Aramus racked his own bolter and poured on more speed.

SERGEANT AVITUS REACHED the end of his heavy bolter's magazine, the firing mechanism clicking on empty. He had expended an entire high-capacity box magazine on the hormagaunt brood, and still they kept coming.

'Barabbas!' Avitus shouted as he yanked the magazine from his heavy bolter and reached for one of the full magazines clipped to his waist. 'Cover me!'

Battle-Brother Barabbas didn't waste breath in replying, but swung the barrel of his meltagun around to spray its heat on the gaunts nearest the sergeant. But even the heat of the melta wasn't enough to destroy the hormagaunts with a single blast, and Barabbas was forced to chase the quickly moving terrors with his aim to do any real damage at all.

There had been perhaps a dozen of the gaunts when they'd first attacked and taken Philetus down beneath their flesh hooks and scything talons. Now, there were no more than a half-dozen of the monsters left. But reducing the brood's number by half had cost the Ninth Squad, and dearly. Philetus was down, never to stand again. Brother Gagan still lived, but the hormagaunts had managed to damage one of his legs quite badly and he was moving now only with difficulty, though he was still able to fire his plasma gun all the same. And Brother Safir had very nearly expended all of his hellfire rounds, and was now forced to employ the far less effective bolter rounds.

Avitus slammed the new magazine home just in time to open fire on a gaunt who had ducked under Barabbas's melta fire and raced right at the sergeant. The tyranid leapt in the air just as Avitus opened fire, and though the hellfire shells ripped into its abdomen, the hormagaunt's momentum carried it forward, talons scything out as toxins dripped from the monster's open maw.

The impact of the hormagaunt knocked Avitus from his feet, and as he toppled backwards, his heavy bolter still firing, the tyranid fell on top of him. The hormagaunt lashed out, knocking the bolter from Avitus's gauntleted hand, and with the mutagenic acid boring through its insides, the tyranid clamped its talons around Avitus's neck, taking him in a dying embrace.

CHAPTER TWELVE

IN THE CLEARING at the centre of the village, as Chaplain Palmarius put a question to one of the last potential aspirants, Librarian Niven was distracted, his attention roving to the dark shadows pressing around the circle of light in which they stood. It was hours before dawn, but none of the villagers had gone to sleep, and many of them were beginning to show clear signs of fatigue and sleep deprivation. Astartes could go for days without sleep, thanks to their catalepsean nodes, and as this was one of the implants already bestowed upon the Blood Raven Scouts, they too were able to continue to function without experiencing any ill effects from their long wakefulness. But the headman and the other villagers shared no such strength, and seemed now to be buoyed only by fear, the terror that had rippled through them on the first report of tyranid contact continuing to rebound among them like the echoing rings of a thrown stone's passage on the surface of a very small pond.

But it wasn't the cold fear of the villagers which brushed Librarian Niven's mind, despite the fact that he'd been forced to block out the terrified thoughts of the headman's people in the hours since Sergeant Aramus first put the village on alert. It was instead the pinprick needling of some entirely alien consciousness, expressing emotions and appetites which could not be readily translated into the language of men.

Niven was hearing the inhuman thoughts of the tyranid hive mind.

But that mind was nowhere near, Niven realized. Though there might be tendrils of it reaching out to grasp Typhon Primaris, though the mycetic spores of a tyranid host might have fallen upon the jungle world and begun the process of infestation, the collective mind which drove the subservient offspring of the Great Devourer was not to be found in those dark jungles, or in orbit above them. It was somewhere else, somewhere relatively close but still beyond his ability to locate with his mind, directing the thoughtless, instinctual movements of the invading tyranids just as a human mind directed the movements of the various parts of the body, large and small. A tyranid hive was, in many ways, only a single organism, a single mind and body incarnate in a multitude of forms. And even if the Blood Ravens were by some miracle able to expunge each of those discrete forms from the midnight jungles around them, the hive itself would remain, the directing mind somewhere out in the dark void of space, seeking the opportunity to reach out and grasp a world yet again.

The cold brush of the tyranid's thoughts against the Librarian's mind was familiar, but only now did he recognize from where. It was the same dark foreboding sensation that Niven had felt all this time, since first arriving in the Aurelia sub-sector, and which had only been intensified when he was revived from his extended hibernation. But the Calderis system was light years from here.

Where, then, was this tyranid hive to be found? And just how *large* was it?

'Avitus! Hold on!'

Battle-Brother Barabbas raced over as the sergeant grappled across the mould-covered ground with the dying hormagaunt.

'N-no,' came Avitus's strained reply over the vox-comms. 'Stand. Back.'

The tyranid had its talons scythed around Avitus's head and neck, doing its best to decapitate the sergeant before the mutagenic acid of the hellfire shells ate it alive from the inside out. But just as fissures began to spider across the ceramite of Avitus's power armour, the sergeant threw aside his heavy bolter, and wrapped his own armoured arms around the hormagaunt's body. Clasping his hands together, the sergeant squeezed for all he was worth, his own enhanced strength redoubled by the servos in his power armour.

'Avitus!' Barabbas shouted again, seeing the gaunt's talons begin to bite through the pitted surface of the sergeant's armour.

'Not. Yet.' Avitus grunted into the vox-comms. 'Almost.'

With a final surge, the sergeant squeezed his arms together in a vice-like embrace, and the chitinous carapace of the hormagaunt cracked open like an egg. The hormagaunt let out a final keening squeal, and then fell silent, slumping forward onto the still-prostrate Avitus.

'There,' Avitus said, catching his breath. Unclasping his hands, he reached up and grabbed hold of a nodule on the gaunt's back, ripped it off, then pushed upwards and shoved the now-dead tyranid off of himself.

'Are you injured?' Barabbas called, rushing to help the sergeant up.

'It's no matter if I am,' Avitus answered, climbing unsteadily to his feet. When he was standing, he held aloft the nodule that he'd yanked off the gaunt's back, which still glistening with the tyranid's ichor.

It was one of the hormagaunt's toxin-sacs.

'Is it contaminated by the hellfire shells?' Barabbas asked, taking the toxin-sac from Avitus's hands. The battle-brother pulled out his auspex and began taking a reading. All around them the other members of the Ninth Squad continued to fire and reload, reload and fire at the remaining monsters of the hormagaunt brood.

'See for yourself,' Avitus said, taking a few steps to where his heavy bolter lay and retrieving the weapon. On his way back to where Barabbas stood the sergeant fired off a stream of shells at another gaunt, this one already wounded enough that it collapsed into paroxysms as the mutagenic acid began to burn.

Barabbas looked up from the severed nodule in his hand. 'No,' he answered, smiling behind his visor. 'There's no trace of mutagen in it. You got it free before the hellfire shells worked their magic on it.'

Avitus nodded. 'Then we may just have what we came for.' He fired another volley of hellfire shells at a hormagaunt who'd come racing towards Barabbas. 'Take a chemical profile and transmit it up to the *Armageddon*.'

'Already in progress, sergeant,' Barabbas answered, as he keyed the commands into his auspex. With the chemical profile of the biotoxin, Apothecary Gordian would be able to begin work on an antitoxin for the poisons that kept Captain Thule at death's door. 'With that done, then perhaps we can get off this ball of muck and mire.'

'If those are our orders,' Avitus replied without a trace of humour or sentiment, 'then yes.'

WITH SERGEANT ARAMUS having rejoined them, the Blood Ravens of the Third Squad had almost managed to eradicate the last of the ripper swarm when Sergeant Avitus voxed confirmation that he and his squad had secured a sample of tyranid toxin.

'Wrap it up here!' Aramus ordered the squad, lobbing a frag grenade at a cluster of rippers that had so far evaded his bolter's hellfire rounds. It exploded in their midst, shredding the monsters nearest the blast to ribbons. 'We're moving out.'

'Acknowledged,' Brother Voire called back, his left arm tucked against his chest. His elbow had been caught between the vicious jaws of one of the rippers, and the joint had been broken before another of the Blood Ravens had been able to pry the monster off.

'All Blood Ravens,' Aramus voxed on an open channel. 'Fall back to the village.'

The runes on the sergeant's visor flashed the squads' acknowledgement, though Aramus could not fail to notice how many of the runes were now glowing red. More brothers fallen.

'Sergeant Cyrus,' Aramus went on.

'Go ahead, sir,' came the Scout sergeant's response.

'Prepare for immediate extraction.'

Sergeant Cyrus signalled acknowledgement without a word wasted.

'Squad,' Aramus called out, unleashing a torrent of hellfire on a ripper that was lunging his direction. 'We're done here. Fastest speed back to the village. Now!'

The Space Marines of the Third Squad, some needing the help of their brothers to remain standing, much less walking, were only too ready to obey.

SERGEANT TARKUS AND the Blood Ravens of First Squad received and acknowledged their orders to withdraw. None was reluctant to turn away from what they had found.

Continuing on into the south-west, they had still to come into close contact with tyranid elements, though they had caught sight of a flight of gargoyles winging their way overhead some time before, too far out of range to waste the bolter rounds in firing upon. And once they had glimpsed what appeared to be a zoanthrope hovering along above the ground a half-kilometre or more away over the swampy lowlands.

But if they had yet to come into direct contact with the tyranid invaders, they had found ample evidence of the monsters' passage. They now found themselves in a landscape of death, stretching out to the south and west as far as their enhanced eyes could see.

The sun was just pinking the skies to the east, and as the dawn slowly flooded across the lowlands, they could better see the effects of the tyranids upon the blighted surroundings. What they had in the darkness taken to be towering trees in the distance were by the first light of day revealed instead to be tyranid bio-structures – spore chimneys, cone-shaped structures hundreds of metres tall, belching mycetic spores into the atmosphere to travel wherever the winds carried them. They were broodhives, in which new monsters were birthed to range out over the land to kill and consume. Sunlight glistened off reclamation pools, miniature lakes of enzymes and acids, in which the bodies of both tyranid victims and tyranids who had outlived their usefulness were rendered down into raw, consumable biomass. There were even the beginnings of capillary towers, which when fully grown would stretch high into the thermosphere, mind-bogglingly tall organic structures through which the biomass of the reclamation pools would eventually be carried up into orbit and transferred to the bellies of spacefaring bio-forms.

This was no initial outbreak, nor was it an infestation that might still be quelled. This was full-scale tyranoforming, the final phase of a tyranid invasion.

'Holy Throne,' Tarkus said in a harsh whisper, surveying the blighted landscape. He remembered another world, half a galaxy away, that had once been a bright and green place, and had ended in just such a nightmare.

The infestation of Typhon Primaris had clearly gone on far longer than any of them had realized, longer than any of them might have even guessed, the effects hidden for too long out in the dark and dense confines of the unpopulated jungles. While the natives had cowered in their villages, fearing the 'jungle spirits' which they believed prowled the darkness, the offspring of the Great Devourer had been steadily converting and consuming the very stuff of the world itself.

And to all appearances, it was far too late in the process to do anything about it.

APOTHECARY GORDIAN HAD received the chemical profile of the biotoxin, and was already well on his way to devising an antitoxin that might serve to purge the poisons that prevented Captain Thule's body from healing itself. As servitors scuttled back and forth across the wide floor of the Apothecarion, Gordian laboured over the narthecium, a full-scale version of the medical kit he carried with him onto the field of battle. Nearby lay the sarcophagus in which Thule lay in a dreamless slumber, his body arrested at the very point of death.

Already Gordian had tried a half-dozen different strains of antitoxin, which had been tested against the samples drawn from Thule's poisoned body, and so far all half-dozen of the strains had failed. But even if the strains had so far failed to completely eradicate the toxins, Gordian had succeeded in creating two that served at least to diminish the amount of the toxin in the sample set. He was, it appeared, on track.

He only hoped that it was worth it. The few scattered reports he'd had from the planet's surface suggested that the Blood Ravens were taking casualties. Sergeant Aramus had sent word that the squads would be retrieving their fallen from the battlefield, and assuming that they were brought back to the *Armageddon* in time, Gordian believed it likely he could still retrieve the gene-seed from their bodies. But the progenoid glands would be at the outer limits of their viability by that point, and any delay would render them useless. And there would be another generation of Blood Ravens lost to the Chapter.

Gordian was beginning to generate a new strain of antitoxin when a voice from behind interrupted his concentration.

'Apothecary?'

Gordian turned to see Lexicanium Konan standing behind him.

'Forgive this intrusion, but I come on an urgent matter at the request of Master Niven.'

Gordian arched an eyebrow, inviting Konan to elaborate.

'Might you be able to provide a cultured sample of the tyranid material, based on the chemical profile you received?' The Lexicanium's tone was quiet, respectful, but there was an urgency beneath his words.

Gordian straightened from the narthecium, his expression thoughtful. 'I suppose I could have a sample fabricated for your use.' He paused, curious. 'To what end?'

Lexicanium Konan leaned forward, and answered in a hushed tone as if he were imparting some precious secret. 'Master Niven, it seems, believes that with such a sample, he can locate the source of the xenos scourge.'

SERGEANT THADDEUS AND the Blood Ravens of the Seventh Squad had nearly reached the village, as ordered, but the action and the withdrawal had come at a heavy price.

Brother Loew had fallen in the early hours of the night, to the claws of the lictor clutch that had burst out of the darkness and attacked them. Brother Shar had succumbed to the deathspitter-symbiote of a ravener only a short while later, the corrosive maggot-like projectiles disgorged by the weapon searing through Shar's helmet like hot rivets dropped on ice, and then melting into and through the face within. Shar's screams of agony had been horrible, made worse by the certain knowledge that, once the deathspitter organisms had eaten their way into his brain, it was only a matter of time.

Counting Thaddeus himself, only six Space Marines of the Seventh Squad were still on their feet, two of them weighted down by the bulk of their fallen brothers' bodies slung over their shoulders.

In a matter of moments, they would reach the village, and the Thunderhawks waiting just beyond it, ready to carry them back to the *Armageddon* in orbit high overhead. In previous undertakings, Thaddeus had always found joy in the knowledge that he had survived another action and would be returning, whether covered in glory or not, to the bosom of his ship. But seeing the lifeless bodies of his battle-brothers Loew and Shar, he found little reason for joy in the present action. The Seventh Squad had boasted a full complement of ten Blood Ravens only weeks before, but after Zalamis, and Calderis, and now Typhon Primaris, their number was reduced to a mere half-dozen. How many more would fall in the coming days, weeks, months?

Thaddeus had for so many years gone into combat with a grin on his lips, and returned from combat the same way.

'Come on, squad,' he called to his men, as the trees pressed closer and closer around them. 'Not much farther, and we'll be off this accursed world. And then we can properly mourn our fallen with the next tolling of the Bell of Souls.'

Now, he wondered if he would ever find reason to grin again.

ONBOARD THE LIGHT cruiser the *Sword of Hadrian*, Admiral Forbes sat on the bunk in her stateroom, eyes losing their focus as the words swam before them on the page. There were only a scant few hours left until the ship's 'day' began, and still Forbes had been unable to surrender herself to slumber. Why she had assumed that the collected writings of

Warmaster Solon might be an appropriate soporific, she now had difficulty remembering.

She was about to flip back a few pages and attempt to approach once more the warmaster's own account of his actions during the Macharian Heresy, in the hopes that there might be some tactical lesson which she might glean from it, when the door chimed, saving her the trouble. Setting the book aside, she rose from the bunk, absent-mindedly pulling straight her tunic.

'Enter,' she said in a loud voice.

The door slid open, and Commander Mitchels stepped in, a data-slate in his hand. Did the first officer ever go *anywhere* without a data-slate?

Forbes imagined that he did not, at that. Mitchels was a man who took his position very seriously, after all, and his responsibilities no less so.

'You're up late, commander,' Forbes said with a slight smile, sitting back down on the edge of her bunk.

'Up early, in fact, admiral,' Mitchels answered, almost apologetically. 'It is technically ship's morning.'

Forbes sighed. Of course he was. 'What service can I do you this morning?'

'We've just received this from the Blood Ravens strike cruiser, ma'am.'

The admiral's eyes narrowed. The news from the planet below had not been good. The most recent report had been dated less than an hour previous, informing the *Sword of Hadrian* that a sample of the biotoxin they sought had been obtained, and that they would shortly be extracting from the planet, returning to their strike cruiser. It appeared that the level of tyranid incursion on Typhon Primaris was severe, but unless and until there was sign of any spaceborne elements of the xenos threat, there was little that Admiral Forbes and her light cruiser could do to assist, short of sending down landing craft to evacuate as much of the civilian population as was practicable. She was not prepared to authorize such an evacuation attempt, though, until she had received the final report from the Blood Ravens officer in charge of the landing party, to gauge his opinion of the situation.

Was this the word on which she'd been waiting? Was it time to order the boats launched, and to have the cargo bays prepared to receive as many as a few hundred refugees? She was sure that Governor Vandis would be less sanguine about receiving the penniless and uncultured refugees of Typhon Primaris than he was about the few hundred wealthy Calderians currently making their way to Meridian. But Admiral Forbes wasn't about to stand idly by doing nothing if there was a chance to save at least a few innocent lives, at no cost or risk to her own vessel.

'What does Sergeant Aramus report?' Forbes asked.

Mitchels shook his head. 'It's not the sergeant sending the message, ma'am, but a Lexicanium Konan.' Seeing her somewhat puzzled expression, he clarified. 'The Librarian serving as the *Armageddon's* astropath.'

Forbes nodded. 'What does he want, then?'

Mitchels handed her the data-slate, covered in what appeared to be complex biochemical information. 'He requests that this be given to our own astropaths, and made available to the Navis dome, as well.'

The admiral looked up from the data-slate with incredulity. 'Whatever for?'

'You SEE, SERGEANT Aramus,' Librarian Niven was explaining to the sergeant, 'there is a tyranid mind out there, however large or small, but it cannot be located from here.'

The two Blood Ravens stood at the centre of the village, while Scouts Xenakis, Jutan, and Watral prepared the Thunderhawks, and Sergeant Cyrus escorted the trio of potential aspirants that had been culled from among the village youth. The evaluations had not been a complete loss, it appeared, but even so there would yet again be no opportunity for Blood Trials, and the aspirants would have to be tested in some other way, at some other time.

'And the chemical profile of the tyranid helps you... How?' Aramus asked.

The sun was creeping up the eastern sky, and the other squads were just now reporting in. Avitus's squad had arrived first, and had already mustered in the long shadows of the Thunderhawks by the time that Aramus and the Third Squad reached the village. Thaddeus and the Seventh arrived a short while later, and began immediately to load their dead and wounded onboard.

Only Sergeant Tarkus's squad remained in the field, and had voxed word that they would be reaching the village at any moment.

'Because, sergeant,' Librarian Niven explained, 'with the sample in hand, it is possible to search for psychic resonances, to attempt to pinpoint the origin of the tyranid thought patterns.'

'So you could find the hive mind?'

'Precisely. If we were to locate the source of the original infestation, then perhaps there might be some way to eradicate it and prevent future outbreaks.'

Aramus scratched his chin with a gauntleted finger, thoughtfully, his helmet held under his arm. 'Then why can't you simply get some of the sample Avitus carries now? And do just the sort of resonance search you outline, but from the surface?'

Niven shook his head, impatiently. 'Because that would simply give us a single vector. Triangulation is required. But with Lexicanium Konan and I on board the *Armageddon*, and the astropaths on board the *Sword of Hadrian* operating at some nontrivial distance, then we would have two vectors with which to operate, and would be able to determine not only the direction, but the distance as well.'

Aramus considered for a moment. 'Very well,' he said, then narrowed his eyes. 'Though I would have preferred you to run this by me before issuing orders to Lexicanium Konan to this effect.'

Niven nodded, absently, and then began turning away to walk towards the Thunderhawks. 'I had considered it a matter of some urgency, sergeant. I thought you would agree.'

WHILE ARAMUS AND his Blood Ravens still gathered on the planet below, the psykers and Navis Nobilite on board the two ships began to extend their senses out into the darkness, searching for resonances with the sample that Librarian Niven had provided.

The Navigators probed the void, searching.

The psykers, Lexicanium and astropath alike, cast their minds into the warp, questing. Niven had told them that the hive mind was most likely on some neighbouring world, an errant spore that had drifted through the cosmos and taken root in the Aurelia sub-sector, and that it was an opportunistic offspring of this isolated infestation that had settled on Typhon Primaris.

Onboard the strike cruiser *Armageddon*, Lexicanium Konan lay on a pallet on the floor of his quarters, his senses stretched to their fullest. He could faintly feel the cold, inhuman impressions that Master Niven had shared with him, and that he had shared with the astropaths on board the *Sword of Hadrian*. Their minds linked, astropath to Lexicanium, they could almost feel that inhuman mind out there, almost touch it, and then…

Konan sat bolt upright, cold sweat poring down his body.

He had touched the mind of the tyranid hive, and it was like nothing he had anticipated.

This was no isolated infestation.

This was a hive fleet.

CHAPTER THIRTEEN

ADMIRAL FORBES REVIEWED the intelligence relayed to her by the astropaths of the *Sword of Hadrian*. The tyranids that had been discovered on the planet below – and brought from there to the desert world of Calderis by persons unknown – were far from being isolated spores that had drifted across space into the Typhon system, to take root in the fertile soil of the jungle world. What had taken Typhon Primaris in its grasp was instead just one of innumerable vast tendrils of a previously unknown hive fleet, pushing deep into the Aurelia sub-sector. They still did not know precisely where the hive mind of the fleet was located, the unholy mother who had birthed the monsters which had infested the world below, but they had been able to chart the range and extent of the tendrils, and it was clear that Typhon Primaris was not the only system under threat.

'How reliable is this intelligence?' Forbes asked her first officer.

'If it were only a single psyker reporting this, ma'am,' Commander Mitchels replied, 'I think there would still be room for doubt.'

'But this isn't a single psyker we're talking about.'

'No, ma'am,' Mitchels allowed. 'Between the astropaths on the *Sword of Hadrian*, and their counterparts on the Blood Ravens strike cruiser, we have independent verification from more than half a dozen sources.'

'So...' Forbes said. She paused, tapping her front teeth with a fingernail. 'Fairly reliable, wouldn't you say?'

Mitchels nodded. 'That was my estimation, ma'am.'

Forbes scowled. The first officer was right, but it was not the answer she'd wanted to hear. She'd clung to the faint hope that these projections might be in error, or that the threat might not be as widespread as the intelligence suggested. But it was foolish to cling to such hopes any longer.

'The Emperor protect us,' Forbes said. She called up a map display on the data-slate, and looked again at the tendrils of the tyranid fleet. Her fingertips brushed the display where the tendrils stretched to encircle distant Meridian, capital of the Aurelia subsector. 'The Emperor protect us all.'

THADDEUS LOOKED UP, his youthful face lined and drawn.

'Meridian?' he repeated, disbelief echoing in his words.

Sergeant Aramus nodded. They were still awaiting the arrival of Sergeant Tarkus and First Squad to the village, but he'd summoned the other squad leaders – Avitus, Thaddeus, and Cyrus – to apprise them of the most recent news from the ships in orbit.

'Emperor's Throne,' Cyrus said, an uncharacteristic display for the stoic veteran.

'We have yet to make contact with Meridian, but Lexicanium Konan and the astropaths on the *Sword of Hadrian* are working in concert to get word through to Governor Vandis and his people. But the fact remains that the tyranid threat will soon reach Meridian, if it hasn't already.'

'But surely the Planetary Defence Force would be in a position to respond to any initial incursion…' Thaddeus began, his voice trailing off as he went.

'When have you known a PDF capable of finding their backsides with both hands and an auspex?' Avitus answered with a snarl.

Aramus met Thaddeus's gaze, and shook his head. 'While I disagree with Sergeant Avitus on the capabilities of PDFs in general – and on the qualities of the Meridian forces in particular – I'm forced to agree that a tyranid invasion is almost certainly beyond the scope of their abilities. And that's assuming that they even discover the infestation in time to respond at all.'

Thaddeus scowled, but knew that Aramus was right. Meridian was a hive world, home to billions of inhabitants. Every square kilometre of the planet was developed to some degree, with habs – enormous cities that stretched from horizon to horizon – covering most of its surface. There were park districts, isolated patches of greenery enjoyed only by the wealthy and powerful – like Aramus's own high-hab family – but a low-hab dweller like Thaddeus had once been would never dream that such places could exist. If a tyranid mycetic spore were to drift to earth and take root in one of the immense 'gardens,' rarely visited and tended only by servitors, or else infest the underhive levels where the authorities never ventured, then the tyranid infestation might progress considerably before those in power even knew it had begun.

'The grim reality that we must face,' Aramus said, pointedly glancing in Cyrus's direction, recalling the Scout sergeant's constant refrain to the neophytes in his charge, 'is that Typhon Primaris is already a lost cause. This world is subject to a late-stage infestation, and we lack the resources and the time to even consider doing anything to reverse it. But Meridian is the capital of the sub-sector, home to billions, and if even some of those billions are to survive what is to follow, then we need to travel to Meridian with all possible speed and stop the tyranid incursion before it has a chance to take root.'

Thaddeus nodded, quickly. 'Yes,' he said. 'Agreed. We must go to Meridian.'

Cyrus glanced over his shoulder at the villagers still gathered in the centre of the village. 'And them?'

'What about them?' Avitus spat.

'What is to be done with them?' Cyrus asked.

'Admiral Forbes intends to evacuate as many as she can, as I understand it,' Aramus answered, 'but as for the rest, may the Emperor protect them, because no one else will.'

He paused, and then motioned to the Thunder-hawks.

'Now get your squads on board and ready to fly. Any moment we waste here is a moment less that we might spend on saving Meridian.'

A SHORT WHILE later, Aramus surveyed the assembled villagers. Except for the three youths selected to accompany the Blood Ravens back to the *Armageddon*, the rest would be staying here, to wait for the creeping tide of tyranid infestation to finally reach this far. Even if he had wished to take the rest of the terrified villagers with them, there wasn't room in the Thunderhawks to carry them, nor space in the strike cruiser for them to be held. He knew that Admiral Forbes intended to begin the evacuation immediately, but with the tyranids encroaching so close, so quickly, he didn't know how her craft would be able to land and take off again safely more than once or twice, if even that often.

Sergeant Tarkus and his squad had arrived only moments before, and waited in the village clearing while the other squads loaded onto the Thunder-hawks. Once they were on board, and First Squad was able to board, they would be ready to lift off, and leave the jungles of Typhon Primaris behind.

Aramus glanced over at Sergeant Tarkus, who stood a few metres off, his attention on the villagers. The headman and his people, none of whom had slept in some thirty hours or more, alternatively wept, or whimpered, or sang songs of praise to the Sky-Father, begging him to deliver them from the evil spirits even now stalking through the forests towards them. The Headman and the others had not understood why it was that the Noble Sons of the Sky-Father were leaving them in their hour of direst need, and Aramus had been unable to explain matters to them.

Tarkus kept looking at the villagers, searching their faces, his own expression unreadable. Aramus wasn't sure what it was that the sergeant was looking for, but suddenly, it appeared that the veteran campaigner had found it. His expression changed to one of stony resolution, and he turned and marched the few metres to stand by Aramus's side.

'Anything the matter, Tarkus?'

'Sergeant Aramus?' Tarkus said, an odd undercurrent to his words. 'Permission to remain on the planet.'

Aramus was startled. 'Remain? Here?'

'Yes,' Tarkus added with a curt nod. 'For myself, and as many of the First Squad who wish to join me.'

'For what purpose?'

Tarkus glanced over at the assembled villagers, his expression softening. 'My homeworld Erinia was lost to tyranids, long after I was recruited to the Blood Ravens. I was half a galaxy away when I learned it had been consumed by the Hive Fleet Behemoth.' He paused, and looked back to meet Aramus's gaze. 'I had family still on Erinia, and there wasn't a single thing I could do for them, or for Erinia, but to mourn.'

'And now…' Aramus began, glancing from the veteran campaigner to the villagers.

'Call it a chance to make amends, if you like,' Tarkus answered. 'I'll stay and try to hold the tyranids off their backs until Admiral Forbes's boats can get them to safety.' Tarkus paused, and smiled slightly. 'If I'm lucky, perhaps the admiral will give *me* a ride, as well.'

APOTHECARY GORDIAN STOOD back, wiping his hands clean on a disinfecting cloth. On the platform before him lay the body of Captain Davian Thule, uncased from its sarcophagus, looking more like a corpse lying in state than a still-living being.

'Begin antitoxin trial Gamma-Nine,' Gordian instructed the medicae servitor who hunched at his side, a syringe held in its mechadendrites. 'Initiate full body readings, recording all findings for later review.'

The servitor flashed its acquiescence.

'Administer sample,' Gordian went on, tossing the cloth onto the floor at his feet. He paid no mind to the tiny servitor who scuttled out from its alcove along the wall to retrieve the discarded cloth.

A tiny drop of amber liquid glinted at the tip of the needle like a gem in the Apothecarion's low light as the medicae servitor brought the syringe near the exposed flesh of Thule's chest. The servitor ratcheted forward, and the needle bit into Thule's chest, the flesh wan and mottled with the effects of toxic shock.

Apothecary Gordian had already generated nearly a dozen antitoxins which appeared to have an effect on the pure biotoxins in the cultured samples, but so far none of them had demonstrated any efficacy when administered to Thule's body itself. If this latest strain didn't have an effect, he would be forced to return Thule's body to the sarcophagus while he started another antitoxin from scratch.

The medicae servitor withdrew the syringe from Thule's flesh, and backed away to await further instructions. The probes and sensors mounted onto the platform itself began their work, scrutinising the captain's bodily processes on a wide variety of wavelengths, capturing a dazzling amount of data. But there was only one datum which Gordian sought – proof of the eradication of the tyranid toxins from Davian Thule's body.

He had worked straight through the night without ceasing, and did not anticipate taking a break any time soon.

'Emperor guide my mind and hand,' Gordian said in a quiet voice. 'Let *this* be the one.'

'Understood, Sergeant Aramus,' Admiral Forbes replied, addressing the vox terminal mounted on the captain's chair. 'Safe hunting. *Sword of Hadrian* out.'

Forbes motioned for the light cruiser's communications officer to cut the vox connection with the *Armageddon*, and swivelled the captain's chair to face Commander Mitchels, who stood to one side of the command dais.

'Permission to speak, admiral?' Mitchels said in a low voice, his eyes cutting from one side to the other as though worried someone might overhear.

Forbes saw the blush rising in Mitchels's cheek, and knew that something was weighing heavily on his thoughts.

'Granted. What's bothering you, commander?'

'Well,' the first officer began, glancing from one side to the other again before continuing, 'are you certain that a planetary evacuation is the best use of our resources at this juncture?' He paused, and leaned in, almost conspiratorially. 'Wouldn't Governor Vandis likely prefer that we proceed to the defence of Meridian with the *Armageddon*?'

A tight smile played across Forbes's lips, and she folded her hands in her lap. 'Leaving aside the fact that we have, as yet, been unable to make contact with Governor Vandis – and far be it from me to second-guess the thoughts of His Most Noble Excellency – we are *not* discussing a planetary evacuation. There isn't time for that many runs down into the gravity well and up again, for one thing, and not enough resources to house them all on board, for another. What we *are* talking about is preserving the life of a scant few hundred Typhonians who, but for our intervention, would very quickly find themselves in the belly of the Great Devourer itself. The rest of the Aurelia Battle-group is already en route to Meridian as we speak, and we should be able to join them within a day or two, at the outside, by which time we'll be in a position to lead an attack against any and all orbital elements of the tyranid fleet, and to provide cover for Sergeant Aramus and his Blood Ravens as they wage the ground war.' She paused, and her tight smile widened, if only fractionally. 'Or, to put it another way, yes, I *am* certain that this is the best use of our resources, commander. Or would *you* prefer to take this seat' – she gestured to the captain's chair on which she rested – 'and instead condemn hundreds of innocents to a painful death for the sake of some slight expediency?'

Mitchels remained stock still, his expression stricken as though he had just been flogged. For one who thrived on his duties, and on the approval of his superiors, even such a minor dressing-down as the admiral had just given him was enough to chastise him.

'Well?' Forbes prompted, arching an eyebrow.

'No, ma'am,' Mitchels hastened to reply.

'Good. In which case I expect my orders to be carried out. Sergeant Tarkus and his team are on the surface now, securing the site for our landing parties. Let's get those birds in the air, and back on board, as quickly as we can. I don't want to spend any more time at this than is absolutely necessary, but let's save as many as we can before duty calls, shall we?'

Mitchels snapped off a crisp salute, and hustled to carry out the admiral's orders.

'Very well, Tarkus,' Forbes said under her breath, her eyes on the forward viewports, 'let's see how many of these poor souls we can grasp from the maw, shall we?'

TARKUS PATROLLED THE boundaries of the village. He could hear the chittering from the lengthening shadows to the south, and knew it was now only a matter of time.

Of the six other Space Marines of the First Squad, five had initially opted to remain behind with the sergeant and safeguard the villagers until the Navy boats arrived to lift them to safety. The sixth Space Marine, Brother Mettius, had at first baulked at the idea, hungry instead to travel to Meridian to scour the tyranid infestation from that world, but when he saw that the rest of his battle-brothers had instead offered to remain behind, he quickly changed his vote. It was a somewhat rare thing for Space Marines to exercise self-determination of this sort, as usually their lot was to follow the orders they were given, no questions asked. But given the unusual nature of the assignment, Tarkus and Aramus had agreed to allow each Space Marine the ability to decide his own fate.

So it was that seven Blood Ravens remained behind on Typhon Primaris when the last of the Thunderhawks rumbled up into the sky, returning Sergeant Aramus and the others back to the *Armageddon*. That had been more than an hour before.

Now, with the first of the transports from the *Sword of Hadrian* already dropping out of the sky towards them, Tarkus and his Space Marines redoubled their watch on the surrounding jungles. The sun was already beginning to set in the west, the end of their second day on the world, and if the experience of the previous night was any guide, the activity of the tyranid invaders would only intensify in the moonless hours of the night.

There had not been an outright attack on the village itself, as yet. Tarkus's auspex was picking up movement out in the trees – a considerable amount of movement, in fact – but thus far none of the tyranids had approached the boundaries of the community.

Tarkus knew that would not last. And if the chittering sounds which grew ever louder were any indication, the tyranid attack would not be long in coming.

The first of the transports from the *Sword of Hadrian* was coming in on an approach vector, and would be landing in moments. From where he stood at the village's edge, Tarkus could see the Headman and the rest of the villagers gathered together in a huddled mass at the edge of the clearing from which the Thunderhawks had lifted off only a short while before.

Had it been like this in the last hours of Erinia, Tarkus wondered? When he pictured the world of his birth, his mind conjured images of the green and growing land of his earliest memories, a peaceful and pastoral world of farms and farmers that provided produce for a dozen other worlds. But having seen the stain of tyranid infestation on other worlds – on Prosperon, now on Typhon Primaris, and on too many others to count – he knew that in its death throes Erinia had no longer been green, and no longer peaceful nor pastoral. It had been overrun by the offspring of the Great Devourer, just as this world was now being overrun before his eyes.

Had the family that Tarkus left behind on Erinia – brothers and sisters, cousins, nieces, and nephews – gathered like the Headman and his villagers now did, desperate to claim the precious few berths on space-bound craft, too few to accommodate even a fraction of them? Had they known, as they huddled together and cast terrified glances at the surrounding shadows, that the slim hope of rescue would be denied so many of them? And when the last transports had come and gone, had they stayed there, watching the skies, looking for one more transport, just one more, knowing that it would never come?

The landing craft set down on the clearing, and as the Navy officers climbed down to supervise the loading of the villagers, the natives pressed forward, threatening to plough the officers under in their mad rush for the transports.

Tarkus considered sending one of this squad to assist in crowd control, but then the chittering from the shadows crescendoed to a fever pitch, and a dozen or more tyranid warriors burst from the trees and hurled themselves towards the village.

The sergeant opened fire with his bolter, hellfire rounds ripping into the advancing wave of warriors. The villagers, and their Navy rescuers, would have to see to themselves. The Blood Ravens had other work to do.

ON DISTANT MERIDIAN, light years away from troubled Typhon Primaris, a rogue trader waited in a secured room in the subterranean levels of the governor's palace. The security personnel who'd escorted him from the space port had divested him of his weaponry before leaving him in the room with the case he carried. They'd taken his duelling pistol, his knives, even the holdout that he kept hidden inside his right boot.

They had, of course, failed to confiscate the ornate signet ring that he wore on the index finger of his right hand. But then, one could hardly expect low-ranking security personnel to recognize Jokaero digital weaponry when they saw it. And they didn't for a moment suspect the surprises loaded into the rogue trader's augmetic eyepatch – he would use them only in an emergency, of course, but it was comforting to know that they were there, if needed.

The rogue trader had been kept waiting for the better part of an hour, but was patient, all the same. The man for whom he waited was an important man, with many demands upon his time, but perhaps even more importantly he was a *wealthy* man, more than willing to make up for a bit of tardiness on his part.

It had been a shame about the seed case from Typhon Primaris. The rogue trader knew that his customer would have paid handsomely to add such a prize to his collection of xenos rarities. But the weapon contained in the case on the table before him would fetch an even grander price, he was sure, especially once the customer learned the circumstances under which the rogue trader had claimed, and just who had wielded, the weapon.

The silence of the room was disrupted by the hiss of a door opening, and the rogue trader smelled the perfumes that wafted ahead of the customer like a cloud. The man always seemed to smell like a hothouse had exploded in his near vicinity in the recent past, the cloyingly sweet scent of flowers wrapped around him like an aromatic shroud.

'Sorry to keep you waiting,' the customer said, his tone making it clear that he wasn't sorry in the slightest. 'I was delayed by the most *tiresome* of men, yammering on about *meteorites*, of all things.'

The rogue trader cocked an eyebrow, but the customer brushed past him, angling right for the case on the table.

'So this is the treasure you told me about, is it?'
The man licked his lips, like a hungry lupine regarding a helpless lamb.

'Yes,' the rogue trader said, reaching over and unlatching the stays that held the case shut. 'Meteorites, did you say?'

The customer nodded, waving a hand in a dismissive gesture. 'He said that some classless low-hab dwellers on the far side claimed to have seen them coming down from the skies, if you can imagine.' He rubbed his hands together in undisguised glee, as the rogue trader removed the protective covering from the weapon, which was as long as a man was tall.

'Meteorites from the skies,' the rogue trader repeated, his single eye narrowing.

'I insisted that what they had seen was merely *weather*, which having been born and raised far from the outdoors they could never have hoped to recognize. But who listens to *me*, I ask you?'

The rogue trader nodded, absently, and removed the last of the protective covering, revealing the weapon in all its glory.

The customer reached a tentative hand out, but stopped with his fingertips only centimetres from the blade. He glanced at the rogue trader, expecting admonishment.

'May I…?' he asked, positively salivating.

The rogue trader nodded, making an expansive gesture. 'By all means, Your Excellency. Assuming, of course, that you authorise payment?'

'Oh, *that*,' the customer said, as though annoyed at the mention of such a triviality. 'Yes, all right, yes.'

He waved his hand at the data-slate the rogue trader produced, authorising the exchange of funds.

'In which case, it is yours,' the rogue trader said, bowing with a flourish.

'Oooh,' the man said, reaching out and touching the flat of the blade. Even powered-down, it still seemed to crackle with life.

'Now,' the rogue trader said, backing away towards the door, 'with your permission I'm afraid I must excuse myself.'

The customer looked up, faint annoyance flittering across his round face. 'So soon?'

'Yes,' the rogue trader answered. 'I'm sorry, but I have an urgent need to return to my ship.'

'Go, then,' the man said, waving the trader away with an imperious gesture.

The rogue trader started towards the door. He'd get his weapons back from the security personnel, get back to the spaceport, and get back to his ship before...

'Shame about the seed case, though,' the customer said, as the rogue trader was slipping out the door.

'Yes,' the rogue trader answered. 'But who knows? Perhaps you'll get another chance to get your hands on a tyranid again. Perhaps even sooner than you think.'

'Oh,' the customer said, rolling his eyes skyward, 'that I should *be* so lucky.'

The rogue trader slipped out the door, and as it hissed shut behind him, he allowed the mask of calm complacency he'd forced on his face to slip.

Meteorites from the skies, the rogue trader thought, already racing down the hallway to the exit.

Spores, more likely. Let the security drones *keep* his pistol and knives and holdout, he could always get more. He knew too well what came in the wake of things that fell from the sky, and he had no intention of lingering on Meridian a single moment longer than was necessary to see it for himself.

CHAPTER FOURTEEN

Sergeant Aramus stood alone at the centre of the empty sparring hall, wearing only a chiton, his arms and legs bare. Eyes closed, he moved through each of the stages of an attack routine, slowly, methodically. Strike, block, punch, kick, block, strike, block – exchanging blows with shadows, concentrating on the sensation of each movement, the pull of muscle over bone and the kiss of wind against bare skin.

The day had yet to begin, with more than an hour until the ship's complement would gather within the company chapel for morning prayer and contemplation. Once Chaplain Palmarius had completed the morning rites, and led the brethren in their daily oaths of loyalty to Chapter and Emperor, then Sergeant Aramus as Commander at Sail would address the brethren, issuing their orders and making any necessary announcements. And had any discipline been required, had any of the brethren, neophytes, or aspirants failed to follow the precepts of Chapter and Codex in the previous day, it would fall to Aramus to dispense summary punishments as required.

Aramus completed the attack routine, then shifted to a defensive rest posture before beginning another set.

With the prayers completed, the brethren would move to the ranges in the ship's armoury to begin the morning firing rites, honing their marksmanship, and then on to battle practice, if time permitted, before their arrival in the Meridian system.

Aramus began another attack routine, this one designed for close-quarters combat against multiple opponents. Starting slowly, he advanced through each of the motions, one after another, his speed increasing as he went. He sparred now with shadows on all sides, and with his eyes closed could almost *sense* the presence of his imaginary foes.

The sergeant began considering the morning's battle practice, his mind wandering as his body was put through its paces. He thought of the fifteen aspirants currently onboard the *Armageddon*, a dozen from Calderis and a further three from Typhon Primaris. Chapter protocols dictated that none of the fifteen could advance to the next stages of the rigorous indoctrination examinations until they had successfully completed – and, more importantly, *survived* – the Blood Trials. But the attacks of the orks on the desert world and the lurking tyranids on the jungle world had prevented the Blood Ravens from conducting their trials. And so, the aspirants onboard were still merely potential candidates, untried and untested in combat. Would it behove the Chapter for Aramus to conduct the Trials onboard the strike cruiser itself, he wondered? Should he do as Chaplain Palmarius had proposed, and bring the fifteen youths into the sparring hall, perhaps during the time set aside for battle practice, issue bladed weapons to each of them and then let the Blood Trials simply commence? Or would it be better to wait until the strike cruiser rejoined the rest of the fleet, and conduct the Blood Trials onboard the fortress-monastery *Scientia Est Potentia* instead?

With the Fifth Company taking such heavy losses in recent actions, it seemed almost criminal to delay even by a matter of days or weeks the induction of new initiates – despite the fact that they would not be ready for battle, even as neophyte Scouts, for years more to come.

Aramus was still grappling with the question, just as he grappled with the shadows on all sides, when his concentration was broken by the sound of the sparring hall's door opening and closing.

'Have you slept, brother-sergeant?' came the voice of Sergeant Thaddeus.

Eyes still closed, Aramus completed the attack routine. 'Some,' he answered. 'A brief while, perhaps.' He finished his routine, and slowly lowered his hands at his sides. Then, opening his eyes he looked in Thaddeus's direction. 'No, I suppose I haven't, at that.'

Thaddeus walked towards the centre of the sparring hall, like Aramus wearing only a blood-red chiton. 'I have not slept, either. Not since Calderis.'

Thanks to their catalepsean node, Space Marines did not truly need sleep, the implant enabling them to rest half of their brain for brief periods while maintaining awareness with the other half. But even vaunted Adeptus Astartes were required to succumb to the circadian rhythms of sleep from time to time, lest they suffer impaired efficiency, or even the onset of personality disorders. And while during the four hours per night in which he lay in a fugue he did not dream, as such, still a Space Marine could find it difficult to slumber if his mind still raced with the concerns of the day.

Occupied with thoughts of their mission, and of the responsibilities of his unanticipated rise in command, Aramus had found it difficult to still his mind sufficiently for his body to lapse into the fugue, and had instead come down to the sparring hall to find some other release for tensions.

Aramus crossed to the nearest wall, and pulled a towel from the railing. Wiping his face and neck dry of the sweat that grimed them, he took a deep breath, his respiration and heart-rate slowing to normal after his hours-long workout. 'Well, what troubles *your* sleep, Thaddeus?'

While Aramus leaned against the rail, Thaddeus began doing stretching exercises, limbering his muscle groups one at a time before beginning his own exercise regimen. 'Not troubled, perhaps,' Thaddeus answered. 'Haunted, one might say?'

'Haunted?' Aramus cocked a brow.

'When I close my eyes, I see the face of Renzo before me. Or Loew. Or Shar. Or Davit. Or any one of the other battle-brothers I've lost over my years as leader of Seventh Squad. I've lost four battle-brothers since Zalamis, more than the Seventh has ever lost in such a short span, at least under my tenure as squad leader, and I cannot help but wonder if the losses should not be laid at my feet. Have I failed them, in not having anticipated the dangers which cost them their lives? Had I been more alert, more attentive, might some of them – might *all* of them – yet live?'

Aramus was silent for a moment before answering. 'I can't help but remember something that Captain Thule told me once, before I was elevated to the command of Third Squad. He told me that command was no honour, but was instead simply another weight to bear.' Aramus called upon the Blood Ravens' fabled memory, which enabled him to recall anything he had experienced since becoming a Space Marine. '"Have faith in your Chapter, in your Emperor, and in your own strength,"' he quoted, '"and your life – and death – will have purpose." If that is true of ourselves – and I believe it is – then it is no less true of those we lead.'

Thaddeus nodded slowly. 'I know you are right,' he said, 'but still… the losses can be difficult to take.' He paused, shifting into a fighting stance, the initial posture of his shadow boxing manoeuvre. 'So when do we expect to reach the Meridian system?'

Aramus draped the towel around his neck. 'The Lord Principal reports that we should translate back into real space by day's end at the latest, perhaps as early as midday.'

Thaddeus struck the empty air with the heel of his palm, then spun around to deliver a roundhouse kick a dozen centimetres below that spot. 'Strange, isn't it?'

'Hmm?' Aramus raised an eyebrow.

'Returning to Meridian, that is.'

Aramus blinked slowly, remembering the planet of his birth, as well as he was able.

It was a strange irony that a Blood Raven could recall in great detail all that befell him since completing his initiating and becoming a full battle-brother, but that his memories of a time before joining the Chapter were often hazy and indistinct. Perhaps it was the aberration in the catalepsean node that was rumoured to be the cause of their eidetic memory that was likewise responsible for the haze that fell over their earlier memories. Perhaps in changing the way that new memories were stored in the mind of the Blood Raven, older memories were lost. It was symbolic, it always seemed to Aramus, of the forgotten memories of the Chapter itself, the Blood Ravens' own lost beginnings. It was fitting, perhaps, that the individual underwent much the same transformation as the Chapter itself, which now recorded its every action and undertaking in exquisite detail, and yet could not recall with any certainty whence it had come.

'It is strange, at that,' Aramus allowed. Neither of the two Space Marines had returned to the world of their birth since the completion of their own Blood Trials there, more than two decades before. And though they had come from different backgrounds – Aramus from the upper classes in the high-habs, Thaddeus a ganger from the low-hab levels – they had grown in the years that followed to accept one another as more than blood kin, but as fellow battle-brothers in the Blood Ravens Chapter.

'Stranger still to return to her in a time of such crisis,' Thaddeus said. 'I've visited countless worlds in my years of service to the Emperor and Chapter, knowing that any of them might fall before the enemy, if that were their fate. But to set out to do battle on our own homeworld, knowing that if we fail then the lives of everyone we once knew – friends, family, even enemies – would then be forfeit...'

'It does seem a heavier burden to bear, doesn't it?' Aramus thought of Sergeant Tarkus, willing to stay behind, to fight and die in the protection of doomed Typhon Primaris, to expunge his feelings of loss and guilt over the death of his own homeworld, Erinia. If Meridian were to be lost, as well, what price would Aramus and Thaddeus one day be required to pay? 'But as Captain Thule pointed out to me, we already carry a heavy burden as members of the Fated.' He paused, and gave Thaddeus a rueful grin. 'What is a little more weight, added to that already heavy load?'

THE MORNING FIRING rites had not yet concluded when the tremors running through the deckplates and the attendant psychic shock signalled that the *Armageddon* had transitioned from the immaterium back into normal space.

A short while later, Librarian Niven waited on the command deck for the Commander at Sail to arrive, a determined look on his face. Niven had been in conference with his junior when the strike cruiser had returned to real space, and as soon as they had cleared the warp both servants of the Librarium had perceived immediately what awaited them. The malevolence he had felt ever since Calderis, and which he had days ago identified as a tyranid hive mind, was even stronger here, the interference redoubled. But both Niven and Konan agreed that they could be no nearer to the hive fleet whose rough location had been triangulated from the two ships in orbit above Typhon Primaris, and if anything might even be farther now from the fleet than they had been before. So why was the interference so much stronger here, why was the malevolence so much more potent?

Sergeant Aramus strode onto the command deck, wearing his full power armour, the bolter at his side still warmed from the rounds fired on the armoury range.

Niven waited atop the command dais for the sergeant's approach, but when Aramus reached his side the Librarian did not pause for formalities but immediately began, all intensity.

'The shadow of a tyranid fleet has fallen over Aurelia,' Niven said, before Aramus had even had the chance to address him. 'Neither Lexicanium Konan nor I can make any astropathic contact outside the *Armageddon*, not even to the *Sword of Hadrian* or any of the other ships of the Aurelia Battlegroup. For reasons I've yet to uncover, the interference of the shadow in the warp is much greater here than elsewhere in the sub-sector, though we appear to be no nearer to the fleet itself.'

'Any suppositions, Librarian?' Aramus asked.

'None, I am ashamed to admit,' Niven answered. 'But be assured that neither Lexicanium Konan nor I will rest until we have divined an answer.'

Aramus nodded. 'Understood. Thank you, Librarian.'

Niven withdrew to the shadows at the command deck's edge, to gather his thoughts and extend his senses, while Aramus busied himself with the running of the ship. In only a matter of hours they would reach Meridian itself. Perhaps an answer would present itself to Niven by then.

ADVANCING AT SUBLIGHT speeds, the journey to the planet Meridian occupied most of the remainder of the day, and it was not until after the evening prayers that Sergeant Aramus summoned the squad leaders to the command deck for their briefing. The Chapter serfs who tended the command deck servitors reported that vox communication with the planet's surface was expected at any moment as the *Armageddon* came within range of the planet-side vox-casters.

Sergeants Avitus, Thaddeus, and Cyrus waited at the Commander at Sail's pleasure when a chime indicated that vox contact had been established, and the Chapter serfs brought word to the command dais that the governor of the sub-sector himself, Governor Vandis, was waiting on the vox-channel to communicate with Sergeant Aramus.

This was an extraordinary breach of protocol. For the governor of any Imperial world, much less an entire sub-sector, to make personal contact over unrestricted vox-channels was all but unheard of. Such officials were creatures of protocols and procedures, usually, who lurked at the centre of vast bureaucracies like immense spiders lounging at the eye of their webs. Either this Governor Vandis was himself extraordinary – which was possible, though vanishingly unlikely – or he found himself in circumstances requiring extraordinary responses.

'Space Marines vessel, this is Governor Vandis, Imperial Authority over the Aurelia Sub-sector. Please respond.'

Aramus glanced at the trio of Blood Ravens at his side. Cyrus's expression was unreadable, Avitus's annoyed, and Thaddeus's a mixture of curiosity and concern.

'This is Brother-Sergeant Aramus of the Blood Ravens Fifth Company, Commander at Sail of the strike cruiser *Armageddon*.' He paused, and then continued, 'We come to your world in…'

'We knew that you'd come, but hadn't *dreamt* it would be so quickly,' the governor interrupted, speaking rapidly. 'Well, *I* knew that you'd come, but some of my *inferiors* insisted that the message hadn't got through. But no matter. Now, how soon do you expect to be finished?'

Aramus, perplexed, raised an eyebrow. 'Finished? And forgive me, but what do you mean, you'd expected us?' Did the governor understand that he was addressing an Adeptus Astartes? Aramus could not recall when he'd been addressed by a normal human with such disregard for niceties, with such brazenness.

'Simple, of course,' Governor Vandis answered. 'I ordered that the call for assistance be sent, and here you are.'

Aramus exchanged a glance with Thaddeus, who shrugged in bafflement. 'Assistance regarding *what* precisely, governor?'

Over the vox-channel, they could hear the governor sighing, dramatically. 'Why, the *tyranids*, of course,' he answered, exasperated.

It HAD NOT proved easy, but in the end Aramus had been able to wring from the governor's report an accurate assessment of the state of affairs on the ground. It appeared that mycetic spores had rained down on the far side of the planet over the course of several days, a week or more before. Some days later, the first attacks were reported. At first the governor and his people had been unable to determine the nature of the attacks or the identity of the attackers, floating theories that it might be the forces of Chaos, whether cultists or actual warp-born daemonspawn, or perhaps even some entirely unknown xenos threat. But when a battalion of the Planetary Defence Forces was dispatched to deal with the matter, it was discovered that the attackers were, in fact, tyranids.

This discovery had, unfortunately, cost the lives of every soldier in that PDF battalion, none of whom survived the first encounter with the tyranids.

The governor had declared an immediate state of emergency, and ordered the planetary astropaths to send a general call for assistance to any Imperium forces in range. The governor had been less than pleased, of course, at the inability of his people to make contact with Fleet Admiral Forbes's flagship, or any of the other vessels of the Aurelia Battlegroup.

The fact that the other two ships of the Aurelia Battlegroup, heavily laden with refugees from Calderis, had failed to reach Meridian as yet was suggestive that something untoward might have befallen them. But since they might have fallen afoul of anything from an attack by spacefaring elements of Gorgrim's horde, to spaceborn offspring of the Great Devourer, or even something as prosaic as the treacherous topologies of warp space, there was little to be gained by worrying about their ultimate fate at this point.

Aramus found it difficult to impress upon Governor Vandis that his people had been right, and that there *were* no communications possible in or out of the Aurelia sub-sector at present. And Aramus likewise found it all but impossible to impress upon Vandis the severity of the threat now facing his world.

Governor Vandis was one of those who had never faced danger first hand. He had heard of the myriad threats to the Imperium, of course, but even having risen in the Imperial bureaucracy to such an elevated post, he had not experienced any of those threats himself. And like one who sees endless images of distant horrors which have never once been visited on him, Vandis had like so many others become inured to the dangers surrounding him on all sides. While he probably was in possession of more *facts* about threats xenos and otherwise than the average hab-dweller on Meridian, he did not *comprehend* what those facts portended, and did not *feel* the terror he should have felt.

It was clear, though, from reading between the governor's words, that the threat was far graver than

Vandis had even imagined. The infestation of Meridian had already begun, and had been allowed to proceed unchecked for more than a week.

Meridian was not a dead world yet, but it had already begun dying. Unless something was done, and soon, it would only be a matter of time.

SERGEANT ARAMUS SURVEYED the squads mustered in the launch bay of the *Armageddon*, as servitors completed the final preparations on the trio of Thunderhawks. At any moment, when the gunships were finished and prepared for take off, Aramus would order the Blood Ravens to load up, and they would descend like lightning bolts on the planet below. He had spent the final hour of their approach to Meridian surveying what they knew of the geography and layout, and taking long-range orbital scans of the planet's surface, identifying locations of densest enemy infestation. With inputs from the other sergeants, Aramus had devised a mission plan that would make the most of their relatively sparse resources, while at the same time producing the greatest results.

The sergeants had not been unanimous in their support of Aramus's plans. The others, Sergeant Cyrus in particular, had not been pleased by his proposal regarding the use of the fifteen aspirants. The youths were even now spending their final moments before the onset of the evening rest period in study with Chaplain Palmarius, but after they awoke when the morning came, they would find even greater tests awaiting them.

But of all the sergeants, Avitus was the most outspoken in his objections to Aramus's plans. Even now, he wore a look of extreme displeasure on his grizzled face, and when Aramus looked his direction, Avitus did not avert his eyes, but raised his chin and spoke. 'It is a waste of manpower and munitions, Aramus, I say it again.'

'Your opinion has been expressed and noted, Avitus,' Aramus replied, his tone level.

'But not understood, it seems,' Avitus said. He paused, and then added, '*Sir*.'

Aramus narrowed his eyes. 'In deference to your years of service, sergeant, I'll grant you one chance to rephrase that.'

Avitus bristled. 'Your pardon,' he said, making the apology sound like a curse. 'But I'll say again that we could get greater and more immediate results if we discarded concerns about collateral damage...'

Aramus held up his hand. 'Let's not use euphemisms, sergeant. You're saying, rather, that we could kill the tyranids faster and easier if we didn't mind killing a few million innocent civilians in the process. Isn't that it?'

'Yes,' Avitus answered without hesitation, his expression grim. 'If it means striking a blow at the hive fleet, then any cost is worth paying.'

'But if we don't protect the innocent,' Thaddeus put in, stepping forward, eyes flashing with barely controlled anger, 'then just what is it we *are* protecting?'

'The Imperium!' Avitus roared in reply. 'We serve the Emperor, not these mewling maggots!'

'Enough!' Aramus shouted, stepping between the two, who looked about to come to blows. 'Enough. Now, I am *not* prepared to abandon the human inhabitants of the planet below us to their fate. We serve the Imperium, and we protect the Emperor's subjects, and that means that we will stand and fight in the defence of Meridian whatever the cost, whatever the odds.'

'If we only had more Space Marines...' Sergeant Cyrus began.

'But we don't,' Aramus said quickly, cutting him off. 'Unless and until we can pierce the shadow in the warp cast by the tyranid fleet, we're on our own.'

'Actually,' interrupted the voice of Librarian Niven, who called to them from the far side of the launch bay. He walked towards them quickly, with Lexicanium Konan following in his wake. 'That may not necessarily be the case.'

CHAPTER FIFTEEN

Brother-Sergeant Aramus and the other five members of Third Squad were arranged in a defensive posture, surveying the area around them as the Thunderhawk rumbled up into the grey Meridian sky, bound for its next landing site. Assuming that the Third Squad was able to accomplish their revised mission goals here, Aramus and the others would proceed to the planet's capital city, Zenith, located on the far side of the world, using whatever transport was available to them. Assuming, of course, that any of them survived.

Librarian Niven's revelation in the final moments before the Thunderhawks departed for planetfall had not affected the missions assigned to the other squads, but it had at least imparted to those plans the faint sense of hope, that their mission objectives might, in the end, actually be accomplishable. The success of all their actions, though, now rested on the shoulders of Sergeant Aramus and the rest of Third Squad.

'Nothing on auspex yet, sergeant,' Battle-Brother Voire reported.

'Keep scanning,' Aramus replied. 'We'll fan out and proceed to the north, but I want everyone to remain within line of sight of the Space Marine to either side of them, and for no one to drift outside of vocal range. Understood?'

The other Blood Ravens acknowledged.

'Then let's move out.'

Aramus knew that Niven had been troubled by the presence of the tyranid hive mind in the Aurelia system, and the Librarian had made mention of the fact that he was unsure why the interference due to the hive fleet's shadow in the warp would be so much stronger here in the Meridian system, ostensibly at a greater remove from the fleet itself than the *Armageddon* had previously been. It wasn't until the strike cruiser came in close approach to the planet Meridian itself, though, that Niven had been able to work out the cause of the discrepancy.

'The vanguard creatures are somewhere in this vicinity, if our intelligence is correct,' Aramus called out to the other Space Marines as they moved steadily towards the north. Their projections had been unable to pinpoint the exact location of the creatures, but they had been able to narrow it to somewhere in this strip of verdant green, one of the sheltered park zones that dotted the face of the planet. 'Keep your eyes and ears open for any sign of movement, and shoot anything that moves.'

Librarian Niven had explained that the hive mind of the tyranid fleet was being reinforced by ground-based tyranid vanguard creatures, specialized variants of the zoanthrope type; brains who acted in concert to extend the shadow in the warp, strengthening the interference. With the fleet so far removed from Meridian, there was no other explanation for the fact that the shadow should fall so far. Niven realised only now that the zoanthropes glimpsed on Typhon Primaris must have been fulfilling a similar role, but knew that the jungle world was already too far gone for the knowledge to have done the Blood Ravens any good.

On Meridian, though, with the infestation still in its early stages, there was still cause for hope. If the vanguard creatures could be located and eliminated, then the interference caused by the shadow in the warp would be lessened, perhaps sufficiently for the *Armageddon* to get an astropathic call out to Blood Ravens elements outside the Aurelia sub-sector. If contact could be made, then reinforcements could be requested, and once they arrived Meridian might still be saved. It was too late for Typhon Primaris, but perhaps if additional Blood Ravens forces arrived in time then no other world in the Aurelia sub-sector needed share the doomed jungle world's fate.

If Aramus and his squad failed, then the only hope that Meridian had was that Admiral Forbes and the Aurelia Battlegroup might be able to cut off the interference at the source, taking the fight to the hive fleet itself. But it was, at best, a distant hope that the *Sword of Hadrian* would be able to survive even the approach to the fleet, much less be victorious in combat against whatever forces protected the tyranid hive mind.

'Sergeant Aramus,' called Battle-Brother Siddig, who had taken up the far left flank position of their formation. 'I may have spotted something.'

Aramus swept his bolter around, eyes narrowed behind his helmet's protective visor.

The grass underfoot was lush and verdant, and the trees and hedges that marched from one side of the immense garden zone to the other in their serried ranks were in full leaf, emerald bright. In inclement weather a force shield extended from atop the walls of the zone, sheltering the plants within, but when the sun shone and the winds died down, the garden zone was open to the grey skies above, to absorb as much sunlight as possible. It must have been a sunny, cloudless day when the mycetic spores of the tyranid invasion drifted down from above, settling here in this little spot of green and taking root. With so much organic material at hand, the spores would have reproduced and grown at an alarming rate, perhaps explaining why this garden appeared to serve as one of the key loci of the invasion.

The hedge in front of which Brother Siddig had halted began to shake, the leaves rustling.

'Something is moving within,' Siddig said in a low voice.

Then the branches suddenly parted and something shot forward, moving almost too quickly to see, with whirring blades in the air.

'Contact!' Siddig shouted, and he, Voire, and a few of the others immediately unleashed a torrent of bolter rounds towards the object.

'Cease fire!' Aramus barked, holding up his fist.

The bolters fell silent, and Aramus strode forward to inspect the carnage.

'A gardening servitor,' he said, nudging the ruined man-machine with the tip of his boot, leaking blood and oil out on the verdant grass. The blades affixed to its arms still clipped and clacked, but would never trim another hedge.

'Sorry, sir,' Siddig said, shamefaced.

'No reason to apologise, Brother,' Aramus said. 'In a contest such as this, better to react too quickly than not at all.' He turned to the others. 'The servitors won't be programmed to notice our presence, so if you're about to have your limbs trimmed or your head pruned off' – he kicked at the still clattering blades of the servitor, each as long and as wickedly sharp as any combat knife – 'don't hesitate to put them down.'

The other Blood Ravens nodded their assent.

'Then let's move out. They're in here somewhere, and it falls to us to find them.'

GOVERNOR VANDIS LOOKED at Sergeant Cyrus and the five Scouts who accompanied him, displeasure evident on his round face. 'I understood that Space Marines were to come to our defence,' the governor said, his tone nasal and almost petulant. He narrowed his eyes, taking in Cyrus's windblown hair and battered scout gear. 'Where is your commander?'

Cyrus straightened, but long years of training restrained him from uttering the first responses that popped into his thoughts. 'I am Sergeant Cyrus of the Blood Ravens Tenth Company, seconded to Captain Davian Thule's Fifth and currently under the direct command of Sergeant Aramus. My Scouts and I have been tasked with reinforcing the defences of Zenith, and with liaising with the Meridian Planetary Defence Forces.'

Vandis waved a hand in Cyrus's direction, as though shooing away a fly. 'I requested *Space Marines*, not Scouts.' He glanced back at the functionaries who had accompanied him to the landing pad, seeking approval. One or two of the functionaries nodded eagerly, but most of them cast worried looks in Cyrus's direction, obviously fearing reprisal.

Cyrus took a single step forward, towering over the governor. 'I am a battle-brother of the Adeptus Astartes, *Excellency*, and have served Chapter and Emperor for the better part of two centuries. And these' – he indicated the five Scouts who stood with him – 'are neophytes of the Blood Ravens Chapter, already blooded and tested in combat and trained in the arts of planetary defence, and they *will* have your respect.'

The governor blanched, unconsciously taking a step backwards, craning his neck to look up and meet Cyrus's smouldering gaze. 'I... that is... but...'

Cyrus held up a hand, palm forward, silencing him. 'We go now to inspect the capital's defences. Have the divisional commanders of the PDF mustered and ready for briefing when we return.'

'But...' the governor began, but Cyrus ignored him and turned away to face the Scouts.

'Watral, you're with me. We'll survey the city perimeter from due west to north-north-east. Tubach and Muren, you're team two, and have north-north-east to south-east, and Jutan and Xenakis are team three with south-east to due west. Mark any defensible positions, any weak points, and any potential barricades. Maintain vox contact at all times, and report back here at 1800 hours. Questions?'

The Scouts shook their heads.

'Then let's get moving.'

With that, the six Blood Ravens split up and moved out at high speed, leaving the governor and his retinue standing alone on the landing pad.

'I shall lodge a complaint,' Governor Vandis said, turning and heading back towards the steps leading back down into the governor's palace. 'See if I don't.'

Behind him, the other members of his retinue exchanged worried glances, but kept their mouths shut.

THADDEUS LOOKED OUT the window as Thunderhawk Two rumbled over the towers and spires of Zenith. Somewhere far below, deep underground, were the darkened, murky warrens of the underhive where he'd spent his formative years, running with the other members of the Lower 40th Ward Riot Boys. He'd killed a man before he'd reached the age of eleven – in self-defence, but the blood was on his hands, all the same – but all these years later he found it difficult to bring the dead man's face to mind. Just as he sometimes found it difficult to remember the sound of his mother's voice, or the cloying stench of the rotgut 'amasec' his father used to drink. But he could remember every wrinkle, scar, and line on the face of every battle-brother who'd been lost these last years, the curse of the Blood Ravens' vaunted memory. Seeing the once familiar and now strange skyline of his home-hab only served to remind him of what he could never remember, and the things he could never forget.

Thaddeus turned away from the window, concentrating on the mission at hand.

They'd just set down atop the governor's palace, to drop off Sergeant Cyrus and his Scout squad, and now Thaddeus and the rest of Seventh Squad were bound for a point some several thousand kilometres to the east. Zenith had been constructed at the point where the planet's equator intersected with the meridian which divided the western and eastern hemispheres – and which gave the planet its name. The first tyranid incursions had been reported on the far side of the world, at the antipodes from Zenith, where the meridian divided east from west. That was where Sergeant Aramus and Third Squad were now, trying to root out the source of the interference which blanketed the entire solar system. But the infestation had already spread thousands of miles, with reports of tyranid sightings in habs, hives, and factories all across the eastern hemisphere. By the Blood Ravens' best estimations, the tyranid reach now extended halfway across the eastern hemisphere towards Zenith, and unless checked in short order, the infestation would swell to consume the capital city itself.

Cyrus and his Scouts had been tasked with preparing the city for the incursion, and Avitus and his

Devastator squad were on their way even now to implement measures to slow the tyranid advance, but in the meantime every effort needed to be made to try to halt the advance altogether. And that task fell on the shoulders of Thaddeus and the Seventh.

The rank and file of a tyranid invasion fleet were mindless creatures, without any independent thought or will of their own. It was only with the guiding influence of the collective minds which directed their movements that the tyranids were any threat at all. Without the beasts who relayed the synapse commands of the hive mind to the lesser forms, the tyranids would be nothing more than mindless beasts, lacking even the appetites and instincts that now drove them.

The synapse beasts that Thaddeus's squad would seek were zoanthropes, close cousins to the vanguard creatures who it was believed were responsible for the blanketing interference of the shadow in the warp. Unlike the vanguard creatures, though, zoanthropes whose psychic potential was geared entirely towards promulgating the warp shadow, the zoanthropes that Thaddeus sought were intended for the battlefield. They possessed not only the power to direct the movements of their hive siblings, but also the ability to fight their enemy directly with claws, teeth, and awesome psychic powers.

'Coming down,' called Battle-Brother Takayo from the commands of the gunship. 'We should touch down in another two minutes, Thaddeus.'

'You heard him, squad,' Thaddeus said, racking his bolt pistol and holstering it at his side. As they emptied out of the Thunderhawk they would don their heavy jump packs, which would allow them to cover ground much faster than they could on foot. 'Be ready.'

The other four Blood Ravens in the transport compartment nodded, checking the action of their own pistols, and loosening their chainswords in their sheaths.

'Knowledge is power…' Thaddeus said in a quiet voice, trying to remember how to forget.

'…GUARD IT WELL!' Sergeant Avitus shouted, completing the Blood Ravens' battle cry as he lobbed another incendiary into the trench cut by Battle-Brother Gagan's meltagun. Already the structures on either side of the trench were licked by tongues of flame, but they had kilometres more work to do before they could move on to their next position, and there was no time to lose.

The fire-bomb went up in a miniature inferno, taking another section of wall with it, but things were still progressing far too slowly for Avitus's taste.

'Dow!' he called to the battle-brother who stood atop the roof of the storage facility a few dozen metres away. 'Target those buildings and fire,' Avitus snarled.

'Right, sir,' Dow said, and fired a ribbon of burning plasma from his gun at the buildings before them.

They'd had no sign of the enemy, and the lack of engagement was wearing on Avitus's nerves. Destroying a few hundred square kilometres of farm and industrial zones served to improve his mood slightly, but it wasn't enough.

'Eyes open, squad,' Avitus said, lobbing another fire-bomb into the gouge carved out by Dow's plasma beam. 'I don't want to be caught napping.'

From the intelligence they'd received, Avitus knew that there were no tyranids within a hundred kilometres of here. But the tyranids to the east of them were advancing on their position quickly, and if it took them another day to close the distance then Avitus would have been surprised. But there was nothing to be gained from being lax, either way.

Some of the inhabitants, hearing reports of the xenos activity to the east, had already fled west toward Zenith, abandoning hive and hab as they sought refugee in the soaring towers of the capital city. The first zone that the Ninth Squad had come to torch had been a farming region, with huge vats of algae and enzymes in culture that could then be reconstituted into the foodstuffs consumed by the lower-hab dwellers of the planet, those who couldn't afford organic foodstuffs imported from off-world. The algae vats were sickly green, repulsive in appearance and even worse in smell, but the worst thing about them was that they were raw, easily processed biomass, such as the tyranids thrived upon. If the vats were still standing when the ripper swarms of the invading tyranids arrived, they would be able to consume it in an eye-blink, preparing it immediately for conversion into yet more tyranids.

Avitus and his Devastator squad had been given the task of removing this asset from the enemy's path. That is, they had been instructed to burn the whole thing to dust. And not just the farm zone itself, but all the buildings and structures surrounding it, kilometres deep and hundreds of kilometres across. Just as firefighters would create a firebreak – cutting down all the trees in the path of a wildfire, employing the axe to spare them the flames – so too did the Blood Ravens have to destroy at times in order to preserve. And there were no Blood Ravens better suited to destruction than a Devastator squad, and no Devastators more qualified for the task than Avitus's Ninth.

Those inhabitants of the area who had not yet fled had, initially, been less than sanguine about the prospect of Imperial forces destroying their homes, their workplaces, everything they had ever known. They had stubbornly refused to accept that the safety of others' homes was worth the sacrifice of their own. Of course, though Avitus had been tempted to rip a few of the dissenters to pieces with his heavy bolter, Sergeant Aramus had ordered in no uncertain terms that the human inhabitants of Meridian were to be safeguarded, whatever the costs. And Aramus would, doubtless, have taken umbrage at Avitus mowing down a few innocent civilians simply in order to make his case with the civilians he *didn't* shoot.

Still, Avitus was not one to coddle, and barred from opening fire on the civilians, he'd simply repeated his order for them to vacate, giving them to the count of one hundred before the Ninth Squad opened fire. If any of the bleating civilians were still in harm's way when the first plasma and melta shots fired the area, it was only because they had refused to listen.

There was no enemy to fire upon… yet. But Avitus had so far managed to keep his temper in check by releasing any frustration he felt on the buildings.

'Knowledge is power!' he shouted, firing his heavy bolter into the bulk of a burning building, watching the flames dance across the green-scummed waters of an algae tank as the liquid accelerants spread. A battle cry issued against standing buildings hardly seemed in the tradition of the Blood Ravens, but it was better than nothing. 'Guard it well!'

CHAPTER SIXTEEN

ONBOARD THE ARMAGEDDON, Apothecary Gordian stepped back from the platform at the centre of the Apothecarion, waiting for any sign of results. The medicae servitor had already trundled off, the latest dose having been administered to the soft flesh of Captain Thule's neck.

The captain's skin was mottled and wan, his complexion sallow and cheeks sunken. The tyranid toxins that had coursed through his system had done considerable harm to his bodily functions, and though periodic stints in the sarcophagus had slowed the advance of the deterioration, the damage was still extensive.

'Report,' Gordian said, almost hesitantly, addressing the servitors which governed the probes and sensors mounted on the platform itself. They bathed the captain's prostrate form with active scans on a wide spectrum, gauging his body's internal and external temperatures, heart and respiration rates, and so on.

This latest antitoxin trial would be the last that Gordian would attempt. If the Omega-Five strain failed to affect the levels of toxins in Thule's system, the captain would be returned to the sarcophagus for the remainder of the undertaking, perhaps indefinitely.

The servitors began to squeal, reeling off the captain's vital signs in binary form.

It was not unheard of for Space Marines to remain in sarcophagi for extended periods. It was told in the pages of the holy text, *Apocrypha Azariah: Travails of Vidya*, that the Great Father Azariah Vidya had been mortally wounded in a terrible battle against the unclean powers, and that enshrined in the hallowed confines of a sarcophagus had floated freely through the black void of space for many decades before finally being recovered by the *Ravenous Spirit*, strike cruiser of the Commander of the Watch.

But wounded as he had been, in body and spirit, Great Father Vidya had not been poisoned by tyranid toxins, his oolitic kidney rendered unable to filter the poisons from his body, Gordian was quick to recall.

The servitors concluded their recitation of the captain's vitals, and Gordian stood stock still.

Had he misheard? Had the servitors just reported the values he *thought* he'd heard?

'Repeat, and elaborate,' Gordian ordered, taking a cautious step towards the platform, his gaze running up and down the length of Captain Thule's weathered form.

The servitors completed their more detailed recitation of the captain's state.

Gordian *had* heard correctly. The toxicity of the captain's blood *was* decreasing.

The Apothecary resisted the urge to utter a prayer of thanks, and instead bent to test the elasticity and tension of the captain's skin with his fingertips. Yes, it was clear now, there were definite signs of improvement.

If antitoxin trial Omega-Five was indeed the elixir for which he'd been searching all these long hours, then there was still a slim hope for Captain Thule. Spared the confines of the sarcophagus, it was just possible that Thule's body might be able to repair itself. But it was still far from certain. Even with the toxins gradually purged from Thule's body, his injuries, internal and external, were still extreme. And it remained to be seen whether the captain's body could heal itself, after all.

There was nothing to do now but wait, and pray.

SERGEANT THADDEUS AND the rest of Seventh Squad made their way down the thoroughfare, eyes watching every shadow. The habs rose on either side of them like mountains of steel-reinforced rockcrete, towering so high that had the thoroughfare not run directly east to west, it was likely that no light would have reached the ground where they walked. As it was, long shadows stretched out as the sun dipped slowly in the west, a sickly white orb in a gun-metal grey sky.

Somewhere just up ahead, Thaddeus knew, the front line of the advancing tyranid forces would be found. Likely it would be lictors who ranged in front, seeking out pockets of enemy resistance, or else locating native life forms that could be easily absorbed by the ripper swarms who followed them. Or perhaps one of the strains of gaunt broods, individually less of a threat than the larger forms, but in their teeming swarms a threat not to be taken lightly. Or perhaps they might encounter gargoyles, taking to the skies on leathery wings, or raveners, slithering like snakes on their serpent-like tails. Worse still would be a biovore, giant war beasts who carried countless spore mines within their very bodies; or one of the largest tyranids of them all, the carnifex, massive engines of destruction as large as any Imperial tank.

But all of them, from the ripper swarms to the mighty carnifex, took their direction from the zoanthrope, who passed along the synapse commands of the hive mind. It was a rare tyranid – like the tyrants and the warriors – who shared its own direct link with the hive mind. The other sibling creatures were ultimately and completely dependent on the psychic resonance of creatures like the zoanthrope. If the zoanthropes were removed from the field of battle, the number of effective combatants among the tyranids would drop precipitously. Tyranid tyrants could still operate on their own, of course, and tyranid warriors could act as psychic resonators on a smaller scale, effectively 'leading' sibling creatures in close range around them, but the rank and file of the tyranid invasion would be incapacitated.

It was unlikely that Seventh Squad would be so lucky as to encounter the zoanthropes first, however, and so the mission plans called for Thaddeus and his squad to punch through the tyranid front lines, pushing deep into enemy-held territory until they located one of the synapse-beasts. Having located one, they would then put it down in the most expedient – and final – way possible, allowing no possibility that the zoanthrope might survive the encounter and continue to function, even in a diminished capacity. And having taken one zoanthrope off the board, they were to continue the operation, searching for another, and another, and another.

Thaddeus, who had so often gone into battle with a grin on his lips, now faced the shadows which lined the deserted thoroughfare with his expression hard and set, his mouth drawn into a line. There was no joy in this action for him, no exultation that he could hope to find in accomplishing a mission. Even if the Seventh Squad succeeded beyond all expectations, and managed to bring down not just one but *all* of the zoanthropes, eliminating the combat-readiness of a majority of the tyranid life-forms on Meridian, the small percentage that still remained would likely still number in the untold thousands, and would still constitute a threat beyond anything that the few dozen Blood Ravens on the planet could hope to stand against.

It was only when taking the missions of the other squads into account that the actions of Seventh Squad had any hope for success. Only if each of the teams accomplished their mission objectives might

Meridian have any hope of survival, and even that hope was a slim one.

As the shadows lengthened before them, a chittering could be heard from beyond the curve of the hab ahead and to their right.

Thaddeus held up his hand in a fist, signalling to the others to halt, but it hadn't been necessary. They'd all heard the sound, and knew all too well what it presaged.

'Brandt, Marr,' Thaddeus voxed to the two Blood Ravens nearest him, his voice scarcely above a whisper. The runes on the inside of Thaddeus's visor flashed green for both of them, signalling that they were listening. 'I want to know what we're walking into, and that means we need aerial. You two hop one hundred metres ahead' – Thaddeus pointed with the barrel of his bolt pistol to the intersection that lay ahead of them, where the thoroughfare met another running north-south – 'with Marr covering left, Brandt right. If you see anything, shoot it. We'll move ahead while you're airborne to give cover for your descent.'

Again the runes flashed green and the two Blood Ravens drew their chainswords, and with the blades whirring in one fist and their bolt pistols in the other, they activated the controls on their jump packs and launched themselves skyward.

'The rest of you advance on my mark,' Thaddeus voxed to the others. 'Takayo and Skander, cover the left approach. Kell, you're with me on the right.'

Three runes flashed green.

Overhead, the two Blood Ravens on their jump packs were about to clear the obstructing habs and get their first glimpse of what lay beyond.

'Mark!' Thaddeus shouted, and drawing his chainsword raced forward towards the intersection.

Far overhead and ahead of them, Brandt opened fire with his bolt pistol, pouring hellfire rounds down. 'I've got lictors,' he voxed, as calm and collected as ever.

To the left, Marr was also firing, and somewhat more agitated than his battle-brother replied, 'And I've got gaunts.'

As Thaddeus and the others pounded across the ferrocrete and into the open, the tyranids rushed out to meet them, dozens of the monsters on either side. It was a riot of scything talons, rending claws, spine-fists and fleshborers, with snapping maws and feeder tendrils lashing the air, hungry to bite into the flesh of their prey.

Lictors and gaunts, then. It wasn't zoanthropes, but it was a start.

Chainsword met talon and claw as the Blood Ravens clashed with the onrushing tyranids, and the battle was on.

IN THE CAPITAL city Zenith, Sergeant Cyrus addressed the mustered ranks of the Planetary Defence Forces, who looked at the Blood Raven with expressions comingling admiration, respect, and fear. Unlike the planetary governor, who appeared so wrapped up in his own skewed view of reality that he was unable to recognize the real threats before him, the soldiers of the PDF were well aware of the gravity of their situation, and how ill-prepared they were to deal with it.

'Now,' Cyrus was saying, 'as far as munitions are concerned, in an ideal universe you'd all be kitted out with hellfire rounds. But I don't have to tell any of you that this universe is far, far from ideal.'

There were several hundred soldiers massed in the pavilion, facing the dais upon which Cyrus stood. The five Scouts of Cyrus's Squad stood on either side of their sergeant, bolt pistols and sniper rifles holstered and slung but in evidence.

One of the soldiers towards the front of the rank, whose insignia marked him as a lieutenant, raised his hand. When Cyrus nodded in his direction, the lieutenant said, 'Hellfire rounds?'

Cyrus nodded. 'Special rounds developed in the early days of the Tyrannic Wars. You take out the core of a bolter round, replace it with thousands of needles full of mutagenic acid encased in a ceramic shell. The round is armour-piercing, just like a standard-issue bolt round, but instead of exploding on impact, the hellfire bleeds the acid inside the target's body, eating it from the inside out.'

Some of the soldiers exchanged glances, nodding appreciatively, while others whistled low, imagining the kind of carnage the sergeant was describing. It was clear that some were even entertaining optimism, having discovered that the Space Marines had developed weapons specially suited to deal with the xenos monsters now invading their world.

'Don't get too excited about it,' Cyrus went on, 'because, as I say, this isn't an ideal universe. Our munitions were already strained after our action against the tyranid on Typhon Primaris, and we've got barely enough hellfire rounds to outfit the Blood Ravens on the ground. But even if we *did* have the rounds to spare, we wouldn't be able to adapt them for use in your autoguns as thrown slugs.'

The expressions on the soldiers' faces showed that the momentary optimism they'd shared was quickly fading.

'Most of you are armed with lasguns. Standard M-G short pattern models, looks like. Now, a single blast from a lasgun isn't likely to do much damage to a tyranid's shell, but pour enough massed fire on and eventually it'll punch through. Any heavy weaponry you've got will just make matters that much simpler. Of course, you've got to know *where* to direct your fire.'

Cyrus paused, casting his glance over the assembled soldiers.

'The Adeptus Astartes have developed whole libraries full of tactics and strategies for dealing with tyranids, but in the end it all boils down to one simple rule: shoot the big ones. Most of the rank and file of a tyranid army are mindless drones, controlled by the bigger brains of the larger creatures. If you can survive long enough to put down one of the big brains, you'll stand a much better chance of staying alive to keep shooting. Once the brain beasts are down, the rest of them will be striking out blindly, without reason or instinct, and are as likely to turn on each other as on you. Pick them off as you can, but always try to keep your distance. Tyranids of all kinds are deadly in close combat, so you're best advised to employ ranged attacks from a safe distance whenever possible.'

The sergeant looked from one side of the room to the other, to see if his words had sunk in.

'Now, are there any questions or requests for clarification?'

A dozen hands shot up.

Cyrus sighed. After decade upon decade of training neophytes of the Blood Ravens Chapter, who took years to grasp the essentials of Codex combat doctrine, he should have expected no better of planet-based infantry. They'd had little experience with anything more threatening than gangers and the occasional riot. How could they be expected to take on board all that a xenos threat like the tyranid entailed? He resisted the urge to find their requests for information a nuisance. After all, every bit of information they absorbed only improved the chances of any of them surviving the first few minutes of their initial encounter with a tyranid.

'Very well,' Cyrus said, as patiently as he could manage, 'let's take it again from the beginning…'

THE SUN HAD disappeared behind the trees to the west, and Sergeant Aramus and the rest of Third Squad moved through the garden zone in the deepening twilight. It had been early morning when they'd unloaded from the Thunderhawk, and in the time since the gunship had lifted off once more they'd covered more than two-thirds of the sprawling greenery, a miniature and well-manicured forest large enough to hide a hundred armoured tanks. So far they'd encountered only foliage and the innumerable gardening servitors which kept the greens meticulously maintained, with no sign yet of the tyranid zoanthropes they'd come in search of. But there was ample evidence of the tyranid presence, for all of that.

'There's another one,' Brother Cirrac said, raising his bolter.

'Shoot it down,' Aramus ordered, and kept moving through the gloom as Cirrac's bolter spat death at the tiny furred creature.

Any animal life native to Meridian had long gone extinct, centuries or millennia before when the Imperium of Man first colonized the planet. But the high-hab nobles who occasionally visited the garden zones liked the illusion of nature that the trees and hedges provided, which was improved by the introduction of various birds, mammals, lizards, amphibians, and fish, that could have been found in a more pristine and less despoiled world. These had been imported from other worlds at considerable cost, and stocked in the garden zones as ornaments to the greenery.

As they'd progressed through the zone, Aramus's squad had found increasing numbers of birds and small mammals who exhibited all the symptoms of advanced mycetic poisoning, either clinging with their last tenacious strength to the branches overhead or already lying sprawled on the garden paths underfoot. And many of the trees and hedges themselves, too, were in advanced stages of mycetic infestation, and here and there the native greenery had already been supplanted by xenos interlopers – loathsome red creepers, clinging mosses, grasping alien fronds. As they moved ever deeper into the garden, the greens had given way to alien hues – sickly yellows and raw-wound reds.

Aramus remembered visiting a garden zone like this one when he had still been a boy, at his parents' side. With his hazy memory of those childhood days, he couldn't recall whether this was the same garden zone, or whether it was another that was as much like this as to be identical. But even so, he recalled the sight of the deep, lush greenery, could remember the scent of the myriad living things all around them. It had been the first time that Aramus had seen more than a handful of living plants in a single place, much less surrounding him on all sides, and it had felt at that young age as though he'd stepped from the real world he knew into some otherworldly existence.

Though he'd known that the garden extended only so far in any direction, bounded by high, impassable walls of adamantium and ferrocrete, in the shaded seclusion of a small clearing ringed by mighty oaks he could easily imagine himself in some forest primeval from the dawn of time. Might primitive warriors, from an age before mankind ever ventured past the confines of Holy Terra's gravity well, lurk somewhere just beyond the next line of trees, ready to fight any monsters that lurked in the shadows? If he just closed his eyes, the young Aramus had imagined, he might well be able to will himself back to such a wild and reckless time, there to see adventure, excitement, and glory.

Now, with the benefit of age and experience, to say nothing of two decades' service to Chapter and Emperor, Aramus found cause to regret those childhood fantasies. There were not primitive warriors from ancient Terra beyond the trees ahead, perhaps, but there *were* inhuman creatures who eclipsed the tepid monsters of his childish imaginings.

Inhuman creatures bent on the destruction of all life on the world, and with only Aramus and the other Blood Ravens to stand in their way.

The sergeant's reveries were interrupted by a ping from his hand-held auspex.

There was movement ahead. And if its mass was any indication, it was no gardening servitor or poisoned squirrel.

'Tighten up,' Aramus voxed to the squad, crouching low. As the others clustered around him, the sergeant pointed to the stand of trees beyond which his auspex had detected motion. 'Zach, scout ahead, but try to keep out of sight.'

The battle-brother flashed his acknowledgement and then crept forward, keeping low to the ground. He stopped a few metres from the stand of trees

'I've got visual,' he voxed back.

Aramus nodded, and tucked his auspex away. 'What can you see?'

'It's difficult to tell through the trees,' Zach answered, 'but one thing's for sure. They're tyranid.'

'Acknowledged,' Aramus answered. He rose up from his crouch, still bent low to the ground. 'You heard him, squad. Either these are the zoanthropes we're after, or they're the tyranids we've got to tear through before we get to them. Either way, here's what we're going to do. Voire and Siddig, flank left. Cirrac and Isek, flank right. Zach, you're with me right up the middle. On my mark break through the trees and open fire on anything that moves. Copy?'

Five runes flashed green in agreement.

'Then let's move out.'

As one, the six Blood Ravens crashed through the trees, bolters raised and ready to fire.

There, in the midst of a small clearing, just like the one in which the young Aramus had dreamt of adventure and glory all those years before, hovered a trio of monsters. Their heads were oversized, monstrously large, their bodies diminutive and withered underneath, and rather than standing upon leg or limb, they levitated in midair, testament to their psychic prowess. The three tyranids faced one another, their eyeless gaze directed within, and they seemed to take no notice of the interloping Space Marines.

Even an individual with a low psychic quotient like Aramus could not fail to detect the buzz of psyker activity crackling all around them. Perhaps it was this background din, beyond the edge of awareness, that blunted his normally keen strategic mind. For in the instant it took for the squad to crash through the trees, it didn't once occur to him to wonder – if this is the synapse vanguard of the invasion force, then where are their guards?

It was only as his feet struck the mutated, otherworldly grass that lined the clearing like a scarlet rug and he raised his bolter to fire upon the zoanthropes that the question occurred to him, and by then it was too late.

'Gaunts!' shouted Battle-Brother Isek as a brood of hormagaunts swarmed from out of the shadows towards them, all scything talons and ripping claws.

As the hormagaunts leapt towards them in prodigious bounds, dozens upon dozens of the beasts propelled by their powerful hind limbs, Aramus raised his bolter and fired upon the nearest of the zoanthrope trio. 'Ignore the swarm!' he shouted to the others. 'We can't take them all, but if we put down the zoanthropes the gaunts will fall on each other.'

It was a sound tactical decision, and Aramus knew it was the only choice they had, but even as he issued the orders he knew that it would mean sacrifice on their part. As the squad opened fire on the zoanthropes, targeting their oversized craniums and pumping round after round of hellfire bolts into the creatures, the gaunts swarmed over Battle-Brother Zach, the nearest of the Blood Ravens to the brood.

Zach's dying screams of agony resounded in Aramus's helmet, booming over the vox-comms, but he didn't allow himself a moment for regret or remorse. This was no time for distraction.

'Krak grenades, at will!' Aramus shouted. Still firing his bolter with one hand, quickly working his way through the magazine, he unclipped a krak grenade from his waist and lobbed it overhand at the nearest zoanthrope.

The krak grenade struck home, and in the next instant the *thwump* of the implosive charge sounded.

Now Voire began to scream as the gaunts ran him down, scything claws tearing at his ceramite power armour, slashing it to pieces. Voire's bolter spat death at the hormagaunts swarming over him, but for every one he hit there were three more behind, and their numbers simply overwhelmed him.

Aramus continued to pour hellfire on the zoanthropes. To his left, Siddig concentrated fire on another of the synapse beasts, and on his right Cirrac and Isek concentrated their fire on the third.

Another *thwump* followed, and a third, and a
fourth, and then one of the trio began to list, like a
sail in a heavy wind, tilting precariously to one side
as it started drifting back down to earth. It was
dying, but just wasn't dead yet.

Isek howled in rage and pain as a talon broke clear
through the ceramite of his power armour, through
his body, and out the other side, impaling him on a
spar of chitin.

As the first zoanthrope began to fall to earth, its
psychic contact with its siblings and with the fleet
hive mind already severed, Aramus joined Siddig in
assaulting the zoanthrope on the left. A final krak
grenade lobbed by Cirrac imploded on the ventral
side of the other zoanthrope's head, and it began to
spin in midair in a final death spiral, ichor spraying
in all directions as it pinwheeled around.

The movements of the hormagaunts became more
sluggish, more confused, and as they crawled over
the still twitching bodies of the fallen Blood Ravens,
advancing on the three Blood Ravens still standing,
the monsters began to snap at one another with
their powerful jaws, jostling for position.

The head of the third and final zoanthrope finally
exploded like an erupting volcano, the cumulative
effect of the krak grenades augmented by the countless hellfire rounds that Aramus and Siddig had
poured into it.

As the last of the synapse beasts fell to earth, the
gaunts lost all sense of direction and purpose, and
the vestigial instincts that remained to them – to
fight, rend, and kill – took precedence. With their
hive siblings the much closer targets than the

remaining trio of Space Marines, the hormagaunts turned on one another, ripping and tearing each other to shreds.

Aramus signalled the other two survivors to withdraw to beyond the treeline, making as little noise as possible. Best to let the mindless beasts dispose of one another, and then return for the fallen Blood Ravens.

It had come at a heavy cost – the loss of half the surviving battle-brothers – but they had taken out the zoanthropes. Now, assuming these *were* the synapse creatures augmenting the shadow in the warp, and with them gone the *Armageddon* could established contact outside the Aurelia sub-sector, then the odds might soon change, and in the Blood Ravens' favour. If not…

Aramus tried not to imagine the alternatives.

CHAPTER SEVENTEEN

TECHMARINE MARTELLUS STOOD on the command deck, listening to the binary squeal of the servitors at their stations. He'd have preferred to be below decks in the enginarium, overseeing the maintenance and repair on the ship's mechanical systems, or better yet personally seeing to the holy Dreadnought assembly that waited below for the biological components that would make it whole, to the greater glory and honour of the Omnissiah. But with the strike cruiser *Armageddon* so short-handed, even more so now than when they had put out from Zalamis, Martellus had once more been dragged from his sacred duties and forced to the upper decks, there to take temporary command of the vessel while the rest of the Blood Ravens carried out their missions on the planet below.

Martellus had been a battle-brother of the Blood Ravens before he had ever been selected as an apprentice by the Master of the Forge, had fought and bled along with his brethren before being sent to complete his studies with the tech-priests of the Adeptus Mechanicus on Mars. And while he had devoted his life in the long years since returning to the Chapter to ministering to the spirits of the machines which served the Blood Ravens, keeping weapons, armour, and equipment in full function, he was still a Space Marine for all of that, and there were times when the call to battle was all but impossible to resist. But Martellus served two masters – Chapter and Machine-God – and to abandon his responsibilities only to indulge himself in the clash and clamour of combat would do disservice to both.

But if he couldn't, at the moment, throw himself into battle along with his brethren, and was denied the liberty to attend his duties in the enginarium, then it meant that he was at complete loose end, required to fulfil a role on board the *Armageddon* which suited neither his strengths nor his temperament. His was not to command, his was to serve. But while he commanded, those spirits he served were left unattended. If he closed his eyes, he could almost hear the machine spirit within the Dreadnought assembly crying out for attention.

Martellus turned from the servitors who monitored and controlled the ship's environmental controls, his augmetic eyes glancing at the command dais which rose above the deck, and the captain's chair which stood high atop it. The chair, and the dais, would remain empty, so long as he was in command. Bad enough that he should be forced to linger on the command deck, but he was not about to compound the indignity by keeping as far away from the ship's controls and processes as the dais would demand. Better to remain down on the deck, near the servitors who kept the systems running. He had only to ignore the Chapter serfs who scurried back and forth, and he could lose himself for a moment in the chorus of binary squeals sounding from all sides.

The Techmarine's concentration was interrupted by the arrival of Librarian Niven and Lexicanium Konan.

'Techmarine Martellus,' Librarian Niven said as he approached, Konan following in his wake at a respectful distance. 'Has there been any word from the surface?'

Martellus shook his head. 'Not since Sergeant Aramus voxed that they had found and eliminated the clutch of vanguard zoanthropes.' He paused, and then asked, 'Does the interference of the warp shadow persist? Should we notify the sergeant to continue the search for other vanguard creatures?'

The corners of Niven's mouth tugged up in a slight smile. 'That won't be necessary, techmarine.' He glanced over his shoulder at Lexicanium Konan, who stood behind him and a pace to the left. 'The effects of Aramus's action appear to have been sufficient. Only moments ago – working in concert to boost our capacities – the Lexicanium and I were able successfully to make contact with a Blood Ravens battlegroup.'

Techmarine Martellus's augmetic eyes flashed excitedly. 'An entire battlegroup?'

Niven nodded. 'The flagship is the *Litany of Fury*, under the command of Captain Gabriel Angelos of the Third Company.'

Martellus considered the implications. The battle-barge *Litany of Fury* was home to the Blood Ravens' Third Company, commanded by Captain Angelos, as well as the Ninth, a reserve company composed mostly of Devastator squads and under the command of Captain Ulantus. Neither company was at full strength, given the recent actions on Tartarus and elsewhere, but even so two partial-strength companies of the Blood Ravens Chapter would be a welcome addition to the mere four squads currently fighting on Meridian, to say nothing of the tactical advantage offered by the battle-barge itself and the strike cruisers and other craft that would be following in its wake.

'Then Meridian is not lost, after all,' Martellus said.

Here the smile on Librarian Niven's face began to fade, and he shook his head slightly. 'It is far too soon to celebrate our victory, I'm afraid,' he said. 'Captain Angelos replies that he will make best speed to the Meridian system, but that his battle-group is a considerable distance from the Aurelia sub-sector. Her Navigators estimate a journey of weeks, perhaps even longer.'

'Weeks?' Techmarine Martellus repeated.

Niven nodded. 'If Meridian is to survive, then our forces on the ground must hold the line in a delaying action until Captain Angelos and his forces can arrive.'

Martellus turned, his augmetic gaze taking in the greyish disc of Meridian turning slowly in the forward viewports. Weeks? Was it even possible that Sergeant Aramus and the others might survive a tyranid onslaught even half so long?

And was there anything that could be done to improve their chances?

Martellus remembered the words of the Cult Mechanicus's Fifteenth Universal Law: 'Flesh is Fallible, but Ritual Honours the Machine Spirit.' Perhaps in the rituals and rites of the Machine God an answer might be found. After all, as the Eighth Universal Law held, 'The Omnissiah Knows All, Comprehends All.'

LIGHT YEARS AWAY, another planet turned slowly beneath an orbiting craft, and others considered whether anything might be done to save the world around which they circled. But here, the planet was verdant green, though quickly turning shades of sickly yellow and red, and the chances for its survival were already nil.

'Sergeant Tarkus,' Fleet Admiral Forbes said, hands held behind her back, 'are all of your men safely aboard?'

Tarkus bristled somewhat at the thought of proud Adeptus Astartes being referred to as mere 'men', but stifled his initial response and nodded. 'Yes, admiral.' He paused, and then added, 'Those of us who are left.'

From Admiral Forbes's expression, Tarkus could tell she knew all too well what it meant to lose troops in battle. 'How many were lost, sergeant?'

'Nearly half, admiral.' Of the seven Blood Ravens who'd remained behind on Typhon Primaris, only four had returned. Brothers Mettius, Eumenis, and Proclus had met their ends at the talons and claws of the tyranid, but had done honour to the Chapter before falling, making the unholy offspring of the Great Devourer pay dearly for their deaths. They would be remembered whenever the Bell of Souls was tolled, Tarkus would see to that.

'You have my sympathies, sergeant,' Admiral Forbes said.

All around them the command deck of the *Sword of Hadrian* was a hive of activity, as officers and crew scurried to ready the ship for an immediate departure from the Typhon system, and the transition to warp space.

'Your sympathies are wasted on a Space Marine,' Tarkus said, with more venom than he'd intended. Then he softened, and added, 'You should save them for those on the planet below who we were not able to save, admiral.'

Forbes's face closed, and she nodded curtly. 'We've carried away as many as we were able.'

'Some thousands, by my count,' Tarkus said.

'Three thousand, two hundred and five, to be exact,' Admiral Forbes corrected.

Tarkus nodded, appreciatively. That the fleet admiral could recite with such exactitude the number of refugees spared the tyranids' wrath suggested that she valued their lives more highly than other Imperial Navy officers might have done, and that the three Blood Ravens who had been left behind on the jungle world had not died in vain.

Commander Mitchels approached the admiral, a data-slate in his hands. 'Your pardon, ma'am, but all stations report readiness. We can depart on your command.'

'Thank you, Mitchels,' Forbes answered, hardly sparing a glance at the data-slate.

'So we're bound for Meridian, then?' Sergeant Tarkus asked.

'Actually,' Admiral Forbes countered, 'I wanted to speak with you regarding our destination. I know that we agreed with your Sergeant Aramus that we would rendezvous with the *Armageddon* in the Meridian system once our mission of mercy was completed here, but circumstances have changed in the intervening days, and I would propose an alteration in our plans.'

'An alteration?' Sergeant Tarkus cocked an eyebrow.

'As you know, we've been operating in imposed silence for days, all astropathic communication blocked by what appears to be a shadow in the warp, the result of the tyranid hive fleet encroaching upon the Aurelia sub-sector. But in the last hours the interference has lifted, at least in part, and the astropathic contact we've established with the *Armageddon* suggests it's your Sergeant Aramus who we have to thank for that.'

Tarkus could not help but feel a small swell of pride. Had it been so long since Aramus had been a complete novice, unskilled in the ways of command, and Tarkus assigned to help shepherd him to his full potential?

'We have *also* regained contact with the other two light cruisers which make up the Aurelia Battlegroup,' Admiral Forbes continued. 'Their journey through the warp from Calderis to Meridian was more lengthy than anticipated, and they have only now emerged at the edge of the Meridian system. Now that they have been apprised as to the nature of the tyranid threat, I have ordered them to divert course immediately, to rendezvous with the *Sword of Hadrian* not in orbit above Meridian, as planned, but instead nearer to the location in interstellar space where our astropaths have estimated that the tyranid hive fleet will be found.'

Tarkus rubbed his grizzled chin with a gauntleted hand. 'We had intended to join in the defence of Meridian with Sergeant Aramus and the others, my squad and I.'

'I can appreciate that,' Admiral Forbes replied, 'but I'm afraid that to transport your squad to Meridian would simply take too much time, time that would be better spent in taking the battle directly to the hive fleet itself. And, in particular, to the hive mind.' She paused, and clasped her hands before her. 'Here is my proposition, Sergeant Tarkus. No offence intended, but four Space Marines one way or the other can matter little in the grand scheme when talking about a planetary defence, but those same four Space Marines acting as a strike force in ship-to-ship vacuum combat could make a very big difference indeed.' She gestured around the command deck. 'My people are well trained for orbital and vacuum manoeuvres, and though we've seen little action in the years we've been assigned to patrol Aurelia, I'd put them up against any spacefaring force of a similar size. But what we lack is boarding parties, vacuum-capable strike troops, and so on – precisely the sort of combat that Astartes are trained to handle.'

Tarkus continued to rub his grizzled chin, thoughtfully. 'Have you any boarding torpedoes?'

Admiral Forbes glanced at her first officer, Commander Mitchels, who still stood by with the data-slate in his hands.

'None on board,' Mitchels reported, without having to check, 'but I have requested the magos technicus to begin work on adapting one of our ordinary torpedoes to that purpose, with life support and rudimentary guidance system.'

'Won't need life support,' Tarkus said to Commander Mitchels, and to illustrate his point rapped his gauntleted knuckles his chest, the ceramite of his plastron resounding with a satisfyingly solid thump. With his helmet fixed on, a Space Marine in full power armour could survive in hard vacuum almost indefinitely. 'So long as you can shoot it and we can steer it, there'll be no complaints from us.'

Tarkus turned from the first officer to the admiral.

'Very well, admiral,' he said, nodding in her direction. 'You've got your strike team.'

DEEP IN THE rockcrete canyons beneath the towering habs of Meridian, Sergeant Thaddeus and the Blood Ravens of the Seventh Squad were in their second day of continuous combat with the tyranid forces, and there was no end in sight.

There had been six Space Marines in the Seventh when they'd jumped into the fray the previous day. Now they numbered only four. Battle-Brother Skander had been lost when a brood of raveners, six in all, had fallen on him from out of the shadows the night before, and had ripped Skander to pieces before Thaddeus and the rest of the squad could come to his aid. Battle-Brother Marr had fallen as the sun rose the following morning when a bio-acid spore mine erupted beneath his feet, the acidic nodules clinging to him until they had eaten clean through his armour's ceramite and then began to dissolve the flesh and bone within.

The spore mine had been hidden beneath refuse that had apparently been discarded in the mad flight of the inhabitants from the hives, and Marr had not seen it until it was too late. But the refuse and broken glass and junked land-vehicles were not the only things left behind in the exodus. Here and there were the bodies of those trampled by their own neighbours in the scramble to depart ahead of the invading monsters, left to rot in the midst of the wide thoroughfares.

But not all who had been left behind were dead, as Thaddeus was to discover.

The mission of the Seventh was to seek out and destroy any tyranids sufficiently developed to act as synapse creatures, those with the ability to receive and retransmit the directives of the hive mind. Their primary targets were the zoanthropes, the most powerful of that sort, but any of the other synapse creatures were also priority targets – hive tyrants, hive warriors, even broodlords if there were any to be found. So far, though, they had managed to locate no zoanthropes, and precious few of the other types, most often encountering lictors, gaunts, and raveners of different varieties.

It was long past the fall of night now, the sun having long disappeared behind the habs to the west, but now that darkness had fallen it appeared that their luck had changed. Though whether for the better or worse, Thaddeus had yet to determine.

'Warriors!' Battle-Brother Takayo shouted, his bolt pistol firing in one fist, his chainsword whirring in the other.

They'd been making their way gradually east since the previous day, plunging deeper and deeper into enemy-held territory. The tyranids were not interested in occupying, though, but merely in overrunning and tainting, and as the Blood Ravens pushed east the tyranids were racing even faster towards the west. So it was that, as Thaddeus and the other surviving members of the Seventh managed to wipe out the last of the hormagaunt brood that they had encountered before sunset, a new wave of tyranid forces raced from the east towards them.

It was tyranid warriors, just the sort of synapse creature they'd been sent to eliminate. But this was no lone warrior, nor even a mere brood of a half-dozen or so creatures. There were dozens of warriors racing towards them, a rolling tide of horrible chittering monsters. Not just dozens, but perhaps even *hundreds*. And all of them barrelling down the thoroughfare on which the Seventh stood, hunger and murder in the tyranids' cold, lifeless eyes.

They were a few hundred metres away, and closing fast.

'We've got to get off this street,' Sergeant Thaddeus said, his eyes cutting back and forth, searching on all sides. Without any cover, standing out in the open as

they were, with nothing but the carcasses of the
fallen gaunts around them, they didn't stand a
chance of surviving an onslaught of so many warriors. They might be able to take a few dozen with
them, perhaps more, but in the end the numbers of
tyranids would overwhelm them. If they were able
to get behind cover, though, barricade themselves
somewhere with a narrow approach, then they
could pick the warriors off in smaller numbers as
they approached, and perhaps stand a chance of getting them all.

To their left rose a hab, looming impossibly tall,
without any break or opening in its rockcrete face.
On their right, though, was another hab, just as tall,
with a narrow opening at ground level. It appeared
to be a service access door of some kind, probably
intended only for use by servitors – habdwellers
would seldom venture out of doors, if they could
help it. But if the footprints and tracks that spread
from the opening were any indication, the doorway
had been used by *many* habdwellers in recent days,
perhaps the entire population as they fled out into
the open and scurried to the west, chased by reports
of marauding monsters from the east.

The door was open, it was narrow – perhaps just
wide enough for a Space Marine in power armour
with jump pack to enter sideways, but not face-on –
and it appeared to be defensible. There were no
other alternatives at hand, and the window to act
was quickly closing.

'There!' Thaddeus said, pointing at the doorway
with the blade of his chainsword. 'Get behind cover,
now!'

Takayo was closest, and went first, approaching the opening sideways and sidling in. As it was, the top of his jump pack scraped the top of the door, sending out a shower of sparks, and his breastplate rubbed against one side of the door while the back of his pack scraped against the other.

'I'm in,' Takayo voxed. 'Looks clear.'

Brother Brandt was next, followed quickly by Brother Kell. Sergeant Thaddeus was last, slipping into the opening just as the first of the tyranid warriors reached their position. As it stabbed its talons in through the opening, about to push its bulk through, Thaddeus fired a barrage of hellfire rounds at the beast, stopping it cold. As it convulsed in the opening, he retreated a little further into the darkness, to find a better vantage point.

'Sergeant?' Takayo called out loud, from deeper in. They were in a service conduit of some kind, a squared-off hallway that continued for a half-dozen metres in either direction before branching off and out of sight. Takayo had ventured deeper into the conduit to scout ahead, after getting through the door. 'There's something back here you should see.'

Thaddeus fired another barrage of hellfire rounds at the next warrior to venture too close to the opening, and then called over to the others. 'Brandt, Kell, cover the door, I'm going to check on Takayo.'

The others flashed their acknowledgement, and Thaddeus pushed past them to follow the sound of Takayo's voice.

When he caught up with his battle-brother, Thaddeus was brought up short.

'What is *this*?' Thaddeus said, lowering his bolt pistol's barrel to the ground.

'I'm Phaeton,' said the young boy who stood blinking in the light cast by Takayo's lamp. He nodded his head at the even younger boy who stood beside him, clutching his hand. 'This is my brother Phoebus. We're lost.' He spoke Low Gothic in a guttural accent, one which Thaddeus found very familiar.

The two boys were covered in dirt and grime, like walking shadows, their eyes and teeth stark white in contrast. Their clothes were tattered and worn, their shoes scuffed and holey, but Thaddeus could see that this clothing had never been finery, even when clean and new. Between the clothes and the boy's accent, it was clear – these were low-hab-dwellers, just as Thaddeus had been, a lifetime ago.

'Everyone else ran away, but we couldn't find our mother,' the younger of the boys said. 'So we stayed to look for her. Have you seen her?'

Thaddeus, who had for years gone into battle with a smile on his lips, and who had in recent actions found himself slipping into a grim moroseness that he could not escape, felt pity welling in his chest for the two boys before him, each a mirror of himself at their age.

'Courage,' Thaddeus said, holstering his bolt pistol and laying a gauntleted hand on the older boy's shoulder. 'We'll look for her together.'

'THIS IS AGAINST Chapter protocol, sir,' Sergeant Cyrus said again, for the tenth time.

'So noted,' Sergeant Aramus replied, his eyes on the Thunderhawk braking for a landing atop the governor's palace. It had been only hours since Aramus and the surviving members of the Third Squad had been ferried back to Zenith on board Thunderhawk One, and with Thunderhawk Two making its final descent from the *Armageddon* the last stage of his emergency strategy was about to begin.

Cyrus scowled and shook his head, his hair whipping around in the backdraft of the Thunderhawk's engines. 'I don't like it...'

Aramus wheeled on him, eyes flashing angrily. 'No one is asking you to *like* it, sergeant. I appreciate your concerns, but these are desperate times, and call for desperate measures.'

'But they're not ready for this, Aramus,' Cyrus said, sounding for all the world like he was still the instructor and Aramus still the neophyte. 'They don't stand a chance.'

Aramus drew his lips into a tight line. The landing pad shuddered as the Thunderhawk touched down and the hatch began to cycle open. 'They stand the same chances as any aspirant walking onto the field of the Blood Trials,' he said, his tone even. 'They will either live, or they won't.'

The hatch opened, and Chaplain Palmarius emerged, the moonlight glinting off the silver metal of his death's-head mask, the ribbons and scrolls of his purity seals fluttering in the wind. He stepped out onto the landing pad, and struck the ferrocrete beneath his feet three times with the butt of his crozius arcanum.

In response to the three resounding thuds of the staff, the other passengers of the Thunderhawk followed the Chaplain down the ramp and stood before him. There were fifteen of them in all, the tallest barely standing as high as the Chaplain's waist, all clad in blood-red bodygloves that covered them from the neck down. All fifteen were armed, some with autoguns, some with shotguns, others with lasguns, the weapons all seemingly ridiculously oversized in their young hands.

'The aspirants stand ready to fight, Sergeant Aramus,' Chaplain Palmarius said, and though his expression was unreadable behind his silver mask, from his tone Aramus could see that the Chaplain no more approved of his plan than Cyrus did.

'And fight they shall,' he said. He strode forward to stand before the assembled youths, who tried valiantly to hide their mounting terror, but failed.

Aramus cast his gaze over the fifteen youths. His head was bare, and he allowed the boys to see the pride in his expression.

'You are not yet Blood Ravens,' he said, his voice booming even over the sound of the Thunderhawk's engines, 'not even yet initiates, but even as bare aspirants you still do our Chapter honour.'

The fifteen youths had been fed well aboard the *Armageddon*, and allowed the benefit of a few days' combat and weapons training, but Cyrus and Chaplain Palmarius both insisted it wasn't enough. It wasn't simply Chapter protocols at issue, they had said, but a matter of simple logic. The youths had scant training, no experience, and none of the physical advantages enjoyed even by a Scout, much less those of a full-fledged Space Marine. But Aramus had insisted that they had potential, and hoped they would be eager to prove their worth.

'Each of you was selected to compete in the Blood Trials, for the honour of initiation into the Blood Ravens Chapter,' Aramus went on. 'Circumstances are such that those Trials could not be held, and so you have waited for the chance to prove yourself worthy.' He waved his hand to the east. 'Out there, in the darkness, are the massed hordes of tyranids, offspring of the Great Devourer, who threaten to overrun this world, and destroy all life on it. Let *this* be your Blood Trial, then. Rather than fighting one another, you will face the tyranid.'

The youths exchanged uneasy glances, as Aramus turned to indicate Sergeant Cyrus, who stood behind him.

'You will serve as a reserve squad, under the direct command of Chaplain Palmarius. Ideally your purpose will be purely defensive, but there is every possibility you may be called upon to come into close combat with the enemy.'

Cyrus scowled, but remained silent.

'The dangers that you face will be legion,' Aramus went on, 'there is no point in hiding it. But know this! Any that survive the coming days will have proven themselves more than worthy to join the Blood Ravens, and should you survive to return to the fleet, you will be welcomed as initiates to the Chapter with open arms.'

Assuming of course, Aramus thought but did not say, that any of them *did* survive and return to the fleet – whether aspirants, neophytes, or Space Marines. It might be weeks before Captain Angelos's battlegroup arrived in the skies over Meridian. By the time he did, would there be anyone left alive on the ground to reinforce?

CHAPTER EIGHTEEN

Apothecary Gordian regarded the immobile, seemingly lifeless body lying atop the platform at the centre of the Apothecarion. If not for the faint rising and falling of Captain Thule's chest with his irregular, ragged breaths, it would be easy to assume that all life had fled, and that it was merely a corpse upon a slab. And even this small glimmer of life would not be possible without the aid of the tubes that snaked from Thule's bruised and bloodied nostrils to the respirator pumps operated by the medicae servitors.

Despite Gordian's best efforts, Thule still hovered on the threshold between life and death. The anti-toxin he'd developed had successfully purged the poisons that had nearly killed Thule on Calderis, but the damage done – by the toxins and by the physical injuries the captain had sustained at the talons of the tyranid – had been too severe. His implanted organs had been rendered all but inoperative by the shock of toxin and bodily trauma, and though Gordian had done everything he could to help the struggling organs repair themselves and the body itself, what little function he'd been able to recover was not sufficient. The cells released by the Larraman's Organ were so pitifully few in number that only the most minor of the captain's cuts and abrasions had begun to scar over and heal, with the majority of the wounds still gaping; and with the oolitic kidney still crippled by injury and the preomnor not operating at full capacity, infection had begun to set in, and the seeping wounds had begun to fester. The smell of putrefaction and rot pervaded the Apothecarion, stinging in Gordian's nostrils.

With the assistance of the medicae servitors, and the various respirator tubes, blood pumps, and intravenous feeds that were connected to all points of Thule's body, Gordian knew that the captain could be kept alive indefinitely. But he also knew that, with so many of the captain's implants already shut down and more of them due to fail in short order, it would never be possible for Thule to regain full use of his body again. In fact, there was some question whether the captain could even be returned to full consciousness in his current state, with it more likely that he could continue to linger on in a perpetual dreamless fugue, hovering at the brink between wakefulness and unconsciousness just as he hovered at the threshold between life and death.

Gordian could not help but be reminded of the words of the Apothecary's Creed, which he kept imprinted in his heart. Normally he recited the creed as he worked as a kind of litany, the familiar phrases acting as a sort of focusing agent for his thoughts, but it did not escape Gordian's notice that since he had begun work on Captain Thule after removing him from the sarcophagus in the skies above Typhon Primaris, that he had not once recited the creed, even silently in his own thoughts.

The Apothecary said them now, aloud but in a voice so quiet it was scarcely above a whisper.

'He that may fight, heal him.'

Gordian ran his gaze along the captain's bruised and battered body, from the suppurating wounds to the massive contusions, bruises still raw purple, that might never grow sickly yellow and green as they healed.

'He that may fight no more, give him peace.'

As it was, Gordian could see no way that Captain Thule would ever be able to stand again, much less stand and fight. It was even possible that he would never regain conscious control of his broken body at all, a healthy mind trapped in a frame too badly damaged to respond.

'He that is dead, take from him the Chapter's due.'

Gordian glanced from the platform to the narthecium at the far side of the Apothecarion, and the reductor which lay upon it, primed and ready to use. Had he reached the stage where there was no other alternative but to give the captain the Emperor's Peace, and to take the reductor in hand?

Turning from the platform, Gordian crossed the floor to the narthecium. It would be the work of only moments to remove the captain's gene-seed, as Gordian had done in recent hours from the fatally wounded and recently dead Blood Ravens ferried up from the planet's surface on the Thunderhawks. Gordian picked up the reductor, turning it over in his hands. By staying at Thule's side for all of these days, he'd been neglecting his other duties, he knew, and though he had been able to retrieve the gene-seed from all of the fallen on Meridian so far, he could not help but feel that he had betrayed his Creed. What if those fallen Space Marines – Voire, Zach, Isek, Skander, Marr – had *not* been returned to the *Armageddon* in time for Gordian to remove their progenoids? Was Thule's life worth the risk of still more potential Astartes that might serve the Chapter for centuries to come?

Was it that a company captain was of more strategic value to the Chapter than the rank and file Space Marines? Or was it a kind of hubris on Gordian's part, to think that he could hold back death?

After so many years of dispensing the Emperor's Peace and taking the Chapter's due, had Gordian finally decided to stand fast, and say, '*No, not this one. This one will live*'…?

Gordian hefted the reductor, and then turned to walk back to the platform on which lay the motionless body of Captain Davian Thule.

'While his gene-seed returns to the Chapter,' Gordian said, quoting the Apothecary's Creed, 'a Space Marine cannot die.'

Gordian raised the reductor over Thule's chest.

'Without death,' he recited, 'pain loses its relevance.'

He began to lower the reductor towards the captain's bruised and bloodied skin, preparing to open Thule's chest cavity and remove the precious gene-seed.

'Hold!' came a voice from behind, staying his hand.

Gordian turned. Techmarine Martellus stood at the open entrance to the Apothecarion, his augmetic eyes flashing in the low light.

'What is Captain Thule's state?' Martellus asked, stepping into the Apothecarion.

'The captain is lost to us,' Gordian said, indicating the body on the platform. He raised the reductor in his hands for the Techmarine to see. 'I am preparing to take the Chapter's due.'

Techmarine Martellus came to stand beside him, looking down at the captain's body. 'Perhaps,' Martellus said in a quiet voice, 'there is another option…'

FAR BELOW THE *Armageddon*, on the surface of Meridian, Sergeant Avitus stood at the edge of the scar he and his Devastator squad had burned in the landscape, peering across the gulf at the massed front line of the tyranid invasion force.

'Sergeant?' Battle-Brother Barabbas said, at Avitus's side. 'Your orders?'

Avitus watched the teeming hordes of tyranids, only a few dozen metres away. The firebreak that the Ninth Squad had cut from north to south still smouldered with flames, hot enough even to crack the chitinous carapaces of the tyranids.

The sergeant removed his helmet and reached up a gauntleted hand to scratch at the side of his head, where augmetic met flesh. The itch was likely psychological, he knew, but he found some comfort in the act, even so. He remembered the battle aboard the hive ship, a lifetime ago, and the norn-queen that had left his chest, neck, and jaw a red ruin, too far gone for even the Apothecaries to repair. Seeing the massed tyranids now brought back the memory of that pain as though it had been only hours before, and not decades.

'Stand fast,' Avitus finally answered. 'The firebreak will slow them, but it won't stop them. Our orders are to hold them here as long as we can, then fall back to the next firebreak.'

Avitus, Barabbas, Gagan, and Safir had remained at the firebreak once it was completed, while Battle-Brothers Dow, Elon, and Pontius withdrew and began cutting another such trench a few dozen kilometres nearer to Zenith. The plan was for the two teams of Blood Ravens, each comprising half of the surviving members of the Ninth Squad, to leapfrog one another, always cutting a new firebreak before the previous one was overrun by the enemy, thereby slowing the tyranid advance to the west as much as possible. With the reinforcements of Captain Angelos's battlegroup still days away, if not more, every additional day that the firebreaks were able to gain the defenders, every additional hour that the tyranid advance was slowed, only served to increase the chances that some of those who now huddled in Zenith might yet survive.

But while the burning firebreaks were serving to slow the advance of the ground-based tyranid forces, it was becoming abundantly clear that the scarred landscape was serving as no impediment to other tyranid elements.

'Spore mine!' Battle-Brother Safir shouted, as a fragmentation spore mine came whistling overhead, launched by the powerful muscle spasms of the biovore gunbeast that hunched on the far side of the firebreak.

The trajectory of the frag spore mine was carrying it directly at Brother Gagan, who dived to one side as the mine exploded, its iron-hard shell splintering into countless razor-sharp shards that scythed out in all directions. Those that pelted against Gagan's body did little more than scratch the ceramite of his armour, but it was not just in their keen edges that the shrapnel posed a threat – the toxins that the mine carried meant that even the tiniest of splinters from a frag spore mine could, if it entered the body, give rise to lethal infection and, eventually, sepsis. Fortunately for Gagan his power armour was proof against the shrapnel, this time at least, and he regained his footing to fire a blast from his meltagun at the biovore.

'Incoming!' Sergeant Avitus called out to the others, swinging up the barrel of his heavy bolter.

There were more than two dozen of the creatures, perhaps even three dozen with more following behind, bat-winged monstrosities with weapons symbiotes slung underneath, a full gargoyle brood on the wing. They resembled nothing so much as gaunts with broad, leathery wings, raking claws, and barbed tails. The advance wave of any tyranid swarm, the gargoyles were not slowed in the slightest by the flames which licked the gouge in the landscape beneath their flight.

Avitus and the others opened fire on the gargoyles, hellfire shells and melta blasts ripping into their leathery wings and hard carapaces. But even as some of the hardest-hit gargoyles pinwheeled down out of the gunmetal grey sky, other gargoyles returned fire, spitting borer beetles and bio-plasma blasts down at the Blood Ravens. One of the gargoyles dived into a strafing run, coming so low as to lash at Barabbas with its barbed tail, but while Avitus poured hellfire shells into the air around the beast its movements were too quick and erratic for him to score more than one or two hits against the gargoyle. The mutagenic acid of the hellfire shell was already coursing through the hellbat's body, but before it fell it would still be able to cover considerable ground, firing from its bio-plasma symbiote as it went.

Some half-dozen hellbats rained down to earth, felled by the weapons-fire of Avitus and his Space Marines, but for every one that fell another four continued to fly, beating their wings on the wind, speeding towards the west and Zenith.

'Stand fast!' Avitus called again, swinging his heavy bolter around and unleashing a torrent of hellfire on the tyranids beyond the firebreak. 'They'll cross, but we'll make them pay dearly for every centimetre of ground they gain.'

KILOMETRES TO THE east of Avitus's firebreak, in the dark shadows beneath a hab whose inhabitants had long since fled, Sergeant Thaddeus and the survivors of Seventh Squad hunted the tyranid warriors who stalked the darkness in pursuit of them. The advantage of numbers was squarely on the side of the tyranids, any one of which was a match for a Space Marine but who in their dozens vastly outnumbered the six Blood Ravens of the assault squad. The Blood Ravens, in turn, were more heavily armed than the warriors, by and large, most of whom were equipped only with rending claws and flesh hook symbiotes.

But in the close confines of the tunnels and corridors that ran through the warrens beneath the hab, the calculus of the conflict quickly took on entirely new dimensions and variables.

With walls no more than a couple of metres apart, and ceiling not much farther from the floor, the vast numbers of tyranids could not throw themselves en masse at the Space Marines, helping to narrow the gulf between the sizes of the two forces. Unfortunately for Thaddeus and his battle-brothers, however, the walls and ceiling of the tunnels themselves offered an advantage to the tyranid, who were able to ascend the sheer walls as though they were ladders, and whose instincts made them especially adept at utilising tunnels to approach their prey. As a result, the Seventh Squad had not merely to watch the ground in either direction, watchful for an approach, but had to be aware of monsters scaling the very walls and dropping from the ceilings just above their heads.

The presence of the two young boys, of course, only made matters that much more difficult.

'Forgive me saying, sir,' Brother Kell began, 'but perhaps we should just leave them behind.' Kell indicated the two boys, Phaeton and Phoebus, with the point of his chainsword. Huddled together at the centre of the ring of Blood Ravens, the boys were all but silent, neither whimpering nor sobbing, though the tracks of tears were traced through the ash and dirt that grimed their faces, streaks of white against the night. 'They won't last long on their own, but with them tagging along we won't last long, either, and....'

Thaddeus held up his hand, cutting his battle-brother off. There had been a time, perhaps, when the sergeant would have responded to such a suggestion with a wry quip, or with a dismissive jibe, but those times were now long past.

'We are *not* leaving them behind,' Thaddeus said, eyes on Kell but addressing the entire squad. 'The next Space Marine to suggest that we should will find *himself* "cut loose", and Emperor help him when he faces the tyranids on his own.' He narrowed his eyes and glanced around, looking at the other five Blood Ravens who stood shoulder to shoulder, facing out into the darkness. 'Is there any confusion on this count?'

The others didn't speak, but only flashed their assent on the runes glowing on Thaddeus's visor.

'Good,' Thaddeus said, with a final sharp glance in Kell's direction.

The squad stood at the intersection of two snaking corridors, deep beneath the hab. For seemingly endless hours they had made their way through the darkness, picking off the warriors who scurried over floor, walls, and ceiling towards them, emerging from hiding from time to time to ensure that the tyranids did not lose the scent. Originally the retreat under the hab had been a temporary measure, seeking momentary refuge from the overwhelming numbers of tyranid warriors swarming from the east, but the warriors were tenacious, and seemed determined to seek out and destroy the Blood Ravens, at any cost. Since their mission objectives were to locate and eradicate as many of the synapse creatures of the tyranid forces as possible, and since warriors were included in that number, Thaddeus had adopted the strategy of remaining in the shadows until they had eliminated as many of the beasts as possible, before emerging into the open once more to continue their hunt.

It was as though the hab was serving as a trap for the tyranids, with the Blood Ravens themselves as bait.

'Sergeant?' The high, piping voice of the younger of the two boys interrupted Thaddeus's thoughts.

'Yes, Phoebus?' The boys were older than Thaddeus had originally assumed, the elder in his twelfth year, the younger a few months shy of his tenth birthday. Poor diet – if not borderline malnutrition – was doubtless the cause of their small stature, and Thaddeus could not help but be reminded of his own relatively small size when he'd walked out onto the killing floor of the Blood Ravens outpost-monastery in Zenith, to compete in the Blood Trials.

'Our mother is dead, isn't she?' the boy asked.

Thaddeus was tempted to lie, to mutter soothing untruths in an attempt to save the youths from the pain of the loss, but looking into their eyes, bright in the low light of the lamps set in the ceiling overhead, the sergeant knew that he could never tell them anything but the truth.

'Yes,' he said, his tone gentle but final. 'Unless she fled with the others, I'm afraid there is no chance that she still lives.'

Phoebus was quiet for a moment, his expression thoughtful. 'And these monsters killed her, didn't they?'

Thaddeus nodded. In their hours of tracking through the darkened corridors, backtracking time and again, they had found evidence of others who, like the two boys, had remained behind when the rest of the inhabitants fled to the west. But in each case, the tyranid warriors who hunted the Blood Ravens had gotten to these isolated holdouts first, and made short work of them. It was possible, for all that Thaddeus knew, that one of the mangled and mutilated bodies they had chanced upon had been that of the boys' mother, mangled beyond all recognition. He had originally assumed that she had fled with the rest, and damned her for abandoning her children, but was forced to admit that she might well have stayed behind, searching for the boys from whom she had gotten separated, moving through darkened halls and shadowed corridors and empty galleries in a fruitless search for her family, only to find her end at the talons and claws of the Great Devourer's own offspring.

'Yes,' Thaddeus answered, after a pause. 'I'm afraid so.'

Phoebus nodded, remaining silent, but his older brother straightened, chin held high and eyes flashing. 'Then *I* will kill them all,' he said, his tone strong and determined.

Thaddeus reached out and put a hand on the boy's shoulder. 'Leave the killing to us, for now.'

It had not escaped the sergeant's notice that both of the boys fit the profile for Chapter aspirants, and the fact that they faced the horrors of the darkness and the monsters who lurked in the shadows without crying out, without wavering, suggested that they were made of just the stuff that the Blood Ravens sought in an initiate. Growing up in the lower-habs had made them that way, Thaddeus knew. They had already seen things in their young lives that the cosseted sons of the high-hab nobility might never experience in their long lifetimes, even before the coming of the tyranids. The underhives and lower-habs were hard places, in which only the hardiest souls survived to adulthood.

Phaeton's hands balled into fists at his sides. 'But when will *we* get to fight?'

A slight smile played about the corners of Thaddeus's mouth, a shadow of the grins he once wore into battle.

'Perhaps one day you'll wear the armour of the Blood Raven,' Thaddeus said, rapping the raven-and-blood-teardrop emblazoned on his chest, 'and with bolter and chainsword can exact revenge on the kin of your mother's killer, and all xenos like them.'

Little Phoebus raised his chin, expression brightening. 'Yes!' he said. 'I want to be a Blood Raven and fight, too!'

Yes, Thaddeus thought, the Chapter could do far worse than to accept these two as initiates. If Thaddeus could only deliver them safely through the countless tyranid that swarmed on all sides.

'Contact!' Brother Takayo shouted, firing his bolt pistol at the warrior who came scuttling across the ceiling towards them.

At the moment, though, it remained to be seen whether any of them survived at all.

SERGEANT ARAMUS REGARDED the data-slates stacked on the table before him, each of them containing reports on the readiness of the city to withstand a full-blown tyranid attack.

He had established a command post in the Blood Ravens outpost-monastery at the heart of Zenith. It was within these same walls that Aramus had fought in the Blood Trials, and when he and Thaddeus had been the last two aspirants left standing they had been taken from the amphitheatre, and led here, to the heart of the outpost-monastery.

Aramus looked up from the data-slates to the altar that dominated the far side of the chamber, dedicated to the Undying Emperor. Behind the altar the walls were covered with intricate carvings, depicting images from the sacred lore of the Blood Ravens, some historical, some legendary, and some a blending of the two. Here were the great Missionary-Chaplains Elizur and Shedeur, planting the Blood Ravens' standard on a jagged mountain peak, representing the countless worlds to which they had brought the light of the Emperor, and on which they had established Chapter monastery-outposts. Here, too, were the great Librarian Fathers, the Chapter Masters from the dim and distant past, back to the Great Father himself, Azariah Vidya, the earliest known Librarian Father in the broken annals of the Blood Ravens.

The Chapter was led now by Secret Masters, their names and faces known only to one another, chosen from amongst the great Librarians, Chaplains, and captains of the Blood Ravens, a legacy of secrecy passed down over the millennia. There was some irony, perhaps, that a Chapter whose battle cry held that knowledge was power should keep so closely guarded information that other Chapters shouted from the rooftops, but if knowledge *was* power, then perhaps it was not so ironic, at that. Power must be marshalled, and protected, lest it be lost, and the knowledge of who at any time served as Master of the Blood Ravens was perhaps the most precious knowledge that the Chapter possessed.

Aramus did not know what the enemies of the Chapter might do with that secret knowledge, but he could guess. He had heard whispered rumours of the secrets that lay hidden in the forbidden pages of the *Grimoire Hereticus* or the *Tactica Adeptus Chaotica*, kept under lock and key within the Librarium Sanctorum on board the Chapter's fortress-monastery the *Omnis Arcanum*, and if only a fraction of those rumours were correct, then the Blood Ravens were right to keep secret the identities of their masters. There were forces in the universe, and beyond, who would do evil to the Chapter otherwise.

'Sergeant Aramus!' Scout Xenakis came running into the chamber, his bolt pistol drawn, his sniper-rifle slung over his shoulder.

Aramus stood up from the bench. 'What is it, scout?'

'The tyranids, sir,' Xenakis answered. 'They've begun to attack the city.'

Aramus was already on his way out the door. 'With me, scout.'

As he burst from the darkened security of the out-post-monastery into the harsh light of day, Aramus knew what to expect. The latest action reports from Sergeant Avitus and his Ninth Squad put the ground forces of the tyranids nearly a hundred kilometres to the east. Avitus's team had yet to report in by vox, but it was anticipated that the advancing front of the tyranid forces would hit the first firebreak today, which was expected to delay their forward motion considerably. Even so, whether the firebreak held them or not, there was no chance that ground forces could have reached Zenith in so short a time.

Which was why, when Aramus rushed outside, he did not look out at the city which stretched as far as the eye could see in either direction, but instead cast his gaze skyward. And there, as he had anticipated, he saw the leathery wings of gargoyle broods darkening the grey skies.

'The fool!' came the voice of Sergeant Cyrus over the microbead in Aramus's ear.

'Cyrus?' Aramus replied, his eyes following the high-flying gargoyles, trying to judge where they would strike.

'It's the Emperor-forsaken governor, sir,' Cyrus voxed back. 'He won't listen to reason.'

The monastery-outpost of the Blood Ravens towered over the streets of Zenith, but even it was dwarfed by the bulk of the governor's palace to the north. In between the two buildings the streets swarmed with people, the city's population swelled by the countless thousands – even millions – of refugees who had fled to the capital city in recent days, ahead of the tyranid advance. The shouts and screams of the terrified crowd rose to slam Aramus like a solid wall of sound, as the huddled masses below pointed in horror at the hellbats which now wheeled high overhead. The gargoyles had not yet attacked, and in fact appeared to be surveying the area first before selecting a target, but Aramus knew that when they began to strafe the streets, the death toll would be tremendous.

'Scout,' Aramus said to Scout Xenakis who'd come to stand at his side. 'Pot a few shots at them with your sniper rifle, see if you can't clip a few wings.'

'Yes, sir,' Xenakis answered, and unslinging his rifle from his shoulder knelt to take aim.

'Now,' Aramus sighed, tapping his microbead and returning his attention to Cyrus, 'what's this about the governor?'

Aramus had expected trouble from the governor. As the tyranid advance had grown ever closer, Governor Vandis had appeared, at long last, to recognize the gravity of their situation and, having spent the first days of the Blood Ravens' presence on Meridian guided by the blind assumption that the Space Marines would quickly and easily put everything to rights, was now caught up in a full-blown panic, demanding immediate action from the Blood Ravens, insisting on personal protection for himself above all else.

In the face of the governor's constant demands, Aramus had been forced to dispatch Sergeant Cyrus, to prevent the governor's people from attempting to barge into the outpost-monastery and demand an answer themselves. He'd hoped that, if Cyrus could hear the governor's concerns in person, then perhaps they might get a small measure of silence from the damnable man and the space in which to work. But it appeared that those hopes had been unfounded.

'He... he's taking off, sir,' Cyrus voxed. 'I tried to stop him.'

'What?' Aramus looked from the skies overhead to the governor's palace to the north.

Atop the palace, Aramus could just make out what appeared to be a shuttle lifting off from the landing pad.

'Cyrus, who's in that ship?'

'It's the governor, Aramus,' Cyrus answered. 'He's in a complete panic, sir. Says that we betrayed him by sending the Aurelia Battlegroup away, and that we're not doing enough to safeguard the city. He says it's only a matter of time before the tyranids overrun Zenith.'

Aramus didn't know that he could argue with the last point, but as for the others...

'Damn the man,' Aramus spat. 'So where's he going?'

'He's trying to contract a rogue trader to take him out of system, but in the meantime he's just intending to wait in orbit in his shuttle.' Cyrus paused. 'I think he's got something in the shuttle he doesn't want us to see. He was very concerned that I not follow him aboard.'

Aramus watched the shuttle arc away from the governor's palace toward the south. Whether the pilot had seen the gargoyle brood wheeling into his path, they would never know.

'Cyrus, take cover!' Aramus shouted.

The bio-plasma bursts of the gargoyle brood lanced into the shuttle's wings. As smoke began to curl up from the shuttle's hull, and debris rained down on the crowds below, the craft began to veer wildly out of control.

'Sir?' Scout Xenakis said, lowering the sniper rifle from his shoulder, his gaze drifting from the out of control shuttle to the crowds massed underneath, already whipped into a frenzy for fear of the hellbats overhead.

'Keep firing at the gargoyles, Scout,' Aramus said, as he made for the steps leading from the monastery-fortress down to the street.

The shuttle plunged to earth, engines screaming but ineffectual.

'What about the people?' Xenakis said, gesturing to the street below.

'Some will die,' Aramus said flatly.

As if in response, the shuttle came crashing down into the street, the sound of its impact accented by the horrified shrieks of those innocents close enough to see the crash but not so close they were killed on impact.

'But if we don't stop those hellbats,' Aramus said, leaping down the steps five at a time, 'more will follow.'

CHAPTER NINETEEN

'DAMAGE REPORT!' ADMIRAL Forbes shouted from the command dais.

All around her on the command deck of the *Sword of Hadrian* the ship's officers were about their business, their attentions fixed on the crystal displays of their stations, monitoring the course of the battle raging all around them.

'We've taken a battery hit to our starboard side,' reported the midshipman monitoring the ship's hull. 'Damage from impact is minimal, with only minor hull penetration, but the resulting fire is raging on the starboard quadrant of deck twenty.'

Forbes scowled. Pyro-acidic batteries were among the most damaging weapons in the tyranid arsenal. Unless the battery were deflected on impact, the ship ran the risk of severe internal damage from the deadly bio-agents contained within. 'Damage control teams to deck twenty,' Forbes ordered. 'If they can't quell it, lock down the quadrant and flush to vacuum.'

'Aye aye, ma'am,' the midshipman replied, already keying in the commands to be transmitted below decks.

'She's coming about,' Commander Mitchels reported, monitoring the motions of the Razorfiend tyranid cruiser through the forward viewports.

'Prepare to fire forward lances on my mark,' Forbes ordered. She leaned forward in the captain's chair, hands gripping the armrests on either side.

'Admiral,' called the lieutenant at the port-side monitoring station, 'we're taking bio-plasma hits from a flight of drones.'

'Increase power to port-side void shields and return fire from the port battery at your discretion.'

'With pleasure, ma'am,' the lieutenant answered, his tone grim.

'She's preparing to launch feeder tentacles, admiral,' Mitchels reported, his attention still on the Razorfiend.

'Forward lances fire,' Forbes barked.

High-powered beams shot out from the energy projectors of the forward lance, searing into the main body of the Razorfiend cruiser.

'Direct hit,' Mitchels said calmly. 'But she's still bringing her tentacles to bear.'

Tentacles, digestive acids, and bio-plasma... Forbes wearied of the tactics of the tyranids, who fought with teeth, claws, and spines rather than thrown slugs and projected energy beams like any civilized foe. What she wouldn't give for an enemy who fought with guns, right about now.

'Starboard battery,' Forbes said, 'target rail guns on Razorfiend and fire when ready.'

'Aye, aye,' chorused the pair of officers who controlled the myriad of weapons housed in the starboard battery.

Forbes leaned back in her seat, as the crew on the command deck carried out her commands. It had been more than two years since they'd been in active combat, more than two years since they'd even encountered another ship in vacuum except for the odd rogue trader who refused to stand down for an inspection boarding party. But it was rare to find a rogue trader who wouldn't back down when a warship's weapons batteries were trained on him, and as a result the *Sword of Hadrian* had not exchanged live fire with an enemy the entire time they'd been stationed to Aurelia, a full two years. That her officers were rising to the occasion, now that they faced the tyranid fleet, only served as proof that Forbes's insistence on regular combat drills had not been time wasted.

So far, the damage sustained by the *Sword of Hadrian* had been relatively minimal, with only minor casualties suffered by her crew. She was sorry that the same could not be said of *The Praetorian*, one of the *Hadrian*'s sister ships.

It wasn't as if Battlegroup Aurelia was a proper 'battlegroup,' not that that was any excuse. The name was just an informal tag for a convoy that was small by Imperial Navy standards to say the least, just three Dauntless-class light cruisers – her own *Sword of Hadrian*, *Trajan's Shield* under the command of Captain Grieve, and Captain Voronin's *The Praetorian*.

'*Trajan's Shield* reports minimal damage, admiral,' called the communications officer. 'Captain Grieve sends his compliments, and asks if there are any new orders?'

Forbes could well imagine what Grieve's 'compliments' might sound like, in this hour. Grieve had been against this plan of attack from the beginning, and doubtless saw the loss of *The Praetorian* only moments before as vindication of his concerns.

'Inform the *Trajan* that losses had been anticipated,' Admiral Forbes answered, her tone level, 'and that the mission will continue as planned.'

'Aye, ma'am.'

Forbes scowled. It seemed an eternity already, but it had been only moments before that the forward sections of *The Praetorian* had been shorn clean off by the massive claws of a tyranid Kraken, like the pincers of an enormous crab tearing right through the cruiser's decks and gantries. There was little doubt that Captain Voronin and the rest of the command crew had died almost immediately, their blood boiling away in the cold vacuum of space in the slim chance that they survived the Kraken's claws themselves, but any hope that the crew in the rest of the ship might survive the attack was lost when the Kraken wrapped its mighty feeder tentacles around *The Praetorian's* bulk and then disgorged countless batteries of pyro-acid into the cruiser. Any that had survived the initial attack had found themselves burned alive, as the bio-agents flooded deck after deck.

'The Razorfiend appears to be listing, ma'am,' called Commander Mitchels.

'Don't let up,' Forbes answered. 'Keep punching until she stops hitting back, and then keep firing until she splits open. We can't chance a rearguard attack as we advance.'

Forbes had never quite known whom she had offended to be given this backwater posting. Seconded to a planetary governor, the admiral had originally assumed that she was merely to rattle the sabre, perhaps even to remind Governor Vandis exactly whence his authority flowed. But when she arrived in the Aurelia system Forbes found new orders from Sector Command waiting, informing her to assist the governor in whatever way possible until new orders were posted. For two years now that had meant acting as little more than a ferrying and messenger service for Meridian's governor, who was the Imperial authority over the entire Aurelia sub-sector. Some 'battle-group,' she scoffed.

Still, the enemy they faced today might serve to balance the lack of action they'd seen these long months, if the last hours had been any indication.

'Admiral, we've got a lock on the hive ship,' called the officer monitoring medium-range scans. 'We should close to firing range within the hour.'

'Keep monitoring, ensign,' Forbes answered. 'If she budges a centimetre I want to hear about it.'

In the end, it had proved almost ridiculously easy to find the hive fleet. With one ship, it might have taken ages, but with all three of the Dauntless-class cruisers at her disposal it had been a matter of surprising ease – though she doubted the battlegroup's astropaths would describe it in quite that way.

It was a well known fact among the Imperial Navy that the gestalt consciousness of a hive – the psychic contact that pervaded the area around a tyrannic fleet – had the effect of distorting warp space for light years in every direction. As a result, travel via the warp became increasingly uncertain the nearer one came to a tyrannic fleet, and astropathic contact became unreliable, sometimes even completely impossible. On the larger scale, this was the cause for the shadow in the warp that had interfered with astrotelepathy in the Aurelia sub-sector these last days and weeks. On the smaller scale, though, and in combat situations in particular, this distortion could have a profoundly unsettling effect on astropaths, many of whom had been known to lose their minds completely in battles with tyranids.

However, just as the astropaths of the *Sword of Hadrian* and the Blood Ravens strike cruiser *Armageddon* had been able to triangulate the general position of the fleet by measuring in which direction the interference was strongest, so too was Admiral Forbes with three ships able to do much the same kind of triangulation to steer the Aurelia Battlegroup physically towards the fleet itself. In essence – and in a move that many in her command considered foolhardy and unnecessarily dangerous, Captain Grieve chief among them – Forbes had simply ordered the three light cruisers to travel *towards* the direction of greatest distortion, reasoning that the greater the distortion, the closer to the hive fleet they would be.

When the battlegroup had emerged in normal space at the far edge of the Aurelia sub-sector, only days before, their long-range scans had immediately detected the vanguard drones of the tyranid fleet, proof positive that they were in close range of the fleet itself. To traverse the remaining distance by warp, though, *was* too foolhardy and dangerous, and so Forbes had ordered the ships to proceed at sublight speeds, making ready to engage with the fleet as soon as they made contact.

As they had closed with the hive fleet, they had quickly gotten a better read on their situation. It came as something of a relief to discover that this was not a full fleet, like the massive Leviathan, Behemoth, and Kraken Fleets of such dark memory, but was instead a splinter fleet, which must have split off from one of the larger bodies at some point in the past. But while it wasn't a full-fledged invasion fleet, it was still a not-inconsiderable threat, the hive ship herself a massive void-swimming gargantuan, attended by a myriad of other vessels ranging in size from the vanguard drone ships who acted as her scouts – small and only lightly armed, but possessing great speed and agility – to the massive Razorfiend cruisers and Kraken predators who swam in the hive ship's wake.

But if Forbes's plan was to have any hope of succeeding, they would need to punch their way through the outer ranks of the splinter fleet, taking the fight directly to the hive ship itself, the seat of the norn-queen and the collective hive mind who directed the movements not only of the spacefaring fleet but also of the ground-based elements on

Meridian, Typhon Primaris, and anywhere else in the sub-sector.

'Razorfiend is down,' Mitchels reported, as the last barrage from the *Hadrian's* starboard batteries found their mark.

'Drones still buzzing our port,' the port-side monitoring officer called out.

'Keep at them, port,' Forbes ordered the monitoring officer. 'Commander Mitchels, come to a new heading, to intercept the hive ship, and all ahead full.'

'Aye, ma'am,' Mitchels replied, and then hurried to relay the orders to the appropriate stations.

Now, they had the hive ship in their sights, and if luck and the Emperor were with them, they could manage to get within torpedo firing range. And then it would all be up to Sergeant Tarkus and his Blood Ravens.

By the time Sergeant Aramus reached the crash site at the heart of Meridian's capital city Zenith, the other two surviving members of his Third Squad, Battle-Brothers Cirrac and Siddig, were already there with fire suppression units, trying to keep the flames that burned on the outer hull of the governor's shuttle from igniting the promethium in its tanks and taking an entire city block up with it.

Fortunately, the shuttle had come down in a reflecting pool, which meant that not only did the waters now boiling off serve to dampen the flames, but that casualties were kept to a relative minimum. A number of civilian bystanders were hit by debris from the impact, some merely wounded and others afflicted with fatal injuries, while more were burned badly by the bio-plasma flames that poured off the craft's hull; but the death toll was a fraction of what it would have been had the shuttle come down directly onto one of the milling crowds.

It remained to be seen, though, whether anyone on board had survived the crash.

'As soon as the flames are doused,' Aramus ordered, 'we'll open her up.' He stepped over the low wall into the reflecting pool, which was now all but completely drained, the water having boiled off as steam from the heat of the shuttle's flames.

Siddig sprayed the last of the foam on the shuttle's mangled wings, and signalled the all-clear to the sergeant.

His own enhanced strength augmented even further by the servos of his power armour, Aramus simply reached down, grabbed hold of the edge of the crumpled starboard-side hatch, and yanked it off. With an ear-splitting sound of metal against metal the hatch tore free, and Aramus tossed it aside without another thought. The shuttle was canted over onto its right side, its nose buried in the cracked base of the pool, and so with the hatch open everything in the cabin that wasn't locked down came tumbling out the starboard hatch, falling at Aramus's feet.

The sergeant reached down to pick up a clear cube, a few centimetres on a side, in which was encased a polished oblong stone about the length of a man's finger. He'd seen such stones before, worn around the necks of eldar warriors.

'This looks like an eldar spirit stone,' Aramus said in disbelief. The sergeant understood little of the hermetic beliefs of the eldar, but enough to know that no eldar would dream of allowing one of their sacred spirit stones to fall into a human's hands.

Aramus looked down at the litter of items scattered at his feet. There were perhaps a dozen or more similar cubes of various sizes. One held what appeared to be a tooth of an ork, another what appeared to be circuitry of Tau design, still another a disc covered in Chaos sigils that made Aramus's eyes ache just to look upon them. And there weren't just the cubes, but a riot of data-slates and books – printed *books* – whose titles were suggestive of daemonic grimoires, as well as hololiths and two-dimensional paintings depicting a wide range of unwholesome subjects.

Aramus recoiled at the sight of the hoard. All of it was forbidden, whether xenos, or heretical, or daemonic. All of it was repulsive, repellent. And all of it, it appeared, was the possession of Governor Vandis himself.

'I... I can explain,' came the tremulous voice of Governor Vandis, who stood awkwardly in the canted hatchway, carrying in his arms an opaque case as long as he was tall. 'It isn't what it appears...'

Aramus didn't bother responding, but reached forward and snatched the long case from Vandis's hands.

'Please,' the governor said, trying to step down from the shuttle and instead sprawling face-forwards onto the mound of forbidden treasures. 'This is just my... collection, you see.' He rose up unsteadily on his knees, hands up in supplication. 'I am a collector, a patron, nothing more.' The governor's dark eyes were wide and frightened in his round face, lips quivering.

The case was heavy in Aramus's hands. He'd taken it from the governor for the simple reason that one didn't let a possessor of heretical items keep anything, for fear that he might carry something he might use against you. But now that Aramus held the case, he could not help but wonder what it held.

'No, don't!' Vandis pleaded, as Aramus undid the clasps that held the case shut. 'I… It was *given* to me, and…'

The case fell open, and inside Aramus saw something he'd not expected ever to lay eyes on again.

Battle-Brothers Siddig and Cirrac had come to stand beside him, but from their vantage points could not see within the case. 'What is it?' Cirrac asked.

Aramus wrapped his hands around the hilt, and lifted the power sword free of the case, holding the blade high overhead.

'Wisdom,' Aramus said, the name on his lips a kind of litany.

The power sword, relic of the Blood Ravens Chapter, so ancient and honoured that it had been granted a name, had been borne into battle by countless champions and heroes of the Chapter over the millennia, back to the earliest days of the Blood Ravens, but the most recent to carry it had been Captain Davian Thule himself.

Wisdom had been lost when Thule had fallen to the talons and toxins of the tyranid on Calderis, and Aramus had thought it would never be found again.

And yet here it was, in the heretical trove of this collector of the perverse, the forbidden, the arcane.

'It was a *gift*...' Vandis pleaded. 'I didn't... I didn't know it was *yours*...'

It wasn't Aramus's, of course. Perhaps the governor merely meant that it belonged to the Chapter. But whomever was the rightful bearer of the blade, now that Thule could no longer wield it, it had no place being tarnished by the touch of such a low creature as Vandis.

'I... I can *pay* you....' Vandis said, nodding in desperation. 'Call it a fine, if you like. I can...'

Aramus activated the power sword, energy coruscating down the length of the blade.

Vandis rose to his feet, hands held up before him, face blanched and bloodless.

'Anything you want!' Vandis screamed. 'I... I'm *sorry*...'

Aramus remained silent as a stone statue, but swung the power sword down in a sweeping arc with all of the strength of his servo-augmented arm.

The governor collapsed to the ground, his shoulders hitting the ground before his legs had begun to topple over.

'Should we not have kept him for the Inquisition?' Brother Siddig asked. 'They might have wanted to interrogate him to track the source of...' – he gestured to the mound of items at Aramus's feet, much of it now incarnadine with the governor's blood – 'all of this.'

Aramus stilled the power sword, and shook his head. 'We don't have the luxury to worry about such things now,' he said, turning away from the shuttle and stepping back over the pool's low wall. 'He was in possession of heretical items, and so secured his own doom.'

'Sergeant?' Brother Cirrac called. 'What do we do with his... collection?'

Aramus glanced back over his shoulder, his expression disgusted.

'Burn it,' he said, jaw set. 'Burn it all.'

SERGEANT TARKUS CROUCHED at the forward end of the cabin, hands on the makeshift guidance controls. There was little room for a Space Marine in full power armour to manoeuvre in the confined space, much less four Adeptus Astartes.

'Closing on target,' came the voice of Commander Mitchels over the vox-comms. 'We should be in firing range in moments.'

'Acknowledged,' Tarkus replied.

Behind him, the other three surviving battle-brothers of First Squad – Battle-Brothers Nord, Tane, and Horatius – checked the actions on their bolters, and secured their grenades and other ordnance for the coming acceleration.

'Be ready, squad,' Tarkus called back to them. 'We launch at any moment, and I want us ready to strike as soon as we punch through.'

The magos technicus of the *Sword of Hadrian* was to be commended, Tarkus thought. The modified torpedo was not the most stylish of conveyances, and not as roomy as boarding torpedoes specifically designed for the task, but it would suit their present needs admirably.

'I wouldn't mind a bit more armament,' Brother Tane said.

'And I wouldn't mind a full company at our backs to do the job with us,' Tarkus answered, 'but we fight with what we've been given.'

Once the First Squad had boarded, the gunnery crew of the *Sword of Hadrian* had loaded the boarding torpedo into the ship's torpedo tubes. It would be fired just like an ordinary torpedo, but unlike the ordinary variety this one could be partially guided in flight.

'I wonder how the others fare on Meridian,' Brother Horatius mused aloud.

'We can be assured that they have done their duty,' Tarkus answered. 'What else is there?'

Since the Aurelia Battlegroup had come in close contact with the tyranid hive fleet all astropathic contact with Meridian had been lost, but the last communications received had indicated that Captain Angelos's battlegroup was inbound for Aurelia. It remained to be seen, though, whether they would reach Meridian in time to save the beleaguered world. As it stood, it seemed likely that the plan that Admiral Forbes and Sergeant Tarkus had devised might well be the best, or perhaps the only, hope that Meridian had.

'We're within firing range now,' Commander Mitchels voxed. 'Preparing to launch.'

'Acknowledged,' Tarkus replied. Then to the others in the squad, he said, 'This is it, squad. Be ready to hit, and hit hard.'

The boarding torpedo would be launched directly at the thorax of the hive ship itself, and provided the gunnery officer did their calculations correctly, then the torpedo's nose would punch through the outer hull of the tyranid craft. Once the hive ship's hull was compromised, Sergeant Tarkus and the others would be disgorged from the boarding torpedo, delivered right into the midst of the enemy.

'Firing boarding torpedo!' came the voice of Commander Mitchels, and Sergeant Tarkus and the others were thrown back against their restraints by the sudden force of acceleration.

'Knowledge is power,' Tarkus called out, as they barrelled towards the heart of the enemy, ' guard it well!'

CHAPTER TWENTY

'FALL BACK!' SERGEANT Avitus voxed, since even his loudest shout would be swallowed by the deafening chittering and shrieks of the tyranid hordes rushing towards them. 'Fall back!'

Avitus spared a last glance at the thrashing form of Battle-Brother Gagan, as the trio of tyrant guards smashed the last life from him with their massive forelimbs. Then he fired an ineffectual burst of hellfire shells at the hive tyrant itself before turning and pounding feet in the opposite direction.

The firebreaks had served to slow the tyranid advance, but not as much as had been hoped. It had taken the tyranids a day and a night and part of a following day to cover ground that they otherwise would have overrun in a matter of hours, it was true, but that came as little comfort to those who had hoped the firebreaks might be a more effective deterrent.

'Avitus, on your right!' voxed Brother Pontius.

Avitus, without pausing, veered left, and turning from the waist fired a few rounds from his heavy bolter at the lictor who loped after him. The hellfire shells pocked the lictor's torso, and while the tyranid didn't fall, its pace was slowed enough for Avitus to outstrip it.

'Elon,' Avitus voxed. 'Flank right, and watch for ripper swarms.'

Brother Elon flashed his acknowledgement on the green-blinking rune on Avitus's visor display.

Avitus and the Ninth Squad had been leapfrogging firebreaks since the previous day, three altogether, and now they were falling back one last time.

'Cyrus,' the sergeant voxed, as he leapt and scrambled over the ruined landscape, 'we're inbound, what's your status?'

A gargoyle flapped on leathery wings overhead, and Avitus potted it with a burst of hellfire shells, ripping the left wing to shreds and pumping mutagenic acid into the creature's abdomen.

'The eastern approaches are covered,' crackled the voice of the Scout sergeant over the comms. 'We should have the west completed by the time the tyranids approach from that vector.'

'Understood,' Avitus replied. 'We should be at the ring in another five.'

'Cyrus out,' came the curt reply.

Avitus scowled, but continued to make the best time possible over the rubble and debris of what had once been a prosperous mercantile region of the capital city. Once, high-hab dwellers and nobles from all over the planet had come here to paw over the offerings of a dozen different systems – over-priced jewellery and baubles, delicacies and comestible rarities, clothes of the finest fabrics and most stylish cuts, ceremonial weapons and more. Now, it looked like nothing but what it was – a war-zone. Buildings had been destroyed by the Blood Ravens and the PDF in their encounters with the iso-lated outriders who had preceded the main body of the tyranid force, the gargoyles who flew overhead and the lictors and gaunts who had made it past the firebreaks to the east.

The most recent firebreak to be abandoned, the last but one to be cut into the landscape, had held through most of that morning, until the arrival of the hive tyrant and his retinue. Sergeant Aramus's orders to Avitus and his squad had been to hold the line as long as possible, giving as much time as they could to Sergeant Cyrus's Scout squad and the PDF forces assisting them in completing the ringed defence around the heart of Zenith itself. Employing the same strategy as the firebreaks, this ring was cut, burned, and blown into the buildings and surrounding land-scapes, but rather than running north and south it curved to the west in either direction, looping gently around until it met itself on the western edge of the city. Or it would, as soon as the western defences were completed. The ring was a moat of dead ground and charred rubble, a no-man's-land that would act a final bulwark against the Great Devourer.

'Spore mine!' shouted Brother Barabbas as a biovore vomited a projectile in their direction.

Zenith would be the last stronghold against the enemy, the final hold-out on Meridian. Any humans who remained outside of the ring – if any survived – would be at the mercy of the tyranids. Of the defenders, once Sergeant Avitus and the survivors of the Ninth Squad got within the ring, only Sergeant Thaddeus and the Seventh Squad would remain outside. The rest of the Blood Ravens, along with the surviving units of the Meridian PDF and the countless millions of civilian refugees, had already withdrawn into the capital city.

Brother Safir had raced ahead, and now reached the defensive ring. He stopped at the edge, and turned back to offer covering fire to the others as they hurried to join him. As soon as the Ninth made it past the ring, the accelerants that Cyrus's squad had laced throughout the moat would be ignited, creating a wall of flame and heat.

'Faster, Avitus,' urged Sergeant Cyrus, who had appeared at Safir's side, potting shots with his sniper rifle at the lictors who raced at Avitus's heels. A pair of Scouts accompanied their sergeant, and stood on the other side of Brother Safir, laying down suppressing fire with their bolt pistols and sniper rifles.

Avitus, already racing as fast as his legs would carry him, only growled in reply.

Brother Pontius leapt the edge of the defensive ring, followed in close order by Brothers Barabbas and Elon. Sergeant Avitus was the last across the line, and then Safir, Cyrus, and the two Scouts fell back as the tyranid raced to close the distance between them.

'Up, up!' urged Cyrus as the others scrambled to climb the inner wall of the moat. Scouts and PDF soldiers stood atop the inner rim, flamers in hand, ready to torch the moat.

By the time Avitus and the others reached the solid ground at the inside of the moat, the first of the tyranids had already scuttled down and into the trench, making good speed for the inside.

'Torch it!' Cyrus yelled out, his hair whipping around his bare head, his voice booming even over the howl of the wind and the skittering and chittering of the tyranids.

Dozens of flamers poured fire down into the trench, and the accelerants and explosives within ignited, throwing up a wall of flame dozens of metres into the air. Any tyranid who had made it into the ring was caught up in the flames, their chitinous carapaces cracking under the immense heat.

Cyrus turned to Sergeant Avitus, an uncharacteristic grin on his weathered face. 'Cutting it a bit fine there, Avitus.'

Avitus pulled off his helmet, the augmetic of his neck and jaw glinting dully in the flickering light of the flames, and answered only with a scowl.

SERGEANT THADDEUS AND the other surviving members of Seventh Squad had fought in the dark shadows beneath the habs for so long it felt as if they'd never see the daylight again. The strategy of luring the warriors in after them and picking them off one by one appeared to be working, though it was clear that for every warrior they put down others passed by their position entirely and continued on towards the west, with the main body of the tyranid forces advancing on Zenith. Thaddeus had been planning to move back out of the habs once the last of the warriors was located and destroyed, to carry the fight deeper into the tyranid-held territory to the east, when orders from Sergeant Aramus called for a change of plans.

'Attention, squad,' Thaddeus said to the others once he'd broken vox contact with Sergeant Aramus. 'We've been ordered to pull back to Zenith.'

'A retreat?' Battle-Brother Brandt asked with evident distaste.

The Blood Ravens Chapter did not adhere as closely to the strictures of the Codex Astartes as other Chapters, but while the Blood Ravens did not refuse to retreat under any circumstances as some Codex Chapters did, still the thought of turning their backs to the enemy was anathema to most Blood Ravens.

'Not a retreat,' Thaddeus corrected, 'but a withdrawal.' He paused, and looked around at the other three Blood Ravens standing in the circle of light cast by the lamps overhead. 'Aramus has decreed that the enemy forces are now too numerous for a direct assault to have any lasting impact, and has decided instead that a defensive posture is the only solution. We are to fall back to Zenith with the others, and help defend the stronghold.'

'So it's to be a siege, then?' Brother Takayo asked.

Thaddeus nodded. 'There is no other choice.'

The others wore grim expressions, and Thaddeus knew that his own could be no less stark. They all knew only too well the chances of a siege defence lasting any appreciable amount of time against such overwhelming numbers. Though they themselves had helped thin the numbers of effective enemy combatants by taking out as many warrior-class

synapse creatures as possible, they knew that a barri-
caded siege against a tyranid invasion was inevitably
doomed to failure.

But they also knew, as Thaddeus did, that there
was no other solution. The Blood Ravens themselves
might survive a frontal assault against the tyranids –
or some percentage of them might, at least – and
could continue to carry out raiding assaults behind
enemy lines almost indefinitely, but unless they
stood and defended the human inhabitants of the
planet, and fought to stop – or at least slow – the
process of tyranoforming, there would very quickly
be nothing left for them to defend but a barren
world overrun by monsters. A siege defence was
doomed to failure, but at least it would ensure the
survival of at least a portion of the human population for longer than any other strategy. And with a
considerable amount of luck, they might be able to
hold out until Captain Angelos's battlegroup could
arrive to reinforce them.

'Sir,' young Phaeton said in a quiet voice, as
though afraid to interrupt the sergeant's thoughts,
'my brother and I are hungry.'

Sergeant Thaddeus looked from the Blood Ravens
to the two youths who accompanied them. The two
had borne up well under the strain of the previous
days, following along with the Seventh Squad just as
Thaddeus had ordered them to do, without com-
ment or complaint. But though they were hardened
by their underhive upbringings, still they were mortal, and were subject to the same failings as any
other humans. When they had grown too tired to
continue walking, Thaddeus and his Space Marines

had carried them in turns, the Blood Ravens continuing to wield their bolt pistols in one hand with a boy thrown over their other shoulder, their chainswords sheathed at their sides. It was a testament either to the depth of the boys' fatigue or else to the conditions under which they were raised that they were able to sleep through the cacophony of bolter fire, the whirr of chainswords, and the shrieking of the dying warriors.

The boys had been awake and moving for hours now, but aside from the small amount of fresh water the squad had been able to find the night before in a cistern, the youths had had nothing to eat or drink since before the habdwellers had fled and they were separated from their mother. That they had gone this long without complaining of hunger was nothing short of remarkable.

'Just a little while longer,' Thaddeus told the boys. 'We'll be joining our friends in the capital soon, and they'll have food and drink for you there.'

Phaeton only nodded, while Phoebus remained silent and still.

'Come on, squad,' Thaddeus said, racking his bolt pistol and drawing his chainsword. 'Let's get moving.'

Despite having spent more than a day and a half wending their way through the catacombs that connected the habs, endless hours moving either through darkness or through twilit corridors, now that it came time to emerge once more into the sunlight it took the squad a surprisingly short amount of time to get out. Only a matter of moments, pausing at one point to rain hellfire on one of the few warriors left lurking in the shadows before them, and the Seventh blew open an access panel and emerged into daylight.

As Thaddeus had anticipated, now that the tyranid main force had continued to the west, the tyranid rearguard would be more sparsely spread, given over largely to ripper swarms who were busy consuming any organic material they could find, and the capillary towers that had just begun to climb towards the sky in the east.

The rippers were innumerable, and despite their small size the relentless eating machines were persistent, and as they became aware of the arrival of the four Space Marines and two human youths in their midst they began to teem towards them, mandibles clacking and claws out and grasping.

Thaddeus picked up Phoebus and held him in the crook of his left arm, while Brother Kell hoisted Phaeton into his arms.

'Jump packs, squad,' Thaddeus said. 'Due west, best possible speed, and the Great Devourer take the hindmost.'

The other three Blood Ravens grinned, recognizing a flash of the old joy that Thaddeus had once found in combat. They signalled their acknowledgement and took to the skies.

'Will there be monsters in the city?' Phoebus asked, looking up into Thaddeus's eye-slits.

'I imagine so,' Thaddeus answered. 'But there are heroes there, too.'

Activating his jump pack, Thaddeus leapt into the grey skies, while the rippers swarmed over the ground where he'd stood, gnashing their teeth, their ravenous hunger denied.

SERGEANT ARAMUS HELD Wisdom overhead, energy coruscating down the length of the power sword's blade, and mouthed the Blood Ravens' battle cry: 'Knowledge is power!'

Now that Sergeant Avitus and his Devastator squad had fallen back within the defensive ring, and the fires had been struck in the moat that surrounded the heart of Zenith, the Blood Ravens' full attentions could be turned to defence – in manning and maintaining the barricades, and in dealing with any enemy elements who made it past the defensive ring and into the defended area within.

The other two surviving members of Third Squad were at Aramus's side, Battle-Brothers Cirrac and Siddig firing their bolters at the hormagaunts who had made it through the flames of the defensive ring and were now ravaging the northern district of the capital. Some half-dozen of the creatures had made it through the ring of fire, and had slaughtered twice that many innocent civilians before Aramus and his squad could reach the site to put them down.

With the runes on his visor display and his hand-held auspex, Aramus was able to track the movements and status of the other Blood Ravens through the city. Avitus and his Devastators had joined Sergeant Cyrus and the Scout Squad in assisting the PDF in manning the barricades, using heavy bolters, meltaguns, and plasma guns to cut down any tyranids who seemed likely to make it through the inferno of the defensive ring. Other units of the

PDF patrolled the city, trying to keep order among the terrified refugees, with varying degrees of success. Chaplain Palmarius, his crozius arcanum in hand, led the fifteen aspirants in their blood-red bodygloves as they moved throughout the city, keeping watch for any stray tyranids that might have slipped through the net. And Librarian Niven, who had come down from the *Armageddon* to join in the effort, used his psyker's senses to help direct the movements of the Thunderhawk gunships who patrolled the skies, shooting down any airborne tyranids they encountered and firing strafing runs on the tyranid forces who had now spread out to surround the city entirely.

Aramus was not happy about having to adopt a siege mentality, knowing that it was doomed to failure in the long run. But the overwhelming numbers of enemy forces had left him with no choice. For every hundred of the monsters stopped by the defensive ring, though, there were always a handful who made it through; and though the clean-up squads led by Aramus and the Chaplain were successful in locating and eradicating the interlopers in time, inevitably the tyranids who made it into the city did considerable damage before they were stopped, wreaking havoc on the defences, the defenders, and the refugees alike. The death toll among the PDF was high, and the numbers of civilians lost was climbing almost as fast, and though the Blood Ravens had lost no more Space Marines since falling back to Zenith their numbers were already so badly depleted by the early actions on Meridian that they were operating at only partial strength.

Up on the *Armageddon*, Lexicanium Konan continued to try to reach other Blood Ravens via astrotelepathy, but since making contact with the astropaths in Captain Angelos's battlegroup he had been unsuccessful in reaching any others elsewhere. Now their only hope of survival lay in holding the city until Angelos arrived, but the chances of them lasting so long were beginning to look bleak.

'Aramus,' came the voice of Sergeant Cyrus buzzing over the vox-comms. 'Scout Jutan reports that tyranids have broken through the ring in the north-west quadrant in numbers.'

'On it,' Aramus replied simply. 'Come on, squad,' he voxed to Cirrac and Siddig, already speeding towards the west along the inner rim of the moat. 'Be ready.'

The Third Squad reached the north-west quadrant of the city to find a hive tyrant slashing through the rubble, his retinue of guards, warriors, and lictors following close behind. The refugees who had been housed in that quadrant were fleeing, but not quickly enough that some of them had not already fallen to the claws and talons of the tyranids, their dying screams still echoing over the stale, smoky air.

Even as he opened fire with his bolter, spitting hellfire at the tyrant and slashing at one of the forerunning lictors with the power sword Wisdom, Aramus knew that the numbers of tyranids in the quadrant were too great to overcome with the forces he had at his disposal. They would be able to pick them off in time, but not before the damage that they did had been irreparable, and the losses of innocent life impossible to calculate.

There was no choice. It was time for the oxbow manoeuvre.

'The north-west quadrant is lost to the enemy,' he voxed to the others on an open channel. 'All personnel pull back. Thunderhawks, initiate oxbow manoeuvre on my mark, centred on my current position.'

When he got the flashing confirmation that all of the Blood Ravens and PDF had pulled back from the wall for dozens of metres in either direction, Aramus signalled to Cirrac and Siddig. The three Blood Ravens lobbed frag and krak grenades at the invaders, then pulled back as quickly as possible while the tyranids regrouped. 'Mark!' Aramus shouted into the vox.

In answer, two Thunderhawks streaked towards his position, one from the north-west and the other from the north-east, high-energy beams lancing down from their dorsal-mounted turbo-lasers while Whirlwind missiles launched from beneath their wings. The two Thunderhawks drew lines of fire in the ground, starting at the defensive ring and arcing inwards until they met only a few dozen metres from where Aramus stood.

Like an oxbow, a semicircular bend in a river that closes off the land within, Aramus's emergency plan called for an oxbow to be cut in the defensive ring, surrendering the land within to the enemy while cutting a new firebreak to be defended.

It was a desperate measure, of course. Use it too often, and the tyranids would succeed in pressing the defenders into an ever decreasing area, making it all the easier to ultimately overrun them entirely. But it was a preferable alternative to standing and fighting a losing battle against an overwhelming force.

The Thunderhawk pilots signalled the movement complete, and peeled away to return to their duties.

'Cyrus, Avitus,' Aramus voxed, 'I want this hole in the net closed up, as fast as possible.' In response, the Blood Ravens and PDF who had moved away from the quadrant only moments before now rushed back to man the new barricades.

Aramus glanced skyward, knowing that somewhere overhead the strike cruiser *Armageddon* orbited. Onboard, Lexicanium Konan would still be trying to reach anyone by astrotelepathy, for all the good it would do them. As it stood, they could not even communicate with anyone in the next system over, much less hundreds or thousands of light years away.

Not only had they been unable to contact anyone outside of the Aurelia sub-sector, but ever since the Aurelia Battlegroup had closed with the hive fleet, they'd lost astropathic contact with Admiral Forbes as well. Aramus only hoped that her forces were still in the fight, and that they might succeed in weakening the tyranid fleet, or distracting it if nothing else.

'EMPEROR'S THRONE!' SERGEANT Tarkus swore as they moved ever deeper into the body of the beast. The floor squelched beneath their feet, and the walls and ceiling pulsed, rhythmically, like a beating heart.

'Sergeant?' Space Marines were never uneasy, but there was almost a quaver of fear running beneath Battle-Brother Horatius's tone. 'Which way is it?'

They stood at a juncture between two corridors. Of course, the tubular passages with their irregular walls were more like arteries than the corridors of a engineer-designed vessel like the *Armageddon*, the juncture more like a chamber, with heart-like valves instead of hatches. But that was hardly surprising, as the hive ship had never been designed by any engineer, but was a living creature, though impossibly large.

Before Tarkus could reply, another collection of the 'bites' came swarming down the artery to their right, teeming over walls, ceiling, and floor. They knew of no other name for them so had called them bites since each appeared to be nothing more than an oversized biting mouth at the end of a stunted, snake-like body.

'Fire!' Tarkus said, and played hellfire over them. The heavy bolters echoed deafeningly in the narrow artery as the Blood Ravens cut them down.

The bites had first swarmed at the location where the boarding torpedo had pierced the outer skin of the hive ship, where Tarkus and the First Squad had been able to gain access to the innards of the gargantuan beast itself.

'Tane, you say those things are like our Larraman cells?' Tarkus said.

Brother Tane had advanced the theory, but it had been little more than a guess. He shrugged. 'Seems reasonable.'

As Tane had opined, like the Larraman cells which coursed to the site of any injury in a Space Marines body, converting into scar tissue and beginning the healing process, the bites might act as defensive cells, rushing to the site of intrusion and sealing the wound, perhaps by devouring any foreign bodies and converting them into 'scab.'

'Then we go *that* way,' Tarkus said, pointing the direction from which the bites had come. 'If the defences are keyed to keep us from that direction, it stands to reason that's where we want to go.'

Tarkus had always known that tyranid hive ships were living creatures, just like all of the warriors and weapons of the tyranid – from the tiniest microscopic spores through the weapons-symbiotes to the most massive carnifex – but until now he had not really contemplated what that suggested. But now, moving through the pulsing arteries of the hive ship, fending off its antibodies and wending their gradual way towards its heart, it finally struck Tarkus that they were not boarding a ship… they were invading a *body*.

The hive ship was, in a sense, the mother of a tyranid hive. Home of the norn-queen, a living bio-factory that constantly gave birth to an unending stream of warriors, weapons, and ships, the ship itself was a living creature incorporating millions of bio-engineered organisms, their genomes spliced and replicated to be perfectly adapted for their tasks. The hive ship followed the rest of the fleet, arriving at an invaded world only at the last stages of assimilation, and with the help of the capillary towers constructed on the surface by its offspring, it would then complete the process of planetary assimilation by consuming even the atmosphere and oceans from a world, until there was nothing left behind but a lifeless husk.

A whistling came down the artery towards them, like a strong wind blowing.

'Incoming,' Tarkus said, raising his bolter. He expected more bites, perhaps defensive organisms of a somewhat larger form.

Six monsters shambled down the artery towards them, burning spittle dripping from their gaping maws, scything blades and serrated fangs sharp as razors, each of them easily twice the size of any one of the Blood Ravens.

Tarkus had expected that the next defenders might be *somewhat* larger than the bites. He was learning that his expectations were, in this and in so many other aspects, woefully short of the true horror to be found in the hive ship.

'At them, Blood Ravens!' Tarkus yelled, firing his bolter as the shambling monsters raced with ungainly gaits towards them. 'Do your duty!'

CHAPTER TWENTY-ONE

SERGEANT THADDEUS ARCED down out of the grey skies, Phoebus in the crook of his left arm, his bolt pistol spitting hellfire in his right hand. Brothers Brandt and Takayo were already on the ground, laying about them on all sides with their chainswords, clearing a landing zone, while Brother Kell with the young Phaeton in his arms was arcing down out of the sky just above and to the left of Thaddeus. All around Brandt and Takayo lay the severed carcasses of rippers, with a couple of gaunts still striking out at them.

As Thaddeus touched down, Takayo used his chainsword to lop the forelimbs from one of the gaunts, and Brandt blew holes in the other's abdomen with his bolt pistol.

'Hang on,' Thaddeus told the boy in his arms, 'we're almost there.' As Kell thudded to the ground behind him, and Brandt and Takayo covered the approaches on all sides, the sergeant pulled out his auspex and oriented their present position. 'That way,' he said, pointing a few degrees off due west. 'Another hop or two and we should be there.'

They'd spent hours like this, completing prodigious leaps, using hellfire and chainswords to clear a patch of ground to land, then jumping off again as soon as they'd got their bearings. As they'd moved further west the numbers of tyranid they encountered had grown more and more concentrated, until now it was as though they were dropping down into an endless sea of the monsters. But at least their jump packs allowed them to leap over hordes that it would have been all but impossible to fight their way through on foot.

'Move out, squad,' Thaddeus ordered, glancing in Kell's direction.

First in the air and last on the ground, Brother Kell's calculated trajectory carried him slower and longer through the air, in deference to the vulnerable youth he carried in his arms. Thaddeus was next, for the same reason, leaving first Brandt and then Takayo to vault into the grey skies as soon as the other two were clear. Brandt and Takayo followed a shallower trajectory that brought them back to earth sooner, to once more use hellfire and chainsword to clear a swathe on which their battle-brothers could land.

As a result of his higher, slower trajectory, Sergeant Thaddeus reached a better vantage point from which to survey the surrounding landscape, and had more time to take in the detail. While he so far had seen nothing but the ruined urban landscape of Meridian's eastern hemisphere, overrun by tyranid monsters, he kept careful watch in the event that he espied any enemy movements that might prove strategically useful to Sergeant Aramus and the others once the Seventh reached Zenith.

Thaddeus approached the apex of his trajectory. In his arms, the young Phoebus shivered as the cold winds whipped around them.

'Not much longer now,' Thaddeus said aloud to the boy, though he doubted his words could be heard over the whistling of the wind. 'Almost there.'

The sergeant's gaze scanned from south to west, surveying the land over which he jumped. The ground swarmed in places with tyranids, like an unbroken carpet of monstrous bugs. Had he been a mortal man, Thaddeus might have felt a shiver up his spine, a quail of terror looking upon such overwhelming numbers of the beast, but even with his system and emotional state carefully regulated by implants and long years of indoctrination he could feel a faint touch of disquietude, the slightest brush of something he might well name fear.

Up ahead, just this side of the horizon, he could see the defensive ring cut around the heart of Zenith. Another jump and they would be there.

He turned his head to the right, as he began to arc downwards to the ground, his gaze scanning from west to north. And there he saw something that caused the faint touch of fear to tighten in a vice-strong grip.

A monstrous creature, living engine of destruction, was approaching Zenith from the northeast.

'Holy Throne,' Thaddeus swore in a harsh whisper. He came down to earth, his bolt pistol still and cold in his hands, and if not for Brandt and Takayo keeping the surging tide of tyranid back he would have fallen before their talons as soon as his boots touched down. 'Emperor preserve us...'

'What is it?' Brother Takayo voxed over, hearing Thaddeus's muttered prayer.

'Just move!' Thaddeus said, immediately preparing his jump pack for a final leap. 'Don't ask, just jump!'

SERGEANT AVITUS PATROLLED the inner rim of the defensive ring, covering the eastern approaches. A trio of lictors from the far side lunged into the ring of flame, intending to race to the other side, and Avitus unleashed hellfire from his heavy bolter at them, slowing them enough to let the heat of the flames do the rest of the work.

The ring had contracted time and again, these last hours, as the inhuman monsters threw body after body into the gap, bridging the moat with their own burning dead. The area held by the defenders had shrunk by perhaps as much as fifteen or twenty per cent since the main assault had begun, and they were losing more ground all the time.

'Blood Ravens,' came a voice crackling over the vox-comms. 'This is Thaddeus. The Seventh approaches from the east, and will pass over the ring in moments.'

'Acknowledged, Thaddeus,' Avitus replied by vox. 'We'll hold the door open for you.' A clutch of warriors dived into the flames from the outer rim of the ring and Avitus opened fire on them, spraying hellfire from side to side indiscriminately. 'But don't tarry. We may have to fall back from this position soon.'

'No worries on that count,' Thaddeus answered. 'Coming in fast and hot.'

As if to punctuate Sergeant Thaddeus's words, a Space Marine with a jump pack on his back came whistling out of the grey sky, passing just above the wall of flame and landing with a thud a few metres behind Avitus. The Space Marine hit the ground on his feet, and without pause turned and trained his bolt pistol back the way he'd come, his chainsword whirring in hand.

'Stand down, brother,' Avitus called over, waving his hand to signal the Space Marine to be at ease. 'We've got your back covered.'

Avitus's heavy bolter fired again down into the moat.

'All units on the eastern ring,' Avitus voxed on an open channel. 'Concentrate your fire into the moat and not at airborne elements. We've got Blood Ravens jumping in, and I don't want any of them shot down in error.'

The others, spread out to the north and south on both sides of Avitus's position, signalled their acknowledgement, as another Blood Raven came arcing down out of the sky. Like the first, this one had a bolt pistol in one hand and a whirring chainsword in the other.

'Stand fast, Brandt,' the first jump pack wearing Blood Raven called to the other as the newcomer hit the ground. 'We're covered.'

'You won't get any complaints from me, Takayo,' the other said, stilling his chainsword and holstering his bolt pistol.

A third Space Marine whistled down out of the sky, this one carrying a human youth cradled in his arms.

'Picked up a passenger out there, did you?' Avitus called over.

The Space Marine set the youth down on the ground. The boy appeared no more than ten or eleven, and Avitus didn't fail to notice that he fit the physiognomy profile for a Blood Ravens aspirant.

'Two, actually, sergeant,' the Space Marine answered. He pulled off his helmet, and Avitus recognized the assault squad member known as Kell. 'We had a time getting them back here in one piece, though.'

'Clear the ground!' came the voice of Sergeant Thaddeus over the vox as a fourth and final Blood Raven came soaring out of the sky. Like Kell, Thaddeus carried a youth in his arms, this one a year or two younger than the first, but looking as much alike that they could be brothers.

Thaddeus hit the ground, but kept the youth cradled in his arms, protectively. Without a word, he went striding up towards Avitus, his eyes on the fiery defensive ring.

'It won't be enough,' Thaddeus said, peering down into the burning scar gouged out of the landscape. The last batch of warriors still writhed and burned in the fires below, having fallen just short of reaching the inner side. 'It won't be near enough.'

Avitus looked from Thaddeus to the moat and back again. He felt the skin of his face and neck itch where it joined with his augmetic, a long-familiar sign of impending danger. 'What is it, Thaddeus? What's the situation out there?'

Thaddeus had glanced down at the boy in his arms, and looked up to meet Avitus's gaze.

'It is bad, brother,' Thaddeus said, 'and it's about to get much worse.'

SERGEANT ARAMUS AND the other two survivors of the Third Squad had joined Chaplain Palmarius and the aspirants in their defence of the north-east quadrant. Two of the aspirants had fallen to the tyranid interlopers already – one of them scythed in half by the talons of a lictor, the other dying painfully when the corrosive maggot-like organisms of a deathspitter symbiote ate their way through the flesh of one shoulder and the side of his head, killing him quickly but not, to the horror of the other aspirants, immediately – and a third was badly injured by a close scrape with a barbed strangler, but still able to stand and fight.

'Come along!' Chaplain Palmarius shouted to the dozen aspirants still on their feet, leading from the front with his crozius arcanum high over his head. 'For the Emperor and all mankind!'

A hormagaunt brood had broken through the defensive ring a short time before, more than two dozen strong, and begun ravaging the territory on the inside of the moat. Before Chaplain Palmarius and his aspirants arrived at the scene entire families had fallen before the talons and weapon-symbiotes of the gaunts – men, women, and children – but once the Blood Ravens Chaplain stormed into the vicinity, swinging his crozius arcanum as though it were a massive battle-axe, charging into the midst of the foul tyranids, no more innocent civilians had been lost. By the time Sergeant Aramus and Battle-Brothers Siddig and Cirrac arrived, the human refugees who'd been housed in the quadrant had fled screaming, deeper into the heart of the capital city.

In time, Aramus knew, there would be nowhere else for them to run. But for now, he was glad not to have the refugees underfoot for a moment, so that he and the others could fight the tyranids without concern for collateral damage.

'Behind you, Chaplain!' Aramus shouted, and fired his bolter at the gaunt who had rushed up at the Chaplain from behind. Then he shifted the power sword Wisdom in his fist, and brought its coruscating blade slicing across the thorax of another gaunt who was within arm's reach.

Aramus had always known that the defence of Zenith would not be easy, and that it would be only a matter of time before the defenders would be overwhelmed. But it appeared to him as if the intensity of the tyranid attacks had grown exponentially in recent hours. There were more tyranids at the barricades with each passing moment, their attacks even more vicious, almost desperate in character. Aramus knew better than to ascribe individual motivations to the tyranids, or to see agency in a creature that was merely a mindless extension of a distant and impassive hive mind, but perhaps instead it was the hive mind itself that was lashing out. Perhaps the hive fleet had been goaded into ever more violent action as a response to the actions of Admiral Forbes and her Aurelia Battlegroup, not in the conscious and calculated manner of a rational being, but more like the instinctual reaction of an aurochethere set to rampaging by the bite of a tiny insect.

Another hormagaunt raced towards Sergeant Aramus's position, and as it neared it shot flesh hooks out at him, a sharp muscle spasm propelling the chitinous sinews directly at the sergeant's head and shoulders. Aramus didn't delay, but brought Wisdom up in a tight arc, the blade of the power sword sweeping the sinews away while severing them from the body of the beast, so that they flopped to the ground like decapitated snakes, writhing and thrashing madly but unable to do any real damage.

Aramus took a single instant to admire the play of the fading sunlight of late afternoon on the blade, which crackled with coruscating energy. Could he, in the brief time given to him to wield the blade, do some little bit to restore the honour to the cherished relic that had been tarnished by the oily touch of the treacherous governor? If he survived the undertaking on Meridian, he would return Wisdom to the Secret Masters of the Chapter, who would bestow it on a worthy champion among the Blood Ravens, but until that time it was Aramus's duty to guard it well, and to use it to the greater glory of Chapter and Emperor alike. It still rankled to know that the holy weapon had been sullied by inclusion in a heretic's collection of forbidden relics, but every time Aramus drew the blade in battle and met tyranid chitin with honest Astartes metal, he could not help but feel that he was helping to cleanse the sword and restore it, if only in part, to its former glory.

'Aramus?' came a voice buzzing over the vox-comms. Aramus glanced at the runes on his visor display, and saw the transmission identified as coming from Sergeant Thaddeus.

'Thaddeus, have you made it safely within the ring?' Aramus replied, impaling a gaunt on the tip of Wisdom and then exploding its head with hellfire rounds.

'Within the ring, brother,' Aramus responded, 'but I can't say much for 'safely'.'

Aramus kicked the decapitated gaunt off the end of Wisdom, and then turned the power sword towards the next opponent. 'Clarify?'

'I'm approaching your position, Aramus,' Thaddeus voxed. 'You're about to need backup, and more than we have on hand to spare.'

'If this is one of your jibes, brother, it's in poor taste.'

Aramus could hear Thaddeus's ragged sigh. 'I've found precious little cause for jests of late, Aramus. And less still after seeing the beast currently trundling your way.'

Aramus fired his bolter at another gaunt, picking it off before it closed with one of the aspirants.

'It's a carnifex,' Thaddeus went on. 'And it's headed your way. Fast.'

Aramus was brought up short by the mere mention of the word. The carnifex was a living engine of destruction, a massive assault organism every bit as big and powerful as one of the Space Marine's enormous Dreadnoughts. For a force with heavy armour at their disposal a carnifex would still be a daunting challenge to face, but for an almost pure infantry force such as Sergeant Aramus's Blood Ravens were currently constituted, a carnifex would be an almost unstoppable opponent.

Though Aramus had no reason to doubt Thaddeus's report, if he'd harboured any doubts they would have been squelched in the next moment as the massive creature appeared through the smoke at the far side of the defensive ring, beyond the wall of flame and the few interloping hormagaunts who still stood. The carnifex towered over the moat, a living engine of destruction as big – and as dangerous – as any tank, so tall that as it crouched and then leapt down into the moat, its forelimbs and head were still above the level of the ground on either side, the flames only lapping its lower extremities.

The carnifex lumbered forward, the pincer-like talons of its upper limbs scything up and down rhythmically, the weapons symbiotes fused to its mid-limbs swivelled up and ready to attack.

Aramus heard a roar from overhead, and looked up to see Thunderhawk One making its routine pass over the quadrant, scouting for any interlopers from the air and prepared to offer suppressing fire if need be.

'Thunderhawk One!' Aramus called out over the vox-comms. 'Target the carnifex in the moat and fire!'

'Acknowledged,' replied the pilot, and Aramus recognized the voice of Scout Tubach, who sounded eager to unleash the gunship's weaponry on such a massive target.

The dorsal-mounted turbo-laser on the gunship opened fire, as Whirlwind missiles screamed from beneath the wings, flying unerringly towards the carnifex who was just now climbing up the inner wall of the moat.

The las-blasts splattered over the carnifex's carapace, and the Whirlwinds exploded with concussive force against its thorax. For a moment, the carnifex was lost in the black smoke of the explosions, and it seemed to Aramus as though the beast might have been felled. Then the winds whipped the smoke away, and the sergeant saw the massive beast still standing, unmarked and unharmed, training the venom cannon weapon-symbiote bound to its right mid-limb at the Thunderhawk as it passed directly overhead.

'Tubach!' Aramus cried out. 'Evasive!'

But it was too late. The venom cannon discharged directly at the prow of the gunship as Thunderhawk One overflew the moat, lascannon still firing, and the highly corrosive poison crystals of the tyranid blast began eating right through the armour plating that very instant.

'Sergeant!' called out Scout Tubach. 'We've lost integrity, and there's some kind of...' The Scout broke off in a coughing fit as the poisonous vapours seeped into the cockpit.

The Thunderhawk began to veer off to the north, erratically.

'Tubach, can you read me?' Aramus voxed. 'Tubach, pull up. Tubach!'

The Thunderhawk slammed down into the tyranid-held territory to the north of the ring of fire,

and immediately went up in flames as the promethium of its tanks ignited.

The carnifex spared the barest of glances off to
its right, at the column of smoke and flame that
was all that remained of the gunship that had
been to it little more than an irritant, and turned
its cold eyes on Sergeant Aramus and the other
defenders.

The carnifex opened its mouth wide, mandibles
spreading, and uttered a deafening and inhuman
shriek.

Suddenly their odds of surviving to see the arrival
of Captain Angelos's battlegroup seemed far, far
longer...

SERGEANT TARKUS FIRED the last of his hellfire rounds
at the shambler who lurched towards him, and then
his bolter clicked on an empty chamber as the magazine was finally spent. The hellfire did its work, the
shambler collapsing at Tarkus's feet with a twitching
spasm as the mutagenic acid ate through it, but there
would be no other rounds to fend off the countless
other creatures who prowled the arteries and chambers of the hive ship.

Tarkus holstered his bolter, drawing his combat
knife. He might have been tempted to simply toss
the bolter aside, as there was no way for him to load
it again – the others had run out of ammunition
long before – but nearly two centuries of service in
the Adeptus Astartes had taught him to cherish the
rare and treasured weapon, and it felt to him like the
worst sort of betrayal to leave it behind, even if it was
of no further use to him.

'Come along, squad,' Tarkus called to Battle-Brothers Nord and Horatius. 'We gain nothing from lingering here.'

Brother Tane had fallen some time before, swarmed by the teeming bites who had brought him down and gnawed their vicious way through the ceramite of his power armour before his battle-brothers could come to his assistance. The defiant screams of Tane's death throes had echoed over the vox-comms, but Tarkus and the others had honoured his memory by eradicating every last one of the bites that had killed their brother, with hellfire and blade.

Now only a handful of grenades and their combat knives were all that stood between the three Blood Ravens and an equally grisly death, but they soldiered on. They had a mission to carry out, and would do so, even if it meant all of their lives in the attempt.

They had found themselves in the sickly green illumination of the reproductive chambers. The walls, floor, and ceiling of the chambers were slicked with mucus, oily and viscous to the touch, and the fouled air was filled with noxious vapours that would have killed them in a single breath had it not been for the enclosed circulatory systems of their power armour. At the centre of the chamber were the bubbling geno-organs that birthed the endless numbers of tyranids in the fleet, and lining the chamber were the cocooned officers of nightmare hordes yet to be born.

'We're getting nearer our goal,' Tarkus said to the others, who followed him in silence. 'With the offspring here, the norn-queen can't be far beyond.'

The others nodded, watching the green-hued shadows on all sides.

From the far side of the chamber came a high-pitched keening noise, followed by the appearance through a valve of another trio of shamblers, the acid of their burning spittle dripping viscously from their mandibles, the blades of their forelimbs scything menacingly.

'For the Emperor!' Tarkus yelled, brandishing his combat knife and rushing full tilt at the shamblers. 'For the Chapter! Only in death does duty end!'

ANOTHER OF THE aspirants, moving too slowly to avoid the lash whip of the carnifex's tail, was ripped in half by the barbs, his lifeblood pouring out, all but invisible against the blood-red hide of his body-glove.

'Faster, Emperor damn you!' Sergeant Aramus shouted, readying a krak grenade in one fist as Wisdom sang in the other. He'd ordered the aspirants to fall back, but the frightened youths had moved too slowly to avoid the carnifex's initial attack.

'Aramus, cover!' came the voice of Thaddeus as he threw a frag grenade at the carnifex's head. The shrapnel sleeted against the behemoth's carapace in the instant after the explosion, but it wasn't clear that it had done any damage at all.

Aramus couldn't help but remember Battle-Brother Durio facing off against the carnifex on Prosperon, what seemed a lifetime before. He hefted the krak grenade in his hand, and prayed to the

Emperor to give him the courage that Durio had displayed.

'Fall back, I said!' Aramus called out, all patience lost. He knew only too well that bolter fire and lasguns and frag grenades would do little more than annoy a living war machine like the carnifex, but with a considerable amount of luck and the willingness for self-sacrifice a Space Marine with a krak grenade and good aim might well be able to bring one down. If he was but a few centimetres off in his delivery, though, he'd find himself imploded to a pulp and the carnifex completely unharmed.

There was nothing else for it. If he perished in the failed attempt to bring down the monster, then it would fall to Thaddeus to try his hand, and should Thaddeus fall one of the others would do the same, and so on, and so on, until either the carnifex fell or the Blood Ravens were wiped out, whichever came first.

He readied himself to rush forward, as soon as the last of the others were clear.

'Aramus, look skyward!' Thaddeus called, pointing with the tip of his chainsword at the heavens above.

Aramus craned his neck back, and saw a white dot flaring out of the grey sky, growing larger with each passing instant.

It was a drop-pod.

'But who…?' Aramus couldn't guess who might be aboard, with all of the Blood Ravens from the *Armageddon* already on Meridian. All except for Apothecary Gordian, Lexicanium Konan, and Techmarine Martellus. Had any of them been so foolish as to leave their posts, despite Aramus's orders, and employed one of the strike cruiser's one-way landing craft?

For the briefest moment, Aramus entertained the notion that it might be a drop-pod from Captain Angelos's *Litany of Fury*, and that the battlegroup had arrived in the Meridian system far ahead of schedule. But as the drop-pod plummeted out of the sky he could see the markings on its hull, the black raven with the teardrop of blood in its heart – it was a Fifth Company craft. So it *had* to be Gordian, Konan, or Martellus onboard. Unless…

As the craft thundered down to the ground, the carnifex reared back, screeching deafening defiance at the interloper, snapping its horrible talons in a martial display.

Mere moments after it had appeared in the skies overhead, the drop-pod landed with a deafening thud only a few dozen metres from Aramus's position, the shockwave of the impact kicking up clouds of dust in all directions.

As soon as the pod had touched down, it cracked open, the five faces of its armoured exterior casing falling open like the petals of a bloom.

No Space Marines poured out, but instead a voice boomed from within.

'Blood Ravens! To arms!'

Aramus recognized the voice, and felt hope flare within his breast.

'Knowledge is power!' came the altered but still unmistakable voice of Davian Thule, as the massive Dreadnought stamped out onto the dusty ground, the sound of its massive footfalls like pealing thunder.

'Guard it well!' shouted Aramus and Thaddeus in unison, raising their weapons on high.

No longer Captain Davian Thule, he was now and forever the Thule Dreadnought, the ultimate fusion between mechanical and biological, with the body of the fallen captain held in amniotic fluids and surgically implanted into the heart of the war machine. Standing three times as tall as a man, plated in thick adamantium and armed with a staggering amount of firepower, the Dreadnought was a mighty engine of war, the perfect union of biological and mechanical, the living embodiment of the Machine-God.

'Face me!' the Thule Dreadnought bellowed, turning towards the carnifex. 'Face Thule and your doom!'

Aramus found himself smiling, to his surprise. The return of Thule to the field of battle, whether under his own power or at the heart of a Dreadnought assembly, gave him hope that they might prevail, at last. If only they could hold out until Captain Angelos arrived…

CHAPTER TWENTY-TWO

Sergeant Aramus was tempted to simply stand and watch the massive war machine do battle with the tyranid engine of destruction, to bask in the glory of the Emperor's might, but he knew that the arrival of the Thule Dreadnought on the field of battle gave them a momentary advantage, not an easy victory.

This was no time to act the spectator. There was still work to be done.

'Knowledge is power!' the Thule Dreadnought repeated, unleashing the fury of the twin-linked autocannons mounted on his right arm while raising the power fist that grasped at the end of his left. Mighty pistons drove the Dreadnought's legs, and he took one step after another towards the carnifex, the destroyed buildings surrounding them echoing with the thunder of his footfalls.

The carnifex lashed out with its whip-like tail, but the barbs only rebounded harmlessly off the cast-adamantium of the Dreadnought's armour plating.

'Guard it well!' the voice of Thule boomed across the ruined city streets.

The carnifex lunged forward, the wicked talons of its forelimbs scything downwards, but in a lightning-fast movement the Thule Dreadnought reached up and grabbed hold of the carnifex's right forelimb with his massive power fist, and as the carnifex's left forelimb completed its arc to collide with the Dreadnought's shoulder, the Thule Dreadnought opened fire with his autocannons at point-blank range.

As carnifex and Dreadnought grappled, Aramus tore his attention away from the contest and back to the other threats facing them. In the wake of the carnifex had followed a host of raveners and horma-gaunts who were racing over the ruined cityscape towards them, all of them directed by the thoughts of a zoanthrope who hovered behind them, the synapse creature governing the movements of all the others from a rearguard position of defence.

'Thaddeus!' Aramus called to his battle-brother, as transfixed by the sight of the glorious Dreadnought as he himself had been. 'The enemy is not yet finished with us.' With the tip of Wisdom he indicated the tyranids rushing towards them from the defensive ring.

Thaddeus raised his own chainsword, the blade whirring. 'And we are not yet finished with them, either.'

'Do you note the zoanthrope, brother?' Aramus asked.

Thaddeus nodded. 'It won't be easy getting to it.'

'Perhaps,' Aramus answered, a slight grin tugging up the corners of his mouth behind his visor. 'But since when did you prefer anything done the *easy* way?'

Thaddeus chuckled, and Aramus could see his eyes smiling through the eye-slits of his visor. 'Better to die in battle than of boredom, eh, brother?'

Aramus responded by turning to meet the onrushing tide, power sword raised high. 'For the Chapter.'

'For the Emperor,' Thaddeus responded.

'For Meridian!' Aramus shouted, rushing forward, bolter kicking in his right fist as Wisdom coruscated in his left.

'For Meridian!' Thaddeus echoed, ploughing into the interlopers with hellfire and chainsword.

SERGEANT AVITUS AND the rest of the Ninth Squad manned the eastern approaches to Zenith. Reports were coming in from all points of the defensive ring that the tyranid were increasingly the intensity and frequency of their attacks at least threefold, and the defenders were now sorely pressed to prevent interlopers from clearing the fiery moat and making it into the defended territory. Sergeant Thaddeus had gone to aid Aramus against the carnifex, while the other three survivors of the Seventh Squad had hurried off to deliver the two young aspirants to safety before joining the fray. As loath as Avitus was to ask another squad for assistance, though, he was beginning to regret letting the newcomers go, as even with a Devastator squad that was five Space Marines strong he was finding it all but impossible to keep the tyranid forces at bay.

A brood of gargoyles wheeled overhead on leathery wings, the air filled with the sound of their horrible keening screeches.

'Squad, eyes up,' Avitus called out, swinging up the barrel of his heavy bolter and targeting the nearest gargoyle.

To his right, Battle-Brother Barabbas fired his melta gun at another of the hellbats, while Battle-Brother Pontius unleashed the hellfire of his heavy bolter, and on his left Brother Safir with his heavy bolter and Brother Elon with his melta picked their targets and fired.

The first barrage from the Devastators sent five of the hellbats plummeting to earth in a death-spiral, but more than a half-dozen remained, swooping down towards them with fleshborers and bio-plasma weapon-symbiotes spitting death.

Brother Safir's heavy bolter hit an empty chamber as his magazine ran dry, and the hellbat diving right towards him knocked him clear off his feet with its raking claws. As the gargoyle beat back up into the sky, though, Brother Elon spun and caught it with a blast from his melta gun, burning off one of its leathery wings entirely, leaving nothing but a charred stump. Its lone wing flapped uselessly as it plummeted back to earth, shrieking in impotent defiance.

It wasn't until the last of the gargoyles had crashed to the ground, and Safir was once more on his feet, loading a new magazine into his heavy bolter, that the squad realized that the gargoyle brood had been merely a diversion, to distract them from the beast already halfway across the fiery moat and closing fast.

It was a hive tyrant, a massive bonesword in one forelimb and a lash whip growing from the other, a venom cannon affixed to its mid-limbs. And in its wake followed its retinue of tyrant guards, ferocious living shields with no eyes of their own, blind and guided only by the psychic power of the synapse creature they protected.

Avitus could not say if this was the same tyrant who had forced them to fall back from the last fire-break, the same tyrant guards who had smashed the life from Battle-Brother Gagan, but in the end it didn't matter. If he could not have his revenge against the one tyrant, any other would suit his vengeance just as well.

'Pick your target and fire at will,' Sergeant Avitus shouted, the machine-like buzz of his augmetic vocal cords even more pronounced than usual. 'But the tyrant is mine!'

LIBRARIAN NIVEN RAISED his force staff overhead, and with a prayer on his lips unleashed the Storm of the Emperor's Wrath on the onrushing tyranids, his psychic power battering against the mindless creatures of pure appetite and instinct.

It had been too long since he had been in combat, Niven knew. He had inspired the Blood Ravens on Calderis, but even then the injuries he'd sustained on Kronus had kept him from fighting at his full strength. And the damage he'd suffered at the hands of the orks on that desert world had kept him from throwing himself into battle on Typhon Primaris against the offspring of the Great Devourer. Now, on Meridian, it seemed that he had regained his full fighting prowess, and there was nothing that would stop him from carrying out his duty.

Chaplain Palmarius was a short distance off, his crozius arcanum in his hands, leading the surviving aspirants in their blood-red bodygloves.

'Fight on!' Chaplain Palmarius shouted to the assembled aspirants, as they fired at the rippers who swarmed underfoot and the hellbats that wheeled overhead. 'The blood of martyrs is the seed of the Imperium!'

Only four of the aspirants who had come down from the strike cruiser *Armageddon* remained, the other eleven having fallen to the tyranids, but they had been joined by the two young Meridian natives whom Sergeant Thaddeus had brought to Zenith in his flight from the east.

'Do not pause to mourn the fallen,' the Chaplain called out, seeing that some of the aspirants kept casting glances at their former companions, who now lay bloodied and lifeless on the rubble around them. 'No man who died in the Emperor's service died in vain.'

Librarian Niven regarded the two Meridian youths. He had scanned them on their arrival, and found them to be free from taint or mental weakness, and as Battle-Brother Kell had said in delivering them they did appear to fit the aspirant profile. Niven had worried on first seeing them that they were not long for this life, though, as after their travails in enemy-held territory the two youths had looked half-starved and ready to collapse at any moment; but after being given a small measure of water and a bite to eat they had rallied. Picking up the weapons dropped by the fallen aspirants, Phaeton with a lasgun and Phoebus taking up a combat shotgun, they were now ready to stand against the tyranid monsters.

'The wise man learns from the deaths of others,' Chaplain Palmarius called out, smiting a low-flying gargoyle with the swept wings of the Imperial eagle that surmounted his crozius arcanum. 'Profit from their mistakes and fight on!'

Librarian Niven had been among those opposed to Sergeant Aramus's plan to use the aspirants in combat, fearing that the untrained youths were not ready for such a contest, but seeing the steely determination in the faces of the six youths now, he knew that Aramus's instincts had been correct. This struggle against the Great Devourer would test their mettle as well as any Blood Trials could, and any of the proud sons of Calderis, Typhon Primaris, and Meridian who survived the defence of Zenith would be welcome additions to the pool of Chapter initiates.

A ripper dived near to Librarian Niven, and he used his psyker abilities to move supernaturally quickly, moving a metre to one side in a fraction of a second and then driving his force staff into the side of the beast, ending its foul existence.

Since he had first accompanied Captain Davian Thule into the Aurelia sub-sector on the recruiting mission, Niven had been plagued by dark impressions which crowded the edges of his awareness, plaguing his thoughts. In time, he'd identified the lurking presence as the foul emanations of a hive mind, and later still as the dark thoughts of a hive fleet itself and of the norn-queen at its heart. Now, for the first time since arriving in Aurelia, Niven felt *another* presence, tantalizingly familiar, tickling at the edge of his awareness.

Librarian Niven glanced skyward. With the psychic interference of so many synapse creatures in close quarters his ability to extend his awareness through the warp was impeded, but he could not escape the impression that *something* was coming...

SERGEANT TARKUS STALKED through the arteries of the hive ship, alone. Brother Nord had finally fallen to a trio of shamblers who had ripped him limb from limb, while Brother Horatius had been bested by a creature which resembled a lictor, but was covered in oozing mucus instead of the diamond-hard chitin of the lictor's carapace.

Tarkus was all but weaponless, now. In one fist he carried his combat knife, its blade gored on the foul ichor of the inhuman monsters who defended the hive ship, and in his other he carried his final krak grenade. His bolter was holstered at his side, spent and useless, but he could not bear to part with it.

He wished that there were some way to contact Admiral Forbes – or anyone else in the Aurelia Battlegroup, for that matter – to learn how the battle progressed, in the vacuum and on distant Meridian. He longed to know whether Sergeant Aramus and the others still stood, still defied the Great Devourer while waiting for the arrival of Captain Angelos and his battlegroup. But he had been unable to raise the *Sword of Hadrian* on vox ever since they had boarded the hive ship, and there was little chance that he would ever do so again.

Tarkus had fought and clawed his way ever deeper into the heart of the hive ship, fighting past the birthing chambers and unborn warriors, the pools of noxious bio-agents and the wombs in which future tyranid strains were even now being spliced and assembled.

Now, at long last, having forced open the valve that ended the last artery, he found himself in a massive chamber. Its ribbed walls rose like the vault of a cathedral, meeting high overhead, and the ground beneath his feet was yielding and slick, like the soft tissue of an internal organ. At the centre of the massive chamber, nearly filling it entirely, hulked the pulsating form of the norn-queen, mother of monsters, who dwarfed the dozens upon dozens of her misbegotten offspring who attended her on all sides.

Tarkus hefted the krak grenade, and tightened his grip around the hilt of his combat knife. He knew there would be no walking away from this fight.

'Come on, then,' he sneered, striding towards the norn-queen, heedless of the danger, 'let us end this, at last.'

ON THE COMMAND deck of the *Sword of Hadrian*, Admiral Forbes turned as Commander Mitchels approached.

'Any word?' Forbes asked. She'd tasked one of the ship's astropaths with attempting to monitor the progress of Tarkus's strike team through the hive ship, which was difficult given the interference in the warp generated by the fleet's hive mind, but had produced some small measure of success. So far they had been able to confirm that, at least, Tarkus still lived.

Mitchels wore a dark expression, and shook his head. 'The news isn't good, I'm afraid, ma'am.'

'Lost contact, or simply lost?'

Mitchels glanced at his ever-present data-slate, as though the answer might lurk there. 'Lost, it would appear.'

The two surviving light cruisers in the Aurelia Battlegroup, Forbes's *Sword of Hadrian* and Captain Grieve's ship, *Trajan's Shield*, had continued to harry the tyranid craft, but while they had been able to inflict considerable damage on the enemy fleet, it had not come without a cost.

'The latest casualty reports, ma'am,' Mitchels said, breaking the momentary silence by handing the data-slate over. 'We've sealed off the portside of deck fifty, but engineering reports that an entire workshift of conscripts was lost when the aft compartments depressurised.'

Forbes skimmed her eyes along the report, as though she hadn't already anticipated everything it contained. She sighed. 'I'm not sure how much longer we'll be able to–'

She was interrupted by a shout from one of her officers. 'Admiral?' It was the ensign monitoring the medium-range scans, looking up from the crystal of his station, wearing a perplexed expression.

'Yes, ensign?' Forbes prompted, handing Mitchels back the data-slate.

'We…' He paused, glanced at the crystal screen, and then looked back at the admiral. 'We've got inbound, ma'am.'

Forbes leaned forward. 'Tyranid?' Could it be another splinter fleet, or perhaps vanguard elements of this same hive fleet rendezvousing after a scouting run?

The ensign shook his head. 'No, ma'am.'

Forbes jumped out of her seat, and leapt down the steps from the command dais to the deck proper. 'Show me!' she ordered.

She peered at the ensign's display, then straightened and turned to her first officer. 'Signal to Captain Grieve,' she ordered. 'Have the *Trajan* fall back.'

'Retreat, ma'am?' Mitchels asked.

Forbes grinned, and shook her head. 'No, Mitchels. *Reinforcements*.'

SERGEANT ARAMUS AND Sergeant Thaddeus, sons of Meridian and proud members of the Blood Ravens Chapter, fought back-to-back against the tyranid horde, with power sword and chainsword in hand. They had come within metres of the zoanthrope, but found their way forward blocked by the raveners and hormagaunts who fought with the zoanthrope's will. Bolter and bolt pistol spat hellfire at the beasts, but for every one that fell there were three more ready to take its place, the fiery wall of the defensive ring doing little to slow the enemy advance at this point.

A short distance off, the Thule Dreadnought still grappled with the carnifex, power fist against talons, autocannons against venom cannon. The Thule Dreadnought was besting the tyranid engine of destruction, but the contest was taking time, and time was a commodity which the Blood Ravens had in short supply.

Via the runes on his helmet's visor display, Aramus could track the progress of the other squads. Sergeant Cyrus and his Scouts had joined the PDF in safeguarding the refugees, whom they had herded into the governor's palace. Sergeant Avitus and his Devastator squad had their hands full with a hive tyrant and its retinue on the eastern approaches. And Librarian Niven and Chaplain Palmarius led the aspirants from the front, taking the fight to the interlopers.

It was only a matter of time now, Aramus knew. The Blood Ravens would stand and fight, but they had lost too much ground to the enemy to be able to defend the capital city indefinitely, even if they were through some miracle able to best all the interlopers currently within the defensive ring.

From overhead, Aramus could hear the screaming of a gunship coming in fast and hot from the west.

Thunderhawk One had been shot from the sky by the carnifex, and Thunderhawk Two was returning from the *Armageddon* with Apothecary Gordian, who having completed his vigil at the side of Captain Davian Thule was coming to the planet's surface to retrieve the Chapter's due from each of the fallen Blood Ravens. Thunderhawk Three was covering the southern approaches to Zenith, where the line of defence had been weakened by repeated enemy attack.

So which Thunderhawk was it, then, that was now diving towards the ruined streets of Zenith?

'Thaddeus?' Aramus glanced up at the sky, while wrenching the blade of the power sword Wisdom from the body of a falling ravener.

It wasn't one Thunderhawk, but six, a full half-dozen gunships screaming out of the grey sky. And as they fell, they opened fire with lascannons, missiles, and heavy bolters, raining fiery death down on the tyranids who threatened to overrun the capital. And even at this great distance the enhanced vision of the Space Marines could make out the midnight-black raven with a teardrop of blood at its heart – the symbol of the Blood Ravens emblazoned on the hull of each and every one of them.

'Blood Ravens!' came a voice booming over the vox-comms on an open channel, broadcast to every Space Marine in the area. 'This is Captain Gabriel Angelos of the Blood Ravens Third Company. Do you still require assistance?'

Aramus could not contain the laughter that burst from his lips. 'Yes!' he voxed back. 'This is Sergeant Aramus, acting Commander at Sail of the strike cruiser *Armageddon*, and we welcome your arrival, captain!'

'Then we are pleased to comply, sergeant,' Captain Angelos replied. 'All units of the Third and Ninth Companies, deploy. For the Great Father and the Emperor!'

'For the Great Father and the Emperor!' Aramus and Thaddeus replied in unison.

Aramus turned in time to see the Thule Dreadnought deliver the final crushing blow to the carnifex, the massive power fist on the war-engine's left forelimb smashing right through the giant monster's body, sending chitin and ichor raining down on all sides. As the broken carnifex crumpled to the ground at the feet of the Thule Dreadnought, the first of the Third Company gunships swooped low enough to deploy an entire squad of Space Marines with heavy weaponry, already firing on the tyranid horde with melta guns, plasma guns, and heavy bolters before their feet even touched the ground.

'You did it, Aramus,' Thaddeus called over his shoulder, watching the newcomers deploy. 'You held us together until reinforcements arrived.'

'I only did my duty, brother,' Aramus replied. 'Too many of our brothers fell to take any pride in the action.'

Thaddeus hefted his chainsword. 'Then we will remember them when the Bell of Souls tolls, and honour their sacrifice now by winning this world in the Emperor's name.'

As Thaddeus swung his chainsword at the head of the nearest ravener, throwing himself once more into the contest, Aramus glanced around at the ruins of the capital which surrounded them. It was unrecognizable as the place that he had been born and lived his earliest years, and for a time it had seemed that the battle to save it might be lost. It had looked likely, he knew, that Meridian might fall to the Great Devourer.

He regarded the power sword in his hands.

Wisdom had been thought lost, too, for a time, but then found again. So, too, would this world be rescued from the enemy's grasp.

The battle was not over, Aramus knew. But with two full Battle Companies on hand to join the fight, there was the chance that they might still win the war.

'Knowledge is power!' Aramus said, raising Wisdom overhead, the battle cry of the Blood Ravens Chapter on his lips as he drove forward towards the enemy. 'Guard it well!'

EPILOGUE

THE BATTLE FOR Meridian still raged on the planet below them, and in the black vacuum above Angelos's battlegroup still strove against the hive fleet itself, but on the command deck of the strike cruiser *Armageddon*, for a moment at least, things were peaceful and still.

Once Angelos's Third Company and Captain Ulantus's Ninth Company had deployed on the planet's surface, Sergeant Aramus had ordered the beleaguered elements of the Fifth Company to withdraw temporarily, to address their injuries and wounds, repair their weapons, and to replenish their armament and ammunition. Apothecary Gordian had retrieved the gene-seed from the fallen, which he was even now putting into secure storage in the Apothecarion, and Techmarine Martellus had gone immediately to work on repairs to the power armour and weapons of the survivors.

Chaplain Palmarius and Librarian Niven had accompanied the six aspirants to the Apothecarion where Gordian would look after their wounds. Of the fifteen aspirants in their blood-red bodygloves who had come down to the planet, only four had survived, two from each of the recruiting worlds they had visited – Calderis and Typhon Primaris – who had been joined with the two brothers recruited from Meridian herself. Now the six were considered to have survived the Blood Trials, and once the *Armageddon* rendezvoused with the Fifth Company battle-barge *Scientia Est Potentia*, they would be inducted as initiates to the Chapter. And then their trials would *truly* begin…

Sergeant Aramus stood in full armour on the command dais, the power sword Wisdom sheathed at his side. He had spoken to Captain Angelos before returning to the *Armageddon*, as Angelos prepared to lead the Third Company onto the field of battle.

'So you carry Wisdom now?' Angelos had asked.

Aramus had shook his head. 'Only until I can return it to the Secret Masters. I expect they will present it to whomever is chosen to lead the Fated next. I would think either Sergeant Hyrcleon of the Second Squad or Sergeant Eleazer of the Fourth are the most likely candidates.'

Angelos, his head bare in the grey light of the Meridian dawn, had given a slight, enigmatic smile. 'Either brother would be a worthy captain for the Fifth, I've no doubt. But such relics are not always carried by captains, it should be remembered. Some of those who have borne Wisdom into battle in its storied history have been mere battle-brothers, but most of them, I think you will find, have been brother-sergeants.'

Aramus was silent, not knowing what to say.

'Treat it well, Sergeant Aramus,' Angelos had said with a smile, lifting his helmet onto his head. 'You may carry Wisdom longer than you expect.'

That had been the last that Aramus had seen of the Third Company's captain before returning to the strike cruiser. He had not yet removed his power armour, but come straight from the launch bay to the command deck. Not until he had received word of Sergeant Tarkus and the others would he stand down and allow the Apothecary to look at his wounds.

'Sir,' said the Chapter serf who had ascended the command dais, eyes averted. 'We have established vox contact with the *Sword of Hadrian*.'

Aramus nodded, stepping over to the captain's chair where a vox transceiver was housed. 'Put it through,' he commanded. '*Sword of Hadrian*? This is Sergeant Aramus on the strike cruiser *Armageddon*.'

'Sergeant Aramus, this is Admiral Forbes,' came the response, laced with static. 'We are inbound to Meridian, after the Blood Ravens battlegroup relieved us at the front.'

'Admiral,' Aramus replied, 'I'd hoped for word of the Blood Ravens who remained with you on Typhon Primaris.'

'You have my apologies, sergeant. In the confusion surrounding the final assaults, well... In any event, Sergeant Tarkus and his men used a boarding torpedo to infiltrate the Hive Ship, and were lost.'

Aramus could imagine how Tarkus would have
reacted to his Space Marines being called 'men,' and
wondered if she had used the same language with
him.

'Understood, admiral,' Aramus said.

'Sergeant Tarkus and his squad have earned the
greatest respect of the Imperial Navy, sergeant,'
Admiral Forbes said, her voice tinged with sadness,
'and my own unending admiration. I only regret
that the deaths of Tarkus and the others was ultimately in vain, without purpose or gain.'

'Without *purpose*, admiral?'

'That is, in as much as the reinforcements arrived
sooner than anticipated, given the vagaries of warp
travel, and had nearly arrived at our location by the
time that the boarding torpedo punched into the
Hive Ship.'

Aramus could not help recalling everything
Sergeant Tarkus had taught him about duty and
responsibility, and the lessons he'd learned from
Sergeant Cyrus when still just a neophyte. He
thought about Captain Thule, now an undying warrior encased at the heart of Dreadnought war
machine, forever on the brink of life and death, and
the example he'd provided to those under his command. He remembered the words of Captain Thule
on Prosperon, so long ago: '*Have faith in your Chapter, in your Emperor, and in your own strength, and your
life – and death – will have purpose.*'

'You misunderstand, admiral,' Aramus replied, his
voice low but level. 'The lives of the Blood Ravens
who fell in the defence of Aurelia – in vacuum, on
Meridian, on Typhon Primaris, and on Calderis –

were *not* thrown away without purpose, Sergeant Tarkus and the First Squad included. It might have been without *gain*, I'll grant you, but the *purpose* was the service of the Emperor, the protection of the Imperium, and the glory of the Blood Ravens Chapter, and there can be no nobler end than that.'

DRAMATIS PERSONAE

Blood Ravens in the Prosperon Undertaking

Captain Davian Thule
Apothecary Gordian
Sergeant Forrin
Brother Vela
Brother Durio
Brother Milius
Brother Qao
Brother Kraal
Brother Javier
Brother Siano
Brother Quinzi
Brother Aramus

Blood Ravens of the Fifth Company in the Calderis Recruitment Mission

Captain Davian Thule
Chaplain Palmarius
Librarian Niven

SCOUT SQUAD
Sergeant Cyrus, squad leader
Scout Xenakis
Scout Jutan
Scout Muren
Scout Tubach
Scout Watral

Blood Ravens of the Fifth Company returning from the Zalamis Undertaking

FIRST SQUAD, TACTICAL
Sergeant Merrik, squad leader
Brother Sten
Brother Xiao
Brother Mettius
Brother Eumenis
Brother Proclus
Brother Tane
Brother Nord
Brother Horatius

THIRD SQUAD, TACTICAL
Sergeant Aramus, squad leader
Sergeant Tarkus
Brother Voire
Brother Zach
Brother Isek
Brother Cirrac
Brother Siddig

SEVENTH SQUAD, ASSAULT
Sergeant Thaddeus, squad leader
Brother Loew
Brother Renzo
Brother Shar
Brother Marr
Brother Skander
Brother Brandt
Brother Takayo
Brother Kell

NINTH SQUAD, DEVASTATOR
Sergeant Avitus, squad leader
Brother Philetus
Brother Gagan
Brother Dow
Brother Barabbas
Brother Safir
Brother Elon
Brother Pontius

ONBOARD THE STRIKE CRUISER *Armageddon*
Techmarine Martellus
Apothecary Gordian
Lexicanium Konan

OFFICERS OF THE IMPERIAL NAVY'S AURELIA BATTLE-GROUP

Sword of Hadrian, a Dauntless-class light cruiser
Fleet Admiral Laren Forbes, commanding officer
Commander Mitchels, first officer

Trajan's Shield, a Dauntless-class light cruiser
Captain Grieve, commanding officer

The Praetorian, a Dauntless-class light cruiser
Captain Voronin, commanding officer

ABOUT THE AUTHOR

Chris Roberson is a respected SF author whose novels include *The Dragon's Nine Sons* (Solaris, 2007) and *Set the Seas on Fire* (Solaris, 2007). Roberson has been a finalist for the World Fantasy Award for Short Fiction, twice for the John W. Campbell Award for Best New Writer, and three times for the Sidewise Award for Best Alternate History Short Form (winning in 2004 with his story 'O One.') He runs the independent press MonkeyBrain books with his partner.

WARHAMMER
40,000

Contains the novels *Soul Drinker*, *The Bleeding Chalice* and *Crimson Tears*

THE SOUL DRINKERS
OMNIBUS

BEN COUNTER

ISBN 978-1-84416-416-5

WARHAMMER
40,000

THE SPACE WOLF
OMNIBUS

Buy these
omnibuses or read
a free extract at
www.blacklibrary.com

WILLIAM KING

SPACE WOLF • RAGNAR'S CLAW • GREY HUNTER

ISBN 978-1-84416-457-8

BY THE BLOOD OF SANGUINIUS!

WARHAMMER 40,000

THE BLOOD ANGELS
OMNIBUS

Contains the novels *Deus Encarmine* and *Deus Sanguinius*

'War-torn tales of loyalty and honour.' – SFX

JAMES SWALLOW

ISBN 978-1-84416-559-9